THE SECOND GHOST STORY MEGAPACK®

IN THE SAME SERIES

The Ghost Story MEGAPACK®
The Second Ghost Story MEGAPACK®
The Third Ghost Story MEGAPACK®
The Fourth Ghost Story MEGAPACK®
The Fifth Ghost Story MEGAPACK®
The Sixth Ghost Story MEGAPACK®
The Seventh Ghost Story MEGAPACK®

THE SECOND GHOST STORY MEGAPACK®

Edited by
JOHN GREGORY BETANCOURT

WILDSIDE PRESS

NOTE

Language has not been updated for "political correctness" and some stories may contain language which some may find offensive. Please note that languages change and evolve, and what was acceptable in the time of original publication may prove offensive to some today.

VERSION

File Version 1.2

CONTENTS

A NOTE FROM THE PUBLISHER 7
THE SIGNAL-MAN, by Charles Dickens 9
THE SOUL OF THE GREAT BELL, by Lafcadio Hearn 17
PRESENT AT A HANGING, by Ambrose Bierce 20
CANON ALBERIC'S SCRAP-BOOK by M. R. James 22
THE MASS OF SHADOWS, by Anatole France 29
THE MAN WHO WENT TOO FAR, by E.F. Benson 33
THE THING AT NOLAN, by Ambrose Bierce 46
THE PHANTOM 'RICKSHAW, by Rudyard Kipling 49
THE RIVAL GHOSTS by Brander Matthews 62
THE INTERVAL, by Vincent O'Sullivan 73
A GHOST, by Guy De Maupassant 78
A COLD GREETING, by Ambrose Bierce 83
THE TURN OF THE SCREW, by Henry James 85
THE SHADOWS ON THE WALL, by Mary E. Wilkins Freeman 149
THE MESSENGER, by Robert W. Chambers 157
THE BEAST WITH FIVE FINGERS, by W. F. Harvey 180
WHAT WAS IT?, by Fitz-James O'Brien .197
THE SHELL OF SENSE, by Olivia Howard Dunbar 205
THE WOMAN AT SEVEN BROTHERS, by Wilbur Daniel Steele 213
AT THE GATE, by Myla Jo Closser 224
LIGEIA, by Edgar Allan Poe 228
THE HAUNTED ORCHARD, by Richard Le Gallienne 238
KERFOL, by Edith Wharton 243
THE WIND IN THE ROSE-BUSH, by Mary E. Wilkins Freeman 257
THE STORY OF MING-Y, by Lafcadio Hearn 268

A NOTE FROM THE PUBLISHER

Over the last year, our MEGAPACK® series of ebook anthologies has proved to be one of our most popular endeavors. (Maybe it helps that we sometimes offer them as premiums to our mailing list!) One question we keep getting asked is, "Who's the editor?"

The MEGAPACK®s (except where specifically credited) are a group effort. Everyone at Wildside works on them. This includes John Betancourt, Carla Coupe, Steve Coupe, Bonner Menking, Colin Azariah-Kribbs, Robert Reginald, A.E. Warren, and many of Wildside's authors...who often suggest stories to include (and not just their own!)

—John Gregory Betancourt
Publisher, Wildside Press

THE SIGNAL-MAN, by Charles Dickens

"Halloa! Below there!"

When he heard a voice thus calling to him, he was standing at the door of his box, with a flag in his hand, furled round its short pole. One would have thought, considering the nature of the ground, that he could not have doubted from what quarter the voice came; but instead of looking up to where I stood on the top of the steep cutting nearly over his head, he turned himself about, and looked down the Line. There was something remarkable in his manner of doing so, though I could not have said for my life what. But I know it was remarkable enough to attract my notice, even though his figure was foreshortened and shadowed, down in the deep trench, and mine was high above him, so steeped in the glow of an angry sunset, that I had shaded my eyes with my hand before I saw him at all.

"Halloa! Below!"

From looking down the Line, he turned himself about again, and, raising his eyes, saw my figure high above him.

"Is there any path by which I can come down and speak to you?"

He looked up at me without replying, and I looked down at him without pressing him too soon with a repetition of my idle question. Just then there came a vague vibration in the earth and air, quickly changing into a violent pulsation, and an oncoming rush that caused me to start back, as though it had force to draw me down. When such vapour as rose to my height from this rapid train had passed me, and was skimming away over the landscape, I looked down again, and saw him refurling the flag he had shown while the train went by.

I repeated my inquiry. After a pause, during which he seemed to regard me with fixed attention, he motioned with his rolled-up flag towards a point on my level, some two or three hundred yards distant. I called down to him, "All right!" and made for that point. There, by dint of looking closely about me, I found a rough zigzag descending path notched out, which I followed.

The cutting was extremely deep, and unusually precipitate. It was made through a clammy stone, that became oozier and wetter as I went down. For these reasons, I found the way long enough to give me time to recall a singular air of reluctance or compulsion with which he had pointed out the path.

When I came down low enough upon the zigzag descent to see him again, I saw that he was standing between the rails on the way by which the train had lately passed, in an attitude as if he were waiting for me to appear. He had his left hand at his chin, and that left elbow rested on his right hand, crossed over his breast. His attitude was one of such expectation and watchfulness that I stopped a moment, wondering at it.

I resumed my downward way, and stepping out upon the level of the railroad, and drawing nearer to him, saw that he was a dark, sallow man, with a dark beard and rather heavy eyebrows. His post was in as solitary and dismal a place as ever I saw. On either side, a dripping-wet wall of jagged stone, excluding all view but a strip of sky; the perspective one way only a crooked prolongation of this great dungeon; the shorter perspective in the other direction terminating in a gloomy red light, and the gloomier entrance to a black tunnel, in whose massive architecture there was a barbarous, depressing, and forbidding air. So little sunlight ever found its way to this spot, that it had an earthy, deadly smell; and so much cold wind rushed through it, that it struck chill to me, as if I had left the natural world.

Before he stirred, I was near enough to him to have touched him. Not even then removing his eyes from mine, he stepped back one step, and lifted his hand.

This was a lonesome post to occupy (I said), and it had riveted my attention when I looked down from up yonder. A visitor was a rarity, I should suppose; not an unwelcome rarity, I hoped? In me, he merely saw a man who had been shut up within narrow limits all his life, and who, being at last set free, had a newly-awakened interest in these great works. To such purpose I spoke to him; but I am far from sure of the terms I used; for, besides that I am not happy in opening any conversation, there was something in the man that daunted me.

He directed a most curious look towards the red light near the tunnel's mouth, and looked all about it, as if something were missing from it, and then looked at me.

That light was part of his charge? Was it not?

He answered in a low voice—"Don't you know it is?"

The monstrous thought came into my mind, as I perused the fixed eyes and the saturnine face, that this was a spirit, not a man. I have speculated since, whether there may have been infection in his mind.

In my turn, I stepped back. But in making the action, I detected in his eyes some latent fear of me. This put the monstrous thought to flight.

"You look at me," I said, forcing a smile, "as if you had a dread of me."

"I was doubtful," he returned, "whether I had seen you before."

"Where?"

He pointed to the red light he had looked at.

"There?" I said.

Intently watchful of me, he replied (but without sound), "Yes."

"My good fellow, what should I do there? However, be that as it may, I never was there, you may swear."

"I think I may," he rejoined. "Yes; I am sure I may."

His manner cleared, like my own. He replied to my remarks with readiness, and in well-chosen words. Had he much to do there? Yes; that was to say, he had enough responsibility to bear; but exactness and watchfulness were what was required of him, and of actual work—manual labour—he had next to none. To change that signal, to trim those lights, and to turn this iron handle now and then, was all he had to do under that head. Regarding those many long and lonely hours of which I seemed to make so much, he could only say that the routine of his life had shaped itself into that form, and he had grown used to it. He had taught himself a language down here,—if only to know it by sight, and to have formed his own crude ideas of its pronunciation, could be called learning it. He had also worked at fractions and decimals, and tried a little algebra; but he was, and had been as a boy, a poor hand at figures. Was it necessary for him when on duty always to remain in that channel of damp air, and could he never rise into the sunshine from between those high stone walls? Why, that depended upon times and circumstances. Under some conditions there would be less upon the Line than under others, and the same held good as to certain hours of the day and night. In bright weather, he did choose occasions for getting a little above these lower shadows; but, being at all times liable to be called by his electric bell, and at such times listening for it with redoubled anxiety, the relief was less than I would suppose.

He took me into his box, where there was a fire, a desk for an official book in which he had to make certain entries, a telegraphic instrument with its dial, face, and needles, and the little bell of which he had spoken. On my trusting that he would excuse the remark that he had been well educated, and (I hoped I might say without offence) perhaps educated above that station, he observed that instances of slight incongruity in such wise would rarely be found wanting among large bodies of men; that he had heard it was so in workhouses, in the police force, even in that last desperate resource, the army; and that he knew it was so, more or less, in any great railway staff. He had been, when young (if I could believe it, sitting in that hut,—he scarcely could), a student of natural philosophy, and had attended lectures; but he had run wild, misused his opportunities, gone down, and never risen again. He had no complaint to offer about that. He had made his bed, and he lay upon it. It was far too late to make another.

All that I have here condensed he said in a quiet manner, with his grave, dark regards divided between me and the fire. He threw in the word, "Sir," from time to time, and especially when he referred to his youth,—as though to request me to understand that he claimed to be nothing but what I found him. He was several times interrupted by the little bell, and had to read off messages, and send replies. Once he had to stand without the door, and display a flag as a train passed, and make some verbal communication to the driver. In the discharge of his duties, I observed him to be remarkably exact and vigilant, breaking off his discourse at a syllable, and remaining silent until what he had to do was done.

In a word, I should have set this man down as one of the safest of men to be employed in that capacity, but for the circumstance that while he was speaking to me he twice broke off with a fallen colour, turned his face towards the little bell when it did NOT ring, opened the door of the hut (which was kept shut to exclude the unhealthy damp), and looked out towards the red light near the mouth of the tunnel. On both of those occasions, he came back to the fire with the inexplicable air upon him which I had remarked, without being able to define, when we were so far asunder.

Said I, when I rose to leave him, "You almost make me think that I have met with a contented man."

(I am afraid I must acknowledge that I said it to lead him on.)

"I believe I used to be so," he rejoined, in the low voice in which he had first spoken; "but I am troubled, sir, I am troubled."

He would have recalled the words if he could. He had said them, however, and I took them up quickly.

"With what? What is your trouble?"

"It is very difficult to impart, sir. It is very, very difficult to speak of. If ever you make me another visit, I will try to tell you."

"But I expressly intend to make you another visit. Say, when shall it be?"

"I go off early in the morning, and I shall be on again at ten to-morrow night, sir."

"I will come at eleven."

He thanked me, and went out at the door with me. "I'll show my white light, sir," he said, in his peculiar low voice, "till you have found the way up. When you have found it, don't call out! And when you are at the top, don't call out!"

His manner seemed to make the place strike colder to me, but I said no more than, "Very well."

"And when you come down to-morrow night, don't call out! Let me ask you a parting question. What made you cry, 'Halloa! Below there!' to-night?"

"Heaven knows," said I. "I cried something to that effect—"

"Not to that effect, sir. Those were the very words. I know them well."

"Admit those were the very words. I said them, no doubt, because I saw you below."

"For no other reason?"

"What other reason could I possibly have?"

"You had no feeling that they were conveyed to you in any supernatural way?"

"No."

He wished me good-night, and held up his light. I walked by the side of the down Line of rails (with a very disagreeable sensation of a train coming behind me) until I found the path. It was easier to mount than to descend, and I got back to my inn without any adventure.

Punctual to my appointment, I placed my foot on the first notch of the zigzag next night, as the distant clocks were striking eleven. He was waiting for me at the bottom, with his white light on. "I have not called out," I said, when we came close together; "may I speak now?" "By all means, sir." "Good-night, then, and here's my hand." "Good-night, sir, and here's mine." With that we walked side by side to his box, entered it, closed the door, and sat down by the fire.

"I have made up my mind, sir," he began, bending forward as soon as we were seated, and speaking in a tone but a little above a whisper, "that you shall not have to ask me twice what troubles me. I took you for some one else yesterday evening. That troubles me."

"That mistake?"

"No. That some one else."

"Who is it?"

"I don't know."

"Like me?"

"I don't know. I never saw the face. The left arm is across the face, and the right arm is waved,—violently waved. This way."

I followed his action with my eyes, and it was the action of an arm gesticulating, with the utmost passion and vehemence, "For God's sake, clear the way!"

"One moonlight night," said the man, "I was sitting here, when I heard a voice cry, 'Halloa! Below there!' I started up, looked from that door, and saw this Some one else standing by the red light near the tunnel, waving as I just now showed you. The voice seemed hoarse with shouting, and it cried, 'Look out! Look out!' And then again, 'Halloa! Below there! Look out!' I caught up my lamp, turned it on red, and ran towards the figure, calling, 'What's wrong? What has happened? Where?' It stood just outside the blackness of the tunnel. I advanced so close upon it that I wondered at its keeping the sleeve across its eyes. I ran right up at it, and had my hand stretched out to pull the sleeve away, when it was gone."

"Into the tunnel?" said I.

"No. I ran on into the tunnel, five hundred yards. I stopped, and held my lamp above my head, and saw the figures of the measured distance, and saw the wet stains stealing down the walls and trickling through the arch. I ran out again faster than I had run in (for I had a mortal abhorrence of the place upon me), and I looked all round the red light with my own red light, and I went up the iron ladder to the gallery atop of it, and I came down again, and ran back here. I telegraphed both ways, 'An alarm has been given. Is anything wrong?' The answer came back, both ways, 'All well.'"

Resisting the slow touch of a frozen finger tracing out my spine, I showed him how that this figure must be a deception of his sense of sight; and how that figures, originating in disease of the delicate nerves that minister to the functions of the eye, were known to have often troubled patients, some of whom had become conscious of the nature of their affliction, and had even proved it by experiments upon themselves. "As to an imaginary cry," said I, "do but listen for a moment to the wind in this unnatural valley while we speak so low, and to the wild harp it makes of the telegraph wires."

That was all very well, he returned, after we had sat listening for a while, and he ought to know something of the wind and the wires,—he who so often passed long winter nights there, alone and watching. But he would beg to remark that he had not finished.

I asked his pardon, and he slowly added these words, touching my arm,—

"Within six hours after the Appearance, the memorable accident on this Line happened, and within ten hours the dead and wounded were brought along through the tunnel over the spot where the figure had stood."

A disagreeable shudder crept over me, but I did my best against it. It was not to be denied, I rejoined, that this was a remarkable coincidence, calculated deeply to impress his mind. But it was unquestionable that remarkable coincidences did continually occur, and they must be taken into account in dealing with such a subject. Though to be sure I must admit, I added (for I thought I saw that he was going to bring the objection to bear upon me), men of common sense did not allow much for coincidences in making the ordinary calculations of life.

He again begged to remark that he had not finished.

I again begged his pardon for being betrayed into interruptions.

"This," he said, again laying his hand upon my arm, and glancing over his shoulder with hollow eyes, "was just a year ago. Six or seven months passed, and I had recovered from the surprise and shock, when one morning, as the day was breaking, I, standing at the door, looked towards the red light, and saw the spectre again." He stopped, with a fixed look at me.

"Did it cry out?"

"No. It was silent."

"Did it wave its arm?"

"No. It leaned against the shaft of the light, with both hands before the face. Like this."

Once more I followed his action with my eyes. It was an action of mourning. I have seen such an attitude in stone figures on tombs.

"Did you go up to it?"

"I came in and sat down, partly to collect my thoughts, partly because it had turned me faint. When I went to the door again, daylight was above me, and the ghost was gone."

"But nothing followed? Nothing came of this?"

He touched me on the arm with his forefinger twice or thrice giving a ghastly nod each time:—

"That very day, as a train came out of the tunnel, I noticed, at a carriage window on my side, what looked like a confusion of hands and heads, and something waved. I saw it just in time to signal the driver, Stop! He shut off, and put his brake on, but the train drifted past here a hundred and fifty yards or more. I ran after it, and, as I went along, heard terrible screams and cries. A beautiful young lady had died instantaneously in one of the compartments, and was brought in here, and laid down on this floor between us."

Involuntarily I pushed my chair back, as I looked from the boards at which he pointed to himself.

"True, sir. True. Precisely as it happened, so I tell it you."

I could think of nothing to say, to any purpose, and my mouth was very dry. The wind and the wires took up the story with a long lamenting wail.

He resumed. "Now, sir, mark this, and judge how my mind is troubled. The spectre came back a week ago. Ever since, it has been there, now and again, by fits and starts."

"At the light?"

"At the Danger-light."

"What does it seem to do?"

He repeated, if possible with increased passion and vehemence, that former gesticulation of, "For God's sake, clear the way!"

Then he went on. "I have no peace or rest for it. It calls to me, for many minutes together, in an agonised manner, 'Below there! Look out! Look out!' It stands waving to me. It rings my little bell—"

I caught at that. "Did it ring your bell yesterday evening when I was here, and you went to the door?"

"Twice."

"Why, see," said I, "how your imagination misleads you. My eyes were on the bell, and my ears were open to the bell, and if I am a living man, it did NOT ring at those times. No, nor at any other time, except when it was rung in the natural course of physical things by the station communicating with you."

He shook his head. "I have never made a mistake as to that yet, sir. I have never confused the spectre's ring with the man's. The ghost's ring is a strange vibration in the bell that it derives from nothing else, and I have not asserted that the bell stirs to the eye. I don't wonder that you failed to hear it. But *I* heard it."

"And did the spectre seem to be there, when you looked out?"

"It WAS there."

"Both times?"

He repeated firmly: "Both times."

"Will you come to the door with me, and look for it now?"

He bit his under lip as though he were somewhat unwilling, but arose. I opened the door, and stood on the step, while he stood in the doorway. There was the Danger-light. There was the dismal mouth of the tunnel. There were the high, wet stone walls of the cutting. There were the stars above them.

"Do you see it?" I asked him, taking particular note of his face. His eyes were prominent and strained, but not very much more so, perhaps, than my own had been when I had directed them earnestly towards the same spot.

"No," he answered. "It is not there."

"Agreed," said I.

We went in again, shut the door, and resumed our seats. I was thinking how best to improve this advantage, if it might be called one, when he took up the conversation in such a matter-of-course way, so assuming that there could be no serious question of fact between us, that I felt myself placed in the weakest of positions.

"By this time you will fully understand, sir," he said, "that what troubles me so dreadfully is the question, What does the spectre mean?"

I was not sure, I told him, that I did fully understand.

"What is its warning against?" he said, ruminating, with his eyes on the fire, and only by times turning them on me. "What is the danger? Where is the danger? There is danger overhanging somewhere on the Line. Some dreadful calamity will happen. It is not to be doubted this third time, after what has gone before. But surely this is a cruel haunting of *me*. What can *I* do?"

He pulled out his handkerchief, and wiped the drops from his heated forehead.

"If I telegraph Danger, on either side of me, or on both, I can give no reason for it," he went on, wiping the palms of his hands. "I should get into trouble, and do no good. They would think I was mad. This is the way it would work,—Message: 'Danger! Take care!' Answer: 'What Danger? Where?' Message: 'Don't know. But, for God's sake, take care!' They would displace me. What else could they do?"

His pain of mind was most pitiable to see. It was the mental torture of a conscientious man, oppressed beyond endurance by an unintelligible responsibility involving life.

"When it first stood under the Danger-light," he went on, putting his dark hair back from his head, and drawing his hands outward across and across his temples in an extremity of feverish distress, "why not tell me where that accident was to happen,—if it must happen? Why not tell me how it could be averted,—if it could have been averted? When on its second coming it hid its face, why not tell me, instead, 'She is going to die. Let them keep her at home'? If it came, on those two occasions, only to show me that its warnings were true, and so to prepare me for the third, why not warn me plainly now? And I, Lord help me! A mere poor signal-man on this solitary station! Why not go to somebody with credit to be believed, and power to act?"

When I saw him in this state, I saw that for the poor man's sake, as well as for the public safety, what I had to do for the time was to compose his mind. Therefore, setting aside all question of reality or unreality between us, I represented to him that whoever thoroughly discharged his duty must do well, and that at least it was his comfort that he understood his duty, though he did not understand these confounding Appearances. In this effort I succeeded far better than in the attempt to reason him out of his conviction. He became calm; the occupations incidental to his post as the night advanced began to make larger demands on his attention: and I left him at two in the morning. I had offered to stay through the night, but he would not hear of it.

That I more than once looked back at the red light as I ascended the pathway, that I did not like the red light, and that I should have slept but poorly if my bed had been under it, I see no reason to conceal. Nor did I like the two sequences of the accident and the dead girl. I see no reason to conceal that either.

But what ran most in my thoughts was the consideration how ought I to act, having become the recipient of this disclosure? I had proved the man to be intelligent, vigilant, painstaking, and exact; but how long might he remain so, in his state of mind? Though in a subordinate position, still he held a most important trust, and would I (for instance) like to stake my own life on the chances of his continuing to execute it with precision?

Unable to overcome a feeling that there would be something treacherous in my communicating what he had told me to his superiors in the Company, without first being plain with himself and proposing a middle course to him, I ultimately resolved to offer to accompany him (otherwise keeping his secret for the present) to the wisest medical practitioner we could hear of in those parts, and to take his opinion. A change in his time of duty would come round next night, he had apprised me, and he would be off an hour or two after sunrise, and on again soon after sunset. I had appointed to return accordingly.

Next evening was a lovely evening, and I walked out early to enjoy it. The sun was not yet quite down when I traversed the field-path near the top of the deep cutting. I would extend my walk for an hour, I said to myself, half an hour on and half an hour back, and it would then be time to go to my signal-man's box.

Before pursuing my stroll, I stepped to the brink, and mechanically looked down, from the point from which I had first seen him. I cannot describe the thrill that seized upon me, when, close at the mouth of the tunnel, I saw the appearance of a man, with his left sleeve across his eyes, passionately waving his right arm.

The nameless horror that oppressed me passed in a moment, for in a moment I saw that this appearance of a man was a man indeed, and that there was a little group of other men, standing at a short distance, to whom he seemed to be rehearsing the gesture he made. The Danger-light was not yet lighted. Against its shaft, a little low hut, entirely new to me, had been made of some wooden supports and tarpaulin. It looked no bigger than a bed.

With an irresistible sense that something was wrong,—with a flashing self-reproachful fear that fatal mischief had come of my leaving the man there, and causing no one to be sent to overlook or correct what he did,—I descended the notched path with all the speed I could make.

"What is the matter?" I asked the men.

"Signal-man killed this morning, sir."

"Not the man belonging to that box?"

"Yes, sir."

"Not the man I know?"

"You will recognise him, sir, if you knew him," said the man who spoke for the others, solemnly uncovering his own head, and raising an end of the tarpaulin, "for his face is quite composed."

"O, how did this happen, how did this happen?" I asked, turning from one to another as the hut closed in again.

"He was cut down by an engine, sir. No man in England knew his work better. But somehow he was not clear of the outer rail. It was just at broad day. He had struck the light, and had the lamp in his hand. As the engine came out of the tunnel, his back was towards her, and she cut him down. That man drove her, and was showing how it happened. Show the gentleman, Tom."

The man, who wore a rough dark dress, stepped back to his former place at the mouth of the tunnel.

"Coming round the curve in the tunnel, sir," he said, "I saw him at the end, like as if I saw him down a perspective-glass. There was no time to check speed, and I knew him to be very careful. As he didn't seem to take heed of the whistle, I shut it off when we were running down upon him, and called to him as loud as I could call."

"What did you say?"

"I said, 'Below there! Look out! Look out! For God's sake, clear the way!'"

I started.

"Ah! it was a dreadful time, sir. I never left off calling to him. I put this arm before my eyes not to see, and I waved this arm to the last; but it was no use."

* * * *

Without prolonging the narrative to dwell on any one of its curious circumstances more than on any other, I may, in closing it, point out the coincidence that the warning of the Engine-Driver included, not only the words which the unfortunate Signal-man had repeated to me as haunting him, but also the words which I myself—not he—had attached, and that only in my own mind, to the gesticulation he had imitated.

THE SOUL OF THE GREAT BELL, by Lafcadio Hearn

She hath spoken, and her words still resound in his ears.
—Hao-Khieou-Tchouan: c. ix.

* * * *

The water-clock marks the hour in the *Ta-chung sz'*,—in the Tower of the Great Bell: now the mallet is lifted to smite the lips of the metal monster,—the vast lips inscribed with Buddhist texts from the sacred *Fa-hwa-King*, from the chapters of the holy *Ling-yen-King*! Hear the great bell responding!—how mighty her voice, though tongueless!—*KO-NGAI!* All the little dragons on the high-tilted eaves of the green roofs shiver to the tips of their gilded tails under that deep wave of sound; all the porcelain gargoyles tremble on their carven perches; all the hundred little bells of the pagodas quiver with desire to speak. *KO-NGAI!*—all the green-and-gold tiles of the temple are vibrating; the wooden goldfish above them are writhing against the sky; the uplifted finger of Fo shakes high over the heads of the worshippers through the blue fog of incense! *KO-NGAI!*—What a thunder tone was that! All the lacquered goblins on the palace cornices wriggle their fire-colored tongues! And after each huge shock, how wondrous the multiple echo and the great golden moan and, at last, the sudden sibilant sobbing in the ears when the immense tone faints away in broken whispers of silver,—as though a woman should whisper, "*Hiai!*" Even so the great bell hath sounded every day for well-nigh five hundred years,—*Ko-Ngai*: first with stupendous clang, then with immeasurable moan of gold, then with silver murmuring of "*Hiai!*" And there is not a child in all the many-colored ways of the old Chinese city who does not know the story of the great bell,—who cannot tell you why the great bell says *Ko-Ngai* and *Hiai*!

* * * *

Now, this is the story of the great bell in the Ta-chung sz', as the same is related in the *Pe-Hiao-Tou-Choue*, written by the learned Yu-Pao-Tchen, of the City of Kwang-tchau-fu.

Nearly five hundred years ago the Celestially August, the Son of Heaven, Yong-Lo, of the "Illustrious," or Ming, dynasty, commanded the worthy official Kouan-Yu that he should have a bell made of such size that the sound thereof might be heard for one hundred *li*. And he further ordained that the voice of the bell should be strengthened with brass, and deepened with gold, and sweetened with silver; and that the face and the great lips of it should be graven with blessed sayings from the sacred books, and that it should be suspended in the centre of the imperial capital, to sound through all the many-colored ways of the City of Pe-king.

Therefore the worthy mandarin Kouan-Yu assembled the master-moulders and the renowned bellsmiths of the empire, and all men of great repute and cunning in foundry work; and they measured the materials for the alloy, and treated them skilfully, and prepared the moulds, the fires, the instruments, and the monstrous melting-pot for fusing the metal. And they labored exceedingly, like giants,—neglecting only rest and sleep and the comforts of life; toiling both night and day in obedience to Kouan-Yu, and striving in all things to do the behest of the Son of Heaven.

But when the metal had been cast, and the earthen mould separated fromthe glowing casting, it was discovered that, despite their great labor and ceaseless care, the result was void of worth; for the metals had rebelled one against the other,—the gold had scorned alliance with the brass, the silver would not mingle with the molten iron. Therefore the moulds had to be once more prepared, and the fires rekindled, and the metal remelted, and all the work tediously and toilsomely repeated. The Son of Heaven heard, and was angry, but spake nothing.

A second time the bell was cast, and the result was even worse. Still the metals obstinately refused to blend one with the other; and there was no uniformity in the bell, and the sides of it were cracked and fissured, and the lips of it were slagged and split asunder; so that all the labor had to be repeated even a third time, to the great dismay of Kouan-Yu. And when the Son of Heaven heard these things, he was angrier than before; and sent his messenger to Kouan-Yu with a letter, written upon lemon-colored silk, and sealed with the seal of the Dragon, containing these words:—

> "From the Mighty Yong-Lo, the Sublime Tait-Sung, the Celestial and August,—whose reign is called 'Ming,'—to Kouan-Yu the Fuh-yin: Twice thou hast betrayed the trust we have deigned graciously to place in thee; if thou fail a third time in fulfilling our command, thy head shall be severed from thy neck. Tremble, and obey!"

* * * *

Now, Kouan-Yu had a daughter of dazzling loveliness, whose name—Ko-Ngai—was ever in the mouths of poets, and whose heart was even more beautiful than her face. Ko-Ngai loved her father with such love that she had refused a hundred worthy suitors rather than make his home desolate by her absence; and when she had seen the awful yellow missive, sealed with the Dragon-Seal, she fainted away with fear for her father's sake. And when her senses and her strength returned to her, she could not rest or sleep for thinking of her parent's danger, until she had secretly sold some of her jewels, and with the money so obtained had hastened to an astrologer, and paid him a great price to advise her by what means her father might be saved from the peril impending over him. So the astrologer made observations of the heavens, and marked the aspect of the Silver Stream (which we call the Milky Way), and examined the signs of the Zodiac,—the *Hwang-tao*, or Yellow Road,—and consulted the table of the Five *Hin*, or Principles of the Universe, and the mystical books of the alchemists. And after a long silence, he made answer to her, saying: "Gold and brass will never meet in wedlock, silver and iron never will embrace, until the flesh of a maiden be melted in the crucible; until the blood of a virgin be mixed with the metals in their fusion." So Ko-Ngai returned home sorrowful at heart; but she kept secret all that she had heard, and told no one what she had done.

* * * *

At last came the awful day when the third and last effort to cast the great bell was to be made; and Ko-Ngai, together with her waiting-woman, accompanied her father to the foundry, and they took their places upon a platform overlooking the toiling of the moulders and the lava of liquefied metal. All the workmen wrought their tasks in silence; there was no sound heard but the muttering of the fires. And the muttering deepened into a roar like the roar of typhoons approaching, and the blood-red lake of metal slowly brightened like the vermilion of a sunrise, and the vermilion was transmuted into a radiant glow of gold, and the gold whitened blindingly, like the silver face of a full moon. Then the workers ceased to feed the raving flame, and all fixed their eyes upon the eyes of Kouan-Yu; and Kouan-Yu prepared to give the signal to cast.

But ere ever he lifted his finger, a cry caused him to turn his head; and all heard the voice of Ko-Ngai sounding sharply sweet as a bird's song above the great thunder of the fires—"*For thy sake, O my Father!*" And even as she cried, she leaped into the white flood of metal; and the lava of the furnace roared to receive her, and spattered monstrous flakes of flame to the roof, and burst over the verge of the earthen crater, and cast up a whirling fountain of many-colored fires, and subsided quakingly, with lightnings and with thunders and with mutterings.

Then the father of Ko-Ngai, wild with his grief, would have leaped in after her, but that strong men held him back and kept firm grasp upon him until he had fainted away and they could bear him like one dead to his home. And the serving-woman of Ko-Ngai, dizzy and speechless for pain, stood before the furnace, still holding in her hands a shoe, a tiny, dainty shoe, with embroidery of pearls and flowers,—the shoe of her beautiful mistress that was. For she had sought to grasp Ko-Ngai by the foot as she leaped, but had only been able to clutch the shoe, and the pretty shoe came off in her hand; and she continued to stare at it like one gone mad.

But in spite of all these things, the command of the Celestial and August had to be obeyed, and the work of the moulders to be finished, hopeless as the result might be. Yet the glow of the metal seemed purer and whiter than before; and there was no sign of the beautiful body that had been entombed therein. So the ponderous casting was made; and lo! when the metal had become cool, it was found that the bell was beautiful to look upon, and perfect in form, and wonderful in color above all other bells. Nor was there any trace found of the body of Ko-Ngai; for it had been totally absorbed by the precious alloy, and blended with the well-blended brass and gold, with the intermingling of the silver and the iron. And when they sounded the bell, its tones were found to be deeper and mellower and mightier than the tones of any other bell,—reaching even beyond the distance of one hundred *li*, like a pealing of summer thunder; and yet also like some vast voice uttering a name, a woman's name,—the name of Ko-Ngai!

* * * *

And still, between each mighty stroke there is a long low moaning heard; and ever the moaning ends with a sound of sobbing and of complaining, as though a weeping woman should murmur, "*Hiai!*" And still, when the people hear that great golden moan they keep silence; but when the sharp, sweet shuddering comes in the air, and the sobbing of "*Hiai!*" then, indeed, all the Chinese mothers in all the many-colored ways of Pe-king whisper to their little ones: "*Listen! that is Ko-Ngai crying for her shoe! That is Ko-Ngai calling for her shoe!*"

PRESENT AT A HANGING, by Ambrose Bierce

An old man named Daniel Baker, living near Lebanon, Iowa, was suspected by his neighbors of having murdered a peddler who had obtained permission to pass the night at his house. This was in 1853, when peddling was more common in the Western country than it is now, and was attended with considerable danger. The peddler with his pack traversed the country by all manner of lonely roads, and was compelled to rely upon the country people for hospitality. This brought him into relation with queer characters, some of whom were not altogether scrupulous in their methods of making a living, murder being an acceptable means to that end. It occasionally occurred that a peddler with diminished pack and swollen purse would be traced to the lonely dwelling of some rough character and never could be traced beyond. This was so in the case of "old man Baker," as he was always called. (Such names are given in the western "settlements" only to elderly persons who are not esteemed; to the general disrepute of social unworth is affixed the special reproach of age.) A peddler came to his house and none went away—that is all that anybody knew.

Seven years later the Rev. Mr. Cummings, a Baptist minister well known in that part of the country, was driving by Baker's farm one night. It was not very dark: there was a bit of moon somewhere above the light veil of mist that lay along the earth. Mr. Cummings, who was at all times a cheerful person, was whistling a tune, which he would occasionally interrupt to speak a word of friendly encouragement to his horse. As he came to a little bridge across a dry ravine he saw the figure of a man standing upon it, clearly outlined against the gray background of a misty forest. The man had something strapped on his back and carried a heavy stick—obviously an itinerant peddler. His attitude had in it a suggestion of abstraction, like that of a sleepwalker. Mr. Cummings reined in his horse when he arrived in front of him, gave him a pleasant salutation and invited him to a seat in the vehicle—"if you are going my way," he added. The man raised his head, looked him full in the face, but neither answered nor made any further movement. The minister, with good-natured persistence, repeated his invitation. At this the man threw his right hand forward from his side and pointed downward as he stood on the extreme edge of the bridge. Mr. Cummings looked past him, over into the ravine, saw nothing unusual and withdrew his eyes to address the man again. He had disappeared. The horse, which all this time had been uncommonly restless, gave at the same moment a snort of terror and started to run away. Before he had regained control of the animal the minister was at the crest of the hill a hundred yards along. He looked back and saw the figure again, at the same place and in the same attitude as when he had first observed it. Then for the first time he was conscious of a sense of the supernatural and drove home as rapidly as his willing horse would go.

On arriving at home he related his adventure to his family, and early the next morning, accompanied by two neighbors, John White Corwell and Abner Raiser, returned to the spot. They found the body of old man Baker hanging by the neck from one of the beams of the bridge, immediately beneath the spot where the apparition had stood. A thick coating of dust, slightly dampened by the mist, covered the floor of the bridge, but the only footprints were those of Mr. Cummings' horse.

In taking down the body, the men disturbed the loose, friable earth of the slope below it, disclosing human bones already nearly uncovered by the action of water and frost. They were identified as those of the lost peddler. At the double inquest the coroner's jury found that Daniel Baker died by his own hand while suffering from temporary insanity, and that Samuel Morritz was murdered by some person or persons to the jury unknown.

CANON ALBERIC'S SCRAP-BOOK
by M. R. James

St. Bertrand de Comminges is a decayed town on the spurs of the Pyrenees, not very far from Toulouse, and still nearer to Bagnères-de-Luchon. It was the site of a bishopric until the Revolution, and has a cathedral which is visited by a certain number of tourists. In the spring of 1883 an Englishman arrived at this old-world place—I can hardly dignify it with the name of city, for there are not a thousand inhabitants. He was a Cambridge man, who had come specially from Toulouse to see St. Bertrand's Church, and had left two friends, who were less keen archæologists than himself, in their hotel at Toulouse, under promise to join him on the following morning. Half an hour at the church would satisfy *them*, and all three could then pursue their journey in the direction of Auch. But our Englishman had come early on the day in question, and proposed to himself to fill a note-book and to use several dozens of plates in the process of describing and photographing every corner of the wonderful church that dominates the little hill of Comminges. In order to carry out this design satisfactorily, it was necessary to monopolize the verger of the church for the day. The verger or sacristan (I prefer the latter appellation, inaccurate as it may be) was accordingly sent for by the somewhat brusque lady who keeps the inn of the Chapeau Rouge; and when he came, the Englishman found him an unexpectedly interesting object of study. It was not in the personal appearance of the little, dry, wizened old man that the interest lay, for he was precisely like dozens of other church-guardians in France, but in a curious furtive, or rather hunted and oppressed, air which he had. He was perpetually half glancing behind him; the muscles of his back and shoulders seemed to be hunched in a continual nervous contraction, as if he were expecting every moment to find himself in the clutch of an enemy. The Englishman hardly knew whether to put him down as a man haunted by a fixed delusion, or as one oppressed by a guilty conscience, or as an unbearably henpecked husband. The probabilities, when reckoned up, certainly pointed to the last idea; but, still, the impression conveyed was that of a more formidable persecutor even than a termagant wife.

However, the Englishman (let us call him Dennistoun) was soon too deep in his note-book and too busy with his camera to give more than an occasional glance to the sacristan. Whenever he did look at him, he found him at no great distance, either huddling himself back against the wall or crouching in one of the gorgeous stalls. Dennistoun became rather fidgety after a time. Mingled suspicions that he was keeping the old man from his *déjeuner*, that he was regarded as likely to make away with St. Bertrand's ivory crozier, or with the dusty stuffed crocodile that hangs over the font, began to torment him.

"Won't you go home?" he said at last; "I'm quite well able to finish my notes alone; you can lock me in if you like. I shall want at least two hours more here, and it must be cold for you, isn't it?"

"Good heavens!" said the little man, whom the suggestion seemed to throw into a state of unaccountable terror, "such a thing cannot be thought of for a moment. Leave monsieur alone in the church? No, no; two hours, three hours, all will be the same to me. I have breakfasted, I am not at all cold, with many thanks to monsieur."

"Very well, my little man," quoth Dennistoun to himself: "you have been warned, and you must take the consequences."

Before the expiration of the two hours, the stalls, the enormous dilapidated organ, the choir-screen of Bishop John de Mauléon, the remnants of glass and tapestry, and the objects in the treasure-chamber, had been well and truly examined; the sacristan still keeping at Dennistoun's heels, and every now and then whipping round as if he had been stung, when one or other of the strange noises that trouble a large empty building fell on his ear. Curious noises they were sometimes.

"Once," Dennistoun said to me, "I could have sworn I heard a thin metallic voice laughing high up in the tower. I darted an inquiring glance at my sacristan. He was white to the lips. 'It is he—that is—it is no one; the door is locked,' was all he said, and we looked at each other for a full minute."

Another little incident puzzled Dennistoun a good deal. He was examining a large dark picture that hangs behind the altar, one of a series illustrating the miracles of St. Bertrand. The composition of the picture is well-nigh indecipherable, but there is a Latin legend below, which runs thus:

"Qualiter S. Bertrandus liberavit hominem quem diabolus diu volebat strangulare."
(How St. Bertrand delivered a man whom the Devil long sought to strangle.)

Dennistoun was turning to the sacristan with a smile and a jocular remark of some sort on his lips, but he was confounded to see the old man on his knees, gazing at the picture with the eye of a suppliant in agony, his hands tightly clasped, and a rain of tears on his cheeks. Dennistoun naturally pretended to have noticed nothing, but the question would not away from him, "Why should a daub of this kind affect any one so strongly?" He seemed to himself to be getting some sort of clue to the reason of the strange look that had been puzzling him all the day: the man must be monomaniac; but what was his monomania?

It was nearly five o'clock; the short day was drawing in, and the church began to fill with shadows, while the curious noises—the muffled footfalls and distant talking voices that had been perceptible all day—seemed, no doubt because of the fading light and the consequently quickened sense of hearing, to become more frequent and insistent.

The sacristan began for the first time to show signs of hurry and impatience. He heaved a sigh of relief when camera and note-book were finally packed up and stowed away, and hurriedly beckoned Dennistoun to the western door of the church, under the tower. It was time to ring the Angelus. A few pulls at the reluctant rope, and the great bell Bertrande, high in the tower, began to speak, and swung her voice up among the pines and down to the valleys, loud with mountain-streams, calling the dwellers on those lonely hills to remember and repeat the salutation of the angel to her whom he called Blessed among women. With that a profound quiet seemed to fall for the first time that day upon the little town, and Dennistoun and the sacristan went out of the church.

On the doorstep they fell into conversation.

"Monsieur seemed to interest himself in the old choir-books in the sacristy."

"Undoubtedly. I was going to ask you if there were a library in the town."

"No, monsieur; perhaps there used to be one belonging to the Chapter, but it is now such a small place—" Here came a strange pause of irresolution, as it seemed; then, with a sort of plunge, he went on: "But if monsieur is *amateur des vieux livres*, I have at home something that might interest him. It is not a hundred yards."

At once all Dennistoun's cherished dreams of finding priceless manuscripts in untrodden corners of France flashed up, to die down again the next moment. It was probably a stupid missal of Plantin's printing, about 1580. Where was the likelihood that a place so near Toulouse would not have been ransacked long ago by collectors? However, it would be foolish not to go; he would reproach himself for ever after if he refused. So they set off. On the way the curious irresolution and sudden determination of the sacristan recurred to Dennistoun, and he wondered in a shamefaced way whether he was being decoyed into some purlieu to be made away with as a supposed rich Englishman. He contrived, therefore, to begin talking with his guide, and to drag in, in a rather clumsy fashion, the fact that he expected two friends to join him early the next morning. To his surprise, the announcement seemed to relieve the sacristan at once of some of the anxiety that oppressed him.

"That is well," he said quite brightly—"that is very well. Monsieur will travel in company with his friends; they will be always near him. It is a good thing to travel thus in company—sometimes."

The last word appeared to be added as an afterthought, and to bring with it a relapse into gloom for the poor little man.

They were soon at the house, which was one rather larger than its neighbors, stone-built, with a shield carved over the door, the shield of Alberic de Mauléon, a collateral descendant, Dennistoun tells me, of Bishop John de Mauléon. This Alberic was a Canon of Comminges from 1680 to 1701. The upper windows of the mansion were boarded up, and the whole place bore, as does the rest of Comminges, the aspect of decaying age.

Arrived on his doorstep, the sacristan paused a moment.

"Perhaps," he said, "perhaps, after all, monsieur has not the time?"

"Not at all—lots of time—nothing to do till to-morrow. Let us see what it is you have got."

The door was opened at this point, and a face looked out, a face far younger than the sacristan's, but bearing something of the same distressing look: only here it seemed to be the mark, not so much of fear for personal safety as of acute anxiety on behalf of another. Plainly, the owner of the face was the sacristan's daughter; and, but for the expression I have described, she was a handsome girl enough. She brightened up considerably on seeing her father accompanied by an able-bodied stranger. A few remarks passed between father and daughter, of which Dennistoun only caught these words, said by the sacristan, "He was laughing in the church," words which were answered only by a look of terror from the girl.

But in another minute they were in the sitting-room of the house, a small, high chamber with a stone floor, full of moving shadows cast by a wood-fire that flickered on a great hearth. Something of the character of an oratory was imparted to it by a tall crucifix, which reached almost to the ceiling on one side; the figure was painted of the natural colors, the cross was black. Under this stood a chest of some age and solidity, and when a lamp had been brought, and chairs set, the sacristan went to this chest, and produced therefrom, with growing excitement and nervousness, as Dennistoun thought, a large book wrapped in a white cloth, on which cloth a cross was rudely embroidered in red thread. Even before the wrapping had been removed, Dennistoun began to be interested by the size and shape of the volume. "Too large for a missal," he thought, "and not the shape of an antiphoner; perhaps it may be something good, after all." The next moment the book was open, and Dennistoun felt that he had at last lit upon something better than good. Before him lay a large folio, bound, perhaps, late in the seventeenth century, with the arms of Canon Alberic de Mauléon stamped in gold on the sides. There may have been a hundred and fifty leaves of paper in the book, and on almost every one of them was fastened a leaf from an illuminated manuscript. Such a collection Dennistoun had hardly dreamed of in his wildest moments. Here were ten leaves from a copy of Genesis, illustrated with pictures, which could not be later than 700 A.D. Further on was a complete set of pictures from a psalter, of English execution, of the very finest kind that the thirteenth century could produce; and, perhaps best of all, there were twenty leaves of uncial writing in Latin, which, as a few words seen here and there told him at once, must belong to some very early unknown patristic treatise. Could it possibly be a fragment of the copy of Papias "On the Words of Our Lord," which was known to have existed as late as the twelfth century at Nîmes? In any case, his mind was made up; that book must return to Cambridge with him, even if he had to draw the whole of his balance from the bank and stay at St. Bertrand till the money came. He glanced up at the sacristan to see if his face yielded any hint that the book was for sale. The sacristan was pale, and his lips were working.

"If monsieur will turn on to the end," he said.

So monsieur turned on, meeting new treasures at every rise of a leaf; and at the end of the book he came upon two sheets of paper, of much more recent date than anything he had yet seen, which puzzled him considerably. They must be contemporary, he decided, with the unprincipled Canon Alberic, who had doubtless plundered the Chapter library of St. Bertrand to form this priceless scrapbook. On the first of the paper sheets was a plan, carefully drawn and instantly recognizable by a person who knew the ground, of the south aisle and cloisters of St. Bertrand's. There were curious signs looking like planetary symbols, and a few Hebrew words in the corners; and in the northwest angle of the cloister was a cross drawn in gold paint. Below the plan were some lines of writing in Latin, which ran thus:

"Responsa 12^mi^ Dec. 1694.
Interrogatum est: Inveniamne?
Responsum est: Invenies.
Fiamne dives? Fies.
Vivamne invidendus? Vives.
Moriarne in lecto meo? Ita."

(Answers of the 12th of December, 1694. It was asked: Shall I find it? Answer: Thou shalt. Shall I become rich? Thou wilt. Shall I live an object of envy? Thou wilt. Shall I die in my bed? Thou wilt.)

"A good specimen of the treasure-hunter's record—quite reminds one of Mr. Minor-Canon Quatremain in 'Old St. Paul's,'" was Dennistoun's comment, and he turned the leaf.

What he then saw impressed him, as he has often told me, more than he could have conceived any drawing or picture capable of impressing him. And, though the drawing he saw is no longer in existence, there is a photograph of it (which I possess) which fully bears out that statement. The picture in question was a sepia drawing at the end of the seventeenth century, representing, one would say at first sight, a Biblical scene; for the architecture (the picture represented an interior) and the figures had that semi-classical flavor about them which the artists of two hundred years ago thought appropriate to illustrations of the Bible. On the right was a king on his throne, the throne elevated on twelve steps, a canopy overhead, soldiers on either side—evidently King Solomon. He was bending forward with outstretched scepter, in attitude of command; his face expressed horror and disgust, yet there was in it also the mark of imperious command and confident power. The left half of the picture was the strangest, however. The interest plainly centered there. On the pavement before the throne were grouped four soldiers, surrounding a crouching figure which must be described in a moment. A fifth soldier lay dead on the pavement, his neck distorted, and his eyeballs starting from his head. The four surrounding guards were looking at the King. In their faces the sentiment of horror was intensified; they seemed, in fact, only restrained from flight by their implicit trust in their master. All this terror was plainly excited by the being that crouched in their midst. I entirely despair of conveying by any words the impression which this figure makes upon any one who looks at it. I recollect once showing the photograph of the drawing to a lecturer on morphology—a person of, I was going to say, abnormally sane and unimaginative habits of mind. He absolutely refused to be alone for the rest of that evening, and he told me afterwards that for many nights he had not dared to put out his light before going to sleep. However, the main traits of the figure I can at least indicate. At first you saw only a mass of coarse, matted black hair; presently it was seen that this covered a body of fearful thinness, almost a skeleton, but with the muscles standing out like wires. The hands were of a dusky pallor, covered, like the body, with long, coarse hairs, and hideously taloned. The eyes, touched in with a burning yellow, had intensely black pupils, and were fixed upon the throned king with a look of beast-like hate. Imagine one of the awful bird-catching spiders of South America translated into human form, and endowed with intelligence just less than human, and you will have some faint conception of the terror inspired by the appalling effigy. One remark is universally made by those to whom I have shown the picture: "It was drawn from the life."

As soon as the first shock of his irresistible fright had subsided, Dennistoun stole a look at his hosts. The sacristan's hands were pressed upon his eyes; his daughter, looking up at the cross on the wall, was telling her beads feverishly.

At last the question was asked, "Is this book for sale?"

There was the same hesitation, the same plunge of determination, that he had noticed before, and then came the welcome answer, "If monsieur pleases."

"How much do you ask for it?"

"I will take two hundred and fifty francs."

This was confounding. Even a collector's conscience is sometimes stirred, and Dennistoun's conscience was tenderer than a collector's.

"My good man!" he said again and again, "your book is worth far more than two hundred and fifty francs, I assure you—far more."

But the answer did not vary: "I will take two hundred and fifty francs, not more."

There was really no possibility of refusing such a chance. The money was paid, the receipt signed, a glass of wine drunk over the transaction, and then the sacristan seemed to become a new man. He stood upright, he ceased to throw those suspicious glances behind him, he actually laughed or tried to laugh. Dennistoun rose to go.

"I shall have the honor of accompanying monsieur to his hotel?" said the sacristan.

"Oh no, thanks! it isn't a hundred yards. I know the way perfectly, and there is a moon."

The offer was pressed three or four times, and refused as often.

"Then, monsieur will summon me if—if he finds occasion; he will keep the middle of the road, the sides are so rough."

"Certainly, certainly," said Dennistoun, who was impatient to examine his prize by himself; and he stepped out into the passage with his book under his arm.

Here he was met by the daughter; she, it appeared, was anxious to do a little business on her own account; perhaps, like Gehazi, to "take somewhat" from the foreigner whom her father had spared.

"A silver crucifix and chain for the neck; monsieur would perhaps be good enough to accept it?"

Well, really, Dennistoun hadn't much use for these things. What did mademoiselle want for it?

"Nothing—nothing in the world. Monsieur is more than welcome to it."

The tone in which this and much more was said was unmistakably genuine, so that Dennistoun was reduced to profuse thanks, and submitted to have the chain put round his neck. It really seemed as if he had rendered the father and daughter some service which they hardly knew how to repay. As he set off with his book they stood at the door looking after him, and they were still looking when he waved them a last good-night from the steps of the Chapeau Rouge.

Dinner was over, and Dennistoun was in his bedroom, shut up alone with his acquisition. The landlady had manifested a particular interest in him since he had told her that he had paid a visit to the sacristan and bought an old book from him. He thought, too, that he had heard a hurried dialogue between her and the said sacristan in the passage outside the *salle à manger;* some words to the effect that "Pierre and Bertrand would be sleeping in the house" had closed the conversation.

At this time a growing feeling of discomfort had been creeping over him—nervous reaction, perhaps, after the delight of his discovery. Whatever it was, it resulted in a conviction that there was some one behind him, and that he was far more comfortable with his back to the wall. All this, of course, weighed light in the balance as against the obvious value of the collection he had acquired. And now, as I said, he was alone in his bedroom, taking stock of Canon Alberic's treasures, in which every moment revealed something more charming.

"Bless Canon Alberic!" said Dennistoun, who had an inveterate habit of talking to himself. "I wonder where he is now? Dear me! I wish that landlady would learn to laugh in a more cheering manner; it makes one feel as if there was some one dead in the house. Half a pipe more, did you say? I think perhaps you are right. I wonder what that crucifix is that the young woman insisted on giving me? Last century, I suppose. Yes, probably. It is rather a nuisance of a thing to have round one's neck—just too heavy. Most likely her father had been wearing it for years. I think I might give it a clean up before I put it away."

He had taken the crucifix off, and laid it on the table, when his attention was caught by an object lying on the red cloth just by his left elbow. Two or three ideas of what it might be flitted through his brain with their own incalculable quickness.

"A penwiper? No, no such thing in the house. A rat? No, too black. A large spider? I trust to goodness not—no. Good God! a hand like the hand in that picture!"

In another infinitesimal flash he had taken it in. Pale, dusky skin, covering nothing but bones and tendons of appalling strength; coarse black hairs, longer than ever grew on a human hand; nails rising from the ends of the fingers and curving sharply down and forward, gray, horny and wrinkled.

He flew out of his chair with deadly, inconceivable terror clutching at his heart. The shape, whose left hand rested on the table, was rising to a standing posture behind his seat, its right hand crooked above his scalp. There was black and tattered drapery about it; the coarse hair covered it as in the drawing. The lower jaw was thin—what can I call it?—shallow, like a beast's; teeth showed behind the black lips; there was no nose; the eyes, of a fiery yellow, against which the pupils showed black and intense, and the exulting hate and thirst to destroy life which shone there, were the most horrifying feature in the whole vision. There was intelligence of a kind in them—intelligence beyond that of a beast, below that of a man.

The feelings which this horror stirred in Dennistoun were the intensest physical fear and the most profound mental loathing. What did he do? What could he do? He has never been quite certain what words he said, but he knows that he spoke, that he grasped blindly at the silver crucifix, that he was conscious of a movement towards him on the part of the demon, and that he screamed with the voice of an animal in hideous pain.

Pierre and Bertrand, the two sturdy little serving-men, who rushed in, saw nothing, but felt themselves thrust aside by something that passed out between them, and found Dennistoun in a swoon. They sat up with him that night, and his two friends were at St. Bertrand by nine o'clock next morning. He himself, though still shaken and nervous, was almost himself by that time, and his story found credence with them, though not until they had seen the drawing and talked with the sacristan.

Almost at dawn the little man had come to the inn on some pretense, and had listened with the deepest interest to the story retailed by the landlady. He showed no surprise.

"It is he—it is he! I have seen him myself," was his only comment; and to all questionings but one reply was vouchsafed: "Deux fois je l'ai vu; mille fois je l'ai senti." He would tell them nothing of the provenance of the book, nor any details of his experiences. "I shall soon sleep, and my rest will be sweet. Why should you trouble me?" he said.

We shall never know what he or Canon Alberic de Mauléon suffered. At the back of that fateful drawing were some lines of writing which may be supposed to throw light on the situation:

"Contradictio Salomonis cum demonio nocturno.
Albericus de Mauleone delineavit.
V. Deus in adiutorium. Ps. Qui habitat.
Sancte Bertrande, demoniorum effugator, intercede pro me miserrimo.
Primum uidi nocte 12mi Dec. 1694: uidebo mox ultimum.

*

Peccaui et passus sum, plura adhuc passurus. Dec. 29, 1701."

I have never quite understood what was Dennistoun's view of the events I have narrated. He quoted to me once a test from Ecclesiasticus: "Some spirits there be that are created for vengeance, and in their fury lay on sore strokes." On another occasion he said: "Isaiah was a very sensible man; doesn't he say something about night monsters living in the ruins of Babylon? These things are rather beyond us at present."

Another confidence of his impressed me rather, and I sympathized with it. We had been, last year, to Comminges, to see Canon Alberic's tomb. It is a great marble erection with an effigy of the Canon in a large wig and soutane, and an elaborate eulogy of his learning below. I saw Dennistoun talking for some time with the Vicar of St. Bertrand's, and as we drove away he said to me: "I hope it isn't wrong: you know I am a Presbyterian—but I—I believe there will be 'saying of Mass and singing of dirges' for Alberic de Mauléon's rest." Then he added, with a touch of the Northern British in his tone, "I had no notion they came so dear."

* * * *

The book is in the Wentworth Collection at Cambridge. The drawing was photographed and then burnt by Dennistoun on the day when he left Comminges on the occasion of his first visit.

THE MASS OF SHADOWS,
by Anatole France

This tale the sacristan of the church of St. Eulalie at Neuville d'Aumont told me, as we sat under the arbor of the White Horse, one fine summer evening, drinking a bottle of old wine to the health of the dead man, now very much at his ease, whom that very morning he had borne to the grave with full honors, beneath a pall powdered with smart silver tears.

"My poor father who is dead" (it is the sacristan who is speaking,) "was in his lifetime a grave-digger. He was of an agreeable disposition, the result, no doubt, of the calling he followed, for it has often been pointed out that people who work in cemeteries are of a jovial turn. Death has no terrors for them; they never give it a thought. I, for instance, monsieur, enter a cemetery at night as little perturbed as though it were the arbor of the White Horse. And if by chance I meet with a ghost, I don't disturb myself in the least about it, for I reflect that he may just as likely have business of his own to attend to as I. I know the habits of the dead, and I know their character. Indeed, so far as that goes, I know things of which the priests themselves are ignorant. If I were to tell you all I have seen, you would be astounded. But a still tongue makes a wise head, and my father, who, all the same, delighted in spinning a yarn, did not disclose a twentieth part of what he knew. To make up for this he often repeated the same stories, and to my knowledge he told the story of Catherine Fontaine at least a hundred times.

"Catherine Fontaine was an old maid whom he well remembered having seen when he was a mere child. I should not be surprised if there were still, perhaps, three old fellows in the district who could remember having heard folks speak of her, for she was very well known and of excellent reputation, though poor enough. She lived at the corner of the Rue aux Nonnes, in the turret which is still to be seen there, and which formed part of an old half-ruined mansion looking on to the garden of the Ursuline nuns. On that turret can still be traced certain figures and half-obliterated inscriptions. The late curé of St. Eulalie, Monsieur Levasseur, asserted that there are the words in Latin, *Love is stronger than death*, 'which is to be understood,' so he would add, 'of divine love.'

"Catherine Fontaine lived by herself in this tiny apartment. She was a lace-maker. You know, of course, that the lace made in our part of the world was formerly held in high esteem. No one knew anything of her relatives or friends. It was reported that when she was eighteen years of age she had loved the young Chevalier d'Aumont-Cléry, and had been secretly affianced to him. But decent folk didn't believe a word of it, and said it was nothing but a tale concocted because Catherine Fontaine's demeanor was that of a lady rather than that of a working woman, and because, moreover, she possessed beneath her white locks the remains of great beauty. Her expression was sorrowful, and on one finger she wore one of those rings fashioned by the goldsmith into the semblance of two tiny hands clasped together. In former days folks were accustomed to exchange such rings at their betrothal ceremony. I am sure you know the sort of thing I mean.

"Catherine Fontaine lived a saintly life. She spent a great deal of time in churches, and every morning, whatever might be the weather, she went to assist at the six o'clock Mass at St. Eulalie.

"Now one December night, whilst she was in her little chamber, she was awakened by the sound of bells, and nothing doubting that they were ringing for the first Mass, the pious woman dressed herself, and came downstairs and out into the street. The night was so obscure that not even the walls of the houses were visible, and not a ray of light shone from the murky sky. And such was the silence amid this black darkness, that there was not even the sound of a distant dog barking, and a feeling of aloofness from every living creature was perceptible. But Catherine Fontaine knew well every single stone she stepped on, and, as she could have found her way to the church with her eyes shut, she reached without difficulty the corner of the Rue aux Nonnes and the Rue de la Paroisse, where the timbered house stands with the tree of Jesse carved on one of its massive beams. When she reached this spot she perceived that the church doors were open, and that a great light was streaming out from the wax tapers. She resumed her journey, and when she had passed through the porch she found herself in the midst of a vast congregation which entirely filled the church. But she did not recognize any of the worshipers and was surprised to observe that all of these people were dressed in velvets and brocades, with feathers in their hats, and that they wore swords in the fashion of days gone by. Here were gentlemen who carried tall canes with gold knobs, and ladies with lace caps fastened with coronet-shaped combs. Chevaliers of the Order of St. Louis extended their hands to these ladies, who concealed behind their fans painted faces, of which only the powdered brow and the patch at the corner of the eye were visible! All of them proceeded to take their places without the slightest sound, and as they moved neither the sound of their footsteps on the pavement, nor the rustle of their garments could be heard. The lower places were filled with a crowd of young artisans in brown jackets, dimity breeches, and blue stockings, with their arms round the waists of pretty blushing girls who lowered their eyes. Near the holy water stoups peasant women, in scarlet petticoats and laced bodices, sat upon the ground as immovable as domestic animals, whilst young lads, standing up behind them, stared out from wide-open eyes and twirled their hats round and round on their fingers, and all these sorrowful countenances seemed centred irremovably on one and the same thought, at once sweet and sorrowful. On her knees, in her accustomed place, Catherine Fontaine saw the priest advance toward the altar, preceded by two servers. She recognized neither priest nor clerks. The Mass began. It was a silent Mass, during which neither the sound of the moving lips nor the tinkle of the bell was audible. Catherine Fontaine felt that she was under the observation and the influence also of her mysterious neighbor, and when, scarcely turning her head, she stole a glance at him, she recognized the young Chevalier d'Aumont-Cléry, who had once loved her, and who had been dead for five and forty years. She recognized him by a small mark which he had over the left ear, and above all by the shadow which his long black eyelashes cast upon his cheeks. He was dressed in his hunting clothes, scarlet with gold lace, the very clothes he wore that day when he met her in St. Leonard's Wood, begged of her a drink, and stole a kiss. He had preserved his youth and good looks. When he smiled, he still displayed magnificent teeth. Catherine said to him in an undertone:

"'Monseigneur, you who were my friend, and to whom in days gone by I gave all that a girl holds most dear, may God keep you in His grace! O, that He would at length inspire me with regret for the sin I committed in yielding to you; for it is a fact that, though my hair is white and I approach my end, I have not yet repented of having loved you. But, dear dead friend and noble seigneur, tell me, who are these folk, habited after the antique fashion, who are here assisting at this silent Mass?'

"The Chevalier d'Aumont-Cléry replied in a voice feebler than a breath, but none the less crystal clear:

"'Catherine, these men and women are souls from purgatory who have grieved God by sinning as we ourselves sinned through love of the creature, but who are not on that account cast off by God, inasmuch as their sin, like ours, was not deliberate.

"'Whilst separated from those whom they loved upon earth, they are purified in the cleansing fires of purgatory, they suffer the pangs of absence, which is for them the most cruel of tortures. They are so unhappy that an angel from heaven takes pity upon their love-torment. By the permission of the Most High, for one hour in the night, he reunites each year lover to loved in their parish church, where they are permitted to assist at the Mass of Shadows, hand clasped in hand. These are the facts. If it has been granted to me to see thee before thy death, Catherine, it is a boon which is bestowed by God's special permission.'

"And Catherine Fontaine answered him:

"'I would die gladly enough, dear, dead lord, if I might recover the beauty that was mine when I gave you to drink in the forest.'

"Whilst they thus conversed under their breath, a very old canon was taking the collection and proffering to the worshipers a great copper dish, wherein they let fall, each in his turn, ancient coins which have long since ceased to pass current: écus of six livres, florins, ducats and ducatoons, jacobuses and rose-nobles, and the pieces fell silently into the dish. When at length it was placed before the Chevalier, he dropped into it a louis which made no more sound than had the other pieces of gold and silver.

"Then the old canon stopped before Catherine Fontaine, who fumbled in her pocket without being able to find a farthing. Then, being unwilling to allow the dish to pass without an offering from herself, she slipped from her finger the ring which the Chevalier had given her the day before his death, and cast it into the copper bowl. As the golden ring fell, a sound like the heavy clang of a bell rang out, and on the stroke of this reverberation the Chevalier, the canon, the celebrant, the servers, the ladies and their cavaliers, the whole assembly vanished utterly; the candles guttered out, and Catherine Fontaine was left alone in the darkness."

Having concluded his narrative after this fashion, the sacristan drank a long draught of wine, remained pensive for a moment, and then resumed his talk in these words:

"I have told you this tale exactly as my father has told it to me over and over again, and I believe that it is authentic, because it agrees in all respects with what I have observed of the manners and customs peculiar to those who have passed away. I have associated a good deal with the dead ever since my childhood, and I know that they are accustomed to return to what they have loved.

"It is on this account that the miserly dead wander at night in the neighborhood of the treasures they conceal during their life time. They keep a strict watch over their gold; but the trouble they give themselves, far from being of service to them, turns to their disadvantage; and it is not a rare thing at all to come upon money buried in the ground on digging in a place haunted by a ghost. In the same way deceased husbands come by night to harass their wives who have made a second matrimonial venture, and I could easily name several who have kept a better watch over their wives since death than they ever did while living.

"That sort of thing is blameworthy, for in all fairness the dead have no business to stir up jealousies. Still I do but tell you what I have observed myself. It is a matter to take into account if one marries a widow. Besides, the tale I have told you is vouchsafed for in the manner following:

"The morning after that extraordinary night Catherine Fontaine was discovered dead in her chamber. And the beadle attached to St. Eulalie found in the copper bowl used for the collection a gold ring with two clasped hands. Besides, I'm not the kind of man to make jokes. Suppose we order another bottle of wine?..."

THE MAN WHO WENT TOO FAR, by E.F. Benson

The little village of St. Faith's nestles in a hollow of wooded hill up on the north bank of the river Fawn in the county of Hampshire, huddling close round its gray Norman church as if for spiritual protection against the fays and fairies, the trolls and "little people," who might be supposed still to linger in the vast empty spaces of the New Forest, and to come after dusk and do their doubtful businesses. Once outside the hamlet you may walk in any direction (so long as you avoid the high road which leads to Brockenhurst) for the length of a summer afternoon without seeing sign of human habitation, or possibly even catching sight of another human being. Shaggy wild ponies may stop their feeding for a moment as you pass, the white scuts of rabbits will vanish into their burrows, a brown viper perhaps will glide from your path into a clump of heather, and unseen birds will chuckle in the bushes, but it may easily happen that for a long day you will see nothing human. But you will not feel in the least lonely; in summer, at any rate, the sunlight will be gay with butterflies, and the air thick with all those woodland sounds which like instruments in an orchestra combine to play the great symphony of the yearly festival of June. Winds whisper in the birches, and sigh among the firs; bees are busy with their redolent labor among the heather, a myriad birds chirp in the green temples of the forest trees, and the voice of the river prattling over stony places, bubbling into pools, chuckling and gulping round corners, gives you the sense that many presences and companions are near at hand.

Yet, oddly enough, though one would have thought that these benign and cheerful influences of wholesome air and spaciousness of forest were very healthful comrades for a man, in so far as nature can really influence this wonderful human genus which has in these centuries learned to defy her most violent storms in its well-established houses, to bridle her torrents and make them light its streets, to tunnel her mountains and plow her seas, the inhabitants of St. Faith's will not willingly venture into the forest after dark. For in spite of the silence and loneliness of the hooded night it seems that a man is not sure in what company he may suddenly find himself, and though it is difficult to get from these villagers any very clear story of occult appearances, the feeling is widespread. One story indeed I have heard with some definiteness, the tale of a monstrous goat that has been seen to skip with hellish glee about the woods and shady places, and this perhaps is connected with the story which I have here attempted to piece together. It too is well-known to them; for all remember the young artist who died here not long ago, a young man, or so he struck the beholder, of great personal beauty, with something about him that made men's faces to smile and brighten when they looked on him. His ghost they will tell you "walks" constantly by the stream and through the woods which he loved so, and in especial it haunts a certain house, the last of the village, where he lived, and its garden in which he was done to death. For my part I am inclined to think that the terror of the Forest dates chiefly from that day. So, such as the story is, I have set it forth in connected form. It is based partly on the accounts of the villagers, but mainly on that of Darcy, a friend of mine and a friend of the man with whom these events were chiefly concerned.

* * * *

The day had been one of untarnished midsummer splendor, and as the sun drew near to its setting, the glory of the evening grew every moment more crystalline, more miraculous. Westward from St. Faith's the beechwood which stretched for some miles toward the heathery upland beyond already cast its veil of clear shadow over the red roofs of the village, but the spire of the gray church, over-topping all, still pointed a flaming orange finger into the sky. The river Fawn, which runs below, lay in sheets of sky-reflected blue, and wound its dreamy devious course round the edge of this wood, where a rough two-planked bridge crossed from the bottom of the garden of the last house in the village, and communicated by means of a little wicker gate with the wood itself. Then once out of the shadow of the wood the stream lay in flaming pools of the molten crimson of the sunset, and lost itself in the haze of woodland distances.

This house at the end of the village stood outside the shadow, and the lawn which sloped down to the river was still flecked with sunlight. Garden-beds of dazzling color lined its gravel walks, and down the middle of it ran a brick pergola, half-hidden in clusters of rambler-rose and purple with starry clematis. At the bottom end of it, between two of its pillars, was slung a hammock containing a shirt-sleeved figure.

The house itself lay somewhat remote from the rest of the village, and a footpath leading across two fields, now tall and fragrant with hay, was its only communication with the high road. It was low-built, only two stories in height, and like the garden, its walls were a mass of flowering roses. A narrow stone terrace ran along the garden front, over which was stretched an awning, and on the terrace a young silent-footed man-servant was busied with the laying of the table for dinner. He was neat-handed and quick with his job, and having finished it he went back into the house, and reappeared again with a large rough bath-towel on his arm. With this he went to the hammock in the pergola.

"Nearly eight, sir," he said.

"Has Mr. Darcy come yet?" asked a voice from the hammock.

"No, sir."

"If I'm not back when he comes, tell him that I'm just having a bathe before dinner."

The servant went back to the house, and after a moment or two Frank Halton struggled to a sitting posture, and slipped out on to the grass. He was of medium height and rather slender in build, but the supple ease and grace of his movements gave the impression of great physical strength: even his descent from the hammock was not an awkward performance. His face and hands were of very dark complexion, either from constant exposure to wind and sun, or, as his black hair and dark eyes tended to show, from some strain of southern blood. His head was small, his face of an exquisite beauty of modeling, while the smoothness of its contour would have led you to believe that he was a beardless lad still in his teens. But something, some look which living and experience alone can give, seemed to contradict that, and finding yourself completely puzzled as to his age, you would next moment probably cease to think about that, and only look at this glorious specimen of young manhood with wondering satisfaction.

He was dressed as became the season and the heat, and wore only a shirt open at the neck, and a pair of flannel trousers. His head, covered very thickly with a somewhat rebellious crop of short curly hair, was bare as he strolled across the lawn to the bathing-place that lay below. Then for a moment there was silence, then the sound of splashed and divided waters, and presently after, a great shout of ecstatic joy, as he swam up-stream with the foamed water standing in a frill round his neck. Then after some five minutes of limb-stretching struggle with the flood, he turned over on his back, and with arms thrown wide, floated down-stream, ripple-cradled and inert. His eyes were shut, and between half-parted lips he talked gently to himself.

"I am one with it," he said to himself, "the river and I, I and the river. The coolness and splash of it is I, and the water-herbs that wave in it are I also. And my strength and my limbs are not mine but the river's. It is all one, all one, dear Fawn."

* * * *

A quarter of an hour later he appeared again at the bottom of the lawn, dressed as before, his wet hair already drying into its crisp short curls again. There he paused a moment, looking back at the stream with the smile with which men look on the face of a friend, then turned towards the house. Simultaneously his servant came to the door leading on to the terrace, followed by a man who appeared to be some half-way through the fourth decade of his years. Frank and he saw each other across the bushes and garden-beds, and each quickening his step, they met suddenly face to face round an angle of the garden walk, in the fragrance of syringa.

"My dear Darcy," cried Frank, "I am charmed to see you."

But the other stared at him in amazement.

"Frank!" he exclaimed.

"Yes, that is my name," he said laughing, "what is the matter?"

Darcy took his hand.

"What have you done to yourself?" he asked. "You are a boy again."

"Ah, I have a lot to tell you," said Frank. "Lots that you will hardly believe, but I shall convince you—"

He broke off suddenly, and held up his hand.

"Hush, there is my nightingale," he said.

The smile of recognition and welcome with which he had greeted his friend faded from his face, and a look of rapt wonder took its place, as of a lover listening to the voice of his beloved. His mouth parted slightly, showing the white line of teeth, and his eyes looked out and out till they seemed to Darcy to be focused on things beyond the vision of man. Then something perhaps startled the bird, for the song ceased.

"Yes, lots to tell you," he said. "Really I am delighted to see you. But you look rather white and pulled down; no wonder after that fever. And there is to be no nonsense about this visit. It is June now, you stop here till you are fit to begin work again. Two months at least."

"Ah, I can't trespass quite to that extent."

Frank took his arm and walked him down the grass.

"Trespass? Who talks of trespass? I shall tell you quite openly when I am tired of you, but you know when we had the studio together, we used not to bore each other. However, it is ill talking of going away on the moment of your arrival. Just a stroll to the river, and then it will be dinner-time."

Darcy took out his cigarette case, and offered it to the other.

Frank laughed.

"No, not for me. Dear me, I suppose I used to smoke once. How very odd!"

"Given it up?"

"I don't know. I suppose I must have. Anyhow I don't do it now. I would as soon think of eating meat."

"Another victim on the smoking altar of vegetarianism?"

"Victim?" asked Frank. "Do I strike you as such?"

He paused on the margin of the stream and whistled softly. Next moment a moor-hen made its splashing flight across the river, and ran up the bank. Frank took it very gently in his hands and stroked its head, as the creature lay against his shirt.

"And is the house among the reeds still secure?" he half-crooned to it. "And is the missus quite well, and are the neighbors flourishing? There, dear, home with you," and he flung it into the air.

"That bird's very tame," said Darcy, slightly bewildered.

"It is rather," said Frank, following its flight.

* * * *

During dinner Frank chiefly occupied himself in bringing himself up-to-date in the movements and achievements of this old friend whom he had not seen for six years. Those six years, it now appeared, had been full of incident and success for Darcy; he had made a name for himself as a portrait painter which bade fair to outlast the vogue of a couple of seasons, and his leisure time had been brief. Then some four months previously he had been through a severe attack of typhoid, the result of which as concerns this story was that he had come down to this sequestered place to recruit.

"Yes, you've got on," said Frank at the end. "I always knew you would. A.R.A. with more in prospect. Money? You roll in it, I suppose, and, O Darcy, how much happiness have you had all these years? That is the only imperishable possession. And how much have you learned? Oh, I don't mean in Art. Even I could have done well in that."

Darcy laughed.

"Done well? My dear fellow, all I have learned in these six years you knew, so to speak, in your cradle. Your old pictures fetch huge prices. Do you never paint now?"

Frank shook his head.

"No, I'm too busy," he said.

"Doing what? Please tell me. That is what every one is for ever asking me."

"Doing? I suppose you would say I do nothing."

Darcy glanced up at the brilliant young face opposite him.

"It seems to suit you, that way of being busy," he said. "Now, it's your turn. Do you read? Do you study? I remember you saying that it would do us all—all us artists, I mean—a great deal of good if we would study any one human face carefully for a year, without recording a line. Have you been doing that?"

Frank shook his head again.

"I mean exactly what I say," he said, "I have been *doing* nothing. And I have never been so occupied. Look at me; have I not done something to myself to begin with?"

"You are two years younger than I," said Darcy, "at least you used to be. You therefore are thirty-five. But had I never seen you before I should say you were just twenty. But was it worth while to spend six years of greatly-occupied life in order to look twenty? Seems rather like a woman of fashion."

Frank laughed boisterously.

"First time I've ever been compared to that particular bird of prey," he said. "No, that has not been my occupation—in fact I am only very rarely conscious that one effect of my occupation has been that. Of course, it must have been if one comes to think of it. It is not very important. Quite true my body has become young. But that is very little; I have become young."

Darcy pushed back his chair and sat sideways to the table looking at the other.

"Has that been your occupation then?" he asked.

"Yes, that anyhow is one aspect of it. Think what youth means! It is the capacity for growth, mind, body, spirit, all grow, all get stronger, all have a fuller, firmer life every day. That is something, considering that every day that passes after the ordinary man reaches the full-blown flower of his strength, weakens his hold on life. A man reaches his prime, and remains, we say, in his prime, for ten years, or perhaps twenty. But after his primest prime is reached, he slowly, insensibly weakens. These are the signs of age in you, in your body, in your art probably, in your mind. You are less electric than you were. But I, when I reach my prime—I am nearing it—ah, you shall see."

The stars had begun to appear in the blue velvet of the sky, and to the east the horizon seen above the black silhouette of the village was growing dove-colored with the approach of moon-rise. White moths hovered dimly over the garden-beds, and the footsteps of night tip-toed through the bushes. Suddenly Frank rose.

"Ah, it is the supreme moment," he said softly. "Now more than at any other time the current of life, the eternal imperishable current runs so close to me that I am almost enveloped in it. Be silent a minute."

He advanced to the edge of the terrace and looked out standing stretched with arms outspread. Darcy heard him draw a long breath into his lungs, and after many seconds expel it again. Six or eight times he did this, then turned back into the lamplight.

"It will sound to you quite mad, I expect," he said, "but if you want to hear the soberest truth I have ever spoken and shall ever speak, I will tell you about myself. But come into the garden if it is not too damp for you. I have never told any one yet, but I shall like to tell you. It is long, in fact, since I have even tried to classify what I have learned."

They wandered into the fragrant dimness of the pergola, and sat down. Then Frank began:

"Years ago, do you remember," he said, "we used often to talk about the decay of joy in the world. Many impulses, we settled, had contributed to this decay, some of which were good in themselves, others that were quite completely bad. Among the good things, I put what we may call certain Christian virtues, renunciation, resignation, sympathy with suffering, and the desire to relieve sufferers. But out of those things spring very bad ones, useless renunciations, asceticism for its own sake, mortification of the flesh with nothing to follow, no corresponding gain that is, and that awful and terrible disease which devastated England some centuries ago, and from which by heredity of spirit we suffer now, Puritanism. That was a dreadful plague, the brutes held and taught that joy and laughter and merriment were evil: it was a doctrine the most profane and wicked. Why, what is the commonest crime one sees? A sullen face. That is the truth of the matter.

"Now all my life I have believed that we are intended to be happy, that joy is of all gifts the most divine. And when I left London, abandoned my career, such as it was, I did so because I intended to devote my life to the cultivation of joy, and, by continuous and unsparing effort, to be happy. Among people, and in constant intercourse with others, I did not find it possible; there were too many distractions in towns and work-rooms, and also too much suffering. So I took one step backwards or forwards, as you may choose to put it, and went straight to Nature, to trees, birds, animals, to all those things which quite clearly pursue one aim only, which blindly follow the great native instinct to be happy without any care at all for morality, or human law or divine law. I wanted, you understand, to get all joy first-hand and unadulterated, and I think it scarcely exists among men; it is obsolete."

Darcy turned in his chair.

"Ah, but what makes birds and animals happy?" he asked. "Food, food and mating."

Frank laughed gently in the stillness.

"Do not think I became a sensualist," he said. "I did not make that mistake. For the sensualist carries his miseries pick-a-back, and round his feet is wound the shroud that shall soon enwrap him. I may be mad, it is true, but I am not so stupid anyhow as to have tried that. No, what is it that makes puppies play with their own tails, that sends cats on their prowling ecstatic errands at night?".

He paused a moment.

"So I went to Nature," he said. "I sat down here in this New Forest, sat down fair and square, and looked. That was my first difficulty, to sit here quiet without being bored, to wait without being impatient, to be receptive and very alert, though for a long time nothing particular happened. The change in fact was slow in those early stages."

"Nothing happened?" asked Darcy rather impatiently, with the sturdy revolt against any new idea which to the English mind is synonymous with nonsense. "Why, what in the world *should* happen?"

Now Frank as he had known him was the most generous but most quick-tempered of mortal men; in other words his anger would flare to a prodigious beacon, under almost no provocation, only to be quenched again under a gust of no less impulsive kindliness. Thus the moment Darcy had spoken, an apology for his hasty question was half-way up his tongue. But there was no need for it to have traveled even so far, for Frank laughed again with kindly, genuine mirth.

"Oh, how I should have resented that a few years ago," he said. "Thank goodness that resentment is one of the things I have got rid of. I certainly wish that you should believe my story—in fact, you are going to—but that you at this moment should imply that you do not, does not concern me."

"Ah, your solitary sojournings have made you inhuman," said Darcy, still very English.

"No, human," said Frank. "Rather more human, at least rather less of an ape."

"Well, that was my first quest," he continued, after a moment, "the deliberate and unswerving pursuit of joy, and my method, the eager contemplation of Nature. As far as motive went, I daresay it was purely selfish, but as far as effect goes, it seems to me about the best thing one can do for one's fellow-creatures, for happiness is more infectious than small-pox. So, as I said, I sat down and waited; I looked at happy things, zealously avoided the sight of anything unhappy, and by degrees a little trickle of the happiness of this blissful world began to filter into me. The trickle grew more abundant, and now, my dear fellow, if I could for a moment divert from me into you one half of the torrent of joy that pours through me day and night, you would throw the world, art, everything aside, and just live, exist. When a man's body dies, it passes into trees and flowers. Well, that is what I have been trying to do with my soul before death."

The servant had brought into the pergola a table with syphons and spirits, and had set a lamp upon it. As Frank spoke he leaned forward towards the other, and Darcy for all his matter-of-fact commonsense could have sworn that his companion's face shone, was luminous in itself. His dark brown eyes glowed from within, the unconscious smile of a child irradiated and transformed his face. Darcy felt suddenly excited, exhilarated.

"Go on," he said. "Go on. I can feel you are somehow telling me sober truth. I daresay you are mad; but I don't see that matters."

Frank laughed again.

"Mad?" he said. "Yes, certainly, if you wish. But I prefer to call it sane. However, nothing matters less than what anybody chooses to call things. God never labels his gifts; He just puts them into our hands; just as he put animals in the garden of Eden, for Adam to name if he felt disposed."

"So by the continual observance and study of things that were happy," continued he, "I got happiness, I got joy. But seeking it, as I did, from Nature, I got much more which I did not seek, but stumbled upon originally by accident. It is difficult to explain, but I will try.

"About three years ago I was sitting one morning in a place I will show you tomorrow. It is down by the river brink, very green, dappled with shade and sun, and the river passes there through some little clumps of reeds. Well, as I sat there, doing nothing, but just looking and listening, I heard the sound quite distinctly of some flute-like instrument playing a strange unending melody. I thought at first it was some musical yokel on the highway and did not pay much attention. But before long the strangeness and indescribable beauty of the tune struck me. It never repeated itself, but it never came to an end, phrase after phrase ran its sweet course, it worked gradually and inevitably up to a climax, and having attained it, it went on; another climax was reached and another and another. Then with a sudden gasp of wonder I localized where it came from. It came from the reeds and from the sky and from the trees. It was everywhere, it was the sound of life. It was, my dear Darcy, as the Greeks would have said, it was Pan playing on his pipes, the voice of Nature. It was the life-melody, the world-melody."

Darcy was far too interested to interrupt, though there was a question he would have liked to ask, and Frank went on:

"Well, for the moment I was terrified, terrified with the impotent horror of nightmare, and I stopped my ears and just ran from the place and got back to the house panting, trembling, literally in a panic. Unknowingly, for at that time I only pursued joy, I had begun, since I drew my joy from Nature, to get in touch with Nature. Nature, force, God, call it what you will, had drawn across my face a little gossamer web of essential life. I saw that when I emerged from my terror, and I went very humbly back to where I had heard the Pan-pipes. But it was nearly six months before I heard them again."

"Why was that?" asked Darcy.

"Surely because I had revolted, rebelled, and worst of all been frightened. For I believe that just as there is nothing in the world which so injures one's body as fear, so there is nothing that so much shuts up the soul. I was afraid, you see, of the one thing in the world which has real existence. No wonder its manifestation was withdrawn."

"And after six months?"

"After six months one blessed morning I heard the piping again. I wasn't afraid that time. And since then it has grown louder, it has become more constant. I now hear it often, and I can put myself into such an attitude towards Nature that the pipes will almost certainly sound. And never yet have they played the same tune, it is always something new, something fuller, richer, more complete than before."

"What do you mean by 'such an attitude towards Nature'?" asked Darcy.

"I can't explain that; but by translating it into a bodily attitude it is this."

Frank sat up for a moment quite straight in his chair, then slowly sunk back with arms outspread and head drooped.

"That," he said, "an effortless attitude, but open, resting, receptive. It is just that which you must do with your soul."

Then he sat up again.

"One word more," he said, "and I will bore you no further. Nor unless you ask me questions shall I talk about it again. You will find me, in fact, quite sane in my mode of life. Birds and beasts you will see behaving somewhat intimately to me, like that moor-hen, but that is all. I will walk with you, ride with you, play golf with you, and talk with you on any subject you like. But I wanted you on the threshold to know what has happened to me. And one thing more will happen."

He paused again, and a slight look of fear crossed his eyes.

"There will be a final revelation," he said, "a complete and blinding stroke which will throw open to me, once and for all, the full knowledge, the full realization and comprehension that I am one, just as you are, with life. In reality there is no 'me,' no 'you,' no 'it.' Everything is part of the one and only thing which is life. I know that that is so, but the realization of it is not yet mine. But it will be, and on that day, so I take it, I shall see Pan. It may mean death, the death of my body, that is, but I don't care. It may mean immortal, eternal life lived here and now and for ever. Then having gained that, ah, my dear Darcy, I shall preach such a gospel of joy, showing myself as the living proof of the truth, that Puritanism, the dismal religion of sour faces, shall vanish like a breath of smoke, and be dispersed and disappear in the sunlit air. But first the full knowledge must be mine."

Darcy watched his face narrowly.

"You are afraid of that moment," he said.

Frank smiled at him.

"Quite true; you are quick to have seen that. But when it comes I hope I shall not be afraid."

For some little time there was silence; then Darcy rose.

"You have bewitched me, you extraordinary boy," he said. "You have been telling me a fairy-story, and I find myself saying, 'Promise me it is true.'"

"I promise you that," said the other.

"And I know I shan't sleep," added Darcy.

Frank looked at him with a sort of mild wonder as if he scarcely understood.

"Well, what does that matter?" he said.

"I assure you it does. I am wretched unless I sleep."

"Of course I can make you sleep if I want," said Frank in a rather bored voice.

"Well, do."

"Very good: go to bed. I'll come upstairs in ten minutes."

Frank busied himself for a little after the other had gone, moving the table back under the awning of the veranda and quenching the lamp. Then he went with his quick silent tread upstairs and into Darcy's room. The latter was already in bed, but very wide-eyed and wakeful, and Frank with an amused smile of indulgence, as for a fretful child, sat down on the edge of the bed.

"Look at me," he said, and Darcy looked.

"The birds are sleeping in the brake," said Frank softly, "and the winds are asleep. The sea sleeps, and the tides are but the heaving of its breast. The stars swing slow, rocked in the great cradle of the Heavens, and—"

He stopped suddenly, gently blew out Darcy's candle, and left him sleeping.

Morning brought to Darcy a flood of hard commonsense, as clear and crisp as the sunshine that filled his room. Slowly as he woke he gathered together the broken threads of the memories of the evening which had ended, so he told himself, in a trick of common hypnotism. That accounted for it all; the whole strange talk he had had was under a spell of suggestion from the extraordinary vivid boy who had once been a man; all his own excitement, his acceptance of the incredible had been merely the effect of a stronger, more potent will imposed on his own. How strong that will was, he guessed from his own instantaneous obedience to Frank's suggestion of sleep. And armed with impenetrable commonsense he came down to breakfast. Frank had already begun, and was consuming a large plateful of porridge and milk with the most prosaic and healthy appetite.

"Slept well?" he asked.

"Yes, of course. Where did you learn hypnotism?"

"By the side of the river."

"You talked an amazing quantity of nonsense last night," remarked Darcy, in a voice prickly with reason.

"Rather. I felt quite giddy. Look, I remembered to order a dreadful daily paper for you. You can read about money markets or politics or cricket matches."

Darcy looked at him closely. In the morning light Frank looked even fresher, younger, more vital than he had done the night before, and the sight of him somehow dinted Darcy's armor of commonsense.

"You are the most extraordinary fellow I ever saw," he said. "I want to ask you some more questions."

"Ask away," said Frank.

* * * *

For the next day or two Darcy plied his friend with many questions, objections and criticisms on the theory of life and gradually got out of him a coherent and complete account of his experience. In brief then, Frank believed that "by lying naked," as he put it, to the force which controls the passage of the stars, the breaking of a wave, the budding of a tree, the love of a youth and maiden, he had succeeded in a way hitherto undreamed of in possessing himself of the essential principle of life. Day by day, so he thought, he was getting nearer to, and in closer union with the great power itself which caused all life to be, the spirit of nature, of force, or the spirit of God. For himself, he confessed to what others would call paganism; it was sufficient for him that there existed a principle of life. He did not worship it, he did not pray to it, he did not praise it. Some of it existed in all human beings, just as it existed in trees and animals; to realize and make living to himself the fact that it was all one, was his sole aim and object.

Here perhaps Darcy would put in a word of warning. "Take care," he said. "To see Pan meant death, did it not?"

Frank's eyebrows would rise at this.

"What does that matter?" he said. "True, the Greeks were always right, and they said so, but there is another possibility. For the nearer I get to it, the more living, the more vital and young I become."

"What then do you expect the final revelation will do for you?"

"I have told you," said he. "It will make me immortal."

But it was not so much from speech and argument that Darcy grew to grasp his friend's conception, as from the ordinary conduct of his life. They were passing, for instance, one morning down the village street, when an old woman, very bent and decrepit, but with an extraordinary cheerfulness of face, hobbled out from her cottage. Frank instantly stopped when he saw her.

"You old darling! How goes it all?" he said.

But she did not answer, her dim old eyes were riveted on his face; she seemed to drink in like a thirsty creature the beautiful radiance which shone there. Suddenly she put her two withered old hands on his shoulders.

"You're just the sunshine itself," she said, and he kissed her and passed on.

But scarcely a hundred yards further a strange contradiction of such tenderness occurred. A child running along the path towards them fell on its face, and set up a dismal cry of fright and pain. A look of horror came into Frank's eyes, and, putting his fingers in his ears, he fled at full speed down the street, and did not pause till he was out of hearing. Darcy, having ascertained that the child was not really hurt, followed him in bewilderment.

"Are you without pity then?" he asked.

Frank shook his head impatiently.

"Can't you see?" he asked. "Can't you understand that that sort of thing, pain, anger, anything unlovely throws me back, retards the coming of the great hour! Perhaps when it comes I shall be able to piece that side of life on to the other, on to the true religion of joy. At present I can't."

"But the old woman. Was she not ugly?"

Frank's radiance gradually returned.

"Ah, no. She was like me. She longed for joy, and knew it when she saw it, the old darling."

Another question suggested itself.

"Then what about Christianity?" asked Darcy.

"I can't accept it. I can't believe in any creed of which the central doctrine is that God who is Joy should have had to suffer. Perhaps it was so; in some inscrutable way I believe it may have been so, but I don't understand how it was possible. So I leave it alone; my affair is joy."

They had come to the weir above the village, and the thunder of riotous cool water was heavy in the air. Trees dipped into the translucent stream with slender trailing branches, and the meadow where they stood was starred with midsummer blossomings. Larks shot up caroling into the crystal dome of blue, and a thousand voices of June sang round them. Frank, bare-headed as was his wont, with his coat slung over his arm and his shirt sleeves rolled up above the elbow, stood there like some beautiful wild animal with eyes half-shut and mouth half-open, drinking in the scented warmth of the air. Then suddenly he flung himself face downwards on the grass at the edge of the stream, burying his face in the daisies and cowslips, and lay stretched there in wide-armed ecstasy, with his long fingers pressing and stroking the dewy herbs of the field. Never before had Darcy seen him thus fully possessed by his idea; his caressing fingers, his half-buried face pressed close to the grass, even the clothed lines of his figure were instinct with a vitality that somehow was different from that of other men. And some faint glow from it reached Darcy, some thrill, some vibration from that charged recumbent body passed to him, and for a moment he understood as he had not understood before, despite his persistent questions and the candid answers they received, how real, and how realized by Frank, his idea was.

Then suddenly the muscles in Frank's neck became stiff and alert, and he half-raised his head, whispering, "The Pan-pipes, the Pan-pipes. Close, oh, so close."

Very slowly, as if a sudden movement might interrupt the melody, he raised himself and leaned on the elbow of his bent arm. His eyes opened wider, the lower lids drooped as if he focused his eyes on something very far away, and the smile on his face broadened and quivered like sunlight on still water, till the exultance of its happiness was scarcely human. So he remained motionless and rapt for some minutes, then the look of listening died from his face, and he bowed his head satisfied.

"Ah, that was good," he said. "How is it possible you did not hear? Oh, you poor fellow! Did you really hear nothing?"

A week of this outdoor and stimulating life did wonders in restoring to Darcy the vigor and health which his weeks of fever had filched from him, and as his normal activity and higher pressure of vitality returned, he seemed to himself to fall even more under the spell which the miracle of Frank's youth cast over him. Twenty times a day he found himself saying to himself suddenly at the end of some ten minutes' silent resistance to the absurdity of Frank's idea: "But it isn't possible; it can't be possible," and from the fact of his having to assure himself so frequently of this, he knew that he was struggling and arguing with a conclusion which already had taken root in his mind. For in any case a visible living miracle confronted him, since it was equally impossible that this youth, this boy, trembling on the verge of manhood, was thirty-five. Yet such was the fact.

July was ushered in by a couple of days of blustering and fretful rain, and Darcy, unwilling to risk a chill, kept to the house. But to Frank this weeping change of weather seemed to have no bearing on the behavior of man, and he spent his days exactly as he did under the suns of June, lying in his hammock, stretched on the dripping grass, or making huge rambling excursions into the forest, the birds hopping from tree to tree after him, to return in the evening, drenched and soaked, but with the same unquenchable flame of joy burning within him.

"Catch cold?" he would ask, "I've forgotten how to do it, I think. I suppose it makes one's body more sensible always to sleep out-of-doors. People who live indoors always remind me of something peeled and skinless."

"Do you mean to say you slept out-of-doors last night in that deluge?" asked Darcy. "And where, may I ask?"

Frank thought a moment.

"I slept in the hammock till nearly dawn," he said. "For I remember the light blinked in the east when I awoke. Then I went—where did I go?—oh, yes, to the meadow where the Pan-pipes sounded so close a week ago. You were with me, do you remember? But I always have a rug if it is wet."

And he went whistling upstairs.

Somehow that little touch, his obvious effort to recall where he had slept, brought strangely home to Darcy the wonderful romance of which he was the still half-incredulous beholder. Sleep till close on dawn in a hammock, then the tramp—or probably scamper—underneath the windy and weeping heavens to the remote and lonely meadow by the weir! The picture of other such nights rose before him; Frank sleeping perhaps by the bathing-place under the filtered twilight of the stars, or the white blaze of moon-shine, a stir and awakening at some dead hour, perhaps a space of silent wide-eyed thought, and then a wandering through the hushed woods to some other dormitory, alone with his happiness, alone with the joy and the life that suffused and enveloped him, without other thought or desire or aim except the hourly and never-ceasing communion with the joy of nature.

They were in the middle of dinner that night, talking on indifferent subjects, when Darcy suddenly broke off in the middle of a sentence.

"I've got it," he said. "At last I've got it."

"Congratulate you," said Frank. "But what?"

"The radical unsoundness of your idea. It is this: All nature from highest to lowest is full, crammed full of suffering; every living organism in nature preys on another, yet in your aim to get close to, to be one with nature, you leave suffering altogether out; you run away from it, you refuse to recognize it. And you are waiting, you say, for the final revelation."

Frank's brow clouded slightly.

"Well?" he asked, rather wearily.

"Cannot you guess then when the final revelation will be? In joy you are supreme, I grant you that; I did not know a man could be so master of it. You have learned perhaps practically all that nature can teach. And if, as you think, the final revelation is coming to you, it will be the revelation of horror, suffering, death, pain in all its hideous forms. Suffering does exist: you hate it and fear it."

Frank held up his hand.

"Stop; let me think," he said.

There was silence for a long minute.

"That never struck me," he said at length. "It is possible that what you suggest is true. Does the sight of Pan mean that, do you think? Is it that nature, take it altogether, suffers horribly, suffers to a hideous inconceivable extent? Shall I be shown all the suffering?"

He got up and came round to where Darcy sat.

"If it is so, so be it," he said. "Because, my dear fellow, I am near, so splendidly near to the final revelation. To-day the pipes have sounded almost without pause. I have even heard the rustle in the bushes, I believe, of Pan's coming. I have seen, yes, I saw to-day, the bushes pushed aside as if by a hand, and piece of a face, not human, peered through. But I was not frightened, at least I did not run away this time."

He took a turn up to the window and back again.

"Yes, there is suffering all through," he said, "and I have left it all out of my search. Perhaps, as you say, the revelation will be that. And in that case, it will be good-bye. I have gone on one line. I shall have gone too far along one road, without having explored the other. But I can't go back now. I wouldn't if I could; not a step would I retrace! In any case, whatever the revelation is, it will be God. I'm sure of that."

The rainy weather soon passed, and with the return of the sun Darcy again joined Frank in long rambling days. It grew extraordinarily hotter, and with the fresh bursting of life, after the rain, Frank's vitality seemed to blaze higher and higher. Then, as is the habit of the English weather, one evening clouds began to bank themselves up in the west, the sun went down in a glare of coppery thunder-rack, and the whole earth broiling under an unspeakable oppression and sultriness paused and panted for the storm. After sunset the remote fires of lightning began to wink and flicker on the horizon, but when bed-time came the storm seemed to have moved no nearer, though a very low unceasing noise of thunder was audible. Weary and oppressed by the stress of the day, Darcy fell at once into a heavy uncomforting sleep.

He woke suddenly into full consciousness, with the din of some appalling explosion of thunder in his ears, and sat up in bed with racing heart. Then for a moment, as he recovered himself from the panic-land which lies between sleeping and waking, there was silence, except for the steady hissing of rain on the shrubs outside his window. But suddenly that silence was shattered and shredded into fragments by a scream from somewhere close at hand outside in the black garden, a scream of supreme and despairing terror. Again, and once again it shrilled up, and then a babble of awful words was interjected. A quivering sobbing voice that he knew, said:

"My God, oh, my God; oh, Christ!"

And then followed a little mocking, bleating laugh. Then was silence again; only the rain hissed on the shrubs.

All this was but the affair of a moment, and without pause either to put on clothes or light a candle, Darcy was already fumbling at his door-handle. Even as he opened it he met a terror-stricken face outside, that of the man-servant who carried a light.

"Did you hear?" he asked.

The man's face was bleached to a dull shining whiteness.
"Yes, sir," he said. "It was the master's voice."

* * * *

Together they hurried down the stairs, and through the dining-room where an orderly table for breakfast had already been laid, and out on to the terrace. The rain for the moment had been utterly stayed, as if the tap of the heavens had been turned off, and under the lowering black sky, not quite dark, since the moon rode somewhere serene behind the conglomerated thunder-clouds, Darcy stumbled into the garden, followed by the servant with the candle. The monstrous leaping shadow of himself was cast before him on the lawn; lost and wandering odors of rose and lily and damp earth were thick about him, but more pungent was some sharp and acrid smell that suddenly reminded him of a certain châlet in which he had once taken refuge in the Alps. In the blackness of the hazy light from the sky, and the vague tossing of the candle behind him, he saw that the hammock in which Frank so often lay was tenanted. A gleam of white shirt was there, as if a man sitting up in it, but across that there was an obscure dark shadow, and as he approached the acrid odor grew more intense.

He was now only some few yards away, when suddenly the black shadow seemed to jump into the air, then came down with tappings of hard hoofs on the brick path that ran down the pergola, and with frolicsome skippings galloped off into the bushes. When that was gone Darcy could see quite clearly that a shirted figure sat up in the hammock. For one moment, from sheer terror of the unseen, he hung on his step, and the servant joining him they walked together to the hammock.

It was Frank. He was in shirt and trousers only, and he sat up with braced arms. For one half-second he stared at them, his face a mask of horrible contorted terror. His upper lip was drawn back so that the gums of the teeth appeared, and his eyes were focused not on the two who approached him but on something quite close to him; his nostrils were widely expanded, as if he panted for breath, and terror incarnate and repulsion and deathly anguish ruled dreadful lines on his smooth cheeks and forehead. Then even as they looked the body sank backwards, and the ropes of the hammock wheezed and strained.

Darcy lifted him out and carried him indoors. Once he thought there was a faint convulsive stir of the limbs that lay with so dead a weight in his arms, but when they got inside, there was no trace of life. But the look of supreme terror and agony of fear had gone from his face, a boy tired with play but still smiling in his sleep was the burden he laid on the floor. His eyes had closed, and the beautiful mouth lay in smiling curves, even as when a few mornings ago, in the meadow by the weir, it had quivered to the music of the unheard melody of Pan's pipes. Then they looked further.

Frank had come back from his bath before dinner that night in his usual costume of shirt and trousers only. He had not dressed, and during dinner, so Darcy remembered, he had rolled up the sleeves of his shirt to above the elbow. Later, as they sat and talked after dinner on the close sultriness of the evening, he had unbuttoned the front of his shirt to let what little breath of wind there was play on his skin. The sleeves were rolled up now, the front of the shirt was unbuttoned, and on his arms and on the brown skin of his chest were strange discolorations which grew momently more clear and defined, till they saw that the marks were pointed prints, as if caused by the hoofs of some monstrous goat that had leaped and stamped upon him.

THE THING AT NOLAN,
by Ambrose Bierce

To the south of where the road between Leesville and Hardy, in the State of Missouri, crosses the east fork of May Creek stands an abandoned house. Nobody has lived in it since the summer of 1879, and it is fast going to pieces. For some three years before the date mentioned above, it was occupied by the family of Charles May, from one of whose ancestors the creek near which it stands took its name.

Mr. May's family consisted of a wife, an adult son and two young girls. The son's name was John—the names of the daughters are unknown to the writer of this sketch.

John May was of a morose and surly disposition, not easily moved to anger, but having an uncommon gift of sullen, implacable hate. His father was quite otherwise; of a sunny, jovial disposition, but with a quick temper like a sudden flame kindled in a wisp of straw, which consumes it in a flash and is no more. He cherished no resentments, and his anger gone, was quick to make overtures for reconciliation. He had a brother living near by who was unlike him in respect of all this, and it was a current witticism in the neighborhood that John had inherited his disposition from his uncle.

One day a misunderstanding arose between father and son, harsh words ensued, and the father struck the son full in the face with his fist. John quietly wiped away the blood that followed the blow, fixed his eyes upon the already penitent offender and said with cold composure,"You will die for that."

The words were overheard by two brothers named Jackson, who were approaching the men at the moment; but seeing them engaged in a quarrel they retired, apparently unobserved. Charles May afterward related the unfortunate occurrence to his wife and explained that he had apologized to the son for the hasty blow, but without avail; the young man not only rejected his overtures, but refused to withdraw his terrible threat. Nevertheless, there was no open rupture of relations: John continued living with the family, and things went on very much as before.

One Sunday morning in June, 1879, about two weeks after what has been related, May senior left the house immediately after breakfast, taking a spade. He said he was going to make an excavation at a certain spring in a wood about a mile away, so that the cattle could obtain water. John remained in the house for some hours, variously occupied in shaving himself, writing letters and reading a newspaper. His manner was very nearly what it usually was; perhaps he was a trifle more sullen and surly.

At two o'clock he left the house. At five, he returned. For some reason not connected with any interest in his movements, and which is not now recalled, the time of his departure and that of his return were noted by his mother and sisters, as was attested at his trial for murder. It was observed that his clothing was wet in spots, as if (so the prosecution afterward pointed out) he had been removing blood-stains from it. His manner was strange, his look wild. He complained of illness, and going to his room took to his bed.

May senior did not return. Later that evening the nearest neighbors were aroused, and during that night and the following day a search was prosecuted through the wood where the spring was. It resulted in little but the discovery of both men's footprints in the clay about the spring. John May in the meantime had grown rapidly worse with what the local physician called brain fever, and in his delirium raved of murder, but did not say whom he conceived to have been murdered, nor whom he imagined to have done the deed. But his threat was recalled by the brothers Jackson and he was arrested on suspicion and a deputy sheriff put in charge of him at his home. Public opinion ran strongly against him and but for his illness he would probably have been hanged by a mob. As it was, a meeting of the neighbors was held on Tuesday and a committee appointed to watch the case and take such action at any time as circumstances might seem to warrant.

On Wednesday all was changed. From the town of Nolan, eight miles away, came a story which put a quite different light on the matter. Nolan consisted of a school house, a blacksmith's shop, a "store"and a half-dozen dwellings. The store was kept by one Henry Odell, a cousin of the elder May. On the afternoon of the Sunday of May's disappearance Mr. Odell and four of his neighbors, men of credibility, were sitting in the store smoking and talking. It was a warm day; and both the front and the back door were open. At about three o'clock Charles May, who was well known to three of them, entered at the front door and passed out at the rear. He was without hat or coat. He did not look at them, nor return their greeting, a circumstance which did not surprise, for he was evidently seriously hurt. Above the left eyebrow was a wound—a deep gash from which the blood flowed, covering the whole left side of the face and neck and saturating his light-gray shirt. Oddly enough, the thought uppermost in the minds of all was that he had been fighting and was going to the brook directly at the back of the store, to wash himself.

Perhaps there was a feeling of delicacy—a backwoods etiquette which restrained them from following him to offer assistance; the court records, from which, mainly, this narrative is drawn, are silent as to anything but the fact. They waited for him to return, but he did not return.

Bordering the brook behind the store is a forest extending for six miles back to the Medicine Lodge Hills. As soon as it became known in the neighborhood of the missing man's dwelling that he had been seen in Nolan there was a marked alteration in public sentiment and feeling. The vigilance committee went out of existence without the formality of a resolution. Search along the wooded bottom lands of May Creek was stopped and nearly the entire male population of the region took to beating the bush about Nolan and in the Medicine Lodge Hills. But of the missing man no trace was found.

One of the strangest circumstances of this strange case is the formal indictment and trial of a man for murder of one whose body no human being professed to have seen—one not known to be dead. We are all more or less familiar with the vagaries and eccentricities of frontier law, but this instance, it is thought, is unique. However that may be, it is of record that on recovering from his illness John May was indicted for the murder of his missing father. Counsel for the defense appears not to have demurred and the case was tried on its merits. The prosecution was spiritless and perfunctory; the defense easily established—with regard to the deceased—an alibi. If during the time in which John May must have killed Charles May, if he killed him at all, Charles May was miles away from where John May must have been, it is plain that the deceased must have come to his death at the hands of someone else.

John May was acquitted, immediately left the country, and has never been heard of from that day. Shortly afterward his mother and sisters removed to St. Louis. The farm having passed into the possession of a man who owns the land adjoining, and has a dwelling of his own, the May house has ever since been vacant, and has the somber reputation of being haunted.

One day after the May family had left the country, some boys, playing in the woods along May Creek, found concealed under a mass of dead leaves, but partly exposed by the rooting of hogs, a spade, nearly new and bright, except for a spot on one edge, which was rusted and stained with blood. The implement had the initials "C. M." cut into the handle.

This discovery renewed, in some degree, the public excitement of a few months before. The earth near the spot where the spade was found was carefully examined, and the result was the finding of the dead body of a man. It had been buried under two or three feet of soil and the spot covered with a layer of dead leaves and twigs. There was but little decomposition, a fact attributed to some preservative property in the mineral-bearing soil.

Above the left eyebrow was a wound—a deep gash from which blood had flowed, covering the whole left side of the face and neck and saturating the light-gray shirt. The skull had been cut through by the blow. The body was that of Charles May.

But what was it that passed through Mr. Odell's store at Nolan?

THE PHANTOM 'RICKSHAW, by Rudyard Kipling

"May no ill dreams disturb my rest,
Nor Powers of Darkness me molest."

—Evening Hymn

One of the few advantages that India has over England is a certain great Knowability. After five years' service a man is directly or indirectly acquainted with the two or three hundred Civilians in his Province, all the Messes of ten or twelve Regiments and Batteries, and some fifteen hundred other people of the non-official castes. In ten years his knowledge should be doubled, and at the end of twenty he knows, or knows something about, almost every Englishman in the Empire, and may travel anywhere and everywhere without paying hotel-bills.

Globe-trotters who expect entertainment as a right, have, even within my memory, blunted this open-heartedness, but, none the less, to-day if you belong to the Inner Circle and are neither a bear nor a black sheep all houses are open to you and our small world is very kind and helpful.

Rickett of Kamartha stayed with Polder of Kumaon, some fifteen years ago. He meant to stay two nights only, but was knocked down by rheumatic fever, and for six weeks disorganized Polder's establishment, stopped Polder's work, and nearly died in Polder's bed-room. Polder behaves as though he had been placed under eternal obligation by Rickett, and yearly sends the little Ricketts a box of presents and toys. It is the same everywhere. The men who do not take the trouble to conceal from you their opinion that you are an incompetent ass, and the women who blacken your character and misunderstand your wife's amusements, will work themselves to the bone in your behalf if you fall sick or into serious trouble.

Heatherlegh, the Doctor, kept, in addition to his regular practice, a hospital on his private account—an arrangement of loose-boxes for Incurables, his friends called it—but it was really a sort of fitting-up shed for craft that had been damaged by stress of weather. The weather in India is often sultry, and since the tale of bricks is a fixed quantity, and the only liberty allowed is permission to work overtime and get no thanks, men occasionally break down and become as mixed as the metaphors in this sentence.

Heatherlegh is the nicest doctor that ever was, and his invariable prescription to all his patients is "lie low, go slow, and keep cool." He says that more men are killed by overwork than the importance of this world justifies. He maintains that overwork slew Pansay who died under his hands about three years ago. He has, of course, the right to speak authoritatively, and he laughs at my theory that there was a crack in Pansay's head and a little bit of the Dark World came through and pressed him to death. "Pansay went off the handle," says Heatherlegh, "after the stimulus of long leave at Home. He may or he may not have behaved like a blackguard to Mrs. Keith-Wessington. My notion is that the work of the Katabundi Settlement ran him off his legs, and that he took to brooding and making much of an ordinary P. & O. flirtation. He certainly was engaged to Miss Mannering, and she certainly broke off the engagement. Then he took a feverish chill and all that nonsense about ghosts developed itself. Overwork started his illness, kept it alight, and killed him, poor devil. Write him off to the System—one man to do the work of two-and-a-half men."

I do not believe this. I used to sit up with Pansay sometimes when Heatherlegh was called out to visit patients and I happened to be within claim. The man would make me most unhappy by describing in a low, even voice the procession of men, women, children, and devils that was always passing at the bottom of his bed. He had a sick man's command of language. When he recovered I suggested that he should write out the whole affair from beginning to end, knowing that ink might assist him to ease his mind. When little boys have learned a new bad word they are never happy till they have chalked it up on a door. And this also is Literature.

He was in a high fever while he was writing, and the blood-and-thunder Magazine style he adopted did not calm him. Two months afterwards he was reported fit for duty, but, in spite of the fact that he was urgently needed to help an undermanned Commission stagger through a deficit, he preferred to die; vowing at the last that he was hag-ridden. I secured his manuscript before he died, and this is his version of the affair, dated 1885:—

* * * *

My doctor tells me that I need rest and change of air. It is not improbable that I shall get both ere long—rest that neither the red-coated orderly nor the mid-day gun can break, and change of air far beyond that which any homeward-bound steamer can give me. In the meantime I am resolved to stay where I am; and, in flat defiance of my doctor's orders, to take all the world into my confidence. You shall learn for yourselves the precise nature of my malady; and shall, too, judge for yourselves whether any man born of woman on this weary earth was ever so tormented as I.

Speaking now as a condemned criminal might speak ere the drop-bolts are drawn, my story, wild and hideously improbable as it may appear, demands at least attention. That it will ever receive credence I utterly disbelieve. Two months ago I should have scouted as mad or drunk the man who had dared tell me the like. Two months ago I was the happiest man in India. To-day, from Peshawar to the sea, there is no one more wretched. My doctor and I are the only two who know this. His explanation is that my brain, digestion and eyesight are all slightly affected; giving rise to my frequent and persistent "delusions." Delusions, indeed! I call him a fool; but he attends me still with the same unwearied smile, the same bland professional manner, the same neatly-trimmed red whiskers, till I begin to suspect that I am an ungrateful, evil-tempered invalid. But you shall judge for yourselves.

Three years ago it was my fortune—my great misfortune—to sail from Gravesend to Bombay, on return from long leave, with one Agnes Keith-Wessington, wife of an officer on the Bombay side. It does not in the least concern you to know what manner of woman she was. Be content with the knowledge that, ere the voyage had ended, both she and I were desperately and unreasonably in love with one another. Heaven knows that I can make the admission now without one particle of vanity. In matters of this sort there is always one who gives and another who accepts. From the first day of our ill-omened attachment, I was conscious that Agnes's passion was a stronger, a more dominant, and—if I may use the expression—a purer sentiment than mine. Whether she recognized the fact then, I do not know. Afterwards it was bitterly plain to both of us.

Arrived at Bombay in the spring of the year, we went our respective ways, to meet no more for the next three or four months, when my leave and her love took us both to Simla. There we spent the season together; and there my fire of straw burnt itself out to a pitiful end with the closing year. I attempt no excuse. I make no apology. Mrs. Wessington had given up much for my sake, and was prepared to give up all. From my own lips, in August, 1882, she learnt that I was sick of her presence, tired of her company, and weary of the sound of her voice. Ninety-nine women out of a hundred would have wearied of me as I wearied of them; seventy-five of that number would have promptly avenged themselves by active and obtrusive flirtation with other men. Mrs. Wessington was the hundredth. On her neither my openly-expressed aversion, nor the cutting brutalities with which I garnished our interviews had the least effect.

"Jack, darling!" was her one eternal cuckoo-cry, "I'm sure it's all a mistake—a hideous mistake; and we'll be good friends again some day. *Please* forgive me, Jack, dear."

I was the offender, and I knew it. That knowledge transformed my pity into passive endurance, and, eventually, into blind hate—the same instinct, I suppose, which prompts a man to savagely stamp on the spider he has but half killed. And with this hate in my bosom the season of 1882 came to an end.

Next year we met again at Simla—she with her monotonous face and timid attempts at reconciliation, and I with loathing of her in every fiber of my frame. Several times I could not avoid meeting her alone; and on each occasion her words were identically the same. Still the unreasoning wail that it was all a "mistake"; and still the hope of eventually "making friends." I might have seen, had I cared to look, that that hope only was keeping her alive. She grew more wan and thin month by month. You will agree with me, at least, that such conduct would have driven any one to despair. It was uncalled for, childish, unwomanly. I maintain that she was much to blame. And again, sometimes, in the black, fever-stricken night watches, I have begun to think that I might have been a little kinder to her. But that really *is* a "delusion." I could not have continued pretending to love her when I didn't; could I? It would have been unfair to us both.

Last year we met again—on the same terms as before. The same weary appeals, and the same curt answers from my lips. At least I would make her see how wholly wrong and hopeless were her attempts at resuming the old relationship. As the season wore on, we fell apart—that is to say, she found it difficult to meet me, for I had other and more absorbing interests to attend to. When I think it over quietly in my sick-room, the season of 1884 seems a confused nightmare wherein light and shade were fantastically intermingled—my courtship of little Kitty Mannering; my hopes, doubts and fears; our long rides together; my trembling avowal of attachment; her reply; and now and again a vision of a white face flitting by in the 'rickshaw with the black and white liveries I once watched for so earnestly; the wave of Mrs. Wessington's gloved hand; and, when she met me alone, which was but seldom, the irksome monotony of her appeal. I loved Kitty Mannering, honestly, heartily loved her, and with my love for her grew my hatred for Agnes. In August Kitty and I were engaged. The next day I met those accursed "magpie" *jhampanies* at the back of Jakko, and, moved by some passing sentiment of pity, stopped to tell Mrs. Wessington everything. She knew it already.

"So I hear you're engaged, Jack dear." Then, without a moment's pause: "I'm sure it's all a mistake—a hideous mistake. We shall be as good friends some day, Jack, as we ever were."

My answer might have made even a man wince. It cut the dying woman before me like the blow of a whip. "Please forgive me, Jack; I didn't mean to make you angry; but it's true, it's true!"

And Mrs. Wessington broke down completely. I turned away and left her to finish her journey in peace, feeling, but only for a moment or two, that I had been an unutterably mean hound. I looked back, and saw that she had turned her 'rickshaw with the idea, I suppose, of overtaking me.

The scene and its surroundings were photographed on my memory. The rain-swept sky (we were at the end of the wet weather), the sodden, dingy pines, the muddy road, and the black powder-riven cliffs formed a gloomy background against which the black and white liveries of the *jhampanies*, the yellow-paneled 'rickshaw and Mrs. Wessington's down-bowed golden head stood out clearly. She was holding her handkerchief in her left hand and was leaning back exhausted against the 'rickshaw cushions. I turned my horse up a bypath near the Sanjowlie Reservoir and literally ran away. Once I fancied I heard a faint call of "Jack!" This may have been imagination. I never stopped to verify it. Ten minutes later I came across Kitty on horseback; and, in the delight of a long ride with her, forgot all about the interview.

A week later Mrs. Wessington died, and the inexpressible burden of her existence was removed from my life. I went Plainsward perfectly happy. Before three months were over I had forgotten all about her, except that at times the discovery of some of her old letters reminded me unpleasantly of our bygone relationship. By January I had disinterred what was left of our correspondence from among my scattered belongings and had burnt it. At the beginning of April of this year, 1885, I was at Simla—semi-deserted Simla—once more, and was deep in lover's talks and walks with Kitty. It was decided that we should be married at the end of June. You will understand, therefore, that, loving Kitty as I did, I am not saying too much when I pronounce myself to have been, at the time, the happiest man in India.

Fourteen delightful days passed almost before I noticed their flight. Then, aroused to the sense of what was proper among mortals circumstanced as we were, I pointed out to Kitty that an engagement-ring was the outward and visible sign of her dignity as an engaged girl; and that she must forthwith come to Hamilton's to be measured for one. Up to that moment, I give you my word, we had completely forgotten so trivial a matter. To Hamilton's we accordingly went on the 15th of April, 1885. Remember that—whatever my doctor may say to the contrary—I was then in perfect health, enjoying a well-balanced mind and an absolutely tranquil spirit. Kitty and I entered Hamilton's shop together, and there, regardless of the order of affairs, I measured Kitty's finger for the ring in the presence of the amused assistant. The ring was a sapphire with two diamonds. We then rode out down the slope that leads to the Combermere Bridge and Peliti's shop.

While my Waler was cautiously feeling his way over the loose shale, and Kitty was laughing and chattering at my side—while all Simla, that is to say as much of it as had then come from the Plains, was grouped round the Reading-room and Peliti's veranda—I was aware that some one, apparently at a vast distance, was calling me by my Christian name. It struck me that I had heard the voice before, but when and where I could not at once determine. In the short space it took to cover the road between the path from Hamilton's shop and the first plank of the Combermere Bridge I had thought over half-a-dozen people who might have committed such a solecism, and had eventually decided that it must have been some singing in my ears. Immediately opposite Peliti's shop my eye was arrested by the sight of four *jhampanies* in black and white livery, pulling a yellow-paneled, cheap, bazar 'rickshaw. In a moment my mind flew back to the previous season and Mrs. Wessington with a sense of irritation and disgust. Was it not enough that the woman was dead and done with, without her black and white servitors re-appearing to spoil the day's happiness? Whoever employed them now I thought I would call upon, and ask as a personal favor to change her *jhampanies'* livery. I would hire the men myself, and, if necessary, buy their coats from off their backs. It is impossible to say here what a flood of undesirable memories their presence evoked.

"Kitty," I cried, "there are poor Mrs. Wessington's *jhampanies* turned up again! I wonder who has them now?"

Kitty had known Mrs. Wessington slightly last season, and had always been interested in the sickly woman.

"What? Where?" she asked. "I can't see them anywhere."

Even as she spoke, her horse, swerving from a laden mule, threw himself directly in front of the advancing 'rickshaw. I had scarcely time to utter a word of warning when, to my unutterable horror, horse and rider passed *through* men and carriage as if they had been thin air.

"What's the matter?" cried Kitty; "what made you call out so foolishly, Jack? If I *am* engaged I don't want all creation to know about it. There was lots of space between the mule and the veranda; and, if you think I can't ride—There!"

Whereupon willful Kitty set off, her dainty little head in the air, at a hand-gallop in the direction of the Band-stand; fully expecting, as she herself afterwards told me, that I should follow her. What was the matter? Nothing, indeed. Either that I was mad or drunk, or that Simla was haunted with devils. I reined in my impatient cob, and turned round. The 'rickshaw had turned too, and now stood immediately facing me, near the left railing of the Combermere Bridge.

"Jack! Jack, darling." (There was no mistake about the words this time: they rang through my brain as if they had been shouted in my ear.) "It's some hideous mistake, I'm sure. *Please* forgive me, Jack, and let's be friends again."

The 'rickshaw-hood had fallen back, and inside, as I hope and daily pray for the death I dread by night, sat Mrs. Keith-Wessington, handkerchief in hand, and golden head bowed on her breast.

How long I stared motionless I do not know. Finally, I was aroused by my groom taking the Waler's bridle and asking whether I was ill. I tumbled off my horse and dashed, half fainting, into Peliti's for a glass of cherry-brandy. There two or three couples were gathered round the coffee-tables discussing the gossip of the day. Their trivialities were more comforting to me just then than the consolations of religion could have been. I plunged into the midst of the conversation at once; chatted, laughed and jested with a face (when I caught a glimpse of it in a mirror) as white and drawn as that of a corpse. Three or four men noticed my condition; and, evidently setting it down to the results of over many pegs, charitably endeavored to draw me apart from the rest of the loungers. But I refused to be led away. I wanted the company of my kind—as a child rushes into the midst of the dinner-party after a fright in the dark. I must have talked for about ten minutes or so, though it seemed an eternity to me, when I heard Kitty's dear voice outside inquiring for me. In another minute she had entered the shop, prepared to roundly upbraid me for failing so signally in my duties. Something in my face stopped her.

"Why, Jack," she cried, "what *have* you been doing? What *has* happened? Are you ill?" Thus driven into a direct lie, I said that the sun had been a little too much for me. It was close upon five o'clock of a cloudy April afternoon, and the sun had been hidden all day. I saw my mistake as soon as the words were out of my mouth: attempted to recover it; blundered hopelessly and followed Kitty, in a regal rage, out of doors, amid the smiles of my acquaintances. I made some excuse (I have forgotten what) on the score of my feeling faint; and cantered away to my hotel, leaving Kitty to finish the ride by herself.

In my room I sat down and tried calmly to reason out the matter. Here was I,

Theobald Jack Pansay, a well-educated Bengal Civilian in the year of grace 1885, presumably sane, certainly healthy, driven in terror from my sweetheart's side by the apparition of a woman who had been dead and buried eight months ago. These were facts that I could not blink. Nothing was further from my thought than any memory of Mrs. Wessington when Kitty and I left Hamilton's shop. Nothing was more utterly commonplace than the stretch of wall opposite Peliti's. It was broad daylight. The road was full of people; and yet here, look you, in defiance of every law of probability, in direct outrage of Nature's ordinance, there had appeared to me a face from the grave.

Kitty's Arab had gone *through* the 'rickshaw: so that my first hope that some woman marvelously like Mrs. Wessington had hired the carriage and the coolies with their old livery was lost. Again and again I went round this treadmill of thought; and again and again gave up baffled and in despair. The voice was as inexplicable as the apparition. I had originally some wild notion of confiding it all to Kitty; of begging her to marry me at once; and in her arms defying the ghostly occupant of the 'rickshaw. "After all," I argued, "the presence of the 'rickshaw is in itself enough to prove the existence of a spectral illusion. One may see ghosts of men and women, but surely never of coolies and carriages. The whole thing is absurd. Fancy the ghost of a hill-man!"

Next morning I sent a penitent note to Kitty, imploring her to overlook my strange conduct of the previous afternoon. My Divinity was still very wroth, and a personal apology was necessary. I explained, with a fluency born of night-long pondering over a falsehood, that I had been attacked with a sudden palpitation of the heart—the result of indigestion. This eminently practical solution had its effect; and Kitty and I rode out that afternoon with the shadow of my first lie dividing us.

Nothing would please her save a canter round Jakko. With my nerves still unstrung from the previous night I feebly protested against the notion, suggesting Observatory Hill, Jutogh, the Boileaugunge road—anything rather than the Jakko round. Kitty was angry and a little hurt, so I yielded from fear of provoking further misunderstanding, and we set out together towards Chota Simla. We walked a greater part of the way, and, according to our custom, cantered from a mile or so below the Convent to the stretch of level road by the Sanjowlie Reservoir. The wretched horses appeared to fly, and my heart beat quicker and quicker as we neared the crest of the ascent. My mind had been full of Mrs. Wessington all the afternoon; and every inch of the Jakko road bore witness to our old-time walks and talks. The boulders were full of it; the pines sang it aloud overhead; the rain-fed torrents giggled and chuckled unseen over the shameful story; and the wind in my ears chanted the iniquity aloud.

As a fitting climax, in the middle of the level men call the Ladies' Mile, the Horror was awaiting me. No other 'rickshaw was in sight—only the four black and white *jhampanies*, the yellow-paneled carriage, and the golden head of the woman within—all apparently just as I had left them eight months and one fortnight ago! For an instant I fancied that Kitty must see what I saw—we were so marvelously sympathetic in all things. Her next words undeceived me—"Not a soul in sight! Come along, Jack, and I'll race you to the Reservoir buildings!" Her wiry little Arab was off like a bird, my Waler following close behind, and in this order we dashed under the cliffs. Half a minute brought us within fifty yards of the 'rickshaw. I pulled my Waler and fell back a little. The 'rickshaw was directly in the middle of the road: and once more the Arab passed through it, my horse following. "Jack, Jack, dear! *Please* forgive me," rang with a wail in my ears, and, after an interval: "It's all a mistake, a hideous mistake!"

I spurred my horse like a man possessed. When I turned my head at the Reservoir works the black and white liveries were still waiting—patiently waiting—under the gray hillside, and the wind brought me a mocking echo of the words I had just heard. Kitty bantered me a good deal on my silence throughout the remainder of the ride. I had been talking up till then wildly and at random. To save my life I could not speak afterwards naturally, and from Sanjowlie to the Church wisely held my tongue.

I was to dine with the Mannerings that night and had barely time to canter home to dress. On the road to Elysium Hill I overheard two men talking together in the dusk—"It's a curious thing," said one, "how completely all trace of it disappeared. You know my wife was insanely fond of the woman (never could see anything in her myself) and wanted me to pick up her old 'rickshaw and coolies if they were to be got for love or money. Morbid sort of fancy I call it, but I've got to do what the *Memsahib* tells me. Would you believe that the man she hired it from tells me that all four of the men, they were brothers, died of cholera, on the way to Hardwár, poor devils; and the 'rickshaw has been broken up by the man himself. Told me he never used a dead *Memsahib's*'rickshaw. Spoilt his luck. Queer notion, wasn't it? Fancy poor little Mrs. Wessington spoiling any one's luck except her own!" I laughed aloud at this point; and my laugh jarred on me as I uttered it. So there *were* ghosts of 'rickshaws after all, and ghostly employments in the other world! How much did Mrs. Wessington give her men? What were their hours? Where did they go?

And for visible answer to my last question I saw the infernal thing blocking my path in the twilight. The dead travel fast and by short-cuts unknown to ordinary coolies. I laughed aloud a second time and checked my laughter suddenly, for I was afraid I was going mad. Mad to a certain extent I must have been, for I recollect that I reined in my horse at the head of the 'rickshaw, and politely wished Mrs. Wessington "good evening." Her answer was one I knew only too well. I listened to the end; and replied that I had heard it all before, but should be delighted if she had anything further to say. Some malignant devil stronger than I must have entered into me that evening, for I have a dim recollection of talking the commonplaces of the day for five minutes to the thing in front of me.

"Mad as a hatter, poor devil—or drunk. Max, try and get him to come home."

Surely *that* was not Mrs. Wessington's voice! The two men had overheard me speaking to the empty air, and had returned to look after me. They were very kind and considerate, and from their words evidently gathered that I was extremely drunk. I thanked them confusedly and cantered away to my hotel, there changed, and arrived at the Mannerings' ten minutes late. I pleaded the darkness of the night as an excuse; was rebuked by Kitty for my unlover-like tardiness; and sat down.

The conversation had already become general; and, under cover of it, I was addressing some tender small talk to my sweetheart when I was aware that at the further end of the table a short red-whiskered man was describing with much broidery his encounter with a mad unknown that evening. A few sentences convinced me that he was repeating the incident of half an hour ago. In the middle of the story he looked round for applause, as professional story-tellers do, caught my eye, and straightway collapsed. There was a moment's awkward silence, and the red-whiskered man muttered something to the effect that he had "forgotten the rest"; thereby sacrificing a reputation as a good story-teller which he had built up for six seasons past. I blessed him from the bottom of my heart and—went on with my fish.

In the fullness of time that dinner came to an end; and with genuine regret I tore myself away from Kitty—as certain as I was of my own existence that It would be waiting for me outside the door. The red-whiskered man, who had been introduced to me as Dr. Heatherlegh of Simla, volunteered to bear me company as far as our roads lay together. I accepted his offer with gratitude.

My instinct had not deceived me. It lay in readiness in the Mall, and, in what seemed devilish mockery of our ways, with a lighted head-lamp. The red-whiskered man went to the point at once, in a manner that showed he had been thinking over it all dinner time.

"I say, Pansay, what the deuce was the matter with you this evening on the Elysium road?" The suddenness of the question wrenched an answer from me before I was aware.

"That!" said I, pointing to It.

"*That* may be either *D.T.* or eyes for aught I know. Now you don't liquor. I saw as much at dinner, so it can't be *D.T.* There's nothing whatever where you're pointing, though you're sweating and trembling with fright like a scared pony. Therefore, I conclude that it's eyes. And I ought to understand all about them. Come along home with me. I'm on the Blessington lower road."

To my intense delight the 'rickshaw instead of waiting for us kept about twenty yards ahead—and this, too, whether we walked, trotted, or cantered. In the course of that long night ride I had told my companion almost as much as I have told you here.

"Well, you've spoilt one of the best tales I've ever laid tongue to," said he, "but I'll forgive you for the sake of what you've gone through. Now come home and do what I tell you; and when I've cured you, young man, let this be a lesson to you to steer clear of women and indigestible food till the day of your death."

The 'rickshaw kept steadily in front; and my red-whiskered friend seemed to derive great pleasure from my account of its exact whereabouts.

"Eyes, Pansay—all eyes, brain and stomach; and the greatest of these three is stomach. You've too much conceited brain, too little stomach, and thoroughly unhealthy eyes. Get your stomach straight and the rest follows. And all that's French for a liver pill. I'll take sole medical charge of you from this hour; for you're too interesting a phenomenon to be passed over."

By this time we were deep in the shadow of the Blessington lower road and the 'rickshaw came to a dead stop under a pine-clad, overhanging shale cliff. Instinctively I halted too, giving my reason. Heatherlegh rapped out an oath.

"Now, if you think I'm going to spend a cold night on the hillside for the sake of a stomach-*cum*-brain-*cum*-eye illusion.... Lord ha' mercy! What's that?"

There was a muffled report, a blinding smother of dust just in front of us, a crack, the noise of rent boughs, and about ten yards of the cliffside—pines, undergrowth, and all—slid down into the road below, completely blocking it up. The uprooted trees swayed and tottered for a moment like drunken giants in the gloom, and then fell prone among their fellows with a thunderous crash. Our two horses stood motionless and sweating with fear. As soon as the rattle of falling earth and stone had subsided, my companion muttered: "Man, if we'd gone forward we should have been ten feet deep in our graves by now! 'There are more things in heaven and earth'... Come home, Pansay, and thank God. I want a drink badly."

We retraced our way over the Church Ridge, and I arrived at Dr. Heatherlegh's house shortly after midnight.

His attempts towards my cure commenced almost immediately, and for a week I never left his sight. Many a time in the course of that week did I bless the good fortune which had thrown me in contact with Simla's best and kindest doctor. Day by day my spirits grew lighter and more equable. Day by day, too, I became more and more inclined to fall in with Heatherlegh's "spectral illusion" theory, implicating eyes, brain, and stomach. I wrote to Kitty, telling her that a slight sprain caused by a fall from my horse kept me indoors for a few days; and that I should be recovered before she had time to regret my absence.

Heatherlegh's treatment was simple to a degree. It consisted of liver-pills, cold-water baths and strong exercise, taken in the dusk or at early dawn—for, as he sagely observed: "A man with a sprained ankle doesn't walk a dozen miles a day, and your young woman might be wondering if she saw you."

At the end of the week, after much examination of pupil and pulse and strict injunctions as to diet and pedestrianism, Heatherlegh dismissed me as brusquely as he had taken charge of me. Here is his parting benediction: "Man, I certify to your mental cure, and that's as much as to say I've cured most of your bodily ailments. Now, get your traps out of this as soon as you can; and be off to make love to Miss Kitty."

I was endeavoring to express my thanks for his kindness. He cut me short:

"Don't think I did this because I like you. I gather that you've behaved like a blackguard all through. But, all the same you're a phenomenon, and as queer a phenomenon as you are a blackguard. Now, go out and see if you can find the eyes-brain-and-stomach business again. I'll give you a lakh for each time you see it."

Half an hour later I was in the Mannerings' drawing-room with Kitty—drunk with the intoxication of present happiness and the foreknowledge that I should never more be troubled with It's hideous presence. Strong in the sense of my new-found security, I proposed a ride at once; and, by preference, a canter round Jakko.

Never have I felt so well, so overladen with vitality and mere animal spirits as I did on the afternoon of the 30th of April. Kitty was delighted at the change in my appearance, and complimented me on it in her delightfully frank and outspoken manner. We left the Mannerings' house together, laughing and talking, and cantered along the Chota Simla road as of old.

I was in haste to reach the Sanjowlie Reservoir and there make my assurance doubly sure. The horses did their best, but seemed all too slow to my impatient mind. Kitty was astonished at my boisterousness. "Why, Jack!" she cried at last, "you are behaving like a child! What are you doing?"

We were just below the Convent, and from sheer wantonness I was making my Waler plunge and curvet across the road as I tickled it with the loop of my riding-whip.

"Doing," I answered, "nothing, dear. That's just it. If you'd been doing nothing for a week except lie up, you'd be as riotous as I.

> *" 'Singing and murmuring in your feastful mirth,*
> *Joying to feel yourself alive;*
> *Lord over nature, Lord of the visible Earth,*
> *Lord of the senses five.' "*

My quotation was hardly out of my lips before we had rounded the corner above the Convent; and a few yards further on could see across to Sanjowlie. In the center of the level road stood the black and white liveries, the yellow-paneled 'rickshaw and Mrs. Keith-Wessington. I pulled up, looked, rubbed my eyes, and, I believe, must have said something. The next thing I knew was that I was lying face downward on the road, with Kitty kneeling above me in tears.

"Has it gone, child?" I gasped. Kitty only wept more bitterly.

"Has what gone? Jack dear: what does it all mean? There must be a mistake somewhere, Jack. A hideous mistake." Her last words brought me to my feet—mad—raving for the time being.

"Yes, there *is* a mistake somewhere." I repeated, "a hideous mistake. Come and look at It!"

I have an indistinct idea that I dragged Kitty by the wrist along the road up to where It stood, and implored her for pity's sake to speak to it; to tell It that we were betrothed! that neither Death nor Hell could break the tie between us; and Kitty only knows how much more to the same effect. Now and again I appealed passionately to the Terror in the 'rickshaw to bear witness to all I had said, and to release me from a torture that was killing me. As I talked I suppose I must have told Kitty of my old relations with Mrs. Wessington, for I saw her listen intently with white face and blazing eyes.

"Thank you, Mr. Pansay," she said, "that's *quite* enough. Bring my horse."

The grooms, impassive as Orientals always are, had come up with the recaptured horses; and as Kitty sprang into her saddle I caught hold of the bridle entreating her to hear me out and forgive. My answer was the cut of her riding-whip across my face from mouth to eye, and a word or two of farewell that even now I cannot write down. So I judged, and judged rightly, that Kitty knew all; and I staggered back to the side of the 'rickshaw. My face was cut and bleeding, and the blow of the riding-whip had raised a livid blue weal on it. I had no self-respect. Just then, Heatherlegh, who must have been following Kitty and me at a distance, cantered up.

"Doctor," I said, pointing to my face, "here's Miss Mannering's signature to my order of dismissal and… I'll thank you for that lakh as soon as convenient."

Heatherlegh's face, even in my abject misery, moved me to laugh.

"I'll stake my professional reputation"—he began. "Don't be a fool," I whispered. "I've lost my life's happiness and you'd better take me home."

As I spoke the 'rickshaw was gone. Then I lost all knowledge of what was passing. The crest of Jakko seemed to heave and roll like the crest of a cloud and fall in upon me.

Seven days later (on the 7th of May, that is to say) I was aware that I was lying in Heatherlegh's room as weak as a little child. Heatherlegh was watching me intently from behind the papers on his writing table. His first words were not very encouraging; but I was too far spent to be much moved by them.

"Here's Miss Kitty has sent back your letters. You corresponded a good deal, you young people. Here's a packet that looks like a ring, and a cheerful sort of a note from Mannering Papa, which I've taken the liberty of reading and burning. The old gentleman's not pleased with you."

"And Kitty?" I asked dully.

"Rather more drawn than her father from what she says. By the same token you must have been letting out any number of queer reminiscences just before I met you. Says that a man who would have behaved to a woman as you did to Mrs. Wessington ought to kill himself out of sheer pity for his kind. She's a hot-headed little virago, your mash. Will have it too that you were suffering from *D.T.* when that row on the Jakko road turned up. Says she'll die before she ever speaks to you again."

I groaned and turned over on the other side.

"Now you've got your choice, my friend. This engagement has to be broken off; and the Mannerings don't want to be too hard on you. Was it broken through *D.T.* or epileptic fits? Sorry I can't offer you a better exchange unless you'd prefer hereditary insanity. Say the word and I'll tell 'em it's fits. All Simla knows about that scene on the Ladies' Mile. Come! I'll give you five minutes to think over it."

During those five minutes I believe that I explored thoroughly the lowest circles of the Inferno which it is permitted man to tread on earth. And at the same time I myself was watching myself faltering through the dark labyrinths of doubt, misery, and utter despair. I wondered, as Heatherlegh in his chair might have wondered, which dreadful alternative I should adopt. Presently I heard myself answering in a voice that I hardly recognized:

"They're confoundedly particular about morality in these parts. Give 'em fits, Heatherlegh, and my love. Now let me sleep a bit longer."

Then my two selves joined, and it was only I (half crazed, devil-driven I) that tossed in my bed, tracing step by step the history of the past month.

"But I am in Simla," I kept repeating to myself. "I, Jack Pansay, am in Simla, and there are no ghosts here. It's unreasonable of that woman to pretend there are. Why couldn't Agnes have left me alone? I never did her any harm. It might just as well have been me as Agnes. Only I'd never have come back on purpose to kill *her*. Why can't I be left alone—left alone and happy?"

It was high noon when I first awoke: and the sun was low in the sky before I slept—slept as the tortured criminal sleeps on his rack, too worn to feel further pain.

Next day I could not leave my bed. Heatherlegh told me in the morning that he had received an answer from Mr. Mannering, and that, thanks to his (Heatherlegh's) friendly offices, the story of my affliction had traveled through the length and breadth of Simla, where I was on all sides much pitied.

"And that's rather more than you deserve," he concluded pleasantly, "though the Lord knows you've been going through a pretty severe mill. Never mind; we'll cure you yet, you perverse phenomenon."

I declined firmly to be cured. "You've been much too good to me already, old man," said I; "but I don't think I need trouble you further."

In my heart I knew that nothing Heatherlegh could do would lighten the burden that had been laid upon me.

With that knowledge came also a sense of hopeless, impotent rebellion against the unreasonableness of it all. There were scores of men no better than I whose punishments had at least been reserved for another world and I felt that it was bitterly, cruelly unfair that I alone should have been singled out for so hideous a fate. This mood would in time give place to another where it seemed that the 'rickshaw and I were the only realities in a world of shadows; that Kitty was a ghost; that Mannering, Heatherlegh, and all the other men and women I knew were all ghosts and the great, gray hills themselves but vain shadows devised to torture me. From mood to mood I tossed backwards and forwards for seven weary days, my body growing daily stronger and stronger, until the bed-room looking-glass told me that I had returned to everyday life, and was as other men once more. Curiously enough, my face showed no signs of the struggle I had gone through. It was pale indeed, but as expressionless and commonplace as ever. I had expected some permanent alteration—visible evidence of the disease that was eating me away. I found nothing.

On the 15th of May I left Heatherlegh's house at eleven o'clock in the morning; and the instinct of the bachelor drove me to the Club. There I found that every man knew my story as told by Heatherlegh, and was, in clumsy fashion, abnormally kind and attentive. Nevertheless I recognized that for the rest of my natural life I should be among, but not of, my fellows; and I envied very bitterly indeed the laughing coolies on the Mall below. I lunched at the Club, and at four o'clock wandered aimlessly down the Mall in the vague hope of meeting Kitty. Close to the Band-stand the black and white liveries joined me; and I heard Mrs. Wessington's old appeal at my side. I had been expecting this ever since I came out; and was only surprised at her delay. The phantom 'rickshaw and I went side by side along the Chota Simla road in silence. Close to the bazaar, Kitty and a man on horseback overtook and passed us. For any sign she gave I might have been a dog in the road. She did not even pay me the compliment of quickening her pace; though the rainy afternoon had served for an excuse.

So Kitty and her companion, and I and my ghostly Light-o'-Love, crept round Jakko in couples. The road was streaming with water; the pines dripped like roof-pipes on the rocks below, and the air was full of fine, driving rain. Two or three times I found myself saying to myself almost aloud: "I'm Jack Pansay on leave at Simla—*at Simla!* Everyday, ordinary Simla. I mustn't forget that—I mustn't forget that." Then I would try to recollect some of the gossip I had heard at the Club; the prices of So-and-So's horses—anything, in fact, that related to the work-a-day Anglo-Indian world I knew so well. I even repeated the multiplication-table rapidly to myself, to make quite sure that I was not taking leave of my senses. It gave me much comfort; and must have prevented my hearing Mrs. Wessington for a time.

Once more I wearily climbed the Convent slope and entered the level road. Here Kitty and the man started off at a canter, and I was left alone with Mrs. Wessington. "Agnes," said I, "will you put back your hood and tell me what it all means?" The hood dropped noiselessly and I was face to face with my dead and buried mistress. She was wearing the dress in which I had last seen her alive: carried the same tiny handkerchief in her right hand; and the same card-case in her left. (A woman eight months dead with a card-case!) I had to pin myself down to the multiplication-table, and to set both hands on the stone parapet of the road to assure myself that that at least was real.

"Agnes," I repeated, "for pity's sake tell me what it all means." Mrs. Wessington leant forward, with that odd, quick turn of the head I used to know so well, and spoke.

If my story had not already so madly overleaped the bounds of all human belief I should apologize to you now. As I know that no one—no, not even Kitty, for whom it is written as some sort of justification of my conduct—will believe me, I will go on. Mrs. Wessington spoke and I walked with her from the Sanjowlie road to the turning below the Commander-in-Chief's house as I might walk by the side of any living woman's 'rickshaw, deep in conversation. The second and most tormenting of my moods of sickness had suddenly laid hold upon me, and like the prince in Tennyson's poem, "I seemed to move amid a world of ghosts." There had been a garden-party at the Commander-in-Chief's, and we two joined the crowd of homeward-bound folk. As I saw them then it seemed that *they* were the shadows—impalpable fantastic shadows—that divided for Mrs. Wessington's 'rickshaw to pass through. What we said during the course of that weird interview I cannot—indeed, I dare not—tell. Heatherlegh's comment would have been a short laugh and a remark that I had been "mashing a brain-eye-and-stomach chimera." It was a ghastly and yet in some indefinable way a marvelously dear experience. Could it be possible, I wondered, that I was in this life to woo a second time the woman I had killed by my own neglect and cruelty?

I met Kitty on the homeward road—a shadow among shadows.

If I were to describe all the incidents of the next fortnight in their order, my story would never come to an end; and your patience would be exhausted. Morning after morning and evening after evening the ghostly 'rickshaw and I used to wander through Simla together. Wherever I went, there the four black and white liveries followed me and bore me company to and from my hotel. At the theater I found them amid the crowd of yelling *jhampanies;* outside the club veranda, after a long evening of whist; at the birthday ball, waiting patiently for my reappearance; and in broad daylight when I went calling. Save that it cast no shadow, the 'rickshaw was in every respect as real to look upon as one of wood and iron. More than once, indeed, I have had to check myself from warning some hard-riding friend against cantering over it. More than once I have walked down the Mall deep in conversation with Mrs. Wessington to the unspeakable amazement of the passers-by.

Before I had been out and about a week I learnt that the "fit" theory had been discarded in favor of insanity. However, I made no change in my mode of life. I called, rode, and dined out as freely as ever. I had a passion for the society of my kind which I had never felt before; I hungered to be among the realities of life; and at the same time I felt vaguely unhappy when I had been separated too long from my ghostly companion. It would be almost impossible to describe my varying moods from the 15th of May up to to-day.

The presence of the 'rickshaw filled me by turns with horror, blind fear, a dim sort of pleasure, and utter despair. I dared not leave Simla; and I knew that my stay there was killing me. I knew, moreover, that it was my destiny to die slowly and a little every day. My only anxiety was to get the penance over as quietly as might be. Alternately I hungered for a sight of Kitty and watched her outrageous flirtations with my successor—to speak more accurately, my successors—with amused interest. She was as much out of my life as I was out of hers. By day I wandered with Mrs. Wessington almost content. By night I implored Heaven to let me return to the world as I used to know it. Above all these varying moods lay the sensation of dull, numbing wonder that the seen and the unseen should mingle so strangely on this earth to hound one poor soul to its grave.

* * * *

August 27th.—Heatherlegh has been indefatigable in his attendance on me; and only yesterday told me that I ought to send in an application for sick-leave. An application to escape the company of a phantom! A request that the Government would graciously permit me to get rid of five ghosts and an airy 'rickshaw by going to England! Heatherlegh's proposition moved me to almost hysterical laughter. I told him that I should await the end quietly at Simla; and I am sure that the end is not far off. Believe me that I dread its advent more than any word can say; and I torture myself nightly with a thousand speculations as to the manner of my death.

Shall I die in my bed decently and as an English gentlemen should die; or, in one last walk on the Mall, will my soul be wrenched from me to take its place for ever and ever by the side of that ghastly phantasm? Shall I return to my old lost allegiance in the next world, or shall I meet Agnes loathing her and bound to her side through all eternity? Shall we two hover over the scene of our lives till the end of time? As the day of my death draws nearer, the intense horror that all living flesh feels towards escaped spirits from beyond the grave grows more and more powerful. It is an awful thing to go down quick among the dead with scarcely one half of your life completed. It is a thousand times more awful to wait as I do in your midst, for I know not what unimaginable terror. Pity me, at least on the score of my "delusion," for I know you will never believe what I have written here. Yet as surely as ever a man was done to death by the Powers of Darkness I am that man.

In justice, too, pity her. For as surely as ever woman was killed by man, I killed Mrs. Wessington. And the last portion of my punishment is even now upon me.

THE RIVAL GHOSTS, by Brander Matthews

The good ship sped on her way across the calm Atlantic. It was an outward passage, according to the little charts which the company had charily distributed, but most of the passengers were homeward bound, after a summer of rest and recreation, and they were counting the days before they might hope to see Fire Island Light. On the lee side of the boat, comfortably sheltered from the wind, and just by the door of the captain's room (which was theirs during the day), sat a little group of returning Americans. The Duchess (she was down on the purser's list as Mrs. Martin, but her friends and familiars called her the Duchess of Washington Square) and Baby Van Rensselaer (she was quite old enough to vote, had her sex been entitled to that duty, but as the younger of two sisters she was still the baby of the family)—the Duchess and Baby Van Rensselaer were discussing the pleasant English voice and the not unpleasant English accent of a manly young lordling who was going to America for sport. Uncle Larry and Dear Jones were enticing each other into a bet on the ship's run of the morrow.

"I'll give you two to one she don't make 420," said Dear Jones.

"I'll take it," answered Uncle Larry. "We made 427 the fifth day last year." It was Uncle Larry's seventeenth visit to Europe, and this was therefore his thirty-fourth voyage.

"And when did you get in?" asked Baby Van Rensselaer. "I don't care a bit about the run, so long as we get in soon."

"We crossed the bar Sunday night, just seven days after we left Queenstown, and we dropped anchor off Quarantine at three o'clock on Monday morning."

"I hope we shan't do that this time. I can't seem to sleep any when the boat stops."

"I can; but I didn't," continued Uncle Larry; "because my state-room was the most for'ard in the boat, and the donkey-engine that let down the anchor was right over my head."

"So you got up and saw the sunrise over the bay," said Dear Jones, "with the electric lights of the city twinkling in the distance, and the first faint flush of the dawn in the east just over Fort Lafayette, and the rosy tinge which spread softly upward, and—"

"Did you both come back together?" asked the Duchess.

"Because he has crossed thirty-four times you must not suppose that he has a monopoly in sunrises," retorted Dear Jones. "No, this was my own sunrise; and a mighty pretty one it was, too."

"I'm not matching sunrises with you," remarked Uncle Larry, calmly; "but I'm willing to back a merry jest called forth by my sunrise against any two merry jests called forth by yours."

"I confess reluctantly that my sunrise evoked no merry jest at all." Dear Jones was an honest man, and would scorn to invent a merry jest on the spur of the moment.

"That's where my sunrise has the call," said Uncle Larry, complacently.

"What was the merry jest?" was Baby Van Rensselaer's inquiry, the natural result of a feminine curiosity thus artistically excited.

"Well, here it is. I was standing aft, near a patriotic American and a wandering Irishman, and the patriotic American rashly declared that you couldn't see a sunrise like that anywhere in Europe, and this gave the Irishman his chance, and he said, 'Sure ye don't have 'em here till we're through with 'em over there.'"

"It is true," said Dear Jones, thoughtfully, "that they do have some things over there better than we do; for instance, umbrellas."

"And gowns," added the Duchess.

"And antiquities,"—this was Uncle Larry's contribution.

"And we do have some things so much better in America!" protested Baby Van Rensselaer, as yet uncorrupted by any worship of the effete monarchies of despotic Europe. "We make lots of things a great deal nicer than you can get them in Europe —especially ice-cream."

"And pretty girls," added Dear Jones; but he did not look at her.

"And spooks," remarked Uncle Larry casually.

"Spooks?" queried the Duchess.

"Spooks. I maintain the word. Ghosts, if you like that better, or specters. We turn out the best quality of spook—"

"You forget the lovely ghost stories about the Rhine, and the Black Forest," interrupted Miss Van Rensselaer, with feminine inconsistency.

"I remember the Rhine and the Black Forest and all the other haunts of elves and fairies and hobgoblins; but for good honest spooks there is no place like home. And what differentiates our spook—*Spiritus Americanus*—from the ordinary ghost of literature is that it responds to the American sense of humor. Take Irving's stories for example. *The Headless Horseman*, that's a comic ghost story. And Rip Van Winkle—consider what humor, and what good-humor, there is in the telling of his meeting with the goblin crew of Hendrik Hudson's men! A still better example of this American way of dealing with legend and mystery is the marvelous tale of the rival ghosts."

"The rival ghosts?" queried the Duchess and Baby Van Rensselaer together. "Who were they?"

"Didn't I ever tell you about them?" answered Uncle Larry, a gleam of approaching joy flashing from his eye.

"Since he is bound to tell us sooner or later, we'd better be resigned and hear it now," said Dear Jones.

"If you are not more eager, I won't tell it at all."

"Oh, do, Uncle Larry; you know I just dote on ghost stories," pleaded Baby Van Rensselaer.

"Once upon a time," began Uncle Larry—"in fact, a very few years ago—there lived in the thriving town of New York a young American called Duncan—Eliphalet Duncan. Like his name, he was half Yankee and half Scotch, and naturally he was a lawyer, and had come to New York to make his way. His father was a Scotchman, who had come over and settled in Boston, and married a Salem girl. When Eliphalet Duncan was about twenty he lost both of his parents. His father left him with enough money to give him a start, and a strong feeling of pride in his Scotch birth; you see there was a title in the family in Scotland, and although Eliphalet's father was the younger son of a younger son, yet he always remembered, and always bade his only son to remember, that his ancestry was noble. His mother left him her full share of Yankee grit, and a little house in Salem which has belonged to her family for more than two hundred years. She was a Hitchcock, and the Hitchcocks had been settled in Salem since the year 1. It was a great-great-grandfather of Mr. Eliphalet Hitchcock who was foremost in the time of the Salem witchcraft craze. And this little old house which she left to my friend Eliphalet Duncan was haunted."

"By the ghost of one of the witches, of course," interrupted Dear Jones.

"Now how could it be the ghost of a witch, since the witches were all burned at the stake? You never heard of anybody who was burned having a ghost, did you?"

"That's an argument in favor of cremation, at any rate," replied Jones, evading the direct question.

"It is, if you don't like ghosts; I do," said Baby Van Rensselaer.

"And so do I," added Uncle Larry. "I love a ghost as dearly as an Englishman loves a lord."

"Go on with your story," said the Duchess, majestically overruling all extraneous discussion.

"This little old house at Salem was haunted," resumed Uncle Larry. "And by a very distinguished ghost—or at least by a ghost with very remarkable attributes."

"What was he like?" asked Baby Van Rensselaer, with a premonitory shiver of anticipatory delight.

"It had a lot of peculiarities. In the first place, it never appeared to the master of the house. Mostly it confined its visitations to unwelcome guests. In the course of the last hundred years it had frightened away four successive mothers-in-law, while never intruding on the head of the household."

"I guess that ghost had been one of the boys when he was alive and in the flesh." This was Dear Jones's contribution to the telling of the tale.

"In the second place," continued Uncle Larry, "it never frightened anybody the first time it appeared. Only on the second visit were the ghost-seers scared; but then they were scared enough for twice, and they rarely mustered up courage enough to risk a third interview. One of the most curious characteristics of this well-meaning spook was that it had no face—or at least that nobody ever saw its face."

"Perhaps he kept his countenance veiled?" queried the Duchess, who was beginning to remember that she never did like ghost stories.

"That was what I was never able to find out. I have asked several people who saw the ghost, and none of them could tell me anything about its face, and yet while in its presence they never noticed its features, and never remarked on their absence or concealment. It was only afterward when they tried to recall calmly all the circumstances of meeting with the mysterious stranger, that they became aware that they had not seen its face. And they could not say whether the features were covered, or whether they were wanting, or what the trouble was. They knew only that the face was never seen. And no matter how often they might see it, they never fathomed this mystery. To this day nobody knows whether the ghost which used to haunt the little old house in Salem had a face, or what manner of face it had."

"How awfully weird!" said Baby Van Rensselaer. "And why did the ghost go away?"

"I haven't said it went away," answered Uncle Larry, with much dignity.

"But you said it *used* to haunt the little old house at Salem, so I supposed it had moved. Didn't it?"

"You shall be told in due time. Eliphalet Duncan used to spend most of his summer vacations at Salem, and the ghost never bothered him at all, for he was the master of the house—much to his disgust, too, because he wanted to see for himself the mysterious tenant at will of his property. But he never saw it, never. He arranged with friends to call him whenever it might appear, and he slept in the next room with the door open; and yet when their frightened cries waked him the ghost was gone, and his only reward was to hear reproachful sighs as soon as he went back to bed. You see, the ghost thought it was not fair of Eliphalet to seek an introduction which was plainly unwelcome."

Dear Jones interrupted the story-teller by getting up and tucking a heavy rug snugly around Baby Van Rensselaer's feet, for the sky was now overcast and gray, and the air was damp and penetrating.

"One fine spring morning," pursued Uncle Larry, "Eliphalet Duncan received great news. I told you that there was a title in the family in Scotland, and that Eliphalet's father was the younger son of a younger son. Well, it happened that all Eliphalet's father's brothers and uncles had died off without male issue except the eldest son of the eldest, and he, of course, bore the title, and was Baron Duncan of Duncan. Now the great news that Eliphalet Duncan received in New York one fine spring morning was that Baron Duncan and his only son had been yachting in the Hebrides, and they had been caught in a black squall, and they were both dead. So my friend Eliphalet Duncan inherited the title and the estates."

"How romantic!" said the Duchess. "So he was a baron!"

"Well," answered Uncle Larry, "he was a baron if he chose. But he didn't choose."

"More fool he," said Dear Jones sententiously.

"Well," answered Uncle Larry, "I'm not so sure of that. You see, Eliphalet Duncan was half Scotch and half Yankee, and he had two eyes to the main chance. He held his tongue about his windfall of luck until he could find out whether the Scotch estates were enough to keep up the Scotch title. He soon discovered that they were not, and that the late Lord Duncan, having married money, kept up such state as he could out of the revenues of the dowry of Lady Duncan. And Eliphalet, he decided that he would rather be a well-fed lawyer in New York, living comfortably on his practice, than a starving lord in Scotland, living scantily on his title."

"But he kept his title?" asked the Duchess.

"Well," answered Uncle Larry, "he kept it quiet. I knew it, and a friend or two more. But Eliphalet was a sight too smart to put Baron Duncan of Duncan, Attorney and Counselor at Law, on his shingle."

"What has all this got to do with your ghost?" asked Dear Jones pertinently.

"Nothing with that ghost, but a good deal with another ghost. Eliphalet was very learned in spirit lore—perhaps because he owned the haunted house at Salem, perhaps because he was a Scotchman by descent. At all events, he had made a special study of the wraiths and white ladies and banshees and bogies of all kinds whose sayings and doings and warnings are recorded in the annals of the Scottish nobility. In fact, he was acquainted with the habits of every reputable spook in the Scotch peerage. And he knew that there was a Duncan ghost attached to the person of the holder of the title of Baron Duncan of Duncan."

"So, besides being the owner of a haunted house in Salem, he was also a haunted man in Scotland?" asked Baby Van Rensselaer.

"Just so. But the Scotch ghost was not unpleasant, like the Salem ghost, although it had one peculiarity in common with its trans-Atlantic fellow-spook. It never appeared to the holder of the title, just as the other never was visible to the owner of the house. In fact, the Duncan ghost was never seen at all. It was a guardian angel only. Its sole duty was to be in personal attendance on Baron Duncan of Duncan, and to warn him of impending evil. The traditions of the house told that the Barons of Duncan had again and again felt a premonition of ill fortune. Some of them had yielded and withdrawn from the venture they had undertaken, and it had failed dismally. Some had been obstinate, and had hardened their hearts, and had gone on reckless of defeat and to death. In no case had a Lord Duncan been exposed to peril without fair warning."

"Then how came it that the father and son were lost in the yacht off the Hebrides?" asked Dear Jones.

"Because they were too enlightened to yield to superstition. There is extant now a letter of Lord Duncan, written to his wife a few minutes before he and his son set sail, in which he tells her how hard he has had to struggle with an almost overmastering desire to give up the trip. Had he obeyed the friendly warning of the family ghost, the latter would have been spared a journey across the Atlantic."

"Did the ghost leave Scotland for America as soon as the old baron died?" asked Baby Van Rensselaer, with much interest.

"How did he come over," queried Dear Jones—"in the steerage, or as a cabin passenger?"

"I don't know," answered Uncle Larry calmly, "and Eliphalet, he didn't know. For as he was in no danger, and stood in no need of warning, he couldn't tell whether the ghost was on duty or not. Of course he was on the watch for it all the time. But he never got any proof of its presence until he went down to the little old house of Salem, just before the Fourth of July. He took a friend down with him—a young fellow who had been in the regular army since the day Fort Sumter was fired on, and who thought that after four years of the little unpleasantness down South, including six months in Libby, and after ten years of fighting the bad Indians on the plains, he wasn't likely to be much frightened by a ghost. Well, Eliphalet and the officer sat out on the porch all the evening smoking and talking over points in military law. A little after twelve o'clock, just as they began to think it was about time to turn in, they heard the most ghastly noise in the house. It wasn't a shriek, or a howl, or a yell, or anything they could put a name to. It was an undeterminate, inexplicable shiver and shudder of sound, which went wailing out of the window. The officer had been at Cold Harbor, but he felt himself getting colder this time. Eliphalet knew it was the ghost who haunted the house. As this weird sound died away, it was followed by another, sharp, short, blood-curdling in its intensity. Something in this cry seemed familiar to Eliphalet, and he felt sure that it proceeded from the family ghost, the warning wraith of the Duncans."

"Do I understand you to intimate that both ghosts were there together?" inquired the Duchess anxiously.

"Both of them were there," answered Uncle Larry. "You see, one of them belonged to the house, and had to be there all the time, and the other was attached to the person of Baron Duncan, and had to follow him there; wherever he was there was the ghost also. But Eliphalet, he had scarcely time to think this out when he heard both sounds again, not one after another, but both together, and something told him—some sort of an instinct he had—that those two ghosts didn't agree, didn't get on together, didn't exactly hit it off; in fact, that they were quarreling."

"Quarreling ghosts! Well, I never!" was Baby Van Rensselaer's remark.

"It is a blessed thing to see ghosts dwell together in unity," said Dear Jones.

And the Duchess added, "It would certainly be setting a better example."

"You know," resumed Uncle Larry, "that two waves of light or of sound may interfere and produce darkness or silence. So it was with these rival spooks. They interfered, but they did not produce silence or darkness. On the contrary, as soon as Eliphalet and the officer went into the house, there began at once a series of spiritualistic manifestations, a regular dark séance. A tambourine was played upon, a bell was rung, and a flaming banjo went singing around the room."

"Where did they get the banjo?" asked Dear Jones skeptically.

"I don't know. Materialized it, maybe, just as they did the tambourine. You don't suppose a quiet New York lawyer kept a stock of musical instruments large enough to fit out a strolling minstrel troupe just on the chance of a pair of ghosts coming to give him a surprise party, do you? Every spook has its own instrument of torture. Angels play on harps, I'm informed, and spirits delight in banjos and tambourines. These spooks of Eliphalet Duncan's were ghosts with all the modern improvements, and I guess they were capable of providing their own musical weapons. At all events, they had them there in the little old house at Salem the night Eliphalet and his friend came down. And they played on them, and they rang the bell, and they rapped here, there, and everywhere. And they kept it up all night."

"All night?" asked the awe-stricken Duchess.

"All night long," said Uncle Larry solemnly; "and the next night, too. Eliphalet did not get a wink of sleep, neither did his friend. On the second night the house ghost was seen by the officer; on the third night it showed itself again; and the next morning the officer packed his grip-sack and took the first train to Boston. He was a New Yorker, but he said he'd sooner go to Boston than see that ghost again. Eliphalet, he wasn't scared at all, partly because he never saw either the domiciliary or the titular spook, and partly because he felt himself on friendly terms with the spirit world, and didn't scare easily. But after losing three nights' sleep and the society of his friend, he began to be a little impatient, and to think that the thing had gone far enough. You see, while in a way he was fond of ghosts, yet he liked them best one at a time. Two ghosts were one too many. He wasn't bent on making a collection of spooks. He and one ghost were company, but he and two ghosts were a crowd."

"What did he do?" asked Baby Van Rensselaer.

"Well, he couldn't do anything. He waited awhile, hoping they would get tired; but he got tired out first. You see, it comes natural to a spook to sleep in the daytime, but a man wants to sleep nights, and they wouldn't let him sleep nights. They kept on wrangling and quarreling incessantly; they manifested and they dark-séanced as regularly as the old clock on the stairs struck twelve; they rapped and they rang bells and they banged the tambourine and they threw the flaming banjo about the house, and worse than all, they swore."

"I did not know that spirits were addicted to bad language," said the Duchess.

"How did he know they were swearing? Could he hear them?" asked Dear Jones.

"That was just it," responded Uncle Larry; "he could not hear them—at least not distinctly. There were inarticulate murmurs and stifled rumblings. But the impression produced on him was that they were swearing. If they had only sworn right out, he would not have minded it so much, because he would have known the worst. But the feeling that the air was full of suppressed profanity was very wearing and after standing it for a week, he gave up in disgust and went to the White Mountains."

"Leaving them to fight it out, I suppose," interjected Baby Van Rensselaer.

"Not at all," explained Uncle Larry. "They could not quarrel unless he was present. You see, he could not leave the titular ghost behind him, and the domiciliary ghost could not leave the house. When he went away he took the family ghost with him, leaving the house ghost behind. Now spooks can't quarrel when they are a hundred miles apart any more than men can."

"And what happened afterward?" asked Baby Van Rensselaer, with a pretty impatience.

"A most marvelous thing happened. Eliphalet Duncan went to the White Mountains, and in the car of the railroad that runs to the top of Mount Washington he met a classmate whom he had not seen for years, and this classmate introduced Duncan to his sister, and this sister was a remarkably pretty girl, and Duncan fell in love with her at first sight, and by the time he got to the top of Mount Washington he was so deep in love that he began to consider his own unworthiness, and to wonder whether she might ever be induced to care for him a little—ever so little."

"I don't think that is so marvelous a thing," said Dear Jones glancing at Baby Van Rensselaer.

"Who was she?" asked the Duchess, who had once lived in Philadelphia.

"She was Miss Kitty Sutton, of San Francisco, and she was a daughter of old Judge Sutton, of the firm of Pixley and Sutton."

"A very respectable family," assented the Duchess.

"I hope she wasn't a daughter of that loud and vulgar old Mrs. Sutton whom I met at Saratoga, one summer, four or five years ago?" said Dear Jones.

"Probably she was."

"She was a horrid old woman. The boys used to call her Mother Gorgon."

"The pretty Kitty Sutton with whom Eliphalet Duncan had fallen in love was the daughter of Mother Gorgon. But he never saw the mother, who was in 'Frisco, or Los Angeles, or Santa Fe, or somewhere out West, and he saw a great deal of the daughter, who was up in the White Mountains. She was traveling with her brother and his wife, and as they journeyed from hotel to hotel, Duncan went with them, and filled out the quartette. Before the end of the summer he began to think about proposing. Of course he had lots of chances, going on excursions as they were every day. He made up his mind to seize the first opportunity, and that very evening he took her out for a moonlight row on Lake Winnipiseogee. As he handed her into the boat he resolved to do it, and he had a glimmer of a suspicion that she knew he was going to do it, too."

"Girls," said Dear Jones, "never go out in a rowboat at night with a young man unless you mean to accept him."

"Sometimes it's best to refuse him, and get it over once for all," said Baby Van Rensselaer.

"As Eliphalet took the oars he felt a sudden chill. He tried to shake it off, but in vain. He began to have a growing consciousness of impending evil. Before he had taken ten strokes—and he was a swift oarsman—he was aware of a mysterious presence between him and Miss Sutton."

"Was it the guardian-angel ghost warning him off the match?" interrupted Dear Jones.

"That's just what it was," said Uncle Larry. "And he yielded to it, and kept his peace, and rowed Miss Sutton back to the hotel with his proposal unspoken."

"More fool he," said Dear Jones. "It will take more than one ghost to keep me from proposing when my mind is made up." And he looked at Baby Van Rensselaer.

"The next morning," continued Uncle Larry, "Eliphalet overslept himself, and when he went down to a late breakfast he found that the Suttons had gone to New York by the morning train. He wanted to follow them at once, and again he felt the mysterious presence overpowering his will. He struggled two days, and at last he roused himself to do what he wanted in spite of the spook. When he arrived in New York it was late in the evening. He dressed himself hastily and went to the hotel where the Suttons put up, in the hope of seeing at least her brother. The guardian angel fought every inch of the walk with him, until he began to wonder whether, if Miss Sutton were to take him, the spook would forbid the banns. At the hotel he saw no one that night, and he went home determined to call as early as he could the next afternoon, and make an end of it. When he left his office about two o'clock the next day to learn his fate, he had not walked five blocks before he discovered that the wraith of the Duncans had withdrawn his opposition to the suit. There was no feeling of impending evil, no resistance, no struggle, no consciousness of an opposing presence. Eliphalet was greatly encouraged. He walked briskly to the hotel; he found Miss Sutton alone. He asked her the question, and got his answer."

"She accepted him, of course," said Baby Van Rensselaer.

"Of course," said Uncle Larry. "And while they were in the first flush of joy, swapping confidences and confessions, her brother came into the parlor with an expression of pain on his face and a telegram in his hand. The former was caused by the latter, which was from 'Frisco, and which announced the sudden death of Mrs. Sutton, their mother."

"And that was why the ghost no longer opposed the match?" questioned Dear Jones.

"Exactly. You see, the family ghost knew that Mother Gorgon was an awful obstacle to Duncan's happiness, so it warned him. But the moment the obstacle was removed, it gave its consent at once."

The fog was lowering its thick damp curtain, and it was beginning to be difficult to see from one end of the boat to the other. Dear Jones tightened the rug which enwrapped Baby Van Rensselaer, and then withdrew again into his own substantial coverings.

Uncle Larry paused in his story long enough to light another of the tiny cigars he always smoked.

"I infer that Lord Duncan"—the Duchess was scrupulous in the bestowal of titles—"saw no more of the ghosts after he was married."

"He never saw them at all, at any time, either before or since. But they came very near breaking off the match, and thus breaking two young hearts."

"You don't mean to say that they knew any just cause or impediment why they should not forever after hold their peace?" asked Dear Jones.

"How could a ghost, or even two ghosts, keep a girl from marrying the man she loved?" This was Baby Van Rensselaer's question.

"It seems curious, doesn't it?" and Uncle Larry tried to warm himself by two or three sharp pulls at his fiery little cigar. "And the circumstances are quite as curious as the fact itself. You see, Miss Sutton wouldn't be married for a year after her mother's death, so she and Duncan had lots of time to tell each other all they knew. Eliphalet, he got to know a good deal about the girls she went to school with, and Kitty, she learned all about his family. He didn't tell her about the title for a long time, as he wasn't one to brag. But he described to her the little old house at Salem. And one evening toward the end of the summer, the wedding-day having been appointed for early in September, she told him that she didn't want to bridal tour at all; she just wanted to go down to the little old house at Salem to spend her honeymoon in peace and quiet, with nothing to do and nobody to bother them. Well, Eliphalet jumped at the suggestion. It suited him down to the ground. All of a sudden he remembered the spooks, and it knocked him all of a heap. He had told her about the Duncan Banshee, and the idea of having an ancestral ghost in personal attendance on her husband tickled her immensely. But he had never said anything about the ghost which haunted the little old house at Salem. He knew she would be frightened out of her wits if the house ghost revealed itself to her, and he saw at once that it would be impossible to go to Salem on their wedding trip. So he told her all about it, and how whenever he went to Salem the two ghosts interfered, and gave dark séances and manifested and materialized and made the place absolutely impossible. Kitty, she listened in silence, and Eliphalet, he thought she had changed her mind. But she hadn't done anything of the kind."

"Just like a man—to think she was going to," remarked Baby Van Rensselaer.

"She just told him she could not bear ghosts herself, but she would not marry a man who was afraid of them."

"Just like a girl—to be so inconsistent," remarked Dear Jones.

Uncle Larry's tiny cigar had long been extinct. He lighted a new one, and continued: "Eliphalet protested in vain. Kitty said her mind was made up. She was determined to pass her honeymoon in the little old house at Salem, and she was equally determined not to go there as long as there were any ghosts there. Until he could assure her that the spectral tenants had received notice to quit, and that there was no danger of manifestations and materializing, she refused to be married at all. She did not intend to have her honeymoon interrupted by two wrangling ghosts, and the wedding could be postponed until he had made ready the house for her."

"She was an unreasonable young woman," said the Duchess.

"Well, that's what Eliphalet thought, much as he was in love with her. And he believed he could talk her out of her determination. But he couldn't. She was set. And when a girl is set, there's nothing to do but yield to the inevitable. And that's just what Eliphalet did. He saw he would either have to give her up or to get the ghosts out; and as he loved her and did not care for the ghosts, he resolved to tackle the ghosts. He had clear grit, Eliphalet had—he was half Scotch and half Yankee, and neither breed turns tail in a hurry. So he made his plans and he went down to Salem. As he said good-by to Kitty he had an impression that she was sorry she had made him go, but she kept up bravely, and put a bold face on it, and saw him off, and went home and cried for an hour, and was perfectly miserable until he came back the next day."

"Did he succeed in driving the ghosts away?" asked Baby Van Rensselaer, with great interest.

"That's just what I'm coming to," said Uncle Larry, pausing at the critical moment, in the manner of the trained story teller. "You see, Eliphalet had got a rather tough job, and he would gladly have had an extension of time on the contract, but he had to choose between the girl and the ghosts, and he wanted the girl. He tried to invent or remember some short and easy way with ghosts, but he couldn't. He wished that somebody had invented a specific for spooks—something that would make the ghosts come out of the house and die in the yard. He wondered if he could not tempt the ghosts to run in debt, so that he might get the sheriff to help him. He wondered also whether the ghosts could not be overcome with strong drink—a dissipated spook, a spook with delirium tremens, might be committed to the inebriate asylum. But none of these things seemed feasible."

"What did he do?" interrupted Dear Jones. "The learned counsel will please speak to the point."

"You will regret this unseemly haste," said Uncle Larry, gravely, "when you know what really happened."

"What was it, Uncle Larry?" asked Baby Van Rensselaer. "I'm all impatience."

And Uncle Larry proceeded:

"Eliphalet went down to the little old house at Salem, and as soon as the clock struck twelve the rival ghosts began wrangling as before. Raps here, there, and everywhere, ringing bells, banging tambourines, strumming banjos sailing about the room, and all the other manifestations and materializations followed one another just as they had the summer before. The only difference Eliphalet could detect was a stronger flavor in the spectral profanity; and this, of course, was only a vague impression, for he did not actually hear a single word. He waited awhile in patience, listening and watching. Of course he never saw either of the ghosts, because neither of them could appear to him. At last he got his dander up, and he thought it was about time to interfere, so he rapped on the table, and asked for silence. As soon as he felt that the spooks were listening to him he explained the situation to them. He told them he was in love, and that he could not marry unless they vacated the house. He appealed to them as old friends, and he laid claim to their gratitude. The titular ghost had been sheltered by the Duncan family for hundreds of years, and the domiciliary ghost had had free lodging in the little old house at Salem for nearly two centuries. He implored them to settle their differences, and to get him out of his difficulty at once. He suggested they'd better fight it out then and there, and see who was master. He had brought down with him all needful weapons. And he pulled out his valise, and spread on the table a pair of navy revolvers, a pair of shot-guns, a pair of dueling swords, and a couple of bowie-knives. He offered to serve as second for both parties, and to give the word when to begin. He also took out of his valise a pack of cards and a bottle of poison, telling them that if they wished to avoid carnage they might cut the cards to see which one should take the poison. Then he waited anxiously for their reply. For a little space there was silence. Then he became conscious of a tremulous shivering in one corner of the room, and he remembered that he had heard from that direction what sounded like a frightened sigh when he made the first suggestion of the duel. Something told him that this was the domiciliary ghost, and that it was badly scared. Then he was impressed by a certain movement in the opposite corner of the room, as though the titular ghost were drawing himself up with offended dignity. Eliphalet couldn't exactly see these things, because he never saw the ghosts, but he felt them. After a silence of nearly a minute a voice came from the corner where the family ghost stood —a voice strong and full, but trembling slightly with suppressed passion. And this voice told Eliphalet it was plain enough that he had not long been the head of the Duncans, and that he had never properly considered the characteristics of his race if now he supposed that one of his blood could draw his sword against a woman. Eliphalet said he had never suggested that the Duncan ghost should raise his hand against a woman and all he wanted was that the Duncan ghost should fight the other ghost. And then the voice told Eliphalet that the other ghost was a woman."

"What?" said Dear Jones, sitting up suddenly. "You don't mean to tell me that the ghost which haunted the house was a woman?"

"Those were the very words Eliphalet Duncan used," said Uncle Larry; "but he did not need to wait for the answer. All at once he recalled the traditions about the domiciliary ghost, and he knew that what the titular ghost said was the fact. He had never thought of the sex of a spook, but there was no doubt whatever that the house ghost was a woman. No sooner was this firmly fixed in Eliphalet's mind than he saw his way out of the difficulty. The ghosts must be married!—for then there would be no more interference, no more quarreling, no more manifestations and materializations, no more dark séances, with their raps and bells and tambourines and banjos. At first the ghosts would not hear of it. The voice in the corner declared that the Duncan wraith had never thought of matrimony. But Eliphalet argued with them, and pleaded and persuaded and coaxed, and dwelt on the advantages of matrimony. He had to confess, of course, that he did not know how to get a clergyman to marry them; but the voice from the corner gravely told him that there need be no difficulty in regard to that, as there was no lack of spiritual chaplains. Then, for the first time, the house ghost spoke, in a low, clear, gentle voice, and with a quaint, old-fashioned New England accent, which contrasted sharply with the broad Scotch speech of the family ghost. She said that Eliphalet Duncan seemed to have forgotten that she was married. But this did not upset Eliphalet at all; he remembered the whole case clearly, and he told her she was not a married ghost, but a widow, since her husband had been hung for murdering her. Then the Duncan ghost drew attention to the great disparity of their ages, saying that he was nearly four hundred and fifty years old, while she was barely two hundred. But Eliphalet had not talked to juries for nothing; he just buckled to, and coaxed those ghosts into matrimony. Afterward he came to the conclusion that they were willing to be coaxed, but at the time he thought he had pretty hard work to convince them of the advantages of the plan."

"Did he succeed?" asked Baby Van Rensselaer, with a young lady's interest in matrimony.

"He did," said Uncle Larry. "He talked the wraith of the Duncans and the specter of the little old house at Salem into a matrimonial engagement. And from the time they were engaged he had no more trouble with them. They were rival ghosts no longer. They were married by their spiritual chaplain the very same day that Eliphalet Duncan met Kitty Sutton in front of the railing of Grace Church. The ghostly bride and bridegroom went away at once on their bridal tour, and Lord and Lady Duncan went down to the little old house at Salem to pass their honeymoon."

Uncle Larry stopped. His tiny cigar was out again. The tale of the rival ghosts was told. A solemn silence fell on the little party on the deck of the ocean steamer, broken harshly by the hoarse roar of the fog-horn.

THE INTERVAL,
by Vincent O'Sullivan

Mrs. Wilton passed through a little alley leading from one of the gates which are around Regent's Park, and came out on the wide and quiet street. She walked along slowly, peering anxiously from side to side so as not to overlook the number. She pulled her furs closer round her; after her years in India this London damp seemed very harsh. Still, it was not a fog to-day. A dense haze, gray and tinged ruddy, lay between the houses, sometimes blowing with a little wet kiss against the face. Mrs. Wilton's hair and eyelashes and her furs were powdered with tiny drops. But there was nothing in the weather to blur the sight; she could see the faces of people some distance off and read the signs on the shops.

Before the door of a dealer in antiques and second-hand furniture she paused and looked through the shabby uncleaned window at an unassorted heap of things, many of them of great value. She read the Polish name fastened on the pane in white letters.

"Yes; this is the place."

She opened the door, which met her entrance with an ill-tempered jangle. From somewhere in the black depths of the shop the dealer came forward. He had a clammy white face, with a sparse black beard, and wore a skull cap and spectacles. Mrs. Wilton spoke to him in a low voice.

A look of complicity, of cunning, perhaps of irony, passed through the dealer's cynical and sad eyes. But he bowed gravely and respectfully.

"Yes, she is here, madam. Whether she will see you or not I do not know. She is not always well; she has her moods. And then, we have to be so careful. The police —Not that they would touch a lady like you. But the poor alien has not much chance these days."

Mrs. Wilton followed him to the back of the shop, where there was a winding staircase. She knocked over a few things in her passage and stooped to pick them up, but the dealer kept muttering, "It does not matter—surely it does not matter." He lit a candle.

"You must go up these stairs. They are very dark; be careful. When you come to a door, open it and go straight in."

He stood at the foot of the stairs holding the light high above his head and she ascended.

The room was not very large, and it seemed very ordinary. There were some flimsy, uncomfortable chairs in gilt and red. Two large palms were in corners. Under a glass cover on the table was a view of Rome. The room had not a business-like look, thought Mrs. Wilton; there was no suggestion of the office or waiting-room where people came and went all day; yet you would not say that it was a private room which was lived in. There were no books or papers about; every chair was in the place it had been placed when the room was last swept; there was no fire and it was very cold.

To the right of the window was a door covered with a plush curtain. Mrs. Wilton sat down near the table and watched this door. She thought it must be through it that the soothsayer would come forth. She laid her hands listlessly one on top of the other on the table. This must be the tenth seer she had consulted since Hugh had been killed. She thought them over. No, this must be the eleventh. She had forgotten that frightening man in Paris who said he had been a priest. Yet of them all it was only he who had told her anything definite. But even he could do no more than tell the past. He told of her marriage; he even had the duration of it right—twenty-one months. He told too of their time in India—at least, he knew that her husband had been a soldier, and said he had been on service in the "colonies." On the whole, though, he had been as unsatisfactory as the others. None of them had given her the consolation she sought. She did not want to be told of the past. If Hugh was gone forever, then with him had gone all her love of living, her courage, all her better self. She wanted to be lifted out of the despair, the dazed aimless drifting from day to day, longing at night for the morning, and in the morning for the fall of night, which had been her life since his death. If somebody could assure her that it was not all over, that he was somewhere, not too far away, unchanged from what he had been here, with his crisp hair and rather slow smile and lean brown face, that he saw her sometimes, that he had not forgotten her....

"Oh, Hugh, darling!"

When she looked up again the woman was sitting there before her. Mrs. Wilton had not heard her come in. With her experience, wide enough now, of seers and fortune-tellers of all kinds, she saw at once that this woman was different from the others. She was used to the quick appraising look, the attempts, sometimes clumsy, but often cleverly disguised, to collect some fragments of information whereupon to erect a plausible vision. But this woman looked as if she took it out of herself.

Not that her appearance suggested intercourse with the spiritual world more than the others had done; it suggested that, in fact, considerably less. Some of the others were frail, yearning, evaporated creatures, and the ex-priest in Paris had something terrible and condemned in his look. He might well sup with the devil, that man, and probably did in some way or other.

But this was a little fat, weary-faced woman about fifty, who only did not look like a cook because she looked more like a sempstress. Her black dress was all covered with white threads. Mrs. Wilton looked at her with some embarrassment. It seemed more reasonable to be asking a woman like this about altering a gown than about intercourse with the dead. That seemed even absurd in such a very commonplace presence. The woman seemed timid and oppressed: she breathed heavily and kept rubbing her dingy hands, which looked moist, one over the other; she was always wetting her lips, and coughed with a little dry cough. But in her these signs of nervous exhaustion suggested overwork in a close atmosphere, bending too close over the sewing-machine. Her uninteresting hair, like a rat's pelt, was eked out with a false addition of another color. Some threads had got into her hair too.

Her harried, uneasy look caused Mrs. Wilton to ask compassionately: "Are you much worried by the police?"

"Oh, the police! Why don't they leave us alone? You never know who comes to see you. Why don't they leave me alone? I'm a good woman. I only think. What I do is no harm to any one."...

She continued in an uneven querulous voice, always rubbing her hands together nervously. She seemed to the visitor to be talking at random, just gabbling, like children do sometimes before they fall asleep.

"I wanted to explain—" hesitated Mrs. Wilton.

But the woman, with her head pressed close against the back of the chair, was staring beyond her at the wall. Her face had lost whatever little expression it had; it was blank and stupid. When she spoke it was very slowly and her voice was guttural.

"Can't you see him? It seems strange to me that you can't see him. He is so near you. He is passing his arm round your shoulders."

This was a frequent gesture of Hugh's. And indeed at that moment she felt that somebody was very near her, bending over her. She was enveloped in tenderness. Only a very thin veil, she felt, prevented her from seeing. But the woman saw. She was describing Hugh minutely, even the little things like the burn on his right hand.

"Is he happy? Oh, ask him does he love me?"

The result was so far beyond anything she had hoped for that she was stunned. She could only stammer the first thing that came into her head. "Does he love me?"

"He loves you. He won't answer, but he loves you. He wants me to make you see him; he is disappointed, I think, because I can't. But I can't unless you do it yourself."

After a while she said:

"I think you will see him again. You think of nothing else. He is very close to us now."

Then she collapsed, and fell into a heavy sleep and lay there motionless, hardly breathing. Mrs. Wilton put some notes on the table and stole out on tip-toe.

* * * *

She seemed to remember that downstairs in the dark shop the dealer with the waxen face detained her to show some old silver and jewelry and such like. But she did not come to herself, she had no precise recollection of anything, till she found herself entering a church near Portland Place. It was an unlikely act in her normal moments. Why did she go in there? She acted like one walking in her sleep.

The church was old and dim, with high black pews. There was nobody there. Mrs. Wilton sat down in one of the pews and bent forward with her face in her hands.

After a few minutes she saw that a soldier had come in noiselessly and placed himself about half-a-dozen rows ahead of her. He never turned round; but presently she was struck by something familiar in the figure. First she thought vaguely that the soldier looked like her Hugh. Then, when he put up his hand, she saw who it was.

She hurried out of the pew and ran towards him. "Oh, Hugh, Hugh, have you come back?"

He looked round with a smile. He had not been killed. It was all a mistake. He was going to speak....

Footsteps sounded hollow in the empty church. She turned and glanced down the dim aisle.

It was an old sexton or verger who approached. "I thought I heard you call," he said.

"I was speaking to my husband." But Hugh was nowhere to be seen.

"He was here a moment ago." She looked about in anguish. "He must have gone to the door."

"There's nobody here," said the old man gently. "Only you and me. Ladies are often taken funny since the war. There was one in here yesterday afternoon said she was married in this church and her husband had promised to meet her here. Perhaps you were married here?"

"No," said Mrs. Wilton, desolately. "I was married in India."

* * * *

It might have been two or three days after that, when she went into a small Italian restaurant in the Bayswater district. She often went out for her meals now: she had developed an exhausting cough, and she found that it somehow became less troublesome when she was in a public place looking at strange faces. In her flat there were all the things that Hugh had used; the trunks and bags still had his name on them with the labels of places where they had been together. They were like stabs. In the restaurant, people came and went, many soldiers too among them, just glancing at her in her corner.

This day, as it chanced, she was rather late and there was nobody there. She was very tired. She nibbled at the food they brought her. She could almost have cried from tiredness and loneliness and the ache in her heart.

Then suddenly he was before her, sitting there opposite at the table. It was as it was in the days of their engagement, when they used sometimes to lunch at restaurants. He was not in uniform. He smiled at her and urged her to eat, just as he used in those days....

I met her that afternoon as she was crossing Kensington Gardens, and she told me about it.

"I have been with Hugh." She seemed most happy.

"Did he say anything?"

"N-no. Yes. I think he did, but I could not quite hear. My head was so very tired. The next time—"

* * * *

I did not see her for some time after that. She found, I think, that by going to places where she had once seen him—the old church, the little restaurant—she was more certain to see him again. She never saw him at home. But in the street or the park he would often walk along beside her. Once he saved her from being run over. She said she actually felt his hand grabbing her arm, suddenly, when the car was nearly upon her.

She had given me the address of the clairvoyant; and it is through that strange woman that I know—or seem to know—what followed.

Mrs. Wilton was not exactly ill last winter, not so ill, at least, as to keep to her bedroom. But she was very thin, and her great handsome eyes always seemed to be staring at some point beyond, searching. There was a look in them that seamen's eyes sometimes have when they are drawing on a coast of which they are not very certain. She lived almost in solitude: she hardly ever saw anybody except when they sought her out. To those who were anxious about her she laughed and said she was very well.

One sunny morning she was lying awake, waiting for the maid to bring her tea. The shy London sunlight peeped through the blinds. The room had a fresh and happy look.

When she heard the door open she thought that the maid had come in. Then she saw that Hugh was standing at the foot of the bed. He was in uniform this time, and looked as he had looked the day he went away.

"Oh, Hugh, speak to me! Will you not say just one word?"

He smiled and threw back his head, just as he used to in the old days at her mother's house when he wanted to call her out of the room without attracting the attention of the others. He moved towards the door, still signing to her to follow him. He picked up her slippers on his way and held them out to her as if he wanted her to put them on. She slipped out of bed hastily....

* * * *

It is strange that when they came to look through her things after her death the slippers could never be found.

A GHOST,
by Guy De Maupassant

Translated by M. Charles Sommer.

We were speaking of sequestration, alluding to a recent lawsuit. It was at the close of a friendly evening in a very old mansion in the Rue de Grenelle, and each of the guests had a story to tell, which he assured us was true.

Then the old Marquis de la Tour-Samuel, eighty-two years of age, rose and came forward to lean on the mantelpiece. He told the following story in his slightly quavering voice.

"I, also, have witnessed a strange thing—so strange that it has been the nightmare of my life. It happened fifty-six years ago, and yet there is not a month when I do not see it again in my dreams. From that day I have borne a mark, a stamp of fear,—do you understand?

"Yes, for ten minutes I was a prey to terror, in such a way that ever since a constant dread has remained in my soul. Unexpected sounds chill me to the heart; objects which I can ill distinguish in the evening shadows make me long to flee. I am afraid at night.

"No! I would not have owned such a thing before reaching my present age. But now I may tell everything. One may fear imaginary dangers at eighty-two years old. But before actual danger I have never turned back, *mesdames*.

"That affair so upset my mind, filled me with such a deep, mysterious unrest that I never could tell it. I kept it in that inmost part, that corner where we conceal our sad, our shameful secrets, all the weaknesses of our life which cannot be confessed.

"I will tell you that strange happening just as it took place, with no attempt to explain it. Unless I went mad for one short hour it must be explainable, though. Yet I was not mad, and I will prove it to you. Imagine what you will. Here are the simple facts:

"It was in 1827, in July. I was quartered with my regiment in Rouen.

"One day, as I was strolling on the quay, I came across a man I believed I recognized, though I could not place him with certainty. I instinctively went more slowly, ready to pause. The stranger saw my impulse, looked at me, and fell into my arms.

"It was a friend of my younger days, of whom I had been very fond. He seemed to have become half a century older in the five years since I had seen him. His hair was white, and he stooped in his walk, as if he were exhausted. He understood my amazement and told me the story of his life.

"A terrible event had broken him down. He had fallen madly in love with a young girl and married her in a kind of dreamlike ecstasy. After a year of unalloyed bliss and unexhausted passion, she had died suddenly of heart disease, no doubt killed by love itself.

"He had left the country on the very day of her funeral, and had come to live in his hotel at Rouen. He remained there, solitary and desperate, grief slowly mining him, so wretched that he constantly thought of suicide.

"'As I thus came across you again,' he said, 'I shall ask a great favor of you. I want you to go to my château and get some papers I urgently need. They are in the writing-desk of my room, of *our* room. I cannot send a servant or a lawyer, as the errand must be kept private. I want absolute silence.

"'I shall give you the key of the room, which I locked carefully myself before leaving, and the key to the writing-desk. I shall also give you a note for the gardener, who will let you in.

"'Come to breakfast with me to-morrow, and we'll talk the matter over.'

"I promised to render him that slight service. It would mean but a pleasant excursion for me, his home not being more than twenty-five miles from Rouen. I could go there in an hour on horseback.

"At ten o'clock the next day I was with him. We breakfasted alone together, yet he did not utter more than twenty words. He asked me to excuse him. The thought that I was going to visit the room where his happiness lay shattered, upset him, he said. Indeed, he seemed perturbed, worried, as if some mysterious struggle were taking place in his soul.

"At last he explained exactly what I was to do. It was very simple. I was to take two packages of letters and some papers, locked in the first drawer at the right of the desk of which I had the key. He added:

"'I need not ask you not to glance at them.'

"I was almost hurt by his words, and told him so, rather sharply. He stammered:

"'Forgive me. I suffer so much!'

"And tears came to his eyes.

"I left about one o'clock to accomplish my errand.

"The day was radiant, and I rushed through the meadows, listening to the song of the larks, and the rhythmical beat of my sword on my riding-boots.

"Then I entered the forest, and I set my horse to walking. Branches of the trees softly caressed my face, and now and then I would catch a leaf between my teeth and bite it with avidity, full of the joy of life, such as fills you without reason, with a tumultuous happiness almost indefinable, a kind of magical strength.

"As I neared the house I took out the letter for the gardener, and noted with surprise that it was sealed. I was so amazed and so annoyed that I almost turned back without fulfilling my mission. Then I thought that I should thus display over-sensitiveness and bad taste. My friend might have sealed it unconsciously, worried as he was.

"The manor looked as though it had been deserted the last twenty years. The gate, wide-open and rotten, held, one wondered how. Grass filled the paths; you could not tell the flower-beds from the lawn.

"At the noise I made kicking a shutter, an old man came out from a side-door and was apparently amazed to see me there. I dismounted from my horse and gave him the letter. He read it once or twice, turned it over, looked at me with suspicion, and asked:

"'Well, what do you want?'

"I answered sharply:

"'You must know it as you have read your master's orders. I want to get in the house.'

"He appeared overwhelmed. He said:

"'So—you are going in—in his room?'

"I was getting impatient.

"'*Parbleu!* Do you intend to question me, by chance?'

"He stammered:

"'No—monsieur—only—it has not been opened since—since the death. If you will wait five minutes, I will go in to see whether—'

"I interrupted angrily:

"'See here, are you joking? You can't go in that room, as I have the key!'

"He no longer knew what to say.

"'Then, monsieur, I will show you the way.'

"'Show me the stairs and leave me alone. I can find it without your help.'

"'But—still—monsieur—'

"Then I lost my temper.

"'Now be quiet! Else you'll be sorry!'

"I roughly pushed him aside and went into the house.

"I first went through the kitchen, then crossed two small rooms occupied by the man and his wife. From there I stepped into a large hall. I went up the stairs, and I recognized the door my friend had described to me.

"I opened it with ease and went in.

"The room was so dark that at first I could not distinguish anything. I paused, arrested by that moldy and stale odor peculiar to deserted and condemned rooms, of dead rooms. Then gradually my eyes grew accustomed to the gloom, and I saw rather clearly a great room in disorder, a bed without sheets having still its mattresses and pillows, one of which bore the deep print of an elbow or a head, as if someone had just been resting on it.

"The chairs seemed all in confusion. I noticed that a door, probably that of a closet, had remained ajar.

"I first went to the window and opened it to get some light, but the hinges of the outside shutters were so rusted that I could not loosen them.

"I even tried to break them with my sword, but did not succeed. As those fruitless attempts irritated me, and as my eyes were by now adjusted to the dim light, I gave up hope of getting more light and went toward the writing-desk.

"I sat down in an arm-chair, folded back the top, and opened the drawer. It was full to the edge. I needed but three packages, which I knew how to distinguish, and I started looking for them.

"I was straining my eyes to decipher the inscriptions, when I thought I heard, or rather felt a rustle behind me. I took no notice, thinking a draft had lifted some curtain. But a minute later, another movement, almost indistinct, sent a disagreeable little shiver over my skin. It was so ridiculous to be moved thus even so slightly, that I would not turn round, being ashamed. I had just discovered the second package I needed, and was on the point of reaching for the third, when a great and sorrowful sigh, close to my shoulder, made me give a mad leap two yards away. In my spring I had turned round, my hand on the hilt of my sword, and surely had I not felt that, I should have fled like a coward.

"A tall woman, dressed in white, was facing me, standing behind the chair in which I had sat a second before.

"Such a shudder ran through me that I almost fell back! Oh, no one who has not felt them can understand those gruesome and ridiculous terrors! The soul melts; your heart seems to stop; your whole body becomes limp as a sponge, and your innermost parts seem collapsing.

"I do not believe in ghosts; and yet I broke down before the hideous fear of the dead; and I suffered, oh, I suffered more in a few minutes, in the irresistible anguish of supernatural dread, than I have suffered in all the rest of my life!

"If she had not spoken, I might have died. But she did speak; she spoke in a soft and plaintive voice which set my nerves vibrating. I could not say that I regained my self-control. No, I was past knowing what I did; but the kind of pride I have in me, as well as a military pride, helped me to maintain, almost in spite of myself, an honorable countenance. I was making a pose, a pose for myself, and for her, for her, whatever she was, woman, or phantom. I realized this later, for at the time of the apparition, I could think of nothing. I was afraid.

"She said:

"'Oh, you can be of great help to me, monsieur!'

"I tried to answer, but I was unable to utter one word. A vague sound came from my throat.

"She continued:

"'Will you? You can save me, cure me. I suffer terribly. I always suffer. I suffer, oh, I suffer!'

"And she sat down gently in my chair. She looked at me.

"'Will you?'

"I nodded my head, being still paralyzed.

"Then she handed me a woman's comb of tortoise-shell, and murmured:

"'Comb my hair! Oh, comb my hair! That will cure me. Look at my head—how I suffer! And my hair—how it hurts!'

"Her loose hair, very long, very black, it seemed to me, hung over the back of the chair, touching the floor.

"Why did I do it? Why did I, shivering, accept that comb, and why did I take between my hands her long hair, which left on my skin a ghastly impression of cold, as if I had handled serpents? I do not know.

"That feeling still clings about my fingers, and I shiver when I recall it.

"I combed her, I handled, I know not how, that hair of ice. I bound and unbound it; I plaited it as one plaits a horse's mane. She sighed, bent her head, seemed happy.

"Suddenly she said, 'Thank you!' tore the comb from my hands, and fled through the door which I had noticed was half opened.

"Left alone, I had for a few seconds the hazy feeling one feels in waking up from a nightmare. Then I recovered myself. I ran to the window and broke the shutters by my furious assault.

"A stream of light poured in. I rushed to the door through which that being had gone. I found it locked and immovable.

"Then a fever of flight seized on me, a panic, the true panic of battle. I quickly grasped the three packages of letters from the open desk; I crossed the room running, I took the steps of the stairway four at a time. I found myself outside, I don't know how, and seeing my horse close by, I mounted in one leap and left at a full gallop.

"I didn't stop till I reached Rouen and drew up in front of my house. Having thrown the reins to my orderly, I flew to my room and locked myself in to think.

"Then for an hour I asked myself whether I had not been the victim of an hallucination. Certainly I must have had one of those nervous shocks, one of those brain disorders such as give rise to miracles, to which the supernatural owes its strength.

"And I had almost concluded that it was a vision, an illusion of my senses, when I came near to the window. My eyes by chance looked down. My tunic was covered with hairs, long woman's hairs which had entangled themselves around the buttons!

"I took them off one by one and threw them out of the window with trembling fingers.

"I then called my orderly. I felt too perturbed, too moved, to go and see my friend on that day. Besides, I needed to think over what I should tell him.

"I had his letters delivered to him. He gave a receipt to the soldier. He inquired after me and was told that I was not well. I had had a sunstroke, or something. He seemed distressed.

"I went to see him the next day, early in the morning, bent on telling him the truth. He had gone out the evening before and had not come back.

"I returned the same day, but he had not been seen. I waited a week. He did not come back. I notified the police. They searched for him everywhere, but no one could find any trace of his passing or of his retreat.

"A careful search was made in the deserted manor. No suspicious clue was discovered.

"There was no sign that a woman had been concealed there.

"The inquest gave no result, and so the search went no further.

"And in fifty-six years I have learned nothing more. I never found out the truth."

A COLD GREETING,
by Ambrose Bierce

This is a story told by the late Benson Foley of San Francisco:

"In the summer of 1881 I met a man named James H. Conway, a resident of Franklin, Tennessee. He was visiting San Francisco for his health, deluded man, and brought me a note of introduction from Mr. Lawrence Barting. I had known Barting as a captain in the Federal army during the civil war. At its close he had settled in Franklin, and in time became, I had reason to think, somewhat prominent as a lawyer. Barting had always seemed to me an honorable and truthful man, and the warm friendship which he expressed in his note for Mr. Conway was to me sufficient evidence that the latter was in every way worthy of my confidence and esteem. At dinner one day Conway told me that it had been solemnly agreed between him and Barting that the one who died first should, if possible, communicate with the other from beyond the grave, in some unmistakable way—just how, they had left (wisely, it seemed to me) to be decided by the deceased, according to the opportunities that his altered circumstances might present.

"A few weeks after the conversation in which Mr. Conway spoke of this agreement, I met him one day, walking slowly down Montgomery street, apparently, from his abstracted air, in deep thought. He greeted me coldly with merely a movement of the head and passed on, leaving me standing on the walk, with half-proffered hand, surprised and naturally somewhat piqued. The next day I met him again in the office of the Palace Hotel, and seeing him about to repeat the disagreeable performance of the day before, intercepted him in a doorway, with a friendly salutation, and bluntly requested an explanation of his altered manner. He hesitated a moment; then, looking me frankly in the eyes, said:

"'I do not think, Mr. Foley, that I have any longer a claim to your friendship, since Mr. Barting appears to have withdrawn his own from me—for what reason, I protest I do not know. If he has not already informed you he probably will do so.'

"'But,' I replied, 'I have not heard from Mr. Barting.'

"'Heard from him!' he repeated, with apparent surprise. 'Why, he is here. I met him yesterday ten minutes before meeting you. I gave you exactly the same greeting that he gave me. I met him again not a quarter of an hour ago, and his manner was precisely the same: he merely bowed and passed on. I shall not soon forget your civility to me. Good morning, or—as it may please you—farewell.'

"All this seemed to me singularly considerate and delicate behavior on the part of Mr. Conway.

"As dramatic situations and literary effects are foreign to my purpose I will explain at once that Mr. Barting was dead. He had died in Nashville four days before this conversation. Calling on Mr. Conway, I apprised him of our friend's death, showing him the letters announcing it. He was visibly affected in a way that forbade me to entertain a doubt of his sincerity.

"'It seems incredible,' he said, after a period of reflection. 'I suppose I must have mistaken another man for Barting, and that man's cold greeting was merely a stranger's civil acknowledgment of my own. I remember, indeed, that he lacked

Barting's mustache.'

"'Doubtless it was another man,' I assented; and the subject was never afterward mentioned between us. But I had in my pocket a photograph of Barting, which had been inclosed in the letter from his widow. It had been taken a week before his death, and was without a mustache."

THE TURN OF THE SCREW, by Henry James

The story had held us, round the fire, sufficiently breathless, but except the obvious remark that it was gruesome, as, on Christmas Eve in an old house, a strange tale should essentially be, I remember no comment uttered till somebody happened to say that it was the only case he had met in which such a visitation had fallen on a child. The case, I may mention, was that of an apparition in just such an old house as had gathered us for the occasion—an appearance, of a dreadful kind, to a little boy sleeping in the room with his mother and waking her up in the terror of it; waking her not to dissipate his dread and soothe him to sleep again, but to encounter also, herself, before she had succeeded in doing so, the same sight that had shaken him. It was this observation that drew from Douglas—not immediately, but later in the evening—a reply that had the interesting consequence to which I call attention. Someone else told a story not particularly effective, which I saw he was not following. This I took for a sign that he had himself something to produce and that we should only have to wait. We waited in fact till two nights later; but that same evening, before we scattered, he brought out what was in his mind.

"I quite agree—in regard to Griffin's ghost, or whatever it was—that its appearing first to the little boy, at so tender an age, adds a particular touch. But it's not the first occurrence of its charming kind that I know to have involved a child. If the child gives the effect another turn of the screw, what do you say to *two* children —?"

"We say, of course," somebody exclaimed, "that they give two turns! Also that we want to hear about them."

I can see Douglas there before the fire, to which he had got up to present his back, looking down at his interlocutor with his hands in his pockets. "Nobody but me, till now, has ever heard. It's quite too horrible." This, naturally, was declared by several voices to give the thing the utmost price, and our friend, with quiet art, prepared his triumph by turning his eyes over the rest of us and going on: "It's beyond everything. Nothing at all that I know touches it."

"For sheer terror?" I remember asking.

He seemed to say it was not so simple as that; to be really at a loss how to qualify it. He passed his hand over his eyes, made a little wincing grimace. "For dreadful—dreadfulness!"

"Oh, how delicious!" cried one of the women.

He took no notice of her; he looked at me, but as if, instead of me, he saw what he spoke of. "For general uncanny ugliness and horror and pain."

"Well then," I said, "just sit right down and begin."

He turned round to the fire, gave a kick to a log, watched it an instant. Then as he faced us again: "I can't begin. I shall have to send to town." There was a unanimous groan at this, and much reproach; after which, in his preoccupied way, he explained. "The story's written. It's in a locked drawer—it has not been out for years. I could write to my man and enclose the key; he could send down the packet as he finds it." It was to me in particular that he appeared to propound this—appeared almost to appeal for aid not to hesitate. He had broken a thickness of ice, the formation of many a winter; had had his reasons for a long silence. The others resented postponement, but it was just his scruples that charmed me. I adjured him to write by the first post and to agree with us for an early hearing; then I asked him if the experience in question had been his own. To this his answer was prompt. "Oh, thank God, no!"

"And is the record yours? You took the thing down?"

"Nothing but the impression. I took that *here*"—he tapped his heart. "I've never lost it."

"Then your manuscript—?"

"Is in old, faded ink, and in the most beautiful hand." He hung fire again. "A woman's. She has been dead these twenty years. She sent me the pages in question before she died." They were all listening now, and of course there was somebody to be arch, or at any rate to draw the inference. But if he put the inference by without a smile it was also without irritation. "She was a most charming person, but she was ten years older than I. She was my sister's governess," he quietly said. "She was the most agreeable woman I've ever known in her position; she would have been worthy of any whatever. It was long ago, and this episode was long before. I was at Trinity, and I found her at home on my coming down the second summer. I was much there that year—it was a beautiful one; and we had, in her off-hours, some strolls and talks in the garden—talks in which she struck me as awfully clever and nice. Oh yes; don't grin: I liked her extremely and am glad to this day to think she liked me, too. If she hadn't she wouldn't have told me. She had never told anyone. It wasn't simply that she said so, but that I knew she hadn't. I was sure; I could see. You'll easily judge why when you hear."

"Because the thing had been such a scare?"

He continued to fix me. "You'll easily judge," he repeated: "*You* will."

I fixed him, too. "I see. She was in love."

He laughed for the first time. "You *are* acute. Yes, she was in love. That is, she had been. That came out—she couldn't tell her story without its coming out. I saw it, and she saw I saw it; but neither of us spoke of it. I remember the time and the place—the corner of the lawn, the shade of the great beeches and the long, hot summer afternoon. It wasn't a scene for a shudder; but oh—!" He quitted the fire and dropped back into his chair.

"You'll receive the packet Thursday morning?" I inquired.

"Probably not till the second post."

"Well then; after dinner—"

"You'll all meet me here?" He looked us round again. "Isn't anybody going?" It was almost the tone of hope.

"Everybody will stay!"

"*I* will"—and "*I* will!" cried the ladies whose departure had been fixed. Mrs. Griffin, however, expressed the need for a little more light. "Who was it she was in love with?"

"The story will tell," I took upon myself to reply.

"Oh, I can't wait for the story!"

"The story *won't* tell," said Douglas; "not in any literal, vulgar way."

"More's the pity, then. That's the only way I ever understand."

"Won't *you* tell, Douglas?" somebody else inquired.

He sprang to his feet again. "Yes—tomorrow. Now I must go to bed. Good night." And quickly catching up a candlestick, he left us slightly bewildered. From our end of the great brown hall we heard his step on the stair; whereupon Mrs. Griffin spoke. "Well, if I don't know who she was in love with, I know who *he* was."

"She was ten years older," said her husband.

"Raison de plus—at that age! But it's rather nice, his long reticence."

"Forty years!" Griffin put in.

"With this outbreak at last."

"The outbreak," I returned, "will make a tremendous occasion of Thursday night;" and everyone so agreed with me that, in the light of it, we lost all attention for everything else. The last story, however incomplete and like the mere opening of a serial, had been told; we handshook and "candlestuck," as somebody said, and went to bed.

I knew the next day that a letter containing the key had, by the first post, gone off to his London apartments; but in spite of—or perhaps just on account of—the eventual diffusion of this knowledge we quite let him alone till after dinner, till such an hour of the evening, in fact, as might best accord with the kind of emotion on which our hopes were fixed. Then he became as communicative as we could desire and indeed gave us his best reason for being so. We had it from him again before the fire in the hall, as we had had our mild wonders of the previous night. It appeared that the narrative he had promised to read us really required for a proper intelligence a few words of prologue. Let me say here distinctly, to have done with it, that this narrative, from an exact transcript of my own made much later, is what I shall presently give. Poor Douglas, before his death—when it was in sight—committed to me the manuscript that reached him on the third of these days and that, on the same spot, with immense effect, he began to read to our hushed little circle on the night of the fourth. The departing ladies who had said they would stay didn't, of course, thank heaven, stay: they departed, in consequence of arrangements made, in a rage of curiosity, as they professed, produced by the touches with which he had already worked us up. But that only made his little final auditory more compact and select, kept it, round the hearth, subject to a common thrill.

The first of these touches conveyed that the written statement took up the tale at a point after it had, in a manner, begun. The fact to be in possession of was therefore that his old friend, the youngest of several daughters of a poor country parson, had, at the age of twenty, on taking service for the first time in the schoolroom, come up to London, in trepidation, to answer in person an advertisement that had already placed her in brief correspondence with the advertiser. This person proved, on her presenting herself, for judgment, at a house in Harley Street, that impressed her as vast and imposing—this prospective patron proved a gentleman, a bachelor in the prime of life, such a figure as had never risen, save in a dream or an old novel, before a fluttered, anxious girl out of a Hampshire vicarage. One could easily fix his type; it never, happily, dies out. He was handsome and bold and pleasant, offhand and gay and kind. He struck her, inevitably, as gallant and splendid, but what took her most of all and gave her the courage she afterward showed was that he put the whole thing to her as a kind of favor, an obligation he should gratefully incur. She conceived him as rich, but as fearfully extravagant—saw him all in a glow of high fashion, of good looks, of expensive habits, of charming ways with women. He had for his own town residence a big house filled with the spoils of travel and the trophies of the chase; but it was to his country home, an old family place in Essex, that he wished her immediately to proceed.

He had been left, by the death of their parents in India, guardian to a small nephew and a small niece, children of a younger, a military brother, whom he had lost two years before. These children were, by the strangest of chances for a man in his position—a lone man without the right sort of experience or a grain of patience

—very heavily on his hands. It had all been a great worry and, on his own part doubtless, a series of blunders, but he immensely pitied the poor chicks and had done all he could; had in particular sent them down to his other house, the proper place for them being of course the country, and kept them there, from the first, with the best people he could find to look after them, parting even with his own servants to wait on them and going down himself, whenever he might, to see how they were doing. The awkward thing was that they had practically no other relations and that his own affairs took up all his time. He had put them in possession of Bly, which was healthy and secure, and had placed at the head of their little establishment—but below stairs only—an excellent woman, Mrs. Grose, whom he was sure his visitor would like and who had formerly been maid to his mother. She was now house-keeper and was also acting for the time as superintendent to the little girl, of whom, without children of her own, she was, by good luck, extremely fond. There were plenty of people to help, but of course the young lady who should go down as governess would be in supreme authority. She would also have, in holidays, to look after the small boy, who had been for a term at school—young as he was to be sent, but what else could be done?—and who, as the holidays were about to begin, would be back from one day to the other. There had been for the two children at first a young lady whom they had had the misfortune to lose. She had done for them quite beautifully—she was a most respectable person—till her death, the great awkwardness of which had, precisely, left no alternative but the school for little Miles. Mrs. Grose, since then, in the way of manners and things, had done as she could for Flora; and there were, further, a cook, a housemaid, a dairywoman, an old pony, an old groom, and an old gardener, all likewise thoroughly respectable.

So far had Douglas presented his picture when someone put a question. "And what did the former governess die of?—of so much respectability?"

Our friend's answer was prompt. "That will come out. I don't anticipate."

"Excuse me—I thought that was just what you *are* doing."

"In her successor's place," I suggested, "I should have wished to learn if the office brought with it—"

"Necessary danger to life?" Douglas completed my thought. "She did wish to learn, and she did learn. You shall hear tomorrow what she learned. Meanwhile, of course, the prospect struck her as slightly grim. She was young, untried, nervous: it was a vision of serious duties and little company, of really great loneliness. She hesitated—took a couple of days to consult and consider. But the salary offered much exceeded her modest measure, and on a second interview she faced the music, she engaged." And Douglas, with this, made a pause that, for the benefit of the company, moved me to throw in—

"The moral of which was of course the seduction exercised by the splendid young man. She succumbed to it."

He got up and, as he had done the night before, went to the fire, gave a stir to a log with his foot, then stood a moment with his back to us. "She saw him only twice."

"Yes, but that's just the beauty of her passion."

A little to my surprise, on this, Douglas turned round to me. "It *was* the beauty of it. There were others," he went on, "who hadn't succumbed. He told her frankly all his difficulty—that for several applicants the conditions had been prohibitive. They were, somehow, simply afraid. It sounded dull—it sounded strange; and all the more so because of his main condition."

"Which was—?"

"That she should never trouble him—but never, never: neither appeal nor complain nor write about anything; only meet all questions herself, receive all moneys from his solicitor, take the whole thing over and let him alone. She promised to do this, and she mentioned to me that when, for a moment, disburdened, delighted, he held her hand, thanking her for the sacrifice, she already felt rewarded."

"But was that all her reward?" one of the ladies asked.

"She never saw him again."

"Oh!" said the lady; which, as our friend immediately left us again, was the only other word of importance contributed to the subject till, the next night, by the corner of the hearth, in the best chair, he opened the faded red cover of a thin old-fashioned gilt-edged album. The whole thing took indeed more nights than one, but on the first occasion the same lady put another question. "What is your title?"

"I haven't one."

"Oh, *I* have!" I said. But Douglas, without heeding me, had begun to read with a fine clearness that was like a rendering to the ear of the beauty of his author's hand.

I

I remember the whole beginning as a succession of flights and drops, a little seesaw of the right throbs and the wrong. After rising, in town, to meet his appeal, I had at all events a couple of very bad days—found myself doubtful again, felt indeed sure I had made a mistake. In this state of mind I spent the long hours of bumping, swinging coach that carried me to the stopping place at which I was to be met by a vehicle from the house. This convenience, I was told, had been ordered, and I found, toward the close of the June afternoon, a commodious fly in waiting for me. Driving at that hour, on a lovely day, through a country to which the summer sweetness seemed to offer me a friendly welcome, my fortitude mounted afresh and, as we turned into the avenue, encountered a reprieve that was probably but a proof of the point to which it had sunk. I suppose I had expected, or had dreaded, something so melancholy that what greeted me was a good surprise. I remember as a most pleasant impression the broad, clear front, its open windows and fresh curtains and the pair of maids looking out; I remember the lawn and the bright flowers and the crunch of my wheels on the gravel and the clustered treetops over which the rooks circled and cawed in the golden sky. The scene had a greatness that made it a different affair from my own scant home, and there immediately appeared at the door, with a little girl in her hand, a civil person who dropped me as decent a curtsy as if I had been the mistress or a distinguished visitor. I had received in Harley Street a narrower notion of the place, and that, as I recalled it, made me think the proprietor still more of a gentleman, suggested that what I was to enjoy might be something beyond his promise.

I had no drop again till the next day, for I was carried triumphantly through the following hours by my introduction to the younger of my pupils. The little girl who accompanied Mrs. Grose appeared to me on the spot a creature so charming as to make it a great fortune to have to do with her. She was the most beautiful child I had ever seen, and I afterward wondered that my employer had not told me more of her. I slept little that night—I was too much excited; and this astonished me, too, I recollect, remained with me, adding to my sense of the liberality with which I was treated. The large, impressive room, one of the best in the house, the great state bed, as I almost felt it, the full, figured draperies, the long glasses in which, for the first time, I could see myself from head to foot, all struck me—like the extraordinary charm of my small charge—as so many things thrown in. It was thrown in as well, from the first moment, that I should get on with Mrs. Grose in a relation over which, on my way, in the coach, I fear I had rather brooded. The only thing indeed that in this early outlook might have made me shrink again was the clear circumstance of her being so glad to see me. I perceived within half an hour that she was so glad—stout, simple, plain, clean, wholesome woman—as to be positively on her guard against showing it too much. I wondered even then a little why she should wish not to show it, and that, with reflection, with suspicion, might of course have made me uneasy.

But it was a comfort that there could be no uneasiness in a connection with anything so beatific as the radiant image of my little girl, the vision of whose angelic beauty had probably more than anything else to do with the restlessness that, before morning, made me several times rise and wander about my room to take in the whole picture and prospect; to watch, from my open window, the faint summer dawn, to look at such portions of the rest of the house as I could catch, and to listen, while, in the fading dusk, the first birds began to twitter, for the possible recurrence of a sound or two, less natural and not without, but within, that I had fancied I heard. There had been a moment when I believed I recognized, faint and far, the cry of a child; there had been another when I found myself just consciously starting as at the passage, before my door, of a light footstep. But these fancies were not marked enough not to be thrown off, and it is only in the light, or the gloom, I should rather say, of other and subsequent matters that they now come back to me. To watch, teach, "form" little Flora would too evidently be the making of a happy and useful life. It had been agreed between us downstairs that after this first occasion I should have her as a matter of course at night, her small white bed being already arranged, to that end, in my room. What I had undertaken was the whole care of her, and she had remained, just this last time, with Mrs. Grose only as an effect of our consideration for my inevitable strangeness and her natural timidity. In spite of this timidity—which the child herself, in the oddest way in the world, had been perfectly frank and brave about, allowing it, without a sign of uncomfortable consciousness, with the deep, sweet serenity indeed of one of Raphael's holy infants, to be discussed, to be imputed to her, and to determine us—I feel quite sure she would presently like me. It was part of what I already liked Mrs. Grose herself for, the pleasure I could see her feel in my admiration and wonder as I sat at supper with four tall candles and with my pupil, in a high chair and a bib, brightly facing me, between them, over bread and milk. There were naturally things that in Flora's presence could pass between us only as prodigious and gratified looks, obscure and roundabout allusions.

"And the little boy—does he look like her? Is he too so very remarkable?"

One wouldn't flatter a child. "Oh, miss, *most* remarkable. If you think well of this one!"—and she stood there with a plate in her hand, beaming at our companion, who looked from one of us to the other with placid heavenly eyes that contained nothing to check us.

"Yes; if I do—?"

"You *will* be carried away by the little gentleman!"

"Well, that, I think, is what I came for—to be carried away. I'm afraid, however," I remember feeling the impulse to add, "I'm rather easily carried away. I was carried away in London!"

I can still see Mrs. Grose's broad face as she took this in. "In Harley Street?"

"In Harley Street."

"Well, miss, you're not the first—and you won't be the last."

"Oh, I've no pretension," I could laugh, "to being the only one. My other pupil, at any rate, as I understand, comes back tomorrow?"

"Not tomorrow—Friday, miss. He arrives, as you did, by the coach, under care of the guard, and is to be met by the same carriage."

I forthwith expressed that the proper as well as the pleasant and friendly thing would be therefore that on the arrival of the public conveyance I should be in waiting for him with his little sister; an idea in which Mrs. Grose concurred so heartily that I somehow took her manner as a kind of comforting pledge—never falsified, thank heaven!—that we should on every question be quite at one. Oh, she was glad I was there!

What I felt the next day was, I suppose, nothing that could be fairly called a reaction from the cheer of my arrival; it was probably at the most only a slight oppression produced by a fuller measure of the scale, as I walked round them, gazed up at them, took them in, of my new circumstances. They had, as it were, an extent and mass for which I had not been prepared and in the presence of which I found myself, freshly, a little scared as well as a little proud. Lessons, in this agitation, certainly suffered some delay; I reflected that my first duty was, by the gentlest arts I could contrive, to win the child into the sense of knowing me. I spent the day with her out-of-doors; I arranged with her, to her great satisfaction, that it should be she, she only, who might show me the place. She showed it step by step and room by room and secret by secret, with droll, delightful, childish talk about it and with the result, in half an hour, of our becoming immense friends. Young as she was, I was struck, throughout our little tour, with her confidence and courage with the way, in empty chambers and dull corridors, on crooked staircases that made me pause and even on the summit of an old machicolated square tower that made me dizzy, her morning music, her disposition to tell me so many more things than she asked, rang out and led me on. I have not seen Bly since the day I left it, and I daresay that to my older and more informed eyes it would now appear sufficiently contracted. But as my little conductress, with her hair of gold and her frock of blue, danced before me round corners and pattered down passages, I had the view of a castle of romance inhabited by a rosy sprite, such a place as would somehow, for diversion of the young idea, take all color out of storybooks and fairytales. Wasn't it just a storybook over which I had fallen adoze and adream? No; it was a big, ugly, antique, but convenient house, embodying a few features of a building still older, half-replaced and half-utilized, in which I had the fancy of our being almost as lost as a handful of passengers in a great drifting ship. Well, I was, strangely, at the helm!

II

This came home to me when, two days later, I drove over with Flora to meet, as Mrs. Grose said, the little gentleman; and all the more for an incident that, presenting itself the second evening, had deeply disconcerted me. The first day had been, on the whole, as I have expressed, reassuring; but I was to see it wind up in keen apprehension. The postbag, that evening—it came late—contained a letter for me, which, however, in the hand of my employer, I found to be composed but of a few words enclosing another, addressed to himself, with a seal still unbroken. "This, I recognize, is from the headmaster, and the headmaster's an awful bore. Read him, please; deal with him; but mind you don't report. Not a word. I'm off!" I broke the seal with a great effort—so great a one that I was a long time coming to it; took the unopened missive at last up to my room and only attacked it just before going to bed. I had better have let it wait till morning, for it gave me a second sleepless night. With no counsel to take, the next day, I was full of distress; and it finally got so the better of me that I determined to open myself at least to Mrs. Grose.

"What does it mean? The child's dismissed his school."

She gave me a look that I remarked at the moment; then, visibly, with a quick blankness, seemed to try to take it back. "But aren't they all—?"

"Sent home—yes. But only for the holidays. Miles may never go back at all."

Consciously, under my attention, she reddened. "They won't take him?"

"They absolutely decline."

At this she raised her eyes, which she had turned from me; I saw them fill with good tears. "What has he done?"

I hesitated; then I judged best simply to hand her my letter—which, however, had the effect of making her, without taking it, simply put her hands behind her. She shook her head sadly. "Such things are not for me, miss."

My counselor couldn't read! I winced at my mistake, which I attenuated as I could, and opened my letter again to repeat it to her; then, faltering in the act and folding it up once more, I put it back in my pocket. "Is he really *bad*?"

The tears were still in her eyes. "Do the gentlemen say so?"

"They go into no particulars. They simply express their regret that it should be impossible to keep him. That can have only one meaning." Mrs. Grose listened with dumb emotion; she forbore to ask me what this meaning might be; so that, presently, to put the thing with some coherence and with the mere aid of her presence to my own mind, I went on: "That he's an injury to the others."

At this, with one of the quick turns of simple folk, she suddenly flamed up. "Master Miles! *Him* an injury?"

There was such a flood of good faith in it that, though I had not yet seen the child, my very fears made me jump to the absurdity of the idea. I found myself, to meet my friend the better, offering it, on the spot, sarcastically. "To his poor little innocent mates!"

"It's too dreadful," cried Mrs. Grose, "to say such cruel things! Why, he's scarce ten years old."

"Yes, yes; it would be incredible."

She was evidently grateful for such a profession. "See him, miss, first. *Then* believe it!" I felt forthwith a new impatience to see him; it was the beginning of a curiosity that, for all the next hours, was to deepen almost to pain. Mrs. Grose was aware, I could judge, of what she had produced in me, and she followed it up with assurance. "You might as well believe it of the little lady. Bless her," she added the next moment, "Look at her!"

I turned and saw that Flora, whom, ten minutes before, I had established in the schoolroom with a sheet of white paper, a pencil, and a copy of nice "round o's," now presented herself to view at the open door. She expressed in her little way an extraordinary detachment from disagreeable duties, looking to me, however, with a great childish light that seemed to offer it as a mere result of the affection she had conceived for my person, which had rendered necessary that she should follow me. I needed nothing more than this to feel the full force of Mrs. Grose's comparison, and, catching my pupil in my arms, covered her with kisses in which there was a sob of atonement.

Nonetheless, the rest of the day I watched for further occasion to approach my colleague, especially as, toward evening, I began to fancy she rather sought to avoid me. I overtook her, I remember, on the staircase; we went down together, and at the bottom I detained her, holding her there with a hand on her arm. "I take what you said to me at noon as a declaration that *you've* never known him to be bad."

She threw back her head; she had clearly, by this time, and very honestly, adopted an attitude. "Oh, never known him—I don't pretend *that*!"

I was upset again. "Then you *have* known him—?"

"Yes indeed, miss, thank God!"

On reflection I accepted this. "You mean that a boy who never is—?"

"Is no boy for *me*!"

I held her tighter. "You like them with the spirit to be naughty?" Then, keeping pace with her answer, "So do I!" I eagerly brought out. "But not to the degree to contaminate—"

"To contaminate?"—my big word left her at a loss. I explained it. "To corrupt."

She stared, taking my meaning in; but it produced in her an odd laugh. "Are you afraid he'll corrupt *you*?" She put the question with such a fine bold humor that, with a laugh, a little silly doubtless, to match her own, I gave way for the time to the apprehension of ridicule.

But the next day, as the hour for my drive approached, I cropped up in another place. "What was the lady who was here before?"

"The last governess? She was also young and pretty—almost as young and almost as pretty, miss, even as you."

"Ah, then, I hope her youth and her beauty helped her!" I recollect throwing off. "He seems to like us young and pretty!"

"Oh, he *did*," Mrs. Grose assented: "it was the way he liked everyone!" She had no sooner spoken indeed than she caught herself up. "I mean that's *his* way—the master's."

I was struck. "But of whom did you speak first?"

She looked blank, but she colored. "Why, of *him*."

"Of the master?"

"Of who else?"

There was so obviously no one else that the next moment I had lost my impression of her having accidentally said more than she meant; and I merely asked what I wanted to know. "Did *she* see anything in the boy—?"

"That wasn't right? She never told me."

I had a scruple, but I overcame it. "Was she careful—particular?"

Mrs. Grose appeared to try to be conscientious. "About some things—yes."

"But not about all?"

Again she considered. "Well, miss—she's gone. I won't tell tales."

"I quite understand your feeling," I hastened to reply; but I thought it, after an instant, not opposed to this concession to pursue: "Did she die here?"

"No—she went off."

I don't know what there was in this brevity of Mrs. Grose's that struck me as ambiguous. "Went off to die?" Mrs. Grose looked straight out of the window, but I felt that, hypothetically, I had a right to know what young persons engaged for Bly were expected to do. "She was taken ill, you mean, and went home?"

"She was not taken ill, so far as appeared, in this house. She left it, at the end of the year, to go home, as she said, for a short holiday, to which the time she had put in had certainly given her a right. We had then a young woman—a nursemaid who had stayed on and who was a good girl and clever; and *she* took the children altogether for the interval. But our young lady never came back, and at the very moment I was expecting her I heard from the master that she was dead."

I turned this over. "But of what?"

"He never told me! But please, miss," said Mrs. Grose, "I must get to my work."

III

Her thus turning her back on me was fortunately not, for my just preoccupations, a snub that could check the growth of our mutual esteem. We met, after I had brought home little Miles, more intimately than ever on the ground of my stupefaction, my general emotion: so monstrous was I then ready to pronounce it that such a child as had now been revealed to me should be under an interdict. I was a little late on the scene, and I felt, as he stood wistfully looking out for me before the door of the inn at which the coach had put him down, that I had seen him, on the instant, without and within, in the great glow of freshness, the same positive fragrance of purity, in which I had, from the first moment, seen his little sister. He was incredibly beautiful, and Mrs. Grose had put her finger on it: everything but a sort of passion of tenderness for him was swept away by his presence. What I then and there took him to my heart for was something divine that I have never found to the same degree in any child—his indescribable little air of knowing nothing in the world but love. It would have been impossible to carry a bad name with a greater sweetness of innocence, and by the time I had got back to Bly with him I remained merely bewildered—so far, that is, as I was not outraged—by the sense of the horrible letter locked up in my room, in a drawer. As soon as I could compass a private word with Mrs. Grose I declared to her that it was grotesque.

She promptly understood me. "You mean the cruel charge—?"

"It doesn't live an instant. My dear woman, *look* at him!"

She smiled at my pretention to have discovered his charm. "I assure you, miss, I do nothing else! What will you say, then?" she immediately added.

"In answer to the letter?" I had made up my mind. "Nothing."

"And to his uncle?"

I was incisive. "Nothing."

"And to the boy himself?"

I was wonderful. "Nothing."

She gave with her apron a great wipe to her mouth. "Then I'll stand by you. We'll see it out."

"We'll see it out!" I ardently echoed, giving her my hand to make it a vow.

She held me there a moment, then whisked up her apron again with her detached hand. "Would you mind, miss, if I used the freedom—"

"To kiss me? No!" I took the good creature in my arms and, after we had embraced like sisters, felt still more fortified and indignant.

This, at all events, was for the time: a time so full that, as I recall the way it went, it reminds me of all the art I now need to make it a little distinct. What I look back at with amazement is the situation I accepted. I had undertaken, with my companion, to see it out, and I was under a charm, apparently, that could smooth away the extent and the far and difficult connections of such an effort. I was lifted aloft on a great wave of infatuation and pity. I found it simple, in my ignorance, my confusion, and perhaps my conceit, to assume that I could deal with a boy whose education for the world was all on the point of beginning. I am unable even to remember at this day what proposal I framed for the end of his holidays and the resumption of his studies. Lessons with me, indeed, that charming summer, we all had a theory that he was to have; but I now feel that, for weeks, the lessons must have been rather my own. I learned something—at first, certainly—that had not been one of the teachings of my small, smothered life; learned to be amused, and even amusing, and not to think for the morrow. It was the first time, in a manner, that I had known space and air and freedom, all the music of summer and all the mystery of nature. And then there was consideration—and consideration was sweet. Oh, it was a trap—not designed, but deep—to my imagination, to my delicacy, perhaps to my vanity; to whatever, in me, was most excitable. The best way to picture it all is to say that I was off my guard. They gave me so little trouble—they were of a gentleness so extraordinary. I used to speculate—but even this with a dim disconnectedness—as to how the rough future (for all futures are rough!) would handle them and might bruise them. They had the bloom of health and happiness; and yet, as if I had been in charge of a pair of little grandees, of princes of the blood, for whom everything, to be right, would have to be enclosed and protected, the only form that, in my fancy, the afteryears could take for them was that of a romantic, a really royal extension of the garden and the park. It may be, of course, above all, that what suddenly broke into this gives the previous time a charm of stillness—that hush in which something gathers or crouches. The change was actually like the spring of a beast.

In the first weeks the days were long; they often, at their finest, gave me what I used to call my own hour, the hour when, for my pupils, teatime and bedtime having come and gone, I had, before my final retirement, a small interval alone. Much as I liked my companions, this hour was the thing in the day I liked most; and I liked it best of all when, as the light faded—or rather, I should say, the day lingered and the last calls of the last birds sounded, in a flushed sky, from the old trees—I could take a turn into the grounds and enjoy, almost with a sense of property that amused and flattered me, the beauty and dignity of the place. It was a pleasure at these moments to feel myself tranquil and justified; doubtless, perhaps, also to reflect that by my discretion, my quiet good sense and general high propriety, I was giving pleasure—if he ever thought of it!—to the person to whose pressure I had responded. What I was doing was what he had earnestly hoped and directly asked of me, and that I *could*, after all, do it proved even a greater joy than I had expected. I daresay I fancied myself, in short, a remarkable young woman and took comfort in the faith that this would more publicly appear. Well, I needed to be remarkable to offer a front to the remarkable things that presently gave their first sign.

It was plump, one afternoon, in the middle of my very hour: the children were tucked away, and I had come out for my stroll. One of the thoughts that, as I don't in the least shrink now from noting, used to be with me in these wanderings was that it would be as charming as a charming story suddenly to meet someone. Someone would appear there at the turn of a path and would stand before me and smile and approve. I didn't ask more than that—I only asked that he should *know*; and the only way to be sure he knew would be to see it, and the kind light of it, in his handsome face. That was exactly present to me—by which I mean the face was—when, on the first of these occasions, at the end of a long June day, I stopped short on emerging from one of the plantations and coming into view of the house. What arrested me on the spot—and with a shock much greater than any vision had allowed for—was the sense that my imagination had, in a flash, turned real. He did stand there!—but high up, beyond the lawn and at the very top of the tower to which, on that first morning, little Flora had conducted me. This tower was one of a pair—square, incongruous, crenelated structures—that were distinguished, for some reason, though I could see little difference, as the new and the old. They flanked opposite ends of the house and were probably architectural absurdities, redeemed in a measure indeed by not being wholly disengaged nor of a height too pretentious, dating, in their gingerbread antiquity, from a romantic revival that was already a respectable past. I admired them, had fancies about them, for we could all profit in a degree, especially when they loomed through the dusk, by the grandeur of their actual battlements; yet it was not at such an elevation that the figure I had so often invoked seemed most in place.

It produced in me, this figure, in the clear twilight, I remember, two distinct gasps of emotion, which were, sharply, the shock of my first and that of my second surprise. My second was a violent perception of the mistake of my first: the man who met my eyes was not the person I had precipitately supposed. There came to me thus a bewilderment of vision of which, after these years, there is no living view that I can hope to give. An unknown man in a lonely place is a permitted object of fear to a young woman privately bred; and the figure that faced me was—a few more seconds assured me—as little anyone else I knew as it was the image that had been in my mind. I had not seen it in Harley Street—I had not seen it anywhere. The place, moreover, in the strangest way in the world, had, on the instant, and by the very fact of its appearance, become a solitude. To me at least, making my statement here with a deliberation with which I have never made it, the whole feeling of the moment returns. It was as if, while I took in—what I did take in—all the rest of the scene had been stricken with death. I can hear again, as I write, the intense hush in which the sounds of evening dropped. The rooks stopped cawing in the golden sky, and the friendly hour lost, for the minute, all its voice. But there was no other change in nature, unless indeed it were a change that I saw with a stranger sharpness. The gold was still in the sky, the clearness in the air, and the man who looked at me over the battlements was as definite as a picture in a frame. That's how I thought, with extraordinary quickness, of each person that he might have been and that he was not. We were confronted across our distance quite long enough for me to ask myself with intensity who then he was and to feel, as an effect of my inability to say, a wonder that in a few instants more became intense.

The great question, or one of these, is, afterward, I know, with regard to certain matters, the question of how long they have lasted. Well, this matter of mine, think what you will of it, lasted while I caught at a dozen possibilities, none of which made a difference for the better, that I could see, in there having been in the house —and for how long, above all?—a person of whom I was in ignorance. It lasted while I just bridled a little with the sense that my office demanded that there should be no such ignorance and no such person. It lasted while this visitant, at all events —and there was a touch of the strange freedom, as I remember, in the sign of familiarity of his wearing no hat—seemed to fix me, from his position, with just the question, just the scrutiny through the fading light, that his own presence provoked. We were too far apart to call to each other, but there was a moment at which, at shorter range, some challenge between us, breaking the hush, would have been the right result of our straight mutual stare. He was in one of the angles, the one away from the house, very erect, as it struck me, and with both hands on the ledge. So I saw him as I see the letters I form on this page; then, exactly, after a minute, as if to add to the spectacle, he slowly changed his place—passed, looking at me hard all the while, to the opposite corner of the platform. Yes, I had the sharpest sense that during this transit he never took his eyes from me, and I can see at this moment the way his hand, as he went, passed from one of the crenelations to the next. He stopped at the other corner, but less long, and even as he turned away still markedly fixed me. He turned away; that was all I knew.

IV

It was not that I didn't wait, on this occasion, for more, for I was rooted as deeply as I was shaken. Was there a "secret" at Bly—a mystery of Udolpho or an insane, an unmentionable relative kept in unsuspected confinement? I can't say how long I turned it over, or how long, in a confusion of curiosity and dread, I remained where I had had my collision; I only recall that when I re-entered the house darkness had quite closed in. Agitation, in the interval, certainly had held me and driven me, for I must, in circling about the place, have walked three miles; but I was to be, later on, so much more overwhelmed that this mere dawn of alarm was a comparatively human chill. The most singular part of it, in fact—singular as the rest had been—was the part I became, in the hall, aware of in meeting Mrs. Grose. This picture comes back to me in the general train—the impression, as I received it on my return, of the wide white panelled space, bright in the lamplight and with its portraits and red carpet, and of the good surprised look of my friend, which immediately told me she had missed me. It came to me straightway, under her contact, that, with plain heartiness, mere relieved anxiety at my appearance, she knew nothing whatever that could bear upon the incident I had there ready for her. I had not suspected in advance that her comfortable face would pull me up, and I somehow measured the importance of what I had seen by my thus finding myself hesitate to mention it. Scarce anything in the whole history seems to me so odd as this fact that my real beginning of fear was one, as I may say, with the instinct of sparing my companion. On the spot, accordingly, in the pleasant hall and with her eyes on me, I, for a reason that I couldn't then have phrased, achieved an inward resolution—offered a vague pretext for my lateness and, with the plea of the beauty of the night and of the heavy dew and wet feet, went as soon as possible to my room.

Here it was another affair; here, for many days after, it was a queer affair enough. There were hours, from day to day—or at least there were moments, snatched even from clear duties—when I had to shut myself up to think. It was not so much yet that I was more nervous than I could bear to be as that I was remarkably afraid of becoming so; for the truth I had now to turn over was, simply and clearly, the truth that I could arrive at no account whatever of the visitor with whom I had been so inexplicably and yet, as it seemed to me, so intimately concerned. It took little time to see that I could sound without forms of inquiry and without exciting remark any domestic complications. The shock I had suffered must have sharpened all my senses; I felt sure, at the end of three days and as the result of mere closer attention, that I had not been practiced upon by the servants nor made the object of any "game." Of whatever it was that I knew, nothing was known around me. There was but one sane inference: someone had taken a liberty rather gross. That was what, repeatedly, I dipped into my room and locked the door to say to myself. We had been, collectively, subject to an intrusion; some unscrupulous traveler, curious in old houses, had made his way in unobserved, enjoyed the prospect from the best point of view, and then stolen out as he came. If he had given me such a bold hard stare, that was but a part of his indiscretion. The good thing, after all, was that we should surely see no more of him.

This was not so good a thing, I admit, as not to leave me to judge that what, essentially, made nothing else much signify was simply my charming work. My charming work was just my life with Miles and Flora, and through nothing could I so like it as through feeling that I could throw myself into it in trouble. The attraction of my small charges was a constant joy, leading me to wonder afresh at the vanity of my original fears, the distaste I had begun by entertaining for the probable gray prose of my office. There was to be no gray prose, it appeared, and no long grind; so how could work not be charming that presented itself as daily beauty? It was all the romance of the nursery and the poetry of the schoolroom. I don't mean by this, of course, that we studied only fiction and verse; I mean I can express no otherwise the sort of interest my companions inspired. How can I describe that except by saying that instead of growing used to them—and it's a marvel for a governess: I call the sisterhood to witness!—I made constant fresh discoveries. There was one direction, assuredly, in which these discoveries stopped: deep obscurity continued to cover the region of the boy's conduct at school. It had been promptly given me, I have noted, to face that mystery without a pang. Perhaps even it would be nearer the truth to say that—without a word—he himself had cleared it up. He had made the whole charge absurd. My conclusion bloomed there with the real rose flush of his innocence: he was only too fine and fair for the little horrid, unclean school world, and he had paid a price for it. I reflected acutely that the sense of such differences, such superiorities of quality, always, on the part of the majority—which could include even stupid, sordid headmasters—turn infallibly to the vindictive.

Both the children had a gentleness (it was their only fault, and it never made Miles a muff) that kept them—how shall I express it?—almost impersonal and certainly quite unpunishable. They were like the cherubs of the anecdote, who had—morally, at any rate—nothing to whack! I remember feeling with Miles in especial as if he had had, as it were, no history. We expect of a small child a scant one, but there was in this beautiful little boy something extraordinarily sensitive, yet extraordinarily happy, that, more than in any creature of his age I have seen, struck me as beginning anew each day. He had never for a second suffered. I took this as a direct disproof of his having really been chastised. If he had been wicked he would have "caught" it, and I should have caught it by the rebound—I should have found the trace. I found nothing at all, and he was therefore an angel. He never spoke of his school, never mentioned a comrade or a master; and I, for my part, was quite too much disgusted to allude to them. Of course I was under the spell, and the wonderful part is that, even at the time, I perfectly knew I was. But I gave myself up to it; it was an antidote to any pain, and I had more pains than one. I was in receipt in these days of disturbing letters from home, where things were not going well. But with my children, what things in the world mattered? That was the question I used to put to my scrappy retirements. I was dazzled by their loveliness.

There was a Sunday—to get on—when it rained with such force and for so many hours that there could be no procession to church; in consequence of which, as the day declined, I had arranged with Mrs. Grose that, should the evening show improvement, we would attend together the late service. The rain happily stopped, and I prepared for our walk, which, through the park and by the good road to the village, would be a matter of twenty minutes. Coming downstairs to meet my colleague in the hall, I remembered a pair of gloves that had required three stitches and that had received them—with a publicity perhaps not edifying—while I sat with the children at their tea, served on Sundays, by exception, in that cold, clean temple of mahogany and brass, the "grown-up" dining room. The gloves had been dropped there, and I turned in to recover them. The day was gray enough, but the afternoon light still lingered, and it enabled me, on crossing the threshold, not only to recognize, on a chair near the wide window, then closed, the articles I wanted, but to become aware of a person on the other side of the window and looking straight in. One step into the room had sufficed; my vision was instantaneous; it was all there. The person looking straight in was the person who had already appeared to me. He appeared thus again with I won't say greater distinctness, for that was impossible, but with a nearness that represented a forward stride in our intercourse and made me, as I met him, catch my breath and turn cold. He was the same—he was the same, and seen, this time, as he had been seen before, from the waist up, the window, though the dining room was on the ground floor, not going down to the terrace on which he stood. His face was close to the glass, yet the effect of this better view was, strangely, only to show me how intense the former had been. He remained but a few seconds—long enough to convince me he also saw and recognized; but it was as if I had been looking at him for years and had known him always. Something, however, happened this time that had not happened before; his stare into my face, through the glass and across the room, was as deep and hard as then, but it quitted me for a moment during which I could still watch it, see it fix successively several other things. On the spot there came to me the added shock of a certitude that it was not for me he had come there. He had come for someone else.

The flash of this knowledge—for it was knowledge in the midst of dread—produced in me the most extraordinary effect, started as I stood there, a sudden vibration of duty and courage. I say courage because I was beyond all doubt already far gone. I bounded straight out of the door again, reached that of the house, got, in an instant, upon the drive, and, passing along the terrace as fast as I could rush, turned a corner and came full in sight. But it was in sight of nothing now—my visitor had vanished. I stopped, I almost dropped, with the real relief of this; but I took in the whole scene—I gave him time to reappear. I call it time, but how long was it? I can't speak to the purpose today of the duration of these things. That kind of measure must have left me: they couldn't have lasted as they actually appeared to me to last. The terrace and the whole place, the lawn and the garden beyond it, all I could see of the park, were empty with a great emptiness. There were shrubberies and big trees, but I remember the clear assurance I felt that none of them concealed him. He was there or was not there: not there if I didn't see him. I got hold of this; then, instinctively, instead of returning as I had come, went to the window. It was confusedly present to me that I ought to place myself where he had stood. I did so; I applied my face to the pane and looked, as he had looked, into the room. As if, at this moment, to show me exactly what his range had been, Mrs. Grose, as I had done for himself just before, came in from the hall. With this I had the full image of a repetition of what had already occurred. She saw me as I had seen my own visitant; she pulled up short as I had done; I gave her something of the shock that I had received. She turned white, and this made me ask myself if I had blanched as much. She stared, in short, and retreated on just *my* lines, and I knew she had then passed out and come round to me and that I should presently meet her. I remained where I was, and while I waited I thought of more things than one. But there's only one I take space to mention. I wondered why *she* should be scared.

V

Oh, she let me know as soon as, round the corner of the house, she loomed again into view. "What in the name of goodness is the matter—?" She was now flushed and out of breath.

I said nothing till she came quite near. "With me?" I must have made a wonderful face. "Do I show it?"

"You're as white as a sheet. You look awful."

I considered; I could meet on this, without scruple, any innocence. My need to respect the bloom of Mrs. Grose's had dropped, without a rustle, from my shoulders, and if I wavered for the instant it was not with what I kept back. I put out my hand to her and she took it; I held her hard a little, liking to feel her close to me. There was a kind of support in the shy heave of her surprise. "You came for me for church, of course, but I can't go."

"Has anything happened?"

"Yes. You must know now. Did I look very queer?"

"Through this window? Dreadful!"

"Well," I said, "I've been frightened." Mrs. Grose's eyes expressed plainly that *she* had no wish to be, yet also that she knew too well her place not to be ready to share with me any marked inconvenience. Oh, it was quite settled that she *must* share! "Just what you saw from the dining room a minute ago was the effect of that. What *I* saw—just before—was much worse."

Her hand tightened. "What was it?"

"An extraordinary man. Looking in."

"What extraordinary man?"

"I haven't the least idea."

Mrs. Grose gazed round us in vain. "Then where is he gone?"

"I know still less."

"Have you seen him before?"

"Yes—once. On the old tower."

She could only look at me harder. "Do you mean he's a stranger?"

"Oh, very much!"

"Yet you didn't tell me?"

"No—for reasons. But now that you've guessed—"

Mrs. Grose's round eyes encountered this charge. "Ah, I haven't guessed!" she said very simply. "How can I if *you* don't imagine?"

"I don't in the very least."

"You've seen him nowhere but on the tower?"

"And on this spot just now."

Mrs. Grose looked round again. "What was he doing on the tower?"

"Only standing there and looking down at me."

She thought a minute. "Was he a gentleman?"

I found I had no need to think. "No." She gazed in deeper wonder. "No."

"Then nobody about the place? Nobody from the village?"

"Nobody—nobody. I didn't tell you, but I made sure."

She breathed a vague relief: this was, oddly, so much to the good. It only went indeed a little way. "But if he isn't a gentleman—"

"What *is* he? He's a horror."

"A horror?"

"He's—God help me if I know *what* he is!"

Mrs. Grose looked round once more; she fixed her eyes on the duskier distance, then, pulling herself together, turned to me with abrupt inconsequence. "It's time we should be at church."

"Oh, I'm not fit for church!"

"Won't it do you good?"

"It won't do *them*—!" I nodded at the house.

"The children?"

"I can't leave them now."

"You're afraid—?"

I spoke boldly. "I'm afraid of *him*."

Mrs. Grose's large face showed me, at this, for the first time, the faraway faint glimmer of a consciousness more acute: I somehow made out in it the delayed dawn of an idea I myself had not given her and that was as yet quite obscure to me. It comes back to me that I thought instantly of this as something I could get from her; and I felt it to be connected with the desire she presently showed to know more. "When was it—on the tower?"

"About the middle of the month. At this same hour."

"Almost at dark," said Mrs. Grose.

"Oh, no, not nearly. I saw him as I see you."

"Then how did he get in?"

"And how did he get out?" I laughed. "I had no opportunity to ask him! This evening, you see," I pursued, "he has not been able to get in."

"He only peeps?"

"I hope it will be confined to that!" She had now let go my hand; she turned away a little. I waited an instant; then I brought out: "Go to church. Goodbye. I must watch."

Slowly she faced me again. "Do you fear for them?"

We met in another long look. "Don't *you*?" Instead of answering she came nearer to the window and, for a minute, applied her face to the glass. "You see how he could see," I meanwhile went on.

She didn't move. "How long was he here?"

"Till I came out. I came to meet him."

Mrs. Grose at last turned round, and there was still more in her face. "*I* couldn't have come out."

"Neither could I!" I laughed again. "But I did come. I have my duty."

"So have I mine," she replied; after which she added: "What is he like?"

"I've been dying to tell you. But he's like nobody."

"Nobody?" she echoed.

"He has no hat." Then seeing in her face that she already, in this, with a deeper dismay, found a touch of picture, I quickly added stroke to stroke. "He has red hair, very red, close-curling, and a pale face, long in shape, with straight, good features and little, rather queer whiskers that are as red as his hair. His eyebrows are, somehow, darker; they look particularly arched and as if they might move a good deal. His eyes are sharp, strange—awfully; but I only know clearly that they're rather small and very fixed. His mouth's wide, and his lips are thin, and except for his little whiskers he's quite clean-shaven. He gives me a sort of sense of looking like an actor."

"An actor!" It was impossible to resemble one less, at least, than Mrs. Grose at that moment.

"I've never seen one, but so I suppose them. He's tall, active, erect," I continued, "but never—no, never!—a gentleman."

My companion's face had blanched as I went on; her round eyes started and her mild mouth gaped. "A gentleman?" she gasped, confounded, stupefied: "a gentleman *he*?"

"You know him then?"

She visibly tried to hold herself. "But he *is* handsome?"

I saw the way to help her. "Remarkably!"

"And dressed—?"

"In somebody's clothes."

"They're smart, but they're not his own."

She broke into a breathless affirmative groan: "They're the master's!"

I caught it up. "You *do* know him?"

She faltered but a second. "Quint!" she cried.

"Quint?"

"Peter Quint—his own man, his valet, when he was here!"

"When the master was?"

Gaping still, but meeting me, she pieced it all together. "He never wore his hat, but he did wear—well, there were waistcoats missed. They were both here—last year. Then the master went, and Quint was alone."

I followed, but halting a little. "Alone?"

"Alone with *us*." Then, as from a deeper depth, "In charge," she added.

"And what became of him?"

She hung fire so long that I was still more mystified. "He went, too," she brought out at last.

"Went where?"

Her expression, at this, became extraordinary. "God knows where! He died."

"Died?" I almost shrieked.

She seemed fairly to square herself, plant herself more firmly to utter the wonder of it. "Yes. Mr. Quint is dead."

VI

It took of course more than that particular passage to place us together in presence of what we had now to live with as we could—my dreadful liability to impressions of the order so vividly exemplified, and my companion's knowledge, henceforth—a knowledge half consternation and half compassion—of that liability. There had been, this evening, after the revelation left me, for an hour, so prostrate—there had been, for either of us, no attendance on any service but a little service of tears and vows, of prayers and promises, a climax to the series of mutual challenges and pledges that had straightway ensued on our retreating together to the schoolroom and shutting ourselves up there to have everything out. The result of our having everything out was simply to reduce our situation to the last rigor of its elements. She herself had seen nothing, not the shadow of a shadow, and nobody in the house but the governess was in the governess's plight; yet she accepted without directly impugning my sanity the truth as I gave it to her, and ended by showing me, on this ground, an awestricken tenderness, an expression of the sense of my more than questionable privilege, of which the very breath has remained with me as that of the sweetest of human charities.

What was settled between us, accordingly, that night, was that we thought we might bear things together; and I was not even sure that, in spite of her exemption, it was she who had the best of the burden. I knew at this hour, I think, as well as I knew later, what I was capable of meeting to shelter my pupils; but it took me some time to be wholly sure of what my honest ally was prepared for to keep terms with so compromising a contract. I was queer company enough—quite as queer as the company I received; but as I trace over what we went through I see how much common ground we must have found in the one idea that, by good fortune, *could* steady us. It was the idea, the second movement, that led me straight out, as I may say, of the inner chamber of my dread. I could take the air in the court, at least, and there Mrs. Grose could join me. Perfectly can I recall now the particular way strength came to me before we separated for the night. We had gone over and over every feature of what I had seen.

"He was looking for someone else, you say—someone who was not you?"

"He was looking for little Miles." A portentous clearness now possessed me. "*That's* whom he was looking for."

"But how do you know?"

"I know, I know, I know!" My exaltation grew. "And *you* know, my dear!"

She didn't deny this, but I required, I felt, not even so much telling as that. She resumed in a moment, at any rate: "What if *he* should see him?"

"Little Miles? That's what he wants!"

She looked immensely scared again. "The child?"

"Heaven forbid! The man. He wants to appear to *them*." That he might was an awful conception, and yet, somehow, I could keep it at bay; which, moreover, as we lingered there, was what I succeeded in practically proving. I had an absolute certainty that I should see again what I had already seen, but something within me said that by offering myself bravely as the sole subject of such experience, by accepting, by inviting, by surmounting it all, I should serve as an expiatory victim and guard the tranquility of my companions. The children, in especial, I should thus fence about and absolutely save. I recall one of the last things I said that night to Mrs. Grose.

"It does strike me that my pupils have never mentioned—"

She looked at me hard as I musingly pulled up. "His having been here and the time they were with him?"

"The time they were with him, and his name, his presence, his history, in any way."

"Oh, the little lady doesn't remember. She never heard or knew."

"The circumstances of his death?" I thought with some intensity. "Perhaps not. But Miles would remember—Miles would know."

"Ah, don't try him!" broke from Mrs. Grose.

I returned her the look she had given me. "Don't be afraid." I continued to think. "It *is* rather odd."

"That he has never spoken of him?"

"Never by the least allusion. And you tell me they were 'great friends'?"

"Oh, it wasn't *him*!" Mrs. Grose with emphasis declared. "It was Quint's own fancy. To play with him, I mean—to spoil him." She paused a moment; then she added: "Quint was much too free."

This gave me, straight from my vision of his face—*such* a face!—a sudden sickness of disgust. "Too free with *my* boy?"

"Too free with everyone!"

I forbore, for the moment, to analyze this description further than by the reflection that a part of it applied to several of the members of the household, of the half-dozen maids and men who were still of our small colony. But there was everything, for our apprehension, in the lucky fact that no discomfortable legend, no perturbation of scullions, had ever, within anyone's memory attached to the kind old place. It had neither bad name nor ill fame, and Mrs. Grose, most apparently, only desired to cling to me and to quake in silence. I even put her, the very last thing of all, to the test. It was when, at midnight, she had her hand on the schoolroom door to take leave. "I have it from you then—for it's of great importance—that he was definitely and admittedly bad?"

"Oh, not admittedly. *I* knew it—but the master didn't."

"And you never told him?"

"Well, he didn't like tale-bearing—he hated complaints. He was terribly short with anything of that kind, and if people were all right to *him*—"

"He wouldn't be bothered with more?" This squared well enough with my impressions of him: he was not a trouble-loving gentleman, nor so very particular perhaps about some of the company *he* kept. All the same, I pressed my interlocutress. "I promise you *I* would have told!"

She felt my discrimination. "I daresay I was wrong. But, really, I was afraid."

"Afraid of what?"

"Of things that man could do. Quint was so clever—he was so deep."

I took this in still more than, probably, I showed. "You weren't afraid of anything else? Not of his effect—?"

"His effect?" she repeated with a face of anguish and waiting while I faltered.

"On innocent little precious lives. They were in your charge."

"No, they were not in mine!" she roundly and distressfully returned. "The master believed in him and placed him here because he was supposed not to be well and the country air so good for him. So he had everything to say. Yes"—she let me have it—"even about *them.*"

"Them—that creature?" I had to smother a kind of howl. "And you could bear it!"

"No. I couldn't—and I can't now!" And the poor woman burst into tears.

A rigid control, from the next day, was, as I have said, to follow them; yet how often and how passionately, for a week, we came back together to the subject! Much as we had discussed it that Sunday night, I was, in the immediate later hours in especial—for it may be imagined whether I slept—still haunted with the shadow of something she had not told me. I myself had kept back nothing, but there was a word Mrs. Grose had kept back. I was sure, moreover, by morning, that this was not from a failure of frankness, but because on every side there were fears. It seems to me indeed, in retrospect, that by the time the morrow's sun was high I had restlessly read into the fact before us almost all the meaning they were to receive from subsequent and more cruel occurrences. What they gave me above all was just the sinister figure of the living man—the dead one would keep awhile!—and of the months he had continuously passed at Bly, which, added up, made a formidable stretch. The limit of this evil time had arrived only when, on the dawn of a winter's morning, Peter Quint was found, by a laborer going to early work, stone dead on the road from the village: a catastrophe explained—superficially at least—by a visible wound to his head; such a wound as might have been produced—and as, on the final evidence, *had* been—by a fatal slip, in the dark and after leaving the public house, on the steepish icy slope, a wrong path altogether, at the bottom of which he lay. The icy slope, the turn mistaken at night and in liquor, accounted for much—practically, in the end and after the inquest and boundless chatter, for everything; but there had been matters in his life—strange passages and perils, secret disorders, vices more than suspected—that would have accounted for a good deal more.

I scarce know how to put my story into words that shall be a credible picture of my state of mind; but I was in these days literally able to find a joy in the extraordinary flight of heroism the occasion demanded of me. I now saw that I had been asked for a service admirable and difficult; and there would be a greatness in letting it be seen—oh, in the right quarter!—that I could succeed where many another girl might have failed. It was an immense help to me—I confess I rather applaud myself as I look back!—that I saw my service so strongly and so simply. I was there to protect and defend the little creatures in the world the most bereaved and the most lovable, the appeal of whose helplessness had suddenly become only too explicit, a deep, constant ache of one's own committed heart. We were cut off, really, together; we were united in our danger. They had nothing but me, and I—well, I had *them.* It was in short a magnificent chance. This chance presented itself to me in an image richly material. I was a screen—I was to stand before them. The more I saw, the less they would. I began to watch them in a stifled suspense, a disguised excitement that might well, had it continued too long, have turned to something like madness. What saved me, as I now see, was that it turned to something else altogether. It didn't last as suspense—it was superseded by horrible proofs. Proofs, I say, yes—from the moment I really took hold.

This moment dated from an afternoon hour that I happened to spend in the grounds with the younger of my pupils alone. We had left Miles indoors, on the red cushion of a deep window seat; he had wished to finish a book, and I had been glad to encourage a purpose so laudable in a young man whose only defect was an occasional excess of the restless. His sister, on the contrary, had been alert to come out, and I strolled with her half an hour, seeking the shade, for the sun was still high and the day exceptionally warm. I was aware afresh, with her, as we went, of how, like her brother, she contrived—it was the charming thing in both children—to let me alone without appearing to drop me and to accompany me without appearing to surround. They were never importunate and yet never listless. My attention to them all really went to seeing them amuse themselves immensely without me: this was a spectacle they seemed actively to prepare and that engaged me as an active admirer. I walked in a world of their invention—they had no occasion whatever to draw upon mine; so that my time was taken only with being, for them, some remarkable person or thing that the game of the moment required and that was merely, thanks to my superior, my exalted stamp, a happy and highly distinguished sinecure. I forget what I was on the present occasion; I only remember that I was something very important and very quiet and that Flora was playing very hard. We were on the edge of the lake, and, as we had lately begun geography, the lake was the Sea of Azof.

Suddenly, in these circumstances, I became aware that, on the other side of the Sea of Azof, we had an interested spectator. The way this knowledge gathered in me was the strangest thing in the world—the strangest, that is, except the very much stranger in which it quickly merged itself. I had sat down with a piece of work—for I was something or other that could sit—on the old stone bench which overlooked the pond; and in this position I began to take in with certitude, and yet without direct vision, the presence, at a distance, of a third person. The old trees, the thick shrubbery, made a great and pleasant shade, but it was all suffused with the brightness of the hot, still hour. There was no ambiguity in anything; none whatever, at least, in the conviction I from one moment to another found myself forming as to what I should see straight before me and across the lake as a consequence of raising my eyes. They were attached at this juncture to the stitching in which I was engaged, and I can feel once more the spasm of my effort not to move them till I should so have steadied myself as to be able to make up my mind what to do. There was an alien object in view—a figure whose right of presence I instantly, passionately questioned. I recollect counting over perfectly the possibilities, reminding myself that nothing was more natural, for instance, then the appearance of one of the men about the place, or even of a messenger, a postman, or a tradesman's boy, from the village. That reminder had as little effect on my practical certitude as I was conscious—still even without looking—of its having upon the character and attitude of our visitor. Nothing was more natural than that these things should be the other things that they absolutely were not.

Of the positive identity of the apparition I would assure myself as soon as the small clock of my courage should have ticked out the right second; meanwhile, with an effort that was already sharp enough, I transferred my eyes straight to little Flora, who, at the moment, was about ten yards away. My heart had stood still for an instant with the wonder and terror of the question whether she too would see; and I held my breath while I waited for what a cry from her, what some sudden innocent sign either of interest or of alarm, would tell me. I waited, but nothing came; then, in the first place—and there is something more dire in this, I feel, than in anything I have to relate—I was determined by a sense that, within a minute, all sounds from her had previously dropped; and, in the second, by the circumstance that, also within the minute, she had, in her play, turned her back to the water. This was her attitude when I at last looked at her—looked with the confirmed conviction that we were still, together, under direct personal notice. She had picked up a small flat piece of wood, which happened to have in it a little hole that had evidently suggested to her the idea of sticking in another fragment that might figure as a mast and make the thing a boat. This second morsel, as I watched her, she was very markedly and intently attempting to tighten in its place. My apprehension of what she was doing sustained me so that after some seconds I felt I was ready for more. Then I again shifted my eyes—I faced what I had to face.

VII

I got hold of Mrs. Grose as soon after this as I could; and I can give no intelligible account of how I fought out the interval. Yet I still hear myself cry as I fairly threw myself into her arms: "They *know*—it's too monstrous: they know, they know!"

"And what on earth—?" I felt her incredulity as she held me.

"Why, all that *we* know—and heaven knows what else besides!" Then, as she released me, I made it out to her, made it out perhaps only now with full coherency even to myself. "Two hours ago, in the garden"—I could scarce articulate—"Flora *saw*!"

Mrs. Grose took it as she might have taken a blow in the stomach. "She has told you?" she panted.

"Not a word—that's the horror. She kept it to herself! The child of eight, *that* child!" Unutterable still, for me, was the stupefaction of it.

Mrs. Grose, of course, could only gape the wider. "Then how do you know?"

"I was there—I saw with my eyes: saw that she was perfectly aware."

"Do you mean aware of *him*?"

"No—of *her*." I was conscious as I spoke that I looked prodigious things, for I got the slow reflection of them in my companion's face. "Another person—this time; but a figure of quite as unmistakable horror and evil: a woman in black, pale and dreadful—with such an air also, and such a face!—on the other side of the lake. I was there with the child—quiet for the hour; and in the midst of it she came."

"Came how—from where?"

"From where they come from! She just appeared and stood there—but not so near."

"And without coming nearer?"

"Oh, for the effect and the feeling, she might have been as close as you!"

My friend, with an odd impulse, fell back a step. "Was she someone you've never seen?"

"Yes. But someone the child has. Someone *you* have." Then, to show how I had thought it all out: "My predecessor—the one who died."

"Miss Jessel?"

"Miss Jessel. You don't believe me?" I pressed.

She turned right and left in her distress. "How can you be sure?"

This drew from me, in the state of my nerves, a flash of impatience. "Then ask Flora—*she's* sure!" But I had no sooner spoken than I caught myself up. "No, for God's sake, *don't*! She'll say she isn't—she'll lie!"

Mrs. Grose was not too bewildered instinctively to protest. "Ah, how *can* you?"

"Because I'm clear. Flora doesn't want me to know."

"It's only then to spare you."

"No, no—there are depths, depths! The more I go over it, the more I see in it, and the more I see in it, the more I fear. I don't know what I *don't* see—what I *don't* fear!"

Mrs. Grose tried to keep up with me. "You mean you're afraid of seeing her again?"

"Oh, no; that's nothing—now!" Then I explained. "It's of *not* seeing her."

But my companion only looked wan. “I don’t understand you.”

“Why, it’s that the child may keep it up—and that the child assuredly *will*—without my knowing it.”

At the image of this possibility Mrs. Grose for a moment collapsed, yet presently to pull herself together again, as if from the positive force of the sense of what, should we yield an inch, there would really be to give way to. “Dear, dear—we must keep our heads! And after all, if she doesn’t mind it—!” She even tried a grim joke. “Perhaps she likes it!”

“Likes *such* things—a scrap of an infant!”

“Isn’t it just a proof of her blessed innocence?” my friend bravely inquired.

She brought me, for the instant, almost round. “Oh, we must clutch at *that*—we must cling to it! If it isn’t a proof of what you say, it’s a proof of—God knows what! For the woman’s a horror of horrors.”

Mrs. Grose, at this, fixed her eyes a minute on the ground; then at last raising them, “Tell me how you know,” she said.

“Then you admit it’s what she was?” I cried.

“Tell me how you know,” my friend simply repeated.

“Know? By seeing her! By the way she looked.”

“At you, do you mean—so wickedly?”

“Dear me, no—I could have borne that. She gave me never a glance. She only fixed the child.”

Mrs. Grose tried to see it. “Fixed her?”

“Ah, with such awful eyes!”

She stared at mine as if they might really have resembled them. “Do you mean of dislike?”

“God help us, no. Of something much worse.”

“Worse than dislike?”—this left her indeed at a loss.

“With a determination—indescribable. With a kind of fury of intention.”

I made her turn pale. “Intention?”

“To get hold of her.” Mrs. Grose—her eyes just lingering on mine—gave a shudder and walked to the window; and while she stood there looking out I completed my statement. “*That’s* what Flora knows.”

After a little she turned round. “The person was in black, you say?”

“In mourning—rather poor, almost shabby. But—yes—with extraordinary beauty.” I now recognized to what I had at last, stroke by stroke, brought the victim of my confidence, for she quite visibly weighed this. “Oh, handsome—very, very,” I insisted; “wonderfully handsome. But infamous.”

She slowly came back to me. “Miss Jessel—*was* infamous.” She once more took my hand in both her own, holding it as tight as if to fortify me against the increase of alarm I might draw from this disclosure. “They were both infamous,” she finally said.

So, for a little, we faced it once more together; and I found absolutely a degree of help in seeing it now so straight. “I appreciate,” I said, “the great decency of your not having hitherto spoken; but the time has certainly come to give me the whole thing.” She appeared to assent to this, but still only in silence; seeing which I went on: “I must have it now. Of what did she die? Come, there was something between them.”

“There was everything.”

“In spite of the difference—?”

“Oh, of their rank, their condition”—she brought it woefully out. “*She* was a lady.”

I turned it over; I again saw. "Yes—she was a lady."

"And he so dreadfully below," said Mrs. Grose.

I felt that I doubtless needn't press too hard, in such company, on the place of a servant in the scale; but there was nothing to prevent an acceptance of my companion's own measure of my predecessor's abasement. There was a way to deal with that, and I dealt; the more readily for my full vision—on the evidence—of our employer's late clever, good-looking "own" man; impudent, assured, spoiled, depraved. "The fellow was a hound."

Mrs. Grose considered as if it were perhaps a little a case for a sense of shades. "I've never seen one like him. He did what he wished."

"With *her*?"

"With them all."

It was as if now in my friend's own eyes Miss Jessel had again appeared. I seemed at any rate, for an instant, to see their evocation of her as distinctly as I had seen her by the pond; and I brought out with decision: "It must have been also what *she* wished!"

Mrs. Grose's face signified that it had been indeed, but she said at the same time: "Poor woman—she paid for it!"

"Then you do know what she died of?" I asked.

"No—I know nothing. I wanted not to know; I was glad enough I didn't; and I thanked heaven she was well out of this!"

"Yet you had, then, your idea—"

"Of her real reason for leaving? Oh, yes—as to that. She couldn't have stayed. Fancy it here—for a governess! And afterward I imagined—and I still imagine. And what I imagine is dreadful."

"Not so dreadful as what *I* do," I replied; on which I must have shown her—as I was indeed but too conscious—a front of miserable defeat. It brought out again all her compassion for me, and at the renewed touch of her kindness my power to resist broke down. I burst, as I had, the other time, made her burst, into tears; she took me to her motherly breast, and my lamentation overflowed. "I don't do it!" I sobbed in despair; "I don't save or shield them! It's far worse than I dreamed—they're lost!"

VIII

What I had said to Mrs. Grose was true enough: there were in the matter I had put before her depths and possibilities that I lacked resolution to sound; so that when we met once more in the wonder of it we were of a common mind about the duty of resistance to extravagant fancies. We were to keep our heads if we should keep nothing else—difficult indeed as that might be in the face of what, in our prodigious experience, was least to be questioned. Late that night, while the house slept, we had another talk in my room, when she went all the way with me as to its being beyond doubt that I had seen exactly what I had seen. To hold her perfectly in the pinch of that, I found I had only to ask her how, if I had "made it up," I came to be able to give, of each of the persons appearing to me, a picture disclosing, to the last detail, their special marks—a portrait on the exhibition of which she had instantly recognized and named them. She wished of course—small blame to her!—to sink the whole subject; and I was quick to assure her that my own interest in it had now violently taken the form of a search for the way to escape from it. I encountered her on the ground of a probability that with recurrence—for recurrence we took for granted—I should get used to my danger, distinctly professing that my personal exposure had suddenly become the least of my discomforts. It was my new suspicion that was intolerable; and yet even to this complication the later hours of the day had brought a little ease.

On leaving her, after my first outbreak, I had of course returned to my pupils, associating the right remedy for my dismay with that sense of their charm which I had already found to be a thing I could positively cultivate and which had never failed me yet. I had simply, in other words, plunged afresh into Flora's special society and there become aware—it was almost a luxury!—that she could put her little conscious hand straight upon the spot that ached. She had looked at me in sweet speculation and then had accused me to my face of having "cried." I had supposed I had brushed away the ugly signs: but I could literally—for the time, at all events—rejoice, under this fathomless charity, that they had not entirely disappeared. To gaze into the depths of blue of the child's eyes and pronounce their loveliness a trick of premature cunning was to be guilty of a cynicism in preference to which I naturally preferred to abjure my judgment and, so far as might be, my agitation. I couldn't abjure for merely wanting to, but I could repeat to Mrs. Grose—as I did there, over and over, in the small hours—that with their voices in the air, their pressure on one's heart, and their fragrant faces against one's cheek, everything fell to the ground but their incapacity and their beauty. It was a pity that, somehow, to settle this once for all, I had equally to re-enumerate the signs of subtlety that, in the afternoon, by the lake had made a miracle of my show of self-possession. It was a pity to be obliged to reinvestigate the certitude of the moment itself and repeat how it had come to me as a revelation that the inconceivable communion I then surprised was a matter, for either party, of habit. It was a pity that I should have had to quaver out again the reasons for my not having, in my delusion, so much as questioned that the little girl saw our visitant even as I actually saw Mrs. Grose herself, and that she wanted, by just so much as she did thus see, to make me suppose she didn't, and at the same time, without showing anything, arrive at a guess as to whether I myself did! It was a pity that I needed once more to describe the portentous little activity by which she sought to divert my attention—the perceptible increase of movement, the greater intensity of play, the singing, the gabbling of nonsense, and the invitation to romp.

Yet if I had not indulged, to prove there was nothing in it, in this review, I should have missed the two or three dim elements of comfort that still remained to me. I should not for instance have been able to asseverate to my friend that I was certain—which was so much to the good—that *I* at least had not betrayed myself. I should not have been prompted, by stress of need, by desperation of mind—I scarce know what to call it—to invoke such further aid to intelligence as might spring from pushing my colleague fairly to the wall. She had told me, bit by bit, under pressure, a great deal; but a small shifty spot on the wrong side of it all still sometimes brushed my brow like the wing of a bat; and I remember how on this occasion—for the sleeping house and the concentration alike of our danger and our watch seemed to help—I felt the importance of giving the last jerk to the curtain. "I don't believe anything so horrible," I recollect saying; "no, let us put it definitely, my dear, that I don't. But if I did, you know, there's a thing I should require now, just without sparing you the least bit more—oh, not a scrap, come!—to get out of you. What was it you had in mind when, in our distress, before Miles came back, over the letter from his school, you said, under my insistence, that you didn't pretend for him that he had not literally *ever* been 'bad'? He has *not* literally 'ever,' in these weeks that I myself have lived with him and so closely watched him; he has been an imperturbable little prodigy of delightful, lovable goodness. Therefore you might perfectly have made the claim for him if you had not, as it happened, seen an exception to take. What was your exception, and to what passage in your personal observation of him did you refer?"

It was a dreadfully austere inquiry, but levity was not our note, and, at any rate, before the gray dawn admonished us to separate I had got my answer. What my friend had had in mind proved to be immensely to the purpose. It was neither more nor less than the circumstance that for a period of several months Quint and the boy had been perpetually together. It was in fact the very appropriate truth that she had ventured to criticize the propriety, to hint at the incongruity, of so close an alliance, and even to go so far on the subject as a frank overture to Miss Jessel. Miss Jessel had, with a most strange manner, requested her to mind her business, and the good woman had, on this, directly approached little Miles. What she had said to him, since I pressed, was that *she* liked to see young gentlemen not forget their station.

I pressed again, of course, at this. "You reminded him that Quint was only a base menial?"

"As you might say! And it was his answer, for one thing, that was bad."

"And for another thing?" I waited. "He repeated your words to Quint?"

"No, not that. It's just what he *wouldn't*!" she could still impress upon me. "I was sure, at any rate," she added, "that he didn't. But he denied certain occasions."

"What occasions?"

"When they had been about together quite as if Quint were his tutor—and a very grand one—and Miss Jessel only for the little lady. When he had gone off with the fellow, I mean, and spent hours with him."

"He then prevaricated about it—he said he hadn't?" Her assent was clear enough to cause me to add in a moment: "I see. He lied."

"Oh!" Mrs. Grose mumbled. This was a suggestion that it didn't matter; which indeed she backed up by a further remark. "You see, after all, Miss Jessel didn't mind. She didn't forbid him."

I considered. "Did he put that to you as a justification?"

At this she dropped again. "No, he never spoke of it."

"Never mentioned her in connection with Quint?"

She saw, visibly flushing, where I was coming out. "Well, he didn't show anything. He denied," she repeated; "he denied."

Lord, how I pressed her now! "So that you could see he knew what was between the two wretches?"

"I don't know—I don't know!" the poor woman groaned.

"You do know, you dear thing," I replied; "only you haven't my dreadful boldness of mind, and you keep back, out of timidity and modesty and delicacy, even the impression that, in the past, when you had, without my aid, to flounder about in silence, most of all made you miserable. But I shall get it out of you yet! There was something in the boy that suggested to you," I continued, "that he covered and concealed their relation."

"Oh, he couldn't prevent—"

"Your learning the truth? I daresay! But, heavens," I fell, with vehemence, athinking, "what it shows that they must, to that extent, have succeeded in making of him!"

"Ah, nothing that's not nice *now*!" Mrs. Grose lugubriously pleaded.

"I don't wonder you looked queer," I persisted, "when I mentioned to you the letter from his school!"

"I doubt if I looked as queer as you!" she retorted with homely force. "And if he was so bad then as that comes to, how is he such an angel now?"

"Yes, indeed—and if he was a fiend at school! How, how, how? Well," I said in my torment, "you must put it to me again, but I shall not be able to tell you for some days. Only, put it to me again!" I cried in a way that made my friend stare. "There are directions in which I must not for the present let myself go." Meanwhile I returned to her first example—the one to which she had just previously referred—of the boy's happy capacity for an occasional slip. "If Quint—on your remonstrance at the time you speak of—was a base menial, one of the things Miles said to you, I find myself guessing, was that you were another." Again her admission was so adequate that I continued: "And you forgave him that?"

"Wouldn't *you*?"

"Oh, yes!" And we exchanged there, in the stillness, a sound of the oddest amusement. Then I went on: "At all events, while he was with the man—"

"Miss Flora was with the woman. It suited them all!"

It suited me, too, I felt, only too well; by which I mean that it suited exactly the particularly deadly view I was in the very act of forbidding myself to entertain. But I so far succeeded in checking the expression of this view that I will throw, just here, no further light on it than may be offered by the mention of my final observation to Mrs. Grose. "His having lied and been impudent are, I confess, less engaging specimens than I had hoped to have from you of the outbreak in him of the little natural man. Still," I mused, "They must do, for they make me feel more than ever that I must watch."

It made me blush, the next minute, to see in my friend's face how much more unreservedly she had forgiven him than her anecdote struck me as presenting to my own tenderness an occasion for doing. This came out when, at the schoolroom door, she quitted me. "Surely you don't accuse *him*—"

"Of carrying on an intercourse that he conceals from me? Ah, remember that, until further evidence, I now accuse nobody." Then, before shutting her out to go, by another passage, to her own place, "I must just wait," I wound up.

IX

I waited and waited, and the days, as they elapsed, took something from my consternation. A very few of them, in fact, passing, in constant sight of my pupils, without a fresh incident, sufficed to give to grievous fancies and even to odious memories a kind of brush of the sponge. I have spoken of the surrender to their extraordinary childish grace as a thing I could actively cultivate, and it may be imagined if I neglected now to address myself to this source for whatever it would yield. Stranger than I can express, certainly, was the effort to struggle against my new lights; it would doubtless have been, however, a greater tension still had it not been so frequently successful. I used to wonder how my little charges could help guessing that I thought strange things about them; and the circumstances that these things only made them more interesting was not by itself a direct aid to keeping them in the dark. I trembled lest they should see that they *were* so immensely more interesting. Putting things at the worst, at all events, as in meditation I so often did, any clouding of their innocence could only be—blameless and foredoomed as they were—a reason the more for taking risks. There were moments when, by an irresistible impulse, I found myself catching them up and pressing them to my heart. As soon as I had done so I used to say to myself: "What will they think of that? Doesn't it betray too much?" It would have been easy to get into a sad, wild tangle about how much I might betray; but the real account, I feel, of the hours of peace that I could still enjoy was that the immediate charm of my companions was a beguilement still effective even under the shadow of the possibility that it was studied. For if it occurred to me that I might occasionally excite suspicion by the little outbreaks of my sharper passion for them, so too I remember wondering if I mightn't see a queerness in the traceable increase of their own demonstrations.

They were at this period extravagantly and preternaturally fond of me; which, after all, I could reflect, was no more than a graceful response in children perpetually bowed over and hugged. The homage of which they were so lavish succeeded, in truth, for my nerves, quite as well as if I never appeared to myself, as I may say, literally to catch them at a purpose in it. They had never, I think, wanted to do so many things for their poor protectress; I mean—though they got their lessons better and better, which was naturally what would please her most—in the way of diverting, entertaining, surprising her; reading her passages, telling her stories, acting her charades, pouncing out at her, in disguises, as animals and historical characters, and above all astonishing her by the "pieces" they had secretly got by heart and could interminably recite. I should never get to the bottom—were I to let myself go even now—of the prodigious private commentary, all under still more private correction, with which, in these days, I overscored their full hours. They had shown me from the first a facility for everything, a general faculty which, taking a fresh start, achieved remarkable flights. They got their little tasks as if they loved them, and indulged, from the mere exuberance of the gift, in the most unimposed little miracles of memory. They not only popped out at me as tigers and as Romans, but as Shakespeareans, astronomers, and navigators. This was so singularly the case that it had presumably much to do with the fact as to which, at the present day, I am at a loss for a different explanation: I allude to my unnatural composure on the subject of another school for Miles. What I remember is that I was content not, for the time, to open the question, and that contentment must have sprung from the sense of his perpetually striking show of cleverness. He was too clever for a bad governess, for a parson's daughter, to spoil; and the strangest if not the brightest thread in the pensive embroidery I just spoke of was the impression I might have got, if I had dared to work it out, that he was under some influence operating in his small intellectual life as a tremendous incitement.

If it was easy to reflect, however, that such a boy could postpone school, it was at least as marked that for such a boy to have been "kicked out" by a schoolmaster was a mystification without end. Let me add that in their company now—and I was careful almost never to be out of it—I could follow no scent very far. We lived in a cloud of music and love and success and private theatricals. The musical sense in each of the children was of the quickest, but the elder in especial had a marvelous knack of catching and repeating. The schoolroom piano broke into all gruesome fancies; and when that failed there were confabulations in corners, with a sequel of one of them going out in the highest spirits in order to "come in" as something new. I had had brothers myself, and it was no revelation to me that little girls could be slavish idolaters of little boys. What surpassed everything was that there was a little boy in the world who could have for the inferior age, sex, and intelligence so fine a consideration. They were extraordinarily at one, and to say that they never either quarreled or complained is to make the note of praise coarse for their quality of sweetness. Sometimes, indeed, when I dropped into coarseness, I perhaps came across traces of little understandings between them by which one of them should keep me occupied while the other slipped away. There is a naive side, I suppose, in all diplomacy; but if my pupils practiced upon me, it was surely with the minimum of grossness. It was all in the other quarter that, after a lull, the grossness broke out.

I find that I really hang back; but I must take my plunge. In going on with the record of what was hideous at Bly, I not only challenge the most liberal faith—for which I little care; but—and this is another matter—I renew what I myself suffered,

I again push my way through it to the end. There came suddenly an hour after which, as I look back, the affair seems to me to have been all pure suffering; but I have at least reached the heart of it, and the straightest road out is doubtless to advance. One evening—with nothing to lead up or to prepare it—I felt the cold touch of the impression that had breathed on me the night of my arrival and which, much lighter then, as I have mentioned, I should probably have made little of in memory had my subsequent sojourn been less agitated. I had not gone to bed; I sat reading by a couple of candles. There was a roomful of old books at Bly—last-century fiction, some of it, which, to the extent of a distinctly deprecated renown, but never to so much as that of a stray specimen, had reached the sequestered home and appealed to the unavowed curiosity of my youth. I remember that the book I had in my hand was Fielding's Amelia; also that I was wholly awake. I recall further both a general conviction that it was horribly late and a particular objection to looking at my watch. I figure, finally, that the white curtain draping, in the fashion of those days, the head of Flora's little bed, shrouded, as I had assured myself long before, the perfection of childish rest. I recollect in short that, though I was deeply interested in my author, I found myself, at the turn of a page and with his spell all scattered, looking straight up from him and hard at the door of my room. There was a moment during which I listened, reminded of the faint sense I had had, the first night, of there being something undefinably astir in the house, and noted the soft breath of the open casement just move the half-drawn blind. Then, with all the marks of a deliberation that must have seemed magnificent had there been anyone to admire it, I laid down my book, rose to my feet, and, taking a candle, went straight out of the room and, from the passage, on which my light made little impression, noiselessly closed and locked the door.

I can say now neither what determined nor what guided me, but I went straight along the lobby, holding my candle high, till I came within sight of the tall window that presided over the great turn of the staircase. At this point I precipitately found myself aware of three things. They were practically simultaneous, yet they had flashes of succession. My candle, under a bold flourish, went out, and I perceived, by the uncovered window, that the yielding dusk of earliest morning rendered it unnecessary. Without it, the next instant, I saw that there was someone on the stair. I speak of sequences, but I required no lapse of seconds to stiffen myself for a third encounter with Quint. The apparition had reached the landing halfway up and was therefore on the spot nearest the window, where at sight of me, it stopped short and fixed me exactly as it had fixed me from the tower and from the garden. He knew me as well as I knew him; and so, in the cold, faint twilight, with a glimmer in the high glass and another on the polish of the oak stair below, we faced each other in our common intensity. He was absolutely, on this occasion, a living, detestable, dangerous presence. But that was not the wonder of wonders; I reserve this distinction for quite another circumstance: the circumstance that dread had unmistakably quitted me and that there was nothing in me there that didn't meet and measure him.

I had plenty of anguish after that extraordinary moment, but I had, thank God, no terror. And he knew I had not—I found myself at the end of an instant magnificently aware of this. I felt, in a fierce rigor of confidence, that if I stood my ground a minute I should cease—for the time, at least—to have him to reckon with; and during the minute, accordingly, the thing was as human and hideous as a real interview: hideous just because it *was* human, as human as to have met alone, in the small hours, in a sleeping house, some enemy, some adventurer, some criminal. It was the dead silence of our long gaze at such close quarters that gave the whole horror, huge as it was, its only note of the unnatural. If I had met a murderer in such a place and at such an hour, we still at least would have spoken. Something would have passed, in life, between us; if nothing had passed, one of us would have moved. The moment was so prolonged that it would have taken but little more to make me doubt if even *I* were in life. I can't express what followed it save by saying that the silence itself—which was indeed in a manner an attestation of my strength—became the element into which I saw the figure disappear; in which I definitely saw it turn as I might have seen the low wretch to which it had once belonged turn on receipt of an order, and pass, with my eyes on the villainous back that no hunch could have more disfigured, straight down the staircase and into the darkness in which the next bend was lost.

X

I remained awhile at the top of the stair, but with the effect presently of understanding that when my visitor had gone, he had gone: then I returned to my room. The foremost thing I saw there by the light of the candle I had left burning was that Flora's little bed was empty; and on this I caught my breath with all the terror that, five minutes before, I had been able to resist. I dashed at the place in which I had left her lying and over which (for the small silk counterpane and the sheets were disarranged) the white curtains had been deceivingly pulled forward; then my step, to my unutterable relief, produced an answering sound: I perceived an agitation of the window blind, and the child, ducking down, emerged rosily from the other side of it. She stood there in so much of her candor and so little of her nightgown, with her pink bare feet and the golden glow of her curls. She looked intensely grave, and I had never had such a sense of losing an advantage acquired (the thrill of which had just been so prodigious) as on my consciousness that she addressed me with a reproach. "You naughty: where *have* you been?"—instead of challenging her own irregularity I found myself arraigned and explaining. She herself explained, for that matter, with the loveliest, eagerest simplicity. She had known suddenly, as she lay there, that I was out of the room, and had jumped up to see what had become of me. I had dropped, with the joy of her reappearance, back into my chair—feeling then, and then only, a little faint; and she had pattered straight over to me, thrown herself upon my knee, given herself to be held with the flame of the candle full in the wonderful little face that was still flushed with sleep. I remember closing my eyes an instant, yieldingly, consciously, as before the excess of something beautiful that shone out of the blue of her own. "You were looking for me out of the window?" I said. "You thought I might be walking in the grounds?"

"Well, you know, I thought someone was"—she never blanched as she smiled out that at me.

Oh, how I looked at her now! "And did you see anyone?"

"Ah, *no*!" she returned, almost with the full privilege of childish inconsequence, resentfully, though with a long sweetness in her little drawl of the negative.

At that moment, in the state of my nerves, I absolutely believed she lied; and if I once more closed my eyes it was before the dazzle of the three or four possible ways in which I might take this up. One of these, for a moment, tempted me with such singular intensity that, to withstand it, I must have gripped my little girl with a spasm that, wonderfully, she submitted to without a cry or a sign of fright. Why not break out at her on the spot and have it all over?—give it to her straight in her lovely little lighted face? "You see, you see, you *know* that you do and that you already quite suspect I believe it; therefore, why not frankly confess it to me, so that we may at least live with it together and learn perhaps, in the strangeness of our fate, where we are and what it means?" This solicitation dropped, alas, as it came: if I could immediately have succumbed to it I might have spared myself—well, you'll see what. Instead of succumbing I sprang again to my feet, looked at her bed, and took a helpless middle way. "Why did you pull the curtain over the place to make me think you were still there?"

Flora luminously considered; after which, with her little divine smile: "Because I don't like to frighten you!"

"But if I had, by your idea, gone out—?"

She absolutely declined to be puzzled; she turned her eyes to the flame of the candle as if the question were as irrelevant, or at any rate as impersonal, as Mrs. Marcet or nine-times-nine. "Oh, but you know," she quite adequately answered, "that you might come back, you dear, and that you *have*!" And after a little, when she had got into bed, I had, for a long time, by almost sitting on her to hold her hand, to prove that I recognized the pertinence of my return.

You may imagine the general complexion, from that moment, of my nights. I repeatedly sat up till I didn't know when; I selected moments when my roommate unmistakably slept, and, stealing out, took noiseless turns in the passage and even pushed as far as to where I had last met Quint. But I never met him there again; and I may as well say at once that I on no other occasion saw him in the house. I just missed, on the staircase, on the other hand, a different adventure. Looking down it from the top I once recognized the presence of a woman seated on one of the lower steps with her back presented to me, her body half-bowed and her head, in an attitude of woe, in her hands. I had been there but an instant, however, when she vanished without looking round at me. I knew, nonetheless, exactly what dreadful face she had to show; and I wondered whether, if instead of being above I had been below, I should have had, for going up, the same nerve I had lately shown Quint. Well, there continued to be plenty of chance for nerve. On the eleventh night after my latest encounter with that gentleman—they were all numbered now—I had an alarm that perilously skirted it and that indeed, from the particular quality of its unexpectedness, proved quite my sharpest shock. It was precisely the first night during this series that, weary with watching, I had felt that I might again without laxity lay myself down at my old hour. I slept immediately and, as I afterward knew, till about one o'clock; but when I woke it was to sit straight up, as completely roused as if a hand had shook me. I had left a light burning, but it was now out, and I felt an instant certainty that Flora had extinguished it. This brought me to my feet and straight, in the darkness, to her bed, which I found she had left. A glance at the window enlightened me further, and the striking of a match completed the picture.

The child had again got up—this time blowing out the taper, and had again, for some purpose of observation or response, squeezed in behind the blind and was peering out into the night. That she now saw—as she had not, I had satisfied myself, the previous time—was proved to me by the fact that she was disturbed neither by my reillumination nor by the haste I made to get into slippers and into a wrap. Hidden, protected, absorbed, she evidently rested on the sill—the casement opened forward—and gave herself up. There was a great still moon to help her, and this fact had counted in my quick decision. She was face to face with the apparition we had met at the lake, and could now communicate with it as she had not then been able to do. What I, on my side, had to care for was, without disturbing her, to reach, from the corridor, some other window in the same quarter. I got to the door without her hearing me; I got out of it, closed it, and listened, from the other side, for some sound from her. While I stood in the passage I had my eyes on her brother's door, which was but ten steps off and which, indescribably, produced in me a renewal of the strange impulse that I lately spoke of as my temptation. What if I should go straight in and march to *his* window?—what if, by risking to his boyish bewilderment a revelation of my motive, I should throw across the rest of the mystery the long halter of my boldness?

This thought held me sufficiently to make me cross to his threshold and pause again. I preternaturally listened; I figured to myself what might portentously be; I wondered if his bed were also empty and he too were secretly at watch. It was a deep, soundless minute, at the end of which my impulse failed. He was quiet; he might be innocent; the risk was hideous; I turned away. There was a figure in the grounds—a figure prowling for a sight, the visitor with whom Flora was engaged; but it was not the visitor most concerned with my boy. I hesitated afresh, but on other grounds and only for a few seconds; then I had made my choice. There were empty rooms at Bly, and it was only a question of choosing the right one. The right one suddenly presented itself to me as the lower one—though high above the gardens—in the solid corner of the house that I have spoken of as the old tower. This was a large, square chamber, arranged with some state as a bedroom, the extravagant size of which made it so inconvenient that it had not for years, though kept by Mrs. Grose in exemplary order, been occupied. I had often admired it and I knew my way about in it; I had only, after just faltering at the first chill gloom of its disuse, to pass across it and unbolt as quietly as I could one of the shutters. Achieving this transit, I uncovered the glass without a sound and, applying my face to the pane, was able, the darkness without being much less than within, to see that I commanded the right direction. Then I saw something more. The moon made the night extraordinarily penetrable and showed me on the lawn a person, diminished by distance, who stood there motionless and as if fascinated, looking up to where I had appeared—looking, that is, not so much straight at me as at something that was apparently above me. There was clearly another person above me—there was a person on the tower; but the presence on the lawn was not in the least what I had conceived and had confidently hurried to meet. The presence on the lawn—I felt sick as I made it out—was poor little Miles himself.

XI

It was not till late next day that I spoke to Mrs. Grose; the rigor with which I kept my pupils in sight making it often difficult to meet her privately, and the more as we each felt the importance of not provoking—on the part of the servants quite as much as on that of the children—any suspicion of a secret flurry or that of a discussion of mysteries. I drew a great security in this particular from her mere smooth aspect. There was nothing in her fresh face to pass on to others my horrible confidences. She believed me, I was sure, absolutely: if she hadn't I don't know what would have become of me, for I couldn't have borne the business alone. But she was a magnificent monument to the blessing of a want of imagination, and if she could see in our little charges nothing but their beauty and amiability, their happiness and cleverness, she had no direct communication with the sources of my trouble. If they had been at all visibly blighted or battered, she would doubtless have grown, on tracing it back, haggard enough to match them; as matters stood, however, I could feel her, when she surveyed them, with her large white arms folded and the habit of serenity in all her look, thank the Lord's mercy that if they were ruined the pieces would still serve. Flights of fancy gave place, in her mind, to a steady fireside glow, and I had already begun to perceive how, with the development of the conviction that—as time went on without a public accident—our young things could, after all, look out for themselves, she addressed her greatest solicitude to the sad case presented by their instructress. That, for myself, was a sound simplification: I could engage that, to the world, my face should tell no tales, but it would have been, in the conditions, an immense added strain to find myself anxious about hers.

At the hour I now speak of she had joined me, under pressure, on the terrace, where, with the lapse of the season, the afternoon sun was now agreeable; and we sat there together while, before us, at a distance, but within call if we wished, the children strolled to and fro in one of their most manageable moods. They moved slowly, in unison, below us, over the lawn, the boy, as they went, reading aloud from a storybook and passing his arm round his sister to keep her quite in touch. Mrs. Grose watched them with positive placidity; then I caught the suppressed intellectual creak with which she conscientiously turned to take from me a view of the back of the tapestry. I had made her a receptacle of lurid things, but there was an odd recognition of my superiority—my accomplishments and my function—in her patience under my pain. She offered her mind to my disclosures as, had I wished to mix a witch's broth and proposed it with assurance, she would have held out a large clean saucepan. This had become thoroughly her attitude by the time that, in my recital of the events of the night, I reached the point of what Miles had said to me when, after seeing him, at such a monstrous hour, almost on the very spot where he happened now to be, I had gone down to bring him in; choosing then, at the window, with a concentrated need of not alarming the house, rather that method than a signal more resonant. I had left her meanwhile in little doubt of my small hope of representing with success even to her actual sympathy my sense of the real splendor of the little inspiration with which, after I had got him into the house, the boy met my final articulate challenge. As soon as I appeared in the moonlight on the terrace, he had come to me as straight as possible; on which I had taken his hand without a word and led him, through the dark spaces, up the staircase where Quint had so hungrily hovered for him, along the lobby where I had listened and trembled, and so to his forsaken room.

Not a sound, on the way, had passed between us, and I had wondered—oh, *how* I had wondered!—if he were groping about in his little mind for something plausible and not too grotesque. It would tax his invention, certainly, and I felt, this time, over his real embarrassment, a curious thrill of triumph. It was a sharp trap for the inscrutable! He couldn't play any longer at innocence; so how the deuce would he get out of it? There beat in me indeed, with the passionate throb of this question an equal dumb appeal as to how the deuce *I* should. I was confronted at last, as never yet, with all the risk attached even now to sounding my own horrid note. I remember in fact that as we pushed into his little chamber, where the bed had not been slept in at all and the window, uncovered to the moonlight, made the place so clear that there was no need of striking a match—I remember how I suddenly dropped, sank upon the edge of the bed from the force of the idea that he must know how he really, as they say, "had" me. He could do what he liked, with all his cleverness to help him, so long as I should continue to defer to the old tradition of the criminality of those caretakers of the young who minister to superstitions and fears. He "had" me indeed, and in a cleft stick; for who would ever absolve me, who would consent that I should go unhung, if, by the faintest tremor of an overture, I were the first to introduce into our perfect intercourse an element so dire? No, no: it was useless to attempt to convey to Mrs. Grose, just as it is scarcely less so to attempt to suggest here, how, in our short, stiff brush in the dark, he fairly shook me with admiration. I was of course thoroughly kind and merciful; never, never yet had I placed on his little shoulders hands of such tenderness as those with which, while I rested against the bed, I held him there well under fire. I had no alternative but, in form at least, to put it to him.

"You must tell me now—and all the truth. What did you go out for? What were you doing there?"

I can still see his wonderful smile, the whites of his beautiful eyes, and the uncovering of his little teeth shine to me in the dusk. "If I tell you why, will you understand?" My heart, at this, leaped into my mouth. *would* he tell me why? I found no sound on my lips to press it, and I was aware of replying only with a vague, repeated, grimacing nod. He was gentleness itself, and while I wagged my head at him he stood there more than ever a little fairy prince. It was his brightness indeed that gave me a respite. Would it be so great if he were really going to tell me? "Well," he said at last, "just exactly in order that you should do this."

"Do what?"

"Think me—for a change—*bad*!" I shall never forget the sweetness and gaiety with which he brought out the word, nor how, on top of it, he bent forward and kissed me. It was practically the end of everything. I met his kiss and I had to make, while I folded him for a minute in my arms, the most stupendous effort not to cry. He had given exactly the account of himself that permitted least of my going behind it, and it was only with the effect of confirming my acceptance of it that, as I presently glanced about the room, I could say—

"Then you didn't undress at all?"

He fairly glittered in the gloom. "Not at all. I sat up and read."

"And when did you go down?"

"At midnight. When I'm bad I *am* bad!"

"I see, I see—it's charming. But how could you be sure I would know it?"

"Oh, I arranged that with Flora." His answers rang out with a readiness! "She was to get up and look out."

"Which is what she did do." It was I who fell into the trap!

"So she disturbed you, and, to see what she was looking at, you also looked—you saw."

"While you," I concurred, "caught your death in the night air!"

He literally bloomed so from this exploit that he could afford radiantly to assent. "How otherwise should I have been bad enough?" he asked. Then, after another embrace, the incident and our interview closed on my recognition of all the reserves of goodness that, for his joke, he had been able to draw upon.

XII

The particular impression I had received proved in the morning light, I repeat, not quite successfully presentable to Mrs. Grose, though I reinforced it with the mention of still another remark that he had made before we separated. "It all lies in half a dozen words," I said to her, "words that really settle the matter. 'Think, you know, what I *might* do!' He threw that off to show me how good he is. He knows down to the ground what he 'might' do. That's what he gave them a taste of at school."

"Lord, you do change!" cried my friend.

"I don't change—I simply make it out. The four, depend upon it, perpetually meet. If on either of these last nights you had been with either child, you would clearly have understood. The more I've watched and waited the more I've felt that if there were nothing else to make it sure it would be made so by the systematic silence of each. *Never*, by a slip of the tongue, have they so much as alluded to either of their old friends, any more than Miles has alluded to his expulsion. Oh, yes, we may sit here and look at them, and they may show off to us there to their fill; but even while they pretend to be lost in their fairytale they're steeped in their vision of the dead restored. He's not reading to her," I declared; "they're talking of *them*—they're talking horrors! I go on, I know, as if I were crazy; and it's a wonder I'm not. What I've seen would have made *you* so; but it has only made me more lucid, made me get hold of still other things."

My lucidity must have seemed awful, but the charming creatures who were victims of it, passing and repassing in their interlocked sweetness, gave my colleague something to hold on by; and I felt how tight she held as, without stirring in the breath of my passion, she covered them still with her eyes. "Of what other things have you got hold?"

"Why, of the very things that have delighted, fascinated, and yet, at bottom, as I now so strangely see, mystified and troubled me. Their more than earthly beauty, their absolutely unnatural goodness. It's a game," I went on; "it's a policy and a fraud!"

"On the part of little darlings—?"

"As yet mere lovely babies? Yes, mad as that seems!" The very act of bringing it out really helped me to trace it—follow it all up and piece it all together. "They haven't been good—they've only been absent. It has been easy to live with them, because they're simply leading a life of their own. They're not mine—they're not ours. They're his and they're hers!"

"Quint's and that woman's?"

"Quint's and that woman's. They want to get to them."

Oh, how, at this, poor Mrs. Grose appeared to study them! "But for what?"

"For the love of all the evil that, in those dreadful days, the pair put into them. And to ply them with that evil still, to keep up the work of demons, is what brings the others back."

"Laws!" said my friend under her breath. The exclamation was homely, but it revealed a real acceptance of my further proof of what, in the bad time—for there had been a worse even than this!—must have occurred. There could have been no such justification for me as the plain assent of her experience to whatever depth of depravity I found credible in our brace of scoundrels. It was in obvious submission of memory that she brought out after a moment: "They *were* rascals! But what can they now do?" she pursued.

"Do?" I echoed so loud that Miles and Flora, as they passed at their distance, paused an instant in their walk and looked at us. "Don't they do enough?" I demanded in a lower tone, while the children, having smiled and nodded and kissed hands to us, resumed their exhibition. We were held by it a minute; then I answered: "They can destroy them!" At this my companion did turn, but the inquiry she launched was a silent one, the effect of which was to make me more explicit. "They don't know, as yet, quite how—but they're trying hard. They're seen only across, as it were, and beyond—in strange places and on high places, the top of towers, the roof of houses, the outside of windows, the further edge of pools; but there's a deep design, on either side, to shorten the distance and overcome the obstacle; and the success of the tempters is only a question of time. They've only to keep to their suggestions of danger."

"For the children to come?"

"And perish in the attempt!" Mrs. Grose slowly got up, and I scrupulously added: "Unless, of course, we can prevent!"

Standing there before me while I kept my seat, she visibly turned things over. "Their uncle must do the preventing. He must take them away."

"And who's to make him?"

She had been scanning the distance, but she now dropped on me a foolish face. "You, miss."

"By writing to him that his house is poisoned and his little nephew and niece mad?"

"But if they *are*, miss?"

"And if I am myself, you mean? That's charming news to be sent him by a governess whose prime undertaking was to give him no worry."

Mrs. Grose considered, following the children again. "Yes, he do hate worry. That was the great reason—"

"Why those fiends took him in so long? No doubt, though his indifference must have been awful. As I'm not a fiend, at any rate, I shouldn't take him in."

My companion, after an instant and for all answer, sat down again and grasped my arm. "Make him at any rate come to you."

I stared. "To *me*?" I had a sudden fear of what she might do. "'Him'?"

"He ought to *be* here—he ought to help."

I quickly rose, and I think I must have shown her a queerer face than ever yet. "You see me asking him for a visit?" No, with her eyes on my face she evidently couldn't. Instead of it even—as a woman reads another—she could see what I myself saw: his derision, his amusement, his contempt for the breakdown of my resignation at being left alone and for the fine machinery I had set in motion to attract his attention to my slighted charms. She didn't know—no one knew—how proud I had been to serve him and to stick to our terms; yet she nonetheless took the measure, I think, of the warning I now gave her. "If you should so lose your head as to appeal to him for me—"

She was really frightened. "Yes, miss?"

"I would leave, on the spot, both him and you."

XIII

It was all very well to join them, but speaking to them proved quite as much as ever an effort beyond my strength—offered, in close quarters, difficulties as insurmountable as before. This situation continued a month, and with new aggravations and particular notes, the note above all, sharper and sharper, of the small ironic consciousness on the part of my pupils. It was not, I am as sure today as I was sure then, my mere infernal imagination: it was absolutely traceable that they were aware of my predicament and that this strange relation made, in a manner, for a long time, the air in which we moved. I don't mean that they had their tongues in their cheeks or did anything vulgar, for that was not one of their dangers: I do mean, on the other hand, that the element of the unnamed and untouched became, between us, greater than any other, and that so much avoidance could not have been so successfully effected without a great deal of tacit arrangement. It was as if, at moments, we were perpetually coming into sight of subjects before which we must stop short, turning suddenly out of alleys that we perceived to be blind, closing with a little bang that made us look at each other—for, like all bangs, it was something louder than we had intended—the doors we had indiscreetly opened. All roads lead to Rome, and there were times when it might have struck us that almost every branch of study or subject of conversation skirted forbidden ground. Forbidden ground was the question of the return of the dead in general and of whatever, in especial, might survive, in memory, of the friends little children had lost. There were days when I could have sworn that one of them had, with a small invisible nudge, said to the other: "She thinks she'll do it this time—but she *won't*!" To "do it" would have been to indulge for instance—and for once in a way—in some direct reference to the lady who had prepared them for my discipline. They had a delightful endless appetite for passages in my own history, to which I had again and again treated them; they were in possession of everything that had ever happened to me, had had, with every circumstance the story of my smallest adventures and of those of my brothers and sisters and of the cat and the dog at home, as well as many particulars of the eccentric nature of my father, of the furniture and arrangement of our house, and of the conversation of the old women of our village. There were things enough, taking one with another, to chatter about, if one went very fast and knew by instinct when to go round. They pulled with an art of their own the strings of my invention and my memory; and nothing else perhaps, when I thought of such occasions afterward, gave me so the suspicion of being watched from under cover. It was in any case over *my* life, *my* past, and *my* friends alone that we could take anything like our ease—a state of affairs that led them sometimes without the least pertinence to break out into sociable reminders. I was invited—with no visible connection—to repeat afresh Goody Gosling's celebrated mot or to confirm the details already supplied as to the cleverness of the vicarage pony.

It was partly at such junctures as these and partly at quite different ones that, with the turn my matters had now taken, my predicament, as I have called it, grew most sensible. The fact that the days passed for me without another encounter ought, it would have appeared, to have done something toward soothing my nerves. Since the light brush, that second night on the upper landing, of the presence of a woman at the foot of the stair, I had seen nothing, whether in or out of the house, that one had better not have seen. There was many a corner round which I expected to come upon Quint, and many a situation that, in a merely sinister way, would have favored the appearance of Miss Jessel. The summer had turned, the summer had gone; the autumn had dropped upon Bly and had blown out half our lights. The place, with its gray sky and withered garlands, its bared spaces and scattered dead leaves, was like a theater after the performance—all strewn with crumpled playbills. There were exactly states of the air, conditions of sound and of stillness, unspeakable impressions of the *kind* of ministering moment, that brought back to me, long enough to catch it, the feeling of the medium in which, that June evening out of doors, I had had my first sight of Quint, and in which, too, at those other instants, I had, after seeing him through the window, looked for him in vain in the circle of shrubbery. I recognized the signs, the portents—I recognized the moment, the spot. But they remained unaccompanied and empty, and I continued unmolested; if unmolested one could call a young woman whose sensibility had, in the most extraordinary fashion, not declined but deepened. I had said in my talk with Mrs. Grose on that horrid scene of Flora's by the lake—and had perplexed her by so saying—that it would from that moment distress me much more to lose my power than to keep it. I had then expressed what was vividly in my mind: the truth that, whether the children really saw or not—since, that is, it was not yet definitely proved—I greatly preferred, as a safeguard, the fullness of my own exposure. I was ready to know the very worst that was to be known. What I had then had an ugly glimpse of was that my eyes might be sealed just while theirs were most opened. Well, my eyes *were* sealed, it appeared, at present—a consummation for which it seemed blasphemous not to thank God. There was, alas, a difficulty about that: I would have thanked him with all my soul had I not had in a proportionate measure this conviction of the secret of my pupils.

How can I retrace today the strange steps of my obsession? There were times of our being together when I would have been ready to swear that, literally, in my presence, but with my direct sense of it closed, they had visitors who were known and were welcome. Then it was that, had I not been deterred by the very chance that such an injury might prove greater than the injury to be averted, my exultation would have broken out. "They're here, they're here, you little wretches," I would have cried, "and you can't deny it now!" The little wretches denied it with all the added volume of their sociability and their tenderness, in just the crystal depths of which—like the flash of a fish in a stream—the mockery of their advantage peeped up. The shock, in truth, had sunk into me still deeper than I knew on the night when, looking out to see either Quint or Miss Jessel under the stars, I had beheld the boy over whose rest I watched and who had immediately brought in with him—had straightway, there, turned it on me—the lovely upward look with which, from the battlements above me, the hideous apparition of Quint had played. If it was a question of a scare, my discovery on this occasion had scared me more than any other, and it was in the condition of nerves produced by it that I made my actual inductions. They harassed me so that sometimes, at odd moments, I shut myself up audibly to rehearse—it was at once a fantastic relief and a renewed despair—the manner in which I might come to the point. I approached it from one side and the other while, in my room, I flung myself about, but I always broke down in the monstrous utterance of names. As they died away on my lips, I said to myself that I should indeed help them to represent something infamous, if, by pronouncing them, I should violate as rare a little case of instinctive delicacy as any schoolroom, probably, had ever known. When I said to myself: "*They* have the manners to be silent, and you, trusted as you are, the baseness to speak!" I felt myself crimson and I covered my face with my hands. After these secret scenes I chattered more than ever, going on volubly enough till one of our prodigious, palpable hushes occurred—I can call them nothing else—the strange, dizzy lift or swim (I try for terms!) into a stillness, a pause of all life, that had nothing to do with the more or less noise that at the moment we might be engaged in making and that I could hear through any deepened exhilaration or quickened recitation or louder strum of the piano. Then it was that the others, the outsiders, were there. Though they were not angels, they "passed," as the French say, causing me, while they stayed, to tremble with the fear of their addressing to their younger victims some yet more infernal message or more vivid image than they had thought good enough for myself.

What it was most impossible to get rid of was the cruel idea that, whatever I had seen, Miles and Flora saw *more*—things terrible and unguessable and that sprang from dreadful passages of intercourse in the past. Such things naturally left on the surface, for the time, a chill which we vociferously denied that we felt; and we had, all three, with repetition, got into such splendid training that we went, each time, almost automatically, to mark the close of the incident, through the very same movements. It was striking of the children, at all events, to kiss me inveterately with a kind of wild irrelevance and never to fail—one or the other—of the precious question that had helped us through many a peril. "When do you think he *will* come? Don't you think we *ought* to write?"—there was nothing like that inquiry, we found by experience, for carrying off an awkwardness. "He" of course was their uncle in Harley Street; and we lived in much profusion of theory that he might at any moment arrive to mingle in our circle. It was impossible to have given less encouragement than he had done to such a doctrine, but if we had not had the doctrine to fall back upon we should have deprived each other of some of our finest exhibitions. He never wrote to them—that may have been selfish, but it was a part of the flattery of his trust of me; for the way in which a man pays his highest tribute to a woman is apt to be but by the more festal celebration of one of the sacred laws of his comfort; and I held that I carried out the spirit of the pledge given not to appeal to him when I let my charges understand that their own letters were but charming literary exercises. They were too beautiful to be posted; I kept them myself; I have them all to this hour. This was a rule indeed which only added to the satiric effect of my being plied with the supposition that he might at any moment be among us. It was exactly as if my charges knew how almost more awkward than anything else that might be for me. There appears to me, moreover, as I look back, no note in all this more extraordinary than the mere fact that, in spite of my tension and of their triumph, I never lost patience with them. Adorable they must in truth have been, I now reflect, that I didn't in these days hate them! Would exasperation, however, if relief had longer been postponed, finally have betrayed me? It little matters, for relief arrived. I call it relief, though it was only the relief that a snap brings to a strain or the burst of a thunderstorm to a day of suffocation. It was at least change, and it came with a rush.

XIV

Walking to church a certain Sunday morning, I had little Miles at my side and his sister, in advance of us and at Mrs. Grose's, well in sight. It was a crisp, clear day, the first of its order for some time; the night had brought a touch of frost, and the autumn air, bright and sharp, made the church bells almost gay. It was an odd accident of thought that I should have happened at such a moment to be particularly and very gratefully struck with the obedience of my little charges. Why did they never resent my inexorable, my perpetual society? Something or other had brought nearer home to me that I had all but pinned the boy to my shawl and that, in the way our companions were marshaled before me, I might have appeared to provide against some danger of rebellion. I was like a gaoler with an eye to possible surprises and escapes. But all this belonged—I mean their magnificent little surrender—just to the special array of the facts that were most abysmal. Turned out for Sunday by his uncle's tailor, who had had a free hand and a notion of pretty waistcoats and of his grand little air, Miles's whole title to independence, the rights of his sex and situation, were so stamped upon him that if he had suddenly struck for freedom I should have had nothing to say. I was by the strangest of chances wondering how I should meet him when the revolution unmistakably occurred. I call it a revolution because I now see how, with the word he spoke, the curtain rose on the last act of my dreadful drama, and the catastrophe was precipitated. "Look here, my dear, you know," he charmingly said, "when in the world, please, am I going back to school?"

Transcribed here the speech sounds harmless enough, particularly as uttered in the sweet, high, casual pipe with which, at all interlocutors, but above all at his eternal governess, he threw off intonations as if he were tossing roses. There was something in them that always made one "catch," and I caught, at any rate, now so effectually that I stopped as short as if one of the trees of the park had fallen across the road. There was something new, on the spot, between us, and he was perfectly aware that I recognized it, though, to enable me to do so, he had no need to look a whit less candid and charming than usual. I could feel in him how he already, from my at first finding nothing to reply, perceived the advantage he had gained. I was so slow to find anything that he had plenty of time, after a minute, to continue with his suggestive but inconclusive smile: "You know, my dear, that for a fellow to be with a lady *always*—!" His "my dear" was constantly on his lips for me, and nothing could have expressed more the exact shade of the sentiment with which I desired to inspire my pupils than its fond familiarity. It was so respectfully easy.

But, oh, how I felt that at present I must pick my own phrases! I remember that, to gain time, I tried to laugh, and I seemed to see in the beautiful face with which he watched me how ugly and queer I looked. "And always with the same lady?" I returned.

He neither blanched nor winked. The whole thing was virtually out between us. "Ah, of course, she's a jolly, 'perfect' lady; but, after all, I'm a fellow, don't you see? that's—well, getting on."

I lingered there with him an instant ever so kindly. "Yes, you're getting on." Oh, but I felt helpless!

I have kept to this day the heartbreaking little idea of how he seemed to know that and to play with it. "And you can't say I've not been awfully good, can you?"

I laid my hand on his shoulder, for, though I felt how much better it would have been to walk on, I was not yet quite able. "No, I can't say that, Miles."

"Except just that one night, you know—!"

"That one night?" I couldn't look as straight as he.

"Why, when I went down—went out of the house."

"Oh, yes. But I forget what you did it for."

"You forget?"—he spoke with the sweet extravagance of childish reproach. "Why, it was to show you I could!"

"Oh, yes, you could."

"And I can again."

I felt that I might, perhaps, after all, succeed in keeping my wits about me. "Certainly. But you won't."

"No, not *that* again. It was nothing."

"It was nothing," I said. "But we must go on."

He resumed our walk with me, passing his hand into my arm. "Then when *am* I going back?"

I wore, in turning it over, my most responsible air. "Were you very happy at school?"

He just considered. "Oh, I'm happy enough anywhere!"

"Well, then," I quavered, "if you're just as happy here—!"

"Ah, but that isn't everything! Of course *you* know a lot—"

"But you hint that you know almost as much?" I risked as he paused.

"Not half I want to!" Miles honestly professed. "But it isn't so much that."

"What is it, then?"

"Well—I want to see more life."

"I see; I see." We had arrived within sight of the church and of various persons, including several of the household of Bly, on their way to it and clustered about the door to see us go in. I quickened our step; I wanted to get there before the question between us opened up much further; I reflected hungrily that, for more than an hour, he would have to be silent; and I thought with envy of the comparative dusk of the pew and of the almost spiritual help of the hassock on which I might bend my knees. I seemed literally to be running a race with some confusion to which he was about to reduce me, but I felt that he had got in first when, before we had even entered the churchyard, he threw out—

"I want my own sort!"

It literally made me bound forward. "There are not many of your own sort, Miles!" I laughed. "Unless perhaps dear little Flora!"

"You really compare me to a baby girl?"

This found me singularly weak. "Don't you, then, *love* our sweet Flora?"

"If I didn't—and you, too; if I didn't—!" he repeated as if retreating for a jump, yet leaving his thought so unfinished that, after we had come into the gate, another stop, which he imposed on me by the pressure of his arm, had become inevitable. Mrs. Grose and Flora had passed into the church, the other worshippers had followed, and we were, for the minute, alone among the old, thick graves. We had paused, on the path from the gate, by a low, oblong, tablelike tomb.

"Yes, if you didn't—?"

He looked, while I waited, at the graves. "Well, you know what!" But he didn't move, and he presently produced something that made me drop straight down on the stone slab, as if suddenly to rest. "Does my uncle think what *you* think?"

I markedly rested. "How do you know what I think?"

"Ah, well, of course I don't; for it strikes me you never tell me. But I mean does *he* know?"

"Know what, Miles?"

"Why, the way I'm going on."

I perceived quickly enough that I could make, to this inquiry, no answer that would not involve something of a sacrifice of my employer. Yet it appeared to me that we were all, at Bly, sufficiently sacrificed to make that venial. "I don't think your uncle much cares."

Miles, on this, stood looking at me. "Then don't you think he can be made to?"

"In what way?"

"Why, by his coming down."

"But who'll get him to come down?"

"*I* will!" the boy said with extraordinary brightness and emphasis. He gave me another look charged with that expression and then marched off alone into church.

XV

The business was practically settled from the moment I never followed him. It was a pitiful surrender to agitation, but my being aware of this had somehow no power to restore me. I only sat there on my tomb and read into what my little friend had said to me the fullness of its meaning; by the time I had grasped the whole of which I had also embraced, for absence, the pretext that I was ashamed to offer my pupils and the rest of the congregation such an example of delay. What I said to myself above all was that Miles had got something out of me and that the proof of it, for him, would be just this awkward collapse. He had got out of me that there was something I was much afraid of and that he should probably be able to make use of my fear to gain, for his own purpose, more freedom. My fear was of having to deal with the intolerable question of the grounds of his dismissal from school, for that was really but the question of the horrors gathered behind. That his uncle should arrive to treat with me of these things was a solution that, strictly speaking, I ought now to have desired to bring on; but I could so little face the ugliness and the pain of it that I simply procrastinated and lived from hand to mouth. The boy, to my deep discomposure, was immensely in the right, was in a position to say to me: "Either you clear up with my guardian the mystery of this interruption of my studies, or you cease to expect me to lead with you a life that's so unnatural for a boy." What was so unnatural for the particular boy I was concerned with was this sudden revelation of a consciousness and a plan.

That was what really overcame me, what prevented my going in. I walked round the church, hesitating, hovering; I reflected that I had already, with him, hurt myself beyond repair. Therefore I could patch up nothing, and it was too extreme an effort to squeeze beside him into the pew: he would be so much more sure than ever to pass his arm into mine and make me sit there for an hour in close, silent contact with his commentary on our talk. For the first minute since his arrival I wanted to get away from him. As I paused beneath the high east window and listened to the sounds of worship, I was taken with an impulse that might master me, I felt, completely should I give it the least encouragement. I might easily put an end to my predicament by getting away altogether. Here was my chance; there was no one to stop me; I could give the whole thing up—turn my back and retreat. It was only a question of hurrying again, for a few preparations, to the house which the attendance at church of so many of the servants would practically have left unoccupied. No one, in short, could blame me if I should just drive desperately off. What was it to get away if I got away only till dinner? That would be in a couple of hours, at the end of which—I had the acute prevision—my little pupils would play at innocent wonder about my nonappearance in their train.

"What *did* you do, you naughty, bad thing? Why in the world, to worry us so—and take our thoughts off, too, don't you know?—did you desert us at the very door?" I couldn't meet such questions nor, as they asked them, their false little lovely eyes; yet it was all so exactly what I should have to meet that, as the prospect grew sharp to me, I at last let myself go.

I got, so far as the immediate moment was concerned, away; I came straight out of the churchyard and, thinking hard, retraced my steps through the park. It seemed to me that by the time I reached the house I had made up my mind I would fly. The Sunday stillness both of the approaches and of the interior, in which I met no one, fairly excited me with a sense of opportunity. Were I to get off quickly, this way, I should get off without a scene, without a word. My quickness would have to be remarkable, however, and the question of a conveyance was the great one to settle. Tormented, in the hall, with difficulties and obstacles, I remember sinking down at the foot of the staircase—suddenly collapsing there on the lowest step and then, with a revulsion, recalling that it was exactly where more than a month before, in the darkness of night and just so bowed with evil things, I had seen the specter of the most horrible of women. At this I was able to straighten myself; I went the rest of the way up; I made, in my bewilderment, for the schoolroom, where there were objects belonging to me that I should have to take. But I opened the door to find again, in a flash, my eyes unsealed. In the presence of what I saw I reeled straight back upon my resistance.

Seated at my own table in clear noonday light I saw a person whom, without my previous experience, I should have taken at the first blush for some housemaid who might have stayed at home to look after the place and who, availing herself of rare relief from observation and of the schoolroom table and my pens, ink, and paper, had applied herself to the considerable effort of a letter to her sweetheart. There was an effort in the way that, while her arms rested on the table, her hands with evident weariness supported her head; but at the moment I took this in I had already become aware that, in spite of my entrance, her attitude strangely persisted. Then it was—with the very act of its announcing itself—that her identity flared up in a change of posture. She rose, not as if she had heard me, but with an indescribable grand melancholy of indifference and detachment, and, within a dozen feet of me, stood there as my vile predecessor. Dishonored and tragic, she was all before me; but even as I fixed and, for memory, secured it, the awful image passed away. Dark as midnight in her black dress, her haggard beauty and her unutterable woe, she had looked at me long enough to appear to say that her right to sit at my table was as good as mine to sit at hers. While these instants lasted, indeed, I had the extraordinary chill of feeling that it was I who was the intruder. It was as a wild protest against it that, actually addressing her—"You terrible, miserable woman!"—I heard myself break into a sound that, by the open door, rang through the long passage and the empty house. She looked at me as if she heard me, but I had recovered myself and cleared the air. There was nothing in the room the next minute but the sunshine and a sense that I must stay.

XVI

I had so perfectly expected that the return of my pupils would be marked by a demonstration that I was freshly upset at having to take into account that they were dumb about my absence. Instead of gaily denouncing and caressing me, they made no allusion to my having failed them, and I was left, for the time, on perceiving that she too said nothing, to study Mrs. Grose's odd face. I did this to such purpose that I made sure they had in some way bribed her to silence; a silence that, however, I would engage to break down on the first private opportunity. This opportunity came before tea: I secured five minutes with her in the housekeeper's room, where, in the twilight, amid a smell of lately baked bread, but with the place all swept and garnished, I found her sitting in pained placidity before the fire. So I see her still, so I see her best: facing the flame from her straight chair in the dusky, shining room, a large clean image of the "put away"—of drawers closed and locked and rest without a remedy.

"Oh, yes, they asked me to say nothing; and to please them—so long as they were there—of course I promised. But what had happened to you?"

"I only went with you for the walk," I said. "I had then to come back to meet a friend."

She showed her surprise. "A friend—*you*?"

"Oh, yes, I have a couple!" I laughed. "But did the children give you a reason?"

"For not alluding to your leaving us? Yes; they said you would like it better. Do you like it better?"

My face had made her rueful. "No, I like it worse!" But after an instant I added: "Did they say why I should like it better?"

"No; Master Miles only said, 'We must do nothing but what she likes!'"

"I wish indeed he would. And what did Flora say?"

"Miss Flora was too sweet. She said, 'Oh, of course, of course!'—and I said the same."

I thought a moment. "You were too sweet, too—I can hear you all. But nonetheless, between Miles and me, it's now all out."

"All out?" My companion stared. "But what, miss?"

"Everything. It doesn't matter. I've made up my mind. I came home, my dear," I went on, "for a talk with Miss Jessel."

I had by this time formed the habit of having Mrs. Grose literally well in hand in advance of my sounding that note; so that even now, as she bravely blinked under the signal of my word, I could keep her comparatively firm. "A talk! Do you mean she spoke?"

"It came to that. I found her, on my return, in the schoolroom."

"And what did she say?" I can hear the good woman still, and the candor of her stupefaction.

"That she suffers the torments—!"

It was this, of a truth, that made her, as she filled out my picture, gape. "Do you mean," she faltered, "—of the lost?"

"Of the lost. Of the damned. And that's why, to share them-" I faltered myself with the horror of it.

But my companion, with less imagination, kept me up. "To share them—?"

"She wants Flora." Mrs. Grose might, as I gave it to her, fairly have fallen away from me had I not been prepared. I still held her there, to show I was. "As I've told you, however, it doesn't matter."

"Because you've made up your mind? But to what?"

"To everything."

"And what do you call 'everything'?"

"Why, sending for their uncle."

"Oh, miss, in pity do," my friend broke out. "ah, but I will, I *will*! I see it's the only way. What's 'out,' as I told you, with Miles is that if he thinks I'm afraid to—and has ideas of what he gains by that—he shall see he's mistaken. Yes, yes; his uncle shall have it here from me on the spot (and before the boy himself, if necessary) that if I'm to be reproached with having done nothing again about more school—"

"Yes, miss—" my companion pressed me.

"Well, there's that awful reason."

There were now clearly so many of these for my poor colleague that she was excusable for being vague. "But—a—which?"

"Why, the letter from his old place."

"You'll show it to the master?"

"I ought to have done so on the instant."

"Oh, no!" said Mrs. Grose with decision.

"I'll put it before him," I went on inexorably, "that I can't undertake to work the question on behalf of a child who has been expelled—"

"For we've never in the least known what!" Mrs. Grose declared.

"For wickedness. For what else—when he's so clever and beautiful and perfect? Is he stupid? Is he untidy? Is he infirm? Is he ill-natured? He's exquisite—so it can be only *that*; and that would open up the whole thing. After all," I said, "it's their uncle's fault. If he left here such people—!"

"He didn't really in the least know them. The fault's mine." She had turned quite pale.

"Well, you shan't suffer," I answered.

"The children shan't!" she emphatically returned.

I was silent awhile; we looked at each other. "Then what am I to tell him?"

"You needn't tell him anything. *I'll* tell him."

I measured this. "Do you mean you'll write—?" Remembering she couldn't, I caught myself up. "How do you communicate?"

"I tell the bailiff. *He* writes."

"And should you like him to write our story?"

My question had a sarcastic force that I had not fully intended, and it made her, after a moment, inconsequently break down. The tears were again in her eyes. "Ah, miss, *you* write!"

"Well—tonight," I at last answered; and on this we separated.

XVII

I went so far, in the evening, as to make a beginning. The weather had changed back, a great wind was abroad, and beneath the lamp, in my room, with Flora at peace beside me, I sat for a long time before a blank sheet of paper and listened to the lash of the rain and the batter of the gusts. Finally I went out, taking a candle; I crossed the passage and listened a minute at Miles's door. What, under my endless obsession, I had been impelled to listen for was some betrayal of his not being at rest, and I presently caught one, but not in the form I had expected. His voice tinkled out. “I say, you there—come in.” It was a gaiety in the gloom!

I went in with my light and found him, in bed, very wide awake, but very much at his ease. “Well, what are *you* up to?” he asked with a grace of sociability in which it occurred to me that Mrs. Grose, had she been present, might have looked in vain for proof that anything was “out.”

I stood over him with my candle. “How did you know I was there?”

“Why, of course I heard you. Did you fancy you made no noise? You’re like a troop of cavalry!” he beautifully laughed.

“Then you weren’t asleep?”

“Not much! I lie awake and think.”

I had put my candle, designedly, a short way off, and then, as he held out his friendly old hand to me, had sat down on the edge of his bed. “What is it,” I asked, “that you think of?”

“What in the world, my dear, but *you*?”

“Ah, the pride I take in your appreciation doesn’t insist on that! I had so far rather you slept.”

“Well, I think also, you know, of this queer business of ours.”

I marked the coolness of his firm little hand. “Of what queer business, Miles?”

“Why, the way you bring me up. And all the rest!”

I fairly held my breath a minute, and even from my glimmering taper there was light enough to show how he smiled up at me from his pillow. “What do you mean by all the rest?”

“Oh, you know, you know!”

I could say nothing for a minute, though I felt, as I held his hand and our eyes continued to meet, that my silence had all the air of admitting his charge and that nothing in the whole world of reality was perhaps at that moment so fabulous as our actual relation. “Certainly you shall go back to school,” I said, “if it be that that troubles you. But not to the old place—we must find another, a better. How could I know it did trouble you, this question, when you never told me so, never spoke of it at all?” His clear, listening face, framed in its smooth whiteness, made him for the minute as appealing as some wistful patient in a children’s hospital; and I would have given, as the resemblance came to me, all I possessed on earth really to be the nurse or the sister of charity who might have helped to cure him. Well, even as it was, I perhaps might help! “Do you know you’ve never said a word to me about your school—I mean the old one; never mentioned it in any way?”

He seemed to wonder; he smiled with the same loveliness. But he clearly gained time; he waited, he called for guidance. “Haven’t I?” It wasn’t for *me* to help him—it was for the thing I had met!

Something in his tone and the expression of his face, as I got this from him, set my heart aching with such a pang as it had never yet known; so unutterably touching was it to see his little brain puzzled and his little resources taxed to play, under the spell laid on him, a part of innocence and consistency. “No, never—from the hour you came back. You’ve never mentioned to me one of your masters, one of your comrades, nor the least little thing that ever happened to you at school. Never, little Miles—no, never—have you given me an inkling of anything that *may* have happened there. Therefore you can fancy how much I’m in the dark. Until you came out, that way, this morning, you had, since the first hour I saw you, scarce even made a reference to anything in your previous life. You seemed so perfectly to accept the present.” It was extraordinary how my absolute conviction of his secret precocity (or whatever I might call the poison of an influence that I dared but half to phrase) made him, in spite of the faint breath of his inward trouble, appear as accessible as an older person—imposed him almost as an intellectual equal. "I thought you wanted to go on as you are."

It struck me that at this he just faintly colored. He gave, at any rate, like a convalescent slightly fatigued, a languid shake of his head. "I don't—I don't. I want to get away."

"You're tired of Bly?"

"Oh, no, I like Bly."

"Well, then—?"

"Oh, *you* know what a boy wants!"

I felt that I didn't know so well as Miles, and I took temporary refuge. "You want to go to your uncle?"

Again, at this, with his sweet ironic face, he made a movement on the pillow. "Ah, you can't get off with that!"

I was silent a little, and it was I, now, I think, who changed color. "My dear, I don't want to get off!"

"You can't, even if you do. You can't, you can't!"—he lay beautifully staring. "My uncle must come down, and you must completely settle things."

"If we do," I returned with some spirit, "you may be sure it will be to take you quite away."

"Well, don't you understand that that's exactly what I'm working for? You'll have to tell him—about the way you've let it all drop: you'll have to tell him a tremendous lot!"

The exultation with which he uttered this helped me somehow, for the instant, to meet him rather more. "And how much will *you*, Miles, have to tell him? There are things he'll ask you!"

He turned it over. "Very likely. But what things?"

"The things you've never told me. To make up his mind what to do with you. He can't send you back—"

"Oh, I don't want to go back!" he broke in. "I want a new field."

He said it with admirable serenity, with positive unimpeachable gaiety; and doubtless it was that very note that most evoked for me the poignancy, the unnatural childish tragedy, of his probable reappearance at the end of three months with all this bravado and still more dishonor. It overwhelmed me now that I should never be able to bear that, and it made me let myself go. I threw myself upon him and in the tenderness of my pity I embraced him. "Dear little Miles, dear little Miles—!"

My face was close to his, and he let me kiss him, simply taking it with indulgent good humor. "Well, old lady?"

"Is there nothing—nothing at all that you want to tell me?"

He turned off a little, facing round toward the wall and holding up his hand to look at as one had seen sick children look. "I've told you—I told you this morning."

Oh, I was sorry for him! "That you just want me not to worry you?"

He looked round at me now, as if in recognition of my understanding him; then ever so gently, "To let me alone," he replied.

There was even a singular little dignity in it, something that made me release him, yet, when I had slowly risen, linger beside him. God knows I never wished to harass him, but I felt that merely, at this, to turn my back on him was to abandon or, to put it more truly, to lose him. "I've just begun a letter to your uncle," I said.

"Well, then, finish it!"

I waited a minute. "What happened before?"

He gazed up at me again. "Before what?"

"Before you came back. And before you went away."

For some time he was silent, but he continued to meet my eyes. "What happened?"

It made me, the sound of the words, in which it seemed to me that I caught for the very first time a small faint quaver of consenting consciousness—it made me drop on my knees beside the bed and seize once more the chance of possessing him. "Dear little Miles, dear little Miles, if you *knew* how I want to help you! It's only that, it's nothing but that, and I'd rather die than give you a pain or do you a wrong—I'd rather die than hurt a hair of you. Dear little Miles"—oh, I brought it out now even if I *should* go too far—"I just want you to help me to save you!" But I knew in a moment after this that I had gone too far. The answer to my appeal was instantaneous, but it came in the form of an extraordinary blast and chill, a gust of frozen air, and a shake of the room as great as if, in the wild wind, the casement had crashed in. The boy gave a loud, high shriek, which, lost in the rest of the shock of sound, might have seemed, indistinctly, though I was so close to him, a note either of jubilation or of terror. I jumped to my feet again and was conscious of darkness. So for a moment we remained, while I stared about me and saw that the drawn curtains were unstirred and the window tight. "Why, the candle's out!" I then cried.

"It was I who blew it, dear!" said Miles.

XVIII

The next day, after lessons, Mrs. Grose found a moment to say to me quietly: "Have you written, miss?"

"Yes—I've written." But I didn't add—for the hour—that my letter, sealed and directed, was still in my pocket. There would be time enough to send it before the messenger should go to the village. Meanwhile there had been, on the part of my pupils, no more brilliant, more exemplary morning. It was exactly as if they had both had at heart to gloss over any recent little friction. They performed the dizziest feats of arithmetic, soaring quite out of *my* feeble range, and perpetrated, in higher spirits than ever, geographical and historical jokes. It was conspicuous of course in Miles in particular that he appeared to wish to show how easily he could let me down. This child, to my memory, really lives in a setting of beauty and misery that no words can translate; there was a distinction all his own in every impulse he revealed; never was a small natural creature, to the uninitiated eye all frankness and freedom, a more ingenious, a more extraordinary little gentleman. I had perpetually to guard against the wonder of contemplation into which my initiated view betrayed me; to check the irrelevant gaze and discouraged sigh in which I constantly both attacked and renounced the enigma of what such a little gentleman could have done that deserved a penalty. Say that, by the dark prodigy I knew, the imagination of all evil *had* been opened up to him: all the justice within me ached for the proof that it could ever have flowered into an act.

He had never, at any rate, been such a little gentleman as when, after our early dinner on this dreadful day, he came round to me and asked if I shouldn't like him, for half an hour, to play to me. David playing to Saul could never have shown a finer sense of the occasion. It was literally a charming exhibition of tact, of magnanimity, and quite tantamount to his saying outright: "The true knights we love to read about never push an advantage too far. I know what you mean now: you mean that—to be let alone yourself and not followed up—you'll cease to worry and spy upon me, won't keep me so close to you, will let me go and come. Well, I 'come,' you see—but I don't go! There'll be plenty of time for that. I do really delight in your society, and I only want to show you that I contended for a principle." It may be imagined whether I resisted this appeal or failed to accompany him again, hand in hand, to the schoolroom. He sat down at the old piano and played as he had never played; and if there are those who think he had better have been kicking a football I can only say that I wholly agree with them. For at the end of a time that under his influence I had quite ceased to measure, I started up with a strange sense of having literally slept at my post. It was after luncheon, and by the schoolroom fire, and yet I hadn't really, in the least, slept: I had only done something much worse—I had forgotten. Where, all this time, was Flora? When I put the question to Miles, he played on a minute before answering and then could only say: "Why, my dear, how do *I* know?"—breaking moreover into a happy laugh which, immediately after, as if it were a vocal accompaniment, he prolonged into incoherent, extravagant song.

I went straight to my room, but his sister was not there; then, before going downstairs, I looked into several others. As she was nowhere about she would surely be with Mrs. Grose, whom, in the comfort of that theory, I accordingly proceeded in quest of. I found her where I had found her the evening before, but she met my quick challenge with blank, scared ignorance. She had only supposed that, after the repast, I had carried off both the children; as to which she was quite in her right, for it was the very first time I had allowed the little girl out of my sight without some special provision. Of course now indeed she might be with the maids, so that the immediate thing was to look for her without an air of alarm. This we promptly arranged between us; but when, ten minutes later and in pursuance of our arrangement, we met in the hall, it was only to report on either side that after guarded inquiries we had altogether failed to trace her. For a minute there, apart from observation, we exchanged mute alarms, and I could feel with what high interest my friend returned me all those I had from the first given her.

"She'll be above," she presently said—"in one of the rooms you haven't searched."

"No; she's at a distance." I had made up my mind. "She has gone out."

Mrs. Grose stared. "Without a hat?"

I naturally also looked volumes. "Isn't that woman always without one?"

"She's with *her*?"

"She's with *her*!" I declared. "We must find them."

My hand was on my friend's arm, but she failed for the moment, confronted with such an account of the matter, to respond to my pressure. She communed, on the contrary, on the spot, with her uneasiness. "And where's Master Miles?"

"Oh, *he's* with Quint. They're in the schoolroom."

"Lord, miss!" My view, I was myself aware—and therefore I suppose my tone—had never yet reached so calm an assurance.

"The trick's played," I went on; "they've successfully worked their plan. He found the most divine little way to keep me quiet while she went off."

"'Divine'?" Mrs. Grose bewilderedly echoed.

"Infernal, then!" I almost cheerfully rejoined. "He has provided for himself as well. But come!"

She had helplessly gloomed at the upper regions. "You leave him—?"

"So long with Quint? Yes—I don't mind that now."

She always ended, at these moments, by getting possession of my hand, and in this manner she could at present still stay me. But after gasping an instant at my sudden resignation, "Because of your letter?" she eagerly brought out.

I quickly, by way of answer, felt for my letter, drew it forth, held it up, and then, freeing myself, went and laid it on the great hall table. "Luke will take it," I said as I came back. I reached the house door and opened it; I was already on the steps.

My companion still demurred: the storm of the night and the early morning had dropped, but the afternoon was damp and gray. I came down to the drive while she stood in the doorway. "You go with nothing on?"

"What do I care when the child has nothing? I can't wait to dress," I cried, "and if you must do so, I leave you. Try meanwhile, yourself, upstairs."

"With *them*?" Oh, on this, the poor woman promptly joined me!

XIX

We went straight to the lake, as it was called at Bly, and I daresay rightly called, though I reflect that it may in fact have been a sheet of water less remarkable than it appeared to my untraveled eyes. My acquaintance with sheets of water was small, and the pool of Bly, at all events on the few occasions of my consenting, under the protection of my pupils, to affront its surface in the old flat-bottomed boat moored there for our use, had impressed me both with its extent and its agitation. The usual place of embarkation was half a mile from the house, but I had an intimate conviction that, wherever Flora might be, she was not near home. She had not given me the slip for any small adventure, and, since the day of the very great one that I had shared with her by the pond, I had been aware, in our walks, of the quarter to which she most inclined. This was why I had now given to Mrs. Grose's steps so marked a direction—a direction that made her, when she perceived it, oppose a resistance that showed me she was freshly mystified. "You're going to the water, Miss?—you think she's *in*—?"

"She may be, though the depth is, I believe, nowhere very great. But what I judge most likely is that she's on the spot from which, the other day, we saw together what I told you."

"When she pretended not to see—?"

"With that astounding self-possession? I've always been sure she wanted to go back alone. And now her brother has managed it for her."

Mrs. Grose still stood where she had stopped. "You suppose they really *talk* of them?"

"I could meet this with a confidence! They say things that, if we heard them, would simply appall us."

"And if she *is* there—"

"Yes?"

"Then Miss Jessel is?"

"Beyond a doubt. You shall see."

"Oh, thank you!" my friend cried, planted so firm that, taking it in, I went straight on without her. By the time I reached the pool, however, she was close behind me, and I knew that, whatever, to her apprehension, might befall me, the exposure of my society struck her as her least danger. She exhaled a moan of relief as we at last came in sight of the greater part of the water without a sight of the child. There was no trace of Flora on that nearer side of the bank where my observation of her had been most startling, and none on the opposite edge, where, save for a margin of some twenty yards, a thick copse came down to the water. The pond, oblong in shape, had a width so scant compared to its length that, with its ends out of view, it might have been taken for a scant river. We looked at the empty expanse, and then I felt the suggestion of my friend's eyes. I knew what she meant and I replied with a negative headshake.

"No, no; wait! She has taken the boat."

My companion stared at the vacant mooring place and then again across the lake. "Then where is it?"

"Our not seeing it is the strongest of proofs. She has used it to go over, and then has managed to hide it."

"All alone—that child?"

"She's not alone, and at such times she's not a child: she's an old, old woman." I scanned all the visible shore while Mrs. Grose took again, into the queer element I offered her, one of her plunges of submission; then I pointed out that the boat might perfectly be in a small refuge formed by one of the recesses of the pool, an indentation masked, for the hither side, by a projection of the bank and by a clump of trees growing close to the water.

"But if the boat's there, where on earth's *she*?" my colleague anxiously asked.

"That's exactly what we must learn." And I started to walk further.

"By going all the way round?"

"Certainly, far as it is. It will take us but ten minutes, but it's far enough to have made the child prefer not to walk. She went straight over."

"Laws!" cried my friend again; the chain of my logic was ever too much for her. It dragged her at my heels even now, and when we had got halfway round—a devious, tiresome process, on ground much broken and by a path choked with overgrowth—I paused to give her breath. I sustained her with a grateful arm, assuring her that she might hugely help me; and this started us afresh, so that in the course of but few minutes more we reached a point from which we found the boat to be where I had supposed it. It had been intentionally left as much as possible out of sight and was tied to one of the stakes of a fence that came, just there, down to the brink and that had been an assistance to disembarking. I recognized, as I looked at the pair of short, thick oars, quite safely drawn up, the prodigious character of the feat for a little girl; but I had lived, by this time, too long among wonders and had panted to too many livelier measures. There was a gate in the fence, through which we passed, and that brought us, after a trifling interval, more into the open. Then, "There she is!" we both exclaimed at once.

Flora, a short way off, stood before us on the grass and smiled as if her performance was now complete. The next thing she did, however, was to stoop straight down and pluck—quite as if it were all she was there for—a big, ugly spray of withered fern. I instantly became sure she had just come out of the copse. She waited for us, not herself taking a step, and I was conscious of the rare solemnity with which we presently approached her. She smiled and smiled, and we met; but it was all done in a silence by this time flagrantly ominous. Mrs. Grose was the first to break the spell: she threw herself on her knees and, drawing the child to her breast, clasped in a long embrace the little tender, yielding body. While this dumb convulsion lasted I could only watch it—which I did the more intently when I saw Flora's face peep at me over our companion's shoulder. It was serious now—the flicker had left it; but it strengthened the pang with which I at that moment envied Mrs. Grose the simplicity of *her* relation. Still, all this while, nothing more passed between us save that Flora had let her foolish fern again drop to the ground. What she and I had virtually said to each other was that pretexts were useless now. When Mrs. Grose finally got up she kept the child's hand, so that the two were still before me; and the singular reticence of our communion was even more marked in the frank look she launched me. "I'll be hanged," it said, "if *I'll* speak!"

It was Flora who, gazing all over me in candid wonder, was the first. She was struck with our bareheaded aspect. "Why, where are your things?"

"Where yours are, my dear!" I promptly returned.

She had already got back her gaiety, and appeared to take this as an answer quite sufficient. "And where's Miles?" she went on.

There was something in the small valor of it that quite finished me: these three words from her were, in a flash like the glitter of a drawn blade, the jostle of the cup that my hand, for weeks and weeks, had held high and full to the brim that now, even before speaking, I felt overflow in a deluge. "I'll tell you if you'll tell *me*—" I heard myself say, then heard the tremor in which it broke.

"Well, what?"

Mrs. Grose's suspense blazed at me, but it was too late now, and I brought the thing out handsomely. "Where, my pet, is Miss Jessel?"

XX

Just as in the churchyard with Miles, the whole thing was upon us. Much as I had made of the fact that this name had never once, between us, been sounded, the quick, smitten glare with which the child's face now received it fairly likened my breach of the silence to the smash of a pane of glass. It added to the interposing cry, as if to stay the blow, that Mrs. Grose, at the same instant, uttered over my violence—the shriek of a creature scared, or rather wounded, which, in turn, within a few seconds, was completed by a gasp of my own. I seized my colleague's arm. "She's there, she's there!"

Miss Jessel stood before us on the opposite bank exactly as she had stood the other time, and I remember, strangely, as the first feeling now produced in me, my thrill of joy at having brought on a proof. She was there, and I was justified; she was there, and I was neither cruel nor mad. She was there for poor scared Mrs. Grose, but she was there most for Flora; and no moment of my monstrous time was perhaps so extraordinary as that in which I consciously threw out to her—with the sense that, pale and ravenous demon as she was, she would catch and understand it—an inarticulate message of gratitude. She rose erect on the spot my friend and I had lately quitted, and there was not, in all the long reach of her desire, an inch of her evil that fell short. This first vividness of vision and emotion were things of a few seconds, during which Mrs. Grose's dazed blink across to where I pointed struck me as a sovereign sign that she too at last saw, just as it carried my own eyes precipitately to the child. The revelation then of the manner in which Flora was affected startled me, in truth, far more than it would have done to find her also merely agitated, for direct dismay was of course not what I had expected. Prepared and on her guard as our pursuit had actually made her, she would repress every betrayal; and I was therefore shaken, on the spot, by my first glimpse of the particular one for which I had not allowed. To see her, without a convulsion of her small pink face, not even feign to glance in the direction of the prodigy I announced, but only, instead of that, turn at *me* an expression of hard, still gravity, an expression absolutely new and unprecedented and that appeared to read and accuse and judge me—this was a stroke that somehow converted the little girl herself into the very presence that could make me quail. I quailed even though my certitude that she thoroughly saw was never greater than at that instant, and in the immediate need to defend myself I called it passionately to witness. "She's there, you little unhappy thing—there, there, *there*, and you see her as well as you see me!" I had said shortly before to Mrs. Grose that she was not at these times a child, but an old, old woman, and that description of her could not have been more strikingly confirmed than in the way in which, for all answer to this, she simply showed me, without a concession, an admission, of her eyes, a countenance of deeper and deeper, of indeed suddenly quite fixed, reprobation. I was by this time—if I can put the whole thing at all together—more appalled at what I may properly call her manner than at anything else, though it was simultaneously with this that I became aware of having Mrs. Grose also, and very formidably, to reckon with. My elder companion, the next moment, at any rate, blotted out everything but her own flushed face and her loud, shocked protest, a burst of high disapproval. "What a dreadful turn, to be sure, miss! Where on earth do you see anything?"

I could only grasp her more quickly yet, for even while she spoke the hideous plain presence stood undimmed and undaunted. It had already lasted a minute, and it lasted while I continued, seizing my colleague, quite thrusting her at it and presenting her to it, to insist with my pointing hand. "You don't see her exactly as *we* see?—you mean to say you don't now—*now*? She's as big as a blazing fire! Only look, dearest woman, *look*—!" She looked, even as I did, and gave me, with her deep groan of negation, repulsion, compassion—the mixture with her pity of her relief at her exemption—a sense, touching to me even then, that she would have backed me up if she could. I might well have needed that, for with this hard blow of the proof that her eyes were hopelessly sealed I felt my own situation horribly crumble, I felt—I saw—my livid predecessor press, from her position, on my defeat, and I was conscious, more than all, of what I should have from this instant to deal with in the astounding little attitude of Flora. Into this attitude Mrs. Grose immediately and violently entered, breaking, even while there pierced through my sense of ruin a prodigious private triumph, into breathless reassurance.

"She isn't there, little lady, and nobody's there—and you never see nothing, my sweet! How can poor Miss Jessel—when poor Miss Jessel's dead and buried? *we* know, don't we, love?"—and she appealed, blundering in, to the child. "It's all a mere mistake and a worry and a joke—and we'll go home as fast as we can!"

Our companion, on this, had responded with a strange, quick primness of propriety, and they were again, with Mrs. Grose on her feet, united, as it were, in pained opposition to me. Flora continued to fix me with her small mask of reprobation, and even at that minute I prayed God to forgive me for seeming to see that, as she stood there holding tight to our friend's dress, her incomparable childish beauty had suddenly failed, had quite vanished. I've said it already—she was literally, she was hideously, hard; she had turned common and almost ugly. "I don't know what you mean. I see nobody. I see nothing. I never *have*. I think you're cruel. I don't like you!" Then, after this deliverance, which might have been that of a vulgarly pert little girl in the street, she hugged Mrs. Grose more closely and buried in her skirts the dreadful little face. In this position she produced an almost furious wail. "Take me away, take me away—oh, take me away from *her*!"

"From *me*?" I panted.

"From you—from you!" she cried.

Even Mrs. Grose looked across at me dismayed, while I had nothing to do but communicate again with the figure that, on the opposite bank, without a movement, as rigidly still as if catching, beyond the interval, our voices, was as vividly there for my disaster as it was not there for my service. The wretched child had spoken exactly as if she had got from some outside source each of her stabbing little words, and I could therefore, in the full despair of all I had to accept, but sadly shake my head at her. "If I had ever doubted, all my doubt would at present have gone. I've been living with the miserable truth, and now it has only too much closed round me. Of course I've lost you: I've interfered, and you've seen—under *her* dictation"—with which I faced, over the pool again, our infernal witness—"the easy and perfect way to meet it. I've done my best, but I've lost you. Goodbye." For Mrs.

Grose I had an imperative, an almost frantic "Go, go!" before which, in infinite distress, but mutely possessed of the little girl and clearly convinced, in spite of her blindness, that something awful had occurred and some collapse engulfed us, she retreated, by the way we had come, as fast as she could move.

Of what first happened when I was left alone I had no subsequent memory. I only knew that at the end of, I suppose, a quarter of an hour, an odorous dampness and roughness, chilling and piercing my trouble, had made me understand that I must have thrown myself, on my face, on the ground and given way to a wildness of grief. I must have lain there long and cried and sobbed, for when I raised my head the day was almost done. I got up and looked a moment, through the twilight, at the gray pool and its blank, haunted edge, and then I took, back to the house, my dreary and difficult course. When I reached the gate in the fence the boat, to my surprise, was gone, so that I had a fresh reflection to make on Flora's extraordinary command of the situation. She passed that night, by the most tacit, and I should add, were not the word so grotesque a false note, the happiest of arrangements, with Mrs. Grose. I saw neither of them on my return, but, on the other hand, as by an ambiguous compensation, I saw a great deal of Miles. I saw—I can use no other phrase—so much of him that it was as if it were more than it had ever been. No evening I had passed at Bly had the portentous quality of this one; in spite of which—and in spite also of the deeper depths of consternation that had opened beneath my feet—there was literally, in the ebbing actual, an extraordinarily sweet sadness. On reaching the house I had never so much as looked for the boy; I had simply gone straight to my room to change what I was wearing and to take in, at a glance, much material testimony to Flora's rupture. Her little belongings had all been removed. When later, by the schoolroom fire, I was served with tea by the usual maid, I indulged, on the article of my other pupil, in no inquiry whatever. He had his freedom now—he might have it to the end! Well, he did have it; and it consisted—in part at least—of his coming in at about eight o'clock and sitting down with me in silence. On the removal of the tea things I had blown out the candles and drawn my chair closer: I was conscious of a mortal coldness and felt as if I should never again be warm. So, when he appeared, I was sitting in the glow with my thoughts. He paused a moment by the door as if to look at me; then—as if to share them—came to the other side of the hearth and sank into a chair. We sat there in absolute stillness; yet he wanted, I felt, to be with me.

XXI

Before a new day, in my room, had fully broken, my eyes opened to Mrs. Grose, who had come to my bedside with worse news. Flora was so markedly feverish that an illness was perhaps at hand; she had passed a night of extreme unrest, a night agitated above all by fears that had for their subject not in the least her former, but wholly her present, governess. It was not against the possible re-entrance of Miss Jessel on the scene that she protested—it was conspicuously and passionately against mine. I was promptly on my feet of course, and with an immense deal to ask; the more that my friend had discernibly now girded her loins to meet me once more. This I felt as soon as I had put to her the question of her sense of the child's sincerity as against my own. "She persists in denying to you that she saw, or has ever seen, anything?"

My visitor's trouble, truly, was great. "Ah, miss, it isn't a matter on which I can push her! Yet it isn't either, I must say, as if I much needed to. It has made her, every inch of her, quite old."

"Oh, I see her perfectly from here. She resents, for all the world like some high little personage, the imputation on her truthfulness and, as it were, her respectability. 'Miss Jessel indeed—*she*!' Ah, she's 'respectable,' the chit! The impression she gave me there yesterday was, I assure you, the very strangest of all; it was quite beyond any of the others. I *did* put my foot in it! She'll never speak to me again."

Hideous and obscure as it all was, it held Mrs. Grose briefly silent; then she granted my point with a frankness which, I made sure, had more behind it. "I think indeed, miss, she never will. She do have a grand manner about it!"

"And that manner"—I summed it up—"is practically what's the matter with her now!"

Oh, that manner, I could see in my visitor's face, and not a little else besides! "She asks me every three minutes if I think you're coming in."

"I see—I see." I, too, on my side, had so much more than worked it out. "Has she said to you since yesterday—except to repudiate her familiarity with anything so dreadful—a single other word about Miss Jessel?"

"Not one, miss. And of course you know," my friend added, "I took it from her, by the lake, that, just then and there at least, there *was* nobody."

"Rather! and, naturally, you take it from her still."

"I don't contradict her. What else can I do?"

"Nothing in the world! You've the cleverest little person to deal with. They've made them—their two friends, I mean—still cleverer even than nature did; for it was wondrous material to play on! Flora has now her grievance, and she'll work it to the end."

"Yes, miss; but to *what* end?"

"Why, that of dealing with me to her uncle. She'll make me out to him the lowest creature—!"

I winced at the fair show of the scene in Mrs. Grose's face; she looked for a minute as if she sharply saw them together. "And him who thinks so well of you!"

"He has an odd way—it comes over me now," I laughed,"—of proving it! But that doesn't matter. What Flora wants, of course, is to get rid of me."

My companion bravely concurred. "Never again to so much as look at you."

"So that what you've come to me now for," I asked, "is to speed me on my way?" Before she had time to reply, however, I had her in check. "I've a better idea—the result of my reflections. My going *would* seem the right thing, and on Sunday I was terribly near it. Yet that won't do. It's *you* who must go. You must take Flora."

My visitor, at this, did speculate. "But where in the world—?"

"Away from here. Away from *them*. Away, even most of all, now, from me. Straight to her uncle."

"Only to tell on you—?"

"No, not 'only'! To leave me, in addition, with my remedy."

She was still vague. "And what *is* your remedy?"

"Your loyalty, to begin with. And then Miles's."

She looked at me hard. "Do you think he—?"

"Won't, if he has the chance, turn on me? Yes, I venture still to think it. At all events, I want to try. Get off with his sister as soon as possible and leave me with him alone." I was amazed, myself, at the spirit I had still in reserve, and therefore perhaps a trifle the more disconcerted at the way in which, in spite of this fine example of it, she hesitated. "There's one thing, of course," I went on: "they mustn't, before she goes, see each other for three seconds." Then it came over me that, in spite of Flora's presumable sequestration from the instant of her return from the pool, it might already be too late. "Do you mean," I anxiously asked, "that they *have* met?"

At this she quite flushed. "Ah, miss, I'm not such a fool as that! If I've been obliged to leave her three or four times, it has been each time with one of the maids, and at present, though she's alone, she's locked in safe. And yet—and yet!" There were too many things.

"And yet what?"

"Well, are you so sure of the little gentleman?"

"I'm not sure of anything but *you.* But I have, since last evening, a new hope. I think he wants to give me an opening. I do believe that—poor little exquisite wretch!—he wants to speak. Last evening, in the firelight and the silence, he sat with me for two hours as if it were just coming."

Mrs. Grose looked hard, through the window, at the gray, gathering day. "And did it come?"

"No, though I waited and waited, I confess it didn't, and it was without a breach of the silence or so much as a faint allusion to his sister's condition and absence that we at last kissed for good night. All the same," I continued, "I can't, if her uncle sees her, consent to his seeing her brother without my having given the boy—and most of all because things have got so bad—a little more time."

My friend appeared on this ground more reluctant than I could quite understand. "What do you mean by more time?"

"Well, a day or two—really to bring it out. He'll then be on *my* side—of which you see the importance. If nothing comes, I shall only fail, and you will, at the worst, have helped me by doing, on your arrival in town, whatever you may have found possible." So I put it before her, but she continued for a little so inscrutably embarrassed that I came again to her aid. "Unless, indeed," I wound up, "you really want *not* to go."

I could see it, in her face, at last clear itself; she put out her hand to me as a pledge. "I'll go—I'll go. I'll go this morning."

I wanted to be very just. "If you *should* wish still to wait, I would engage she shouldn't see me."

"No, no: it's the place itself. She must leave it." She held me a moment with heavy eyes, then brought out the rest. "Your idea's the right one. I myself, miss—"

"Well?"

"I can't stay."

The look she gave me with it made me jump at possibilities. "You mean that, since yesterday, you *have* seen—?"

She shook her head with dignity. "I've *heard*—!"

"Heard?"

"From that child—horrors! There!" she sighed with tragic relief. "On my honor, miss, she says things—!" But at this evocation she broke down; she dropped, with a sudden sob, upon my sofa and, as I had seen her do before, gave way to all the grief of it.

It was quite in another manner that I, for my part, let myself go. "Oh, thank God!"

She sprang up again at this, drying her eyes with a groan."'Thank God'?"

"It so justifies me!"

"It does that, miss!"

I couldn't have desired more emphasis, but I just hesitated. "She's so horrible?"

I saw my colleague scarce knew how to put it. "Really shocking."

"And about me?"

"About you, miss—since you must have it. It's beyond everything, for a young lady; and I can't think wherever she must have picked up—"

"The appalling language she applied to me? I can, then!" I broke in with a laugh that was doubtless significant enough.

It only, in truth, left my friend still more grave. "Well, perhaps I ought to also—since I've heard some of it before! Yet I can't bear it," the poor woman went on while, with the same movement, she glanced, on my dressing table, at the face of my watch. "But I must go back."

I kept her, however. "Ah, if you can't bear it—!"

"How can I stop with her, you mean? Why, just *for* that: to get her away. Far from this," she pursued, "far from *them*—"

"She may be different? She may be free?" I seized her almost with joy. "Then, in spite of yesterday, you *believe*—"

"In such doings?" Her simple description of them required, in the light of her expression, to be carried no further, and she gave me the whole thing as she had never done. "I believe."

Yes, it was a joy, and we were still shoulder to shoulder: if I might continue sure of that I should care but little what else happened. My support in the presence of disaster would be the same as it had been in my early need of confidence, and if my friend would answer for my honesty, I would answer for all the rest. On the point of taking leave of her, nonetheless, I was to some extent embarrassed. "There's one thing, of course—it occurs to me—to remember. My letter, giving the alarm, will have reached town before you."

I now perceived still more how she had been beating about the bush and how weary at last it had made her. "Your letter won't have got there. Your letter never went."

"What then became of it?"

"Goodness knows! Master Miles—"

"Do you mean *he* took it?" I gasped.

She hung fire, but she overcame her reluctance. "I mean that I saw yesterday, when I came back with Miss Flora, that it wasn't where you had put it. Later in the evening I had the chance to question Luke, and he declared that he had neither noticed nor touched it." We could only exchange, on this, one of our deeper mutual soundings, and it was Mrs. Grose who first brought up the plumb with an almost elated "You see!"

"Yes, I see that if Miles took it instead he probably will have read it and destroyed it."

"And don't you see anything else?"

I faced her a moment with a sad smile. "It strikes me that by this time your eyes are open even wider than mine."

They proved to be so indeed, but she could still blush, almost, to show it. "I make out now what he must have done at school." And she gave, in her simple sharpness, an almost droll disillusioned nod. "He stole!"

I turned it over—I tried to be more judicial. "Well—perhaps."

She looked as if she found me unexpectedly calm. "He stole *letters*!"

She couldn't know my reasons for a calmness after all pretty shallow; so I showed them off as I might. "I hope then it was to more purpose than in this case! The note, at any rate, that I put on the table yesterday," I pursued, "will have given him so scant an advantage—for it contained only the bare demand for an interview—that he is already much ashamed of having gone so far for so little, and that what he had on his mind last evening was precisely the need of confession." I seemed to myself, for the instant, to have mastered it, to see it all. "Leave us, leave us"—I was already, at the door, hurrying her off. "I'll get it out of him. He'll meet me—he'll confess. If he confesses, he's saved. And if he's saved—"

"Then *you* are?" The dear woman kissed me on this, and I took her farewell. "I'll save you without him!" she cried as she went.

XXII

Yet it was when she had got off—and I missed her on the spot—that the great pinch really came. If I had counted on what it would give me to find myself alone with Miles, I speedily perceived, at least, that it would give me a measure. No hour of my stay in fact was so assailed with apprehensions as that of my coming down to learn that the carriage containing Mrs. Grose and my younger pupil had already rolled out of the gates. Now I *was*, I said to myself, face to face with the elements, and for much of the rest of the day, while I fought my weakness, I could consider that I had been supremely rash. It was a tighter place still than I had yet turned round in; all the more that, for the first time, I could see in the aspect of others a confused reflection of the crisis. What had happened naturally caused them all to stare; there was too little of the explained, throw out whatever we might, in the suddenness of my colleague's act. The maids and the men looked blank; the effect of which on my nerves was an aggravation until I saw the necessity of making it a positive aid. It was precisely, in short, by just clutching the helm that I avoided total wreck; and I dare say that, to bear up at all, I became, that morning, very grand and very dry. I welcomed the consciousness that I was charged with much to do, and I caused it to be known as well that, left thus to myself, I was quite remarkably firm. I wandered with that manner, for the next hour or two, all over the place and looked, I have no doubt, as if I were ready for any onset. So, for the benefit of whom it might concern, I paraded with a sick heart.

The person it appeared least to concern proved to be, till dinner, little Miles himself. My perambulations had given me, meanwhile, no glimpse of him, but they had tended to make more public the change taking place in our relation as a consequence of his having at the piano, the day before, kept me, in Flora's interest, so beguiled and befooled. The stamp of publicity had of course been fully given by her confinement and departure, and the change itself was now ushered in by our nonobservance of the regular custom of the schoolroom. He had already disappeared when, on my way down, I pushed open his door, and I learned below that he had breakfasted—in the presence of a couple of the maids—with Mrs. Grose and his sister. He had then gone out, as he said, for a stroll; than which nothing, I reflected, could better have expressed his frank view of the abrupt transformation of my office. What he would not permit this office to consist of was yet to be settled: there was a queer relief, at all events—I mean for myself in especial—in the renouncement of one pretension. If so much had sprung to the surface, I scarce put it too strongly in saying that what had perhaps sprung highest was the absurdity of our prolonging the fiction that I had anything more to teach him. It sufficiently stuck out that, by tacit little tricks in which even more than myself he carried out the care for my dignity, I had had to appeal to him to let me off straining to meet him on the ground of his true capacity. He had at any rate his freedom now; I was never to touch it again; as I had amply shown, moreover, when, on his joining me in the schoolroom the previous night, I had uttered, on the subject of the interval just concluded, neither challenge nor hint. I had too much, from this moment, my other ideas. Yet when he at last arrived, the difficulty of applying them, the accumulations of my problem, were brought straight home to me by the beautiful little presence on which what had occurred had as yet, for the eye, dropped neither stain nor shadow.

To mark, for the house, the high state I cultivated I decreed that my meals with the boy should be served, as we called it, downstairs; so that I had been awaiting him in the ponderous pomp of the room outside of the window of which I had had from Mrs. Grose, that first scared Sunday, my flash of something it would scarce have done to call light. Here at present I felt afresh—for I had felt it again and again—how my equilibrium depended on the success of my rigid will, the will to shut my eyes as tight as possible to the truth that what I had to deal with was, revoltingly, against nature. I could only get on at all by taking "nature" into my confidence and my account, by treating my monstrous ordeal as a push in a direction unusual, of course, and unpleasant, but demanding, after all, for a fair front, only another turn of the screw of ordinary human virtue. No attempt, nonetheless, could well require more tact than just this attempt to supply, one's self, *all* the nature. How could I put even a little of that article into a suppression of reference to what had occurred? How, on the other hand, could I make reference without a new plunge into the hideous obscure? Well, a sort of answer, after a time, had come to me, and it was so far confirmed as that I was met, incontestably, by the quickened vision of what was rare in my little companion. It was indeed as if he had found even now—as he had so often found at lessons—still some other delicate way to ease me off. Wasn't there light in the fact which, as we shared our solitude, broke out with a specious glitter it had never yet quite worn?—the fact that (opportunity aiding, precious opportunity which had now come) it would be preposterous, with a child so endowed, to forego the help one might wrest from absolute intelligence? What had his intelligence been given him for but to save him? Mightn't one, to reach his mind, risk the stretch of an angular arm over his character? It was as if, when we were face to face in the dining room, he had literally shown me the way. The roast mutton was on the table, and I had dispensed with attendance. Miles, before he sat down, stood a moment with his hands in his pockets and looked at the joint, on which he seemed on the point of passing some humorous judgment. But what he presently produced was: "I say, my dear, is she really very awfully ill?"

"Little Flora? Not so bad but that she'll presently be better. London will set her up. Bly had ceased to agree with her. Come here and take your mutton."

He alertly obeyed me, carried the plate carefully to his seat, and, when he was established, went on. "Did Bly disagree with her so terribly suddenly?"

"Not so suddenly as you might think. One had seen it coming on."

"Then why didn't you get her off before?"

"Before what?"

"Before she became too ill to travel."

I found myself prompt. "She's *not* too ill to travel: she only might have become so if she had stayed. This was just the moment to seize. The journey will dissipate the influence"—oh, I was grand!—"and carry it off."

"I see, I see"—Miles, for that matter, was grand, too. He settled to his repast with the charming little "table manner" that, from the day of his arrival, had relieved me of all grossness of admonition. Whatever he had been driven from school for, it was not for ugly feeding. He was irreproachable, as always, today; but he was unmistakably more conscious. He was discernibly trying to take for granted more things than he found, without assistance, quite easy; and he dropped into peaceful silence while he felt his situation. Our meal was of the briefest—mine a vain pretense, and I had the things immediately removed. While this was done Miles stood again with his hands in his little pockets and his back to me—stood and looked out of the wide window through which, that other day, I had seen what pulled me up. We continued silent while the maid was with us—as silent, it whimsically occurred to me, as some young couple who, on their wedding journey, at the inn, feel shy in the presence of the waiter. He turned round only when the waiter had left us. "Well—so we're alone!"

XXIII

"Oh, more or less." I fancy my smile was pale. "Not absolutely. We shouldn't like that!" I went on.

"No—I suppose we shouldn't. Of course we have the others."

"We have the others—we have indeed the others," I concurred.

"Yet even though we have them," he returned, still with his hands in his pockets and planted there in front of me, "they don't much count, do they?"

I made the best of it, but I felt wan. "It depends on what you call 'much'!"

"Yes"—with all accommodation—"everything depends!" On this, however, he faced to the window again and presently reached it with his vague, restless, cogitating step. He remained there awhile, with his forehead against the glass, in contemplation of the stupid shrubs I knew and the dull things of November. I had always my hypocrisy of "work," behind which, now, I gained the sofa. Steadying myself with it there as I had repeatedly done at those moments of torment that I have described as the moments of my knowing the children to be given to something from which I was barred, I sufficiently obeyed my habit of being prepared for the worst. But an extraordinary impression dropped on me as I extracted a meaning from the boy's embarrassed back—none other than the impression that I was not barred now. This inference grew in a few minutes to sharp intensity and seemed bound up with the direct perception that it was positively *he* who was. The frames and squares of the great window were a kind of image, for him, of a kind of failure. I felt that I saw him, at any rate, shut in or shut out. He was admirable, but not comfortable: I took it in with a throb of hope. Wasn't he looking, through the haunted pane, for something he couldn't see?—and wasn't it the first time in the whole business that he had known such a lapse? The first, the very first: I found it a splendid portent. It made him anxious, though he watched himself; he had been anxious all day and, even while in his usual sweet little manner he sat at table, had needed all his small strange genius to give it a gloss. When he at last turned round to meet me, it was almost as if this genius had succumbed. "Well, I think I'm glad Bly agrees with *me*!"

"You would certainly seem to have seen, these twenty-four hours, a good deal more of it than for some time before. I hope," I went on bravely, "that you've been enjoying yourself."

"Oh, yes, I've been ever so far; all round about—miles and miles away. I've never been so free."

He had really a manner of his own, and I could only try to keep up with him. "Well, do you like it?"

He stood there smiling; then at last he put into two words—"Do *you*?"—more discrimination than I had ever heard two words contain. Before I had time to deal with that, however, he continued as if with the sense that this was an impertinence to be softened. "Nothing could be more charming than the way you take it, for of course if we're alone together now it's you that are alone most. But I hope," he threw in, "you don't particularly mind!"

"Having to do with you?" I asked. "My dear child, how can I help minding? Though I've renounced all claim to your company—you're so beyond me—I at least greatly enjoy it. What else should I stay on for?"

He looked at me more directly, and the expression of his face, graver now, struck me as the most beautiful I had ever found in it. "You stay on just for *that*?"

"Certainly. I stay on as your friend and from the tremendous interest I take in you till something can be done for you that may be more worth your while. That needn't surprise you." My voice trembled so that I felt it impossible to suppress the shake. "Don't you remember how I told you, when I came and sat on your bed the night of the storm, that there was nothing in the world I wouldn't do for you?"

"Yes, yes!" He, on his side, more and more visibly nervous, had a tone to master; but he was so much more successful than I that, laughing out through his gravity, he could pretend we were pleasantly jesting. "Only that, I think, was to get me to do something for *you*!"

"It was partly to get you to do something," I conceded. "But, you know, you didn't do it."

"Oh, yes," he said with the brightest superficial eagerness, "you wanted me to tell you something."

"That's it. Out, straight out. What you have on your mind, you know."

"Ah, then, is *that* what you've stayed over for?"

He spoke with a gaiety through which I could still catch the finest little quiver of resentful passion; but I can't begin to express the effect upon me of an implication of surrender even so faint. It was as if what I had yearned for had come at last only to astonish me. "Well, yes—I may as well make a clean breast of it, it was precisely for that."

He waited so long that I supposed it for the purpose of repudiating the assumption on which my action had been founded; but what he finally said was: "Do you mean now—here?"

"There couldn't be a better place or time." He looked round him uneasily, and I had the rare—oh, the queer!—impression of the very first symptom I had seen in him of the approach of immediate fear. It was as if he were suddenly afraid of me—which struck me indeed as perhaps the best thing to make him. Yet in the very pang of the effort I felt it vain to try sternness, and I heard myself the next instant so gentle as to be almost grotesque. "You want so to go out again?"

"Awfully!" He smiled at me heroically, and the touching little bravery of it was enhanced by his actually flushing with pain. He had picked up his hat, which he had brought in, and stood twirling it in a way that gave me, even as I was just nearly reaching port, a perverse horror of what I was doing. To do it in *any* way was an act of violence, for what did it consist of but the obtrusion of the idea of grossness and guilt on a small helpless creature who had been for me a revelation of the possibilities of beautiful intercourse? Wasn't it base to create for a being so exquisite a mere alien awkwardness? I suppose I now read into our situation a clearness it couldn't have had at the time, for I seem to see our poor eyes already lighted with some spark of a prevision of the anguish that was to come. So we circled about, with terrors and scruples, like fighters not daring to close. But it was for each other we feared! That kept us a little longer suspended and unbruised. "I'll tell you everything," Miles said—"I mean I'll tell you anything you like. You'll stay on with me, and we shall both be all right, and I *will* tell you—I *will*. But not now."

"Why not now?"

My insistence turned him from me and kept him once more at his window in a silence during which, between us, you might have heard a pin drop. Then he was before me again with the air of a person for whom, outside, someone who had frankly to be reckoned with was waiting. "I have to see Luke."

I had not yet reduced him to quite so vulgar a lie, and I felt proportionately ashamed. But, horrible as it was, his lies made up my truth. I achieved thoughtfully a few loops of my knitting. "Well, then, go to Luke, and I'll wait for what you promise. Only, in return for that, satisfy, before you leave me, one very much smaller request."

He looked as if he felt he had succeeded enough to be able still a little to bargain. "Very much smaller—?"

"Yes, a mere fraction of the whole. Tell me"—oh, my work preoccupied me, and I was offhand!—"if, yesterday afternoon, from the table in the hall, you took, you know, my letter."

XXIV

My sense of how he received this suffered for a minute from something that I can describe only as a fierce split of my attention—a stroke that at first, as I sprang straight up, reduced me to the mere blind movement of getting hold of him, drawing him close, and, while I just fell for support against the nearest piece of furniture, instinctively keeping him with his back to the window. The appearance was full upon us that I had already had to deal with here: Peter Quint had come into view like a sentinel before a prison. The next thing I saw was that, from outside, he had reached the window, and then I knew that, close to the glass and glaring in through it, he offered once more to the room his white face of damnation. It represents but grossly what took place within me at the sight to say that on the second my decision was made; yet I believe that no woman so overwhelmed ever in so short a time recovered her grasp of the *act*. It came to me in the very horror of the immediate presence that the act would be, seeing and facing what I saw and faced, to keep the boy himself unaware. The inspiration—I can call it by no other name—was that I felt how voluntarily, how transcendently, I *might*. It was like fighting with a demon for a human soul, and when I had fairly so appraised it I saw how the human soul—held out, in the tremor of my hands, at arm's length—had a perfect dew of sweat on a lovely childish forehead. The face that was close to mine was as white as the face against the glass, and out of it presently came a sound, not low nor weak, but as if from much further away, that I drank like a waft of fragrance.

"Yes—I took it."

At this, with a moan of joy, I enfolded, I drew him close; and while I held him to my breast, where I could feel in the sudden fever of his little body the tremendous pulse of his little heart, I kept my eyes on the thing at the window and saw it move and shift its posture. I have likened it to a sentinel, but its slow wheel, for a moment, was rather the prowl of a baffled beast. My present quickened courage, however, was such that, not too much to let it through, I had to shade, as it were, my flame. Meanwhile the glare of the face was again at the window, the scoundrel fixed as if to watch and wait. It was the very confidence that I might now defy him, as well as the positive certitude, by this time, of the child's unconsciousness, that made me go on. "What did you take it for?"

"To see what you said about me."

"You opened the letter?"

"I opened it."

My eyes were now, as I held him off a little again, on Miles's own face, in which the collapse of mockery showed me how complete was the ravage of uneasiness. What was prodigious was that at last, by my success, his sense was sealed and his communication stopped: he knew that he was in presence, but knew not of what, and knew still less that I also was and that I did know. And what did this strain of trouble matter when my eyes went back to the window only to see that the air was clear again and—by my personal triumph—the influence quenched? There was nothing there. I felt that the cause was mine and that I should surely get *all.* "And you found nothing!"—I let my elation out.

He gave the most mournful, thoughtful little headshake. "Nothing."

"Nothing, nothing!" I almost shouted in my joy.

"Nothing, nothing," he sadly repeated.

I kissed his forehead; it was drenched. "So what have you done with it?"

"I've burned it."

"Burned it?" It was now or never. "Is that what you did at school?"

Oh, what this brought up! "At school?"

"Did you take letters?—or other things?"

"Other things?" He appeared now to be thinking of something far off and that reached him only through the pressure of his anxiety. Yet it did reach him. "Did I *steal*?"

I felt myself redden to the roots of my hair as well as wonder if it were more strange to put to a gentleman such a question or to see him take it with allowances that gave the very distance of his fall in the world. "Was it for that you mightn't go back?"

The only thing he felt was rather a dreary little surprise. "Did you know I mightn't go back?"

"I know everything."

He gave me at this the longest and strangest look. "Everything?"

"Everything. Therefore *did* you—?" But I couldn't say it again.

Miles could, very simply. "No. I didn't steal."

My face must have shown him I believed him utterly; yet my hands—but it was for pure tenderness—shook him as if to ask him why, if it was all for nothing, he had condemned me to months of torment. "What then did you do?"

He looked in vague pain all round the top of the room and drew his breath, two or three times over, as if with difficulty. He might have been standing at the bottom of the sea and raising his eyes to some faint green twilight. "Well—I said things."

"Only that?"

"They thought it was enough!"

"To turn you out for?"

Never, truly, had a person "turned out" shown so little to explain it as this little person! He appeared to weigh my question, but in a manner quite detached and almost helpless. "Well, I suppose I oughtn't."

"But to whom did you say them?"

He evidently tried to remember, but it dropped—he had lost it. "I don't know!"

He almost smiled at me in the desolation of his surrender, which was indeed practically, by this time, so complete that I ought to have left it there. But I was infatuated—I was blind with victory, though even then the very effect that was to have brought him so much nearer was already that of added separation. "Was it to everyone?" I asked.

"No; it was only to—" But he gave a sick little headshake. "I don't remember their names."

"Were they then so many?"

"No—only a few. Those I liked."

Those he liked? I seemed to float not into clearness, but into a darker obscure, and within a minute there had come to me out of my very pity the appalling alarm of his being perhaps innocent. It was for the instant confounding and bottomless, for if he *were* innocent, what then on earth was *I*? Paralyzed, while it lasted, by the mere brush of the question, I let him go a little, so that, with a deep-drawn sigh, he turned away from me again; which, as he faced toward the clear window, I suffered, feeling that I had nothing now there to keep him from. "And did they repeat what you said?" I went on after a moment.

He was soon at some distance from me, still breathing hard and again with the air, though now without anger for it, of being confined against his will. Once more, as he had done before, he looked up at the dim day as if, of what had hitherto sustained him, nothing was left but an unspeakable anxiety. "Oh, yes," he nevertheless replied—"they must have repeated them. To those *they* liked," he added.

There was, somehow, less of it than I had expected; but I turned it over. "And these things came round—?"

"To the masters? Oh, yes!" he answered very simply. "But I didn't know they'd tell."

"The masters? They didn't—they've never told. That's why I ask you."

He turned to me again his little beautiful fevered face. "Yes, it was too bad."

"Too bad?"

"What I suppose I sometimes said. To write home."

I can't name the exquisite pathos of the contradiction given to such a speech by such a speaker; I only know that the next instant I heard myself throw off with homely force: "Stuff and nonsense!" But the next after that I must have sounded stern enough. "What *were* these things?"

My sternness was all for his judge, his executioner; yet it made him avert himself again, and that movement made *me*, with a single bound and an irrepressible cry, spring straight upon him. For there again, against the glass, as if to blight his confession and stay his answer, was the hideous author of our woe—the white face of damnation. I felt a sick swim at the drop of my victory and all the return of my battle, so that the wildness of my veritable leap only served as a great betrayal. I saw him, from the midst of my act, meet it with a divination, and on the perception that even now he only guessed, and that the window was still to his own eyes free, I let the impulse flame up to convert the climax of his dismay into the very proof of his liberation. "No more, no more, no more!" I shrieked, as I tried to press him against me, to my visitant.

"Is she *here*?" Miles panted as he caught with his sealed eyes the direction of my words. Then as his strange "she" staggered me and, with a gasp, I echoed it, "Miss Jessel, Miss Jessel!" he with a sudden fury gave me back.

I seized, stupefied, his supposition—some sequel to what we had done to Flora, but this made me only want to show him that it was better still than that. "It's not Miss Jessel! But it's at the window—straight before us. It's *there*—the coward horror, there for the last time!"

At this, after a second in which his head made the movement of a baffled dog's on a scent and then gave a frantic little shake for air and light, he was at me in a white rage, bewildered, glaring vainly over the place and missing wholly, though it now, to my sense, filled the room like the taste of poison, the wide, overwhelming presence. "It's *he*?"

I was so determined to have all my proof that I flashed into ice to challenge him. "Whom do you mean by 'he'?"

"Peter Quint—you devil!" His face gave again, round the room, its convulsed supplication. "*Where*?"

They are in my ears still, his supreme surrender of the name and his tribute to my devotion. "What does he matter now, my own?—what will he *Ever* matter? *I* have you," I launched at the beast, "but he has lost you forever!" Then, for the demonstration of my work, "There, *there*!" I said to Miles.

But he had already jerked straight round, stared, glared again, and seen but the quiet day. With the stroke of the loss I was so proud of he uttered the cry of a creature hurled over an abyss, and the grasp with which I recovered him might have been that of catching him in his fall. I caught him, yes, I held him—it may be imagined with what a passion; but at the end of a minute I began to feel what it truly was that I held. We were alone with the quiet day, and his little heart, dispossessed, had stopped.

THE SHADOWS ON THE WALL, by Mary E. Wilkins Freeman

"Henry had words with Edward in the study the night before Edward died," said Caroline Glynn.

She spoke not with acrimony, but with grave severity. Rebecca Ann Glynn gasped by way of assent. She sat in a wide flounce of black silk in the corner of the sofa, and rolled terrified eyes from her sister Caroline to her sister Mrs. Stephen Brigham, who had been Emma Glynn, the one beauty of the family. The latter was beautiful still, with a large, splendid, full-blown beauty, she filled a great rocking-chair with her superb bulk of femininity, and swayed gently back and forth, her black silks whispering and her black frills fluttering. Even the shock of death—for her brother Edward lay dead in the house—could not disturb her outward serenity of demeanor.

But even her expression of masterly placidity changed before her sister Caroline's announcement and her sister Rebecca Ann's gasp of terror and distress in response.

"I think Henry might have controlled his temper, when poor Edward was so near his end," she said with an asperity which disturbed slightly the roseate curves of her beautiful mouth.

"Of course he did not *know*," murmured Rebecca Ann in a faint tone.

"Of course he did not know it," said Caroline quickly. She turned on her sister with a strange, sharp look of suspicion. Then she shrank as if from the other's possible answer.

Rebecca gasped again. The married sister, Mrs. Emma Brigham, was now sitting up straight in her chair; she had ceased rocking, and was eyeing them both intently with a sudden accentuation of family likeness in her face.

"What do you mean?" said she impartially to them both. Then she, too, seemed to shrink before a possible answer. She even laughed an evasive sort of laugh.

"Nobody means anything," said Caroline firmly. She rose and crossed the room toward the door with grim decisiveness.

"Where are you going?" asked Mrs. Brigham.

"I have something to see to," replied Caroline, and the others at once knew by her tone that she had some solemn and sad duty to perform in the chamber of death.

"Oh," said Mrs. Brigham.

After the door had closed behind Caroline, she turned to Rebecca.

"Did Henry have many words with him?" she asked.

"They were talking very loud," replied Rebecca evasively.

Mrs. Brigham looked at her. She had not resumed rocking. She still sat up straight, with a slight knitting of intensity on her fair forehead, between the pretty rippling curves of her auburn hair.

"Did you—ever hear anything?" she asked in a low voice with a glance toward the door.

"I was just across the hall in the south parlor, and that door was open and this door ajar," replied Rebecca with a slight flush.

"Then you must have—"
"I couldn't help it."
"Everything?"
"Most of it."
"What was it?"
"The old story."
"I suppose Henry was mad, as he always was, because Edward was living on here for nothing, when he had wasted all the money father left him."
Rebecca nodded, with a fearful glance at the door.
When Emma spoke again her voice was still more hushed. "I know how he felt," said she. "It must have looked to him as if Edward was living at his expense, but he wasn't."
"No, he wasn't."
"And Edward had a right here according to the terms of father's will, and Henry ought to have remembered it."
"Yes, he ought."
"Did he say hard things?"
"Pretty hard, from what I heard."
"What?"
"I heard him tell Edward that he had no business here at all, and he thought he had better go away."
"What did Edward say?"
"That he would stay here as long as he lived and afterward, too, if he was a mind to, and he would like to see Henry get him out; and then—"
"What?"
"Then he laughed."
"What did Henry say?"
"I didn't hear him say anything, but—"
"But what?"
"I saw him when he came out of this room."
"He looked mad?"
"You've seen him when he looked so."
Emma nodded. The expression of horror on her face had deepened.
"Do you remember that time he killed the cat because she had scratched him?"
"Yes. Don't!"
Then Caroline reentered the room; she went up to the stove, in which a wood fire was burning—it was a cold, gloomy day of fall—and she warmed her hands, which were reddened from recent washing in cold water.
Mrs. Brigham looked at her and hesitated. She glanced at the door, which was still ajar; it did not easily shut, being still swollen with the damp weather of the summer. She rose and pushed it together with a sharp thud, which jarred the house. Rebecca started painfully with a half-exclamation. Caroline looked at her disapprovingly.
"It is time you controlled your nerves, Rebecca," she said.
Mrs. Brigham, returning from the closed door, said imperiously that it ought to be fixed, it shut so hard.
"It will shrink enough after we have had the fire a few days," replied Caroline.
"I think Henry ought to be ashamed of himself for talking as he did to Edward," said Mrs. Brigham abruptly, but in an almost inaudible voice.
"Hush," said Caroline, with a glance of actual fear at the closed door.
"Nobody can hear with the door shut. I say again I think Henry ought to be

ashamed of himself. I shouldn't think he'd ever get over it, having words with poor Edward the very night before he died. Edward was enough sight better disposition than Henry, with all his faults."

"I never heard him speak a cross word, unless he spoke cross to Henry that last night. I don't know but he did from what Rebecca overheard."

"Not so much cross, as sort of soft, and sweet, and aggravating," sniffed Rebecca.

"What do you really think ailed Edward?" asked Emma in hardly more than a whisper. She did not look at her sister.

"I know you said that he had terrible pains in his stomach, and had spasms, but what do you think made him have them?"

"Henry called it gastric trouble. You know Edward has always had dyspepsia."

Mrs. Brigham hesitated a moment. "Was there any talk of an—examination?" said she.

Then Caroline turned on her fiercely.

"No," said she in a terrible voice. "No."

The three sisters' souls seemed to meet on one common ground of terrified understanding through their eyes.

The old-fashioned latch of the door was heard to rattle, and a push from without made the door shake ineffectually. "It's Henry," Rebecca sighed rather than whispered. Mrs. Brigham settled herself, after a noiseless rush across the floor, into her rocking-chair again, and was swaying back and forth with her head comfortably leaning back, when the door at last yielded and Henry Glynn entered. He cast a covertly sharp, comprehensive glance at Mrs. Brigham with her elaborate calm; at Rebecca quietly huddled in the corner of the sofa with her handkerchief to her face and only one small uncovered reddened ear as attentive as a dog's, and at Caroline sitting with a strained composure in her armchair by the stove. She met his eyes quite firmly with a look of inscrutable fear, and defiance of the fear and of him.

Henry Glynn looked more like this sister than the others. Both had the same hard delicacy of form and aquilinity of feature. They confronted each other with the pitiless immovability of two statues in whose marble lineaments emotions were fixed for all eternity.

Then Henry Glynn smiled and the smile transformed his face. He looked suddenly years younger, and an almost boyish recklessness appeared in his face. He flung himself into a chair with a gesture which was bewildering from its incongruity with his general appearance. He leaned his head back, flung one leg over the other, and looked laughingly at Mrs. Brigham.

"I declare, Emma, you grow younger every year," he said.

She flushed a little, and her placid mouth widened at the corners. She was susceptible to praise.

"Our thoughts to-day ought to belong to the one of us who will *never* grow older," said Caroline in a hard voice.

Henry looked at her, still smiling. "Of course, we none of us forget that," said he, in a deep, gentle voice; "but we have to speak to the living, Caroline, and I have not seen Emma for a long time, and the living are as dear as the dead."

"Not to me," said Caroline.

She rose and went abruptly out of the room again. Rebecca also rose and hurried after her, sobbing loudly.

Henry looked slowly after them.

"Caroline is completely unstrung," said he.

Mrs. Brigham rocked. A confidence in him inspired by his manner was stealing over her. Out of that confidence she spoke quite easily and naturally.

"His death was very sudden," said she.

Henry's eyelids quivered slightly but his gaze was unswerving.

"Yes," said he, "it was very sudden. He was sick only a few hours."

"What did you call it?"

"Gastric."

"You did not think of an examination?"

"There was no need. I am perfectly certain as to the cause of his death."

Suddenly Mrs. Brigham felt a creep as of some live horror over her very soul. Her flesh prickled with cold, before an inflection of his voice. She rose, tottering on weak knees.

"Where are you going?" asked Henry in a strange, breathless voice.

Mrs. Brigham said something incoherent about some sewing which she had to do—some black for the funeral—and was out of the room. She went up to the front chamber which she occupied. Caroline was there. She went close to her and took her hands, and the two sisters looked at each other.

"Don't speak, don't, I won't have it!" said Caroline finally in an awful whisper.

"I won't," replied Emma.

That afternoon the three sisters were in the study.

Mrs. Brigham was hemming some black material. At last she laid her work on her lap.

"It's no use, I cannot see to sew another stitch until we have a light," said she.

Caroline, who was writing some letters at the table, turned to Rebecca, in her usual place on the sofa.

"Rebecca, you had better get a lamp," she said.

Rebecca started up; even in the dusk her face showed her agitation.

"It doesn't seem to me that we need a lamp quite yet," she said in a piteous, pleading voice like a child's.

"Yes, we do," returned Mrs. Brigham peremptorily. "I can't see to sew another stitch."

Rebecca rose and left the room. Presently she entered with a lamp. She set it on the table, an old-fashioned card-table which was placed against the opposite wall from the window. That opposite wall was taken up with three doors; the one small space was occupied by the table.

"What have you put that lamp over there for?" asked Mrs. Brigham, with more of impatience than her voice usually revealed. "Why didn't you set it in the hall, and have done with it? Neither Caroline nor I can see if it is on that table."

"I thought perhaps you would move," replied Rebecca hoarsely.

"If I do move, we can't both sit at that table. Caroline has her paper all spread around. Why don't you set the lamp on the study table in the middle of the room, then we can both see?"

Rebecca hesitated. Her face was very pale. She looked with an appeal that was fairly agonizing at her sister Caroline.

"Why don't you put the lamp on this table, as she says?" asked Caroline, almost fiercely. "Why do you act so, Rebecca?"

Rebecca took the lamp and set it on the table in the middle of the room without another word. Then she seated herself on the sofa and placed a hand over her eyes as if to shade them, and remained so.

"Does the light hurt your eyes, and is that the reason why you didn't want the lamp?" asked Mrs. Brigham kindly.

"I always like to sit in the dark," replied Rebecca chokingly. Then she snatched her handkerchief hastily from her pocket and began to weep. Caroline continued to write, Mrs. Brigham to sew.

Suddenly Mrs. Brigham as she sewed glanced at the opposite wall. The glance became a steady stare. She looked intently, her work suspended in her hands. Then she looked away again and took a few more stitches, then she looked again, and again turned to her task. At last she laid her work in her lap and stared concentratedly. She looked from the wall round the room, taking note of the various objects. Then she turned to her sisters.

"What *is* that?" said she.

"What?" asked Caroline harshly.

"That strange shadow on the wall," replied Mrs. Brigham.

Rebecca sat with her face hidden; Caroline dipped her pen in the inkstand.

"Why don't you turn around and look?" asked Mrs. Brigham in a wondering and somewhat aggrieved way.

"I am in a hurry to finish this letter," replied Caroline shortly.

Mrs. Brigham rose, her work slipping to the floor, and began walking round the room, moving various articles of furniture, with her eyes on the shadow.

Then suddenly she shrieked out:

"Look at this awful shadow! What is it? Caroline, look, look! Rebecca, look! What is it?"

All Mrs. Brigham's triumphant placidity was gone. Her handsome face was livid with horror. She stood stiffly pointing at the shadow.

Then after a shuddering glance at the wall Rebecca burst out in a wild wail.

"Oh, Caroline, there it is again, there it is again!"

"Caroline Glynn, you look!" said Mrs. Brigham. "Look! What is that dreadful shadow?"

Caroline rose, turned, and stood confronting the wall.

"How should I know?" she said.

"It has been there every night since he died!" cried Rebecca.

"Every night?"

"Yes; he died Thursday and this is Saturday; that makes three nights," said Caroline rigidly. She stood as if holding her calm with a vise of concentrated will.

"It—it looks like—like—" stammered Mrs. Brigham in a tone of intense horror.

"I know what it looks like well enough," said Caroline. "I've got eyes in my head."

"It looks like Edward," burst out Rebecca in a sort of frenzy of fear. "Only—"

"Yes, it does," assented Mrs. Brigham, whose horror-stricken tone matched her sisters', "only—Oh, it is awful! What is it, Caroline?"

"I ask you again, how should I know?" replied Caroline. "I see it there like you. How should I know any more than you?"

"It *must* be something in the room," said Mrs. Brigham, staring wildly around.

"We moved everything in the room the first night it came," said Rebecca; "it is not anything in the room."

Caroline turned upon her with a sort of fury. "Of course it is something in the room," said she. "How you act! What do you mean talking so? Of course it is something in the room."

"Of course it is," agreed Mrs. Brigham, looking at Caroline suspiciously. "It must be something in the room."

"It is not anything in the room," repeated Rebecca with obstinate horror.

The door opened suddenly and Henry Glynn entered. He began to speak, then his eyes followed the direction of the others. He stood staring at the shadow on the wall.

"What is that?" he demanded in a strange voice.

"It must be due to something in the room," Mrs. Brigham said faintly.

Henry Glynn stood and stared a moment longer. His face showed a gamut of emotions. Horror, conviction, then furious incredulity. Suddenly he began hastening hither and thither about the room. He moved the furniture with fierce jerks, turning ever to see the effect upon the shadow on the wall. Not a line of its terrible outlines wavered.

"It must be something in the room!" he declared in a voice which seemed to snap like a lash.

His face changed, the inmost secrecy of his nature seemed evident upon his face, until one almost lost sight of his lineaments. Rebecca stood close to her sofa, regarding him with woeful, fascinated eyes. Mrs. Brigham clutched Caroline's hand. They both stood in a corner out of his way. For a few moments he raged about the room like a caged wild animal. He moved every piece of furniture; when the moving of a piece did not affect the shadow he flung it to the floor.

Then suddenly he desisted. He laughed.

"What an absurdity," he said easily. "Such a to-do about a shadow."

"That's so," assented Mrs. Brigham, in a scared voice which she tried to make natural. As she spoke she lifted a chair near her.

"I think you have broken the chair that Edward was fond of," said Caroline.

Terror and wrath were struggling for expression on her face. Her mouth was set, her eyes shrinking. Henry lifted the chair with a show of anxiety.

"Just as good as ever," he said pleasantly. He laughed again, looking at his sisters. "Did I scare you?" he said. "I should think you might be used to me by this time. You know my way of wanting to leap to the bottom of a mystery, and that shadow does look—queer, like—and I thought if there was any way of accounting for it I would like to without any delay."

"You don't seem to have succeeded," remarked Caroline dryly, with a slight glance at the wall.

Henry's eyes followed hers and he quivered perceptibly.

"Oh, there is no accounting for shadows," he said, and he laughed again. "A man is a fool to try to account for shadows."

Then the supper bell rang, and they all left the room, but Henry kept his back to the wall—as did, indeed, the others.

Henry led the way with an alert motion like a boy; Rebecca brought up the rear. She could scarcely walk, her knees trembled so.

"I can't sit in that room again this evening," she whispered to Caroline after supper.

"Very well; we will sit in the south room," replied Caroline. "I think we will sit in the south parlor," she said aloud; "it isn't as damp as the study, and I have a cold."

So they all sat in the south room with their sewing. Henry read the newspaper, his chair drawn close to the lamp on the table. About nine o'clock he rose abruptly and crossed the hall to the study. The three sisters looked at one another. Mrs. Brigham rose, folded her rustling skirts compactly round her, and began tiptoeing toward the door.

"What are you going to do?" inquired Rebecca agitatedly.

"I am going to see what he is about," replied Mrs. Brigham cautiously.

As she spoke she pointed to the study door across the hall; it was ajar. Henry had striven to pull it together behind him, but it had somehow swollen beyond the limit with curious speed. It was still ajar and a streak of light showed from top to bottom.

Mrs. Brigham folded her skirts so tightly that her bulk with its swelling curves was revealed in a black silk sheath, and she went with a slow toddle across the hall to the study door. She stood there, her eye at the crack.

In the south room Rebecca stopped sewing and sat watching with dilated eyes. Caroline sewed steadily. What Mrs. Brigham, standing at the crack in the study door, saw was this:

Henry Glynn, evidently reasoning that the source of the strange shadow must be between the table on which the lamp stood and the wall, was making systematic passes and thrusts with an old sword which had belonged to his father all over and through the intervening space. Not an inch was left unpierced. He seemed to have divided the space into mathematical sections. He brandished the sword with a sort of cold fury and calculation; the blade gave out flashes of light, the shadow remained unmoved. Mrs. Brigham, watching, felt herself cold with horror.

Finally Henry ceased and stood with the sword in hand and raised as if to strike, surveying the shadow on the wall threateningly. Mrs. Brigham toddled back across the hall and shut the south room door behind her before she related what she had seen.

"He looked like a demon," she said again. "Have you got any of that old wine in the house, Caroline? I don't feel as if I could stand much more."

"Yes, there's plenty," said Caroline; "you can have some when you go to bed."

"I think we had all better take some," said Mrs. Brigham. "Oh, Caroline, what —"

"Don't ask; don't speak," said Caroline.

"No, I'm not going to," replied Mrs. Brigham; "but—"

Soon the three sisters went to their chambers and the south parlor was deserted. Caroline called to Henry in the study to put out the light before he came upstairs. They had been gone about an hour when he came into the room bringing the lamp which had stood in the study. He set it on the table, and waited a few minutes, pacing up and down. His face was terrible, his fair complexion showed livid, and his blue eyes seemed dark blanks of awful reflections.

Then he took up the lamp and returned to the library. He set the lamp on the center table and the shadow sprang out on the wall. Again he studied the furniture and moved it about, but deliberately, with none of his former frenzy. Nothing affected the shadow. Then he returned to the south room with the lamp and again waited. Again he returned to the study and placed the lamp on the table, and the shadow sprang out upon the wall. It was midnight before he went upstairs. Mrs. Brigham and the other sisters, who could not sleep, heard him.

The next day was the funeral. That evening the family sat in the south room. Some relatives were with them. Nobody entered the study until Henry carried a lamp in there after the others had retired for the night. He saw again the shadow on the wall leap to an awful life before the light.

The next morning at breakfast Henry Glynn announced that he had to go to the city for three days. The sisters looked at him with surprise. He very seldom left home, and just now his practice had been neglected on account of Edward's death.

"How can you leave your patients now?" asked Mrs. Brigham wonderingly.

"I don't know how to, but there is no other way," replied Henry easily. "I have had a telegram from Dr. Mitford."

"Consultation?" inquired Mrs. Brigham.

"I have business," replied Henry.

Doctor Mitford was an old classmate of his who lived in a neighboring city and who occasionally called upon him in the case of a consultation.

After he had gone, Mrs. Brigham said to Caroline that, after all, Henry had not said that he was going to consult with Doctor Mitford, and she thought it very strange.

"Everything is very strange," said Rebecca with a shudder.

"What do you mean?" inquired Caroline.

"Nothing," replied Rebecca.

Nobody entered the study that day, nor the next. The third day Henry was expected home, but he did not arrive and the last train from the city had come.

"I call it pretty queer work," said Mrs. Brigham. "The idea of a doctor leaving his patients at such a time as this, and the idea of a consultation lasting three days! There is no sense in it, and *now* he has not come. I don't understand it, for my part."

"I don't either," said Rebecca.

They were all in the south parlor. There was no light in the study; the door was ajar.

Presently Mrs. Brigham rose—she could not have told why; something seemed to impel her—some will outside her own. She went out of the room, again wrapping her rustling skirts round that she might pass noiselessly, and began pushing at the swollen door of the study.

"She has not got any lamp," said Rebecca in a shaking voice.

Caroline, who was writing letters, rose again, took the only remaining lamp in the room, and followed her sister. Rebecca had risen, but she stood trembling, not venturing to follow.

The doorbell rang, but the others did not hear it; it was on the south door on the other side of the house from the study. Rebecca, after hesitating until the bell rang the second time, went to the door; she remembered that the servant was out.

Caroline and her sister Emma entered the study. Caroline set the lamp on the table. They looked at the wall, and there were two shadows. The sisters stood clutching each other, staring at the awful things on the wall. Then Rebecca came in, staggering, with a telegram in her hand. "Here is—a telegram," she gasped. "Henry is—dead."

THE MESSENGER, by Robert W. Chambers

Little gray messenger,
Robed like painted Death,
Your robe is dust.
Whom do you seek
Among lilies and closed buds
At dusk?

Among lilies and closed buds
At dusk,
Whom do you seek,
Little gray messenger,
Robed in the awful panoply
Of painted Death?

*

All-wise,
Hast thou seen all there is to see with thy two eyes?
Dost thou know all there is to know, and so,
Omniscient,
Darest thou still to say thy brother lies?

I

"The bullet entered here," said Max Fortin, and he placed his middle finger over a smooth hole exactly in the center of the forehead.

I sat down upon a mound of dry seaweed and unslung my fowling piece.

The little chemist cautiously felt the edges of the shot-hole, first with his middle finger, and then with his thumb.

"Let me see the skull again," said I.

Max Fortin picked it up from the sod.

"It's like all the others," he repeated, wiping his glasses on his handkerchief. "I thought you might care to see one of the skulls, so I brought this over from the gravel pit. The men from Bannalec are digging yet. They ought to stop."

"How many skulls are there altogether?" I inquired.

"They found thirty-eight skulls; there are thirty-nine noted in the list. They lie piled up in the gravel pit on the edge of Le Bihan's wheat field. The men are at work yet. Le Bihan is going to stop them."

"Let's go over," said I; and I picked up my gun and started across the cliffs, Portin on one side, Môme on the other.

"Who has the list?" I asked, lighting my pipe. "You say there is a list?"

"The list was found rolled up in a brass cylinder," said the chemist. He added: "You should not smoke here. You know that if a single spark drifted into the wheat —"

"Ah, but I have a cover to my pipe," said I, smiling.

Fortin watched me as I closed the pepper-box arrangement over the glowing bowl of the pipe. Then he continued:

"The list was made out on thick yellow paper; the brass tube has preserved it. It is as fresh to-day as it was in 1760. You shall see it."

"Is that the date?"

"The list is dated 'April, 1760.' The Brigadier Durand has it. It is not written in French."

"Not written in French!" I exclaimed.

"No," replied Fortin solemnly, "it is written in Breton."

"But," I protested, "the Breton language was never written or printed in 1760."

"Except by priests," said the chemist.

"I have heard of but one priest who ever wrote the Breton language," I began.

Fortin stole a glance at my face.

"You mean—the Black Priest?" he asked.

I nodded.

Fortin opened his mouth to speak again, hesitated, and finally shut his teeth obstinately over the wheat stem that he was chewing.

"And the Black Priest?" I suggested encouragingly. But I knew it was useless; for it is easier to move the stars from their courses than to make an obstinate Breton talk. We walked on for a minute or two in silence.

"Where is the Brigadier Durand?" I asked, motioning Môme to come out of the wheat, which he was trampling as though it were heather. As I spoke we came in sight of the farther edge of the wheat field and the dark, wet mass of cliffs beyond.

"Durand is down there—you can see him; he stands just behind the mayor of St. Gildas."

"I see," said I; and we struck straight down, following a sun-baked cattle path across the heather.

When we reached the edge of the wheat field, Le Bihan, the mayor of St. Gildas, called to me, and I tucked my gun under my arm and skirted the wheat to where he stood.

"Thirty-eight skulls," he said in his thin, high-pitched voice; "there is but one more, and I am opposed to further search. I suppose Fortin told you?"

I shook hands with him, and returned the salute of the Brigadier Durand.

"I am opposed to further search," repeated Le Bihan, nervously picking at the mass of silver buttons which covered the front of his velvet and broadcloth jacket like a breastplate of scale armor.

Durand pursed up his lips, twisted his tremendous mustache, and hooked his thumbs in his saber belt.

"As for me," he said, "I am in favor of further search."

"Further search for what—for the thirty-ninth skull?" I asked.

Le Bihan nodded. Durand frowned at the sunlit sea, rocking like a bowl of molten gold from the cliffs to the horizon. I followed his eyes. On the dark glistening cliffs, silhouetted against the glare of the sea, sat a cormorant, black, motionless, its horrible head raised toward heaven.

"Where is that list, Durand?" I asked.

The gendarme rummaged in his despatch pouch and produced a brass cylinder about a foot long. Very gravely he unscrewed the head and dumped out a scroll of thick yellow paper closely covered with writing on both sides. At a nod from Le Bihan he handed me the scroll. But I could make nothing of the coarse writing, now faded to a dull brown.

"Come, come, Le Bihan," I said impatiently, "translate it, won't you? You and Max Fortin make a lot of mystery out of nothing, it seems."

Le Bihan went to the edge of the pit where the three Bannalec men were digging, gave an order or two in Breton, and turned to me.

As I came to the edge of the pit the Bannalec men were removing a square piece of sailcloth from what appeared to be a pile of cobblestones.

"Look!" said Le Bihan shrilly. I looked. The pile below was a heap of skulls. After a moment I clambered down the gravel sides of the pit and walked over to the men of Bannalec. They saluted me gravely, leaning on their picks and shovels, and wiping their sweating faces with sunburned hands.

"How many?" said I in Breton.

"Thirty-eight," they replied.

I glanced around. Beyond the heap of skulls lay two piles of human bones. Beside these was a mound of broken, rusted bits of iron and steel. Looking closer, I saw that this mound was composed of rusty bayonets, saber blades, scythe blades, with here and there a tarnished buckle attached to a bit of leather hard as iron.

I picked up a couple of buttons and a belt plate. The buttons bore the royal arms of England; the belt plate was emblazoned with the English arms and also with the number "27."

"I have heard my grandfather speak of the terrible English regiment, the 27th Foot, which landed and stormed the fort up there," said one of the Bannalec men.

"Oh!" said I; "then these are the bones of English soldiers?"

"Yes," said the men of Bannalec.

Le Bihan was calling to me from the edge of the pit above, and I handed the belt plate and buttons to the men and climbed the side of the excavation.

"Well," said I, trying to prevent Môme from leaping up and licking my face as I emerged from the pit, "I suppose you know what these bones are. What are you going to do with them?"

"There was a man," said Le Bihan angrily, "an Englishman, who passed here in a dog-cart on his way to Quimper about an hour ago, and what do you suppose he wished to do?"

"Buy the relics?" I asked, smiling.

"Exactly—the pig!" piped the mayor of St. Gildas. "Jean Marie Tregunc, who found the bones, was standing there where Max Fortin stands, and do you know what he answered? He spat upon the ground, and said: 'Pig of an Englishman, do you take me for a desecrator of graves?'"

I knew Tregunc, a sober, blue-eyed Breton, who lived from one year's end to the other without being able to afford a single bit of meat for a meal.

"How much did the Englishman offer Tregunc?" I asked.

"Two hundred francs for the skulls alone."

I thought of the relic hunters and the relic buyers on the battlefields of our civil war.

"Seventeen hundred and sixty is long ago," I said.

"Respect for the dead can never die," said Fortin.

"And the English soldiers came here to kill your fathers and burn your homes," I continued.

"They were murderers and thieves, but—they are dead," said Tregunc, coming up from the beach below, his long sea rake balanced on his dripping jersey.

"How much do you earn every year, Jean Marie?" I asked, turning to shake hands with him.

"Two hundred and twenty francs, monsieur."

"Forty-five dollars a year," I said. "Bah! you are worth more, Jean. Will you take care of my garden for me? My wife wished me to ask you. I think it would be worth one hundred francs a month to you and to me. Come on, Le Bihan—come along, Fortin—and you, Durand. I want somebody to translate that list into French for me."

Tregunc stood gazing at me, his blue eyes dilated.

"You may begin at once," I said, smiling, "if the salary suits you?"

"It suits," said Tregunc, fumbling for his pipe in a silly way that annoyed Le Bihan.

"Then go and begin your work," cried the mayor impatiently; and Tregunc started across the moors toward St. Gildas, taking off his velvet-ribboned cap to me and gripping his sea rake very hard.

"You offer him more than my salary," said the mayor, after a moment's contemplation of his silver buttons.

"Pooh!" said I, "what do you do for your salary except play dominoes with Max Portin at the Groix Inn?"

Le Bihan turned red, but Durand rattled his saber and winked at Max Fortin, and I slipped my arm through the arm of the sulky magistrate, laughing.

"There's a shady spot under the cliff," I said; "come on, Le Bihan, and read me what is in the scroll."

In a few moments we reached the shadow of the cliff, and I threw myself upon the turf, chin on hand, to listen.

The gendarme, Durand, also sat down, twisting his mustache into needlelike points. Fortin leaned against the cliff, polishing his glasses and examining us with vague, near-sighted eyes; and Le Bihan, the mayor, planted himself in our midst, rolling up the scroll and tucking it under his arm.

"First of all," he began in a shrill voice, "I am going to light my pipe, and while lighting it I shall tell you what I have heard about the attack on the fort yonder. My father told me; his father told him."

He jerked his head in the direction of the ruined fort, a small, square stone structure on the sea cliff, now nothing but crumbling walls. Then he slowly produced a tobacco pouch, a bit of flint and tinder, and a long-stemmed pipe fitted with a microscopical bowl of baked clay. To fill such a pipe requires ten minutes' close attention. To smoke it to a finish takes but four puffs. It is very Breton, this Breton pipe. It is the crystallization of everything Breton.

"Go on," said I, lighting a cigarette.

"The fort," said the mayor, "was built by Louis XIV, and was dismantled twice by the English. Louis XV restored it in 1730. In 1760 it was carried by assault by the English. They came across from the island of Groix—three shiploads, and they stormed the fort and sacked St. Julien yonder, and they started to burn St. Gildas—you can see the marks of their bullets on my house yet; but the men of Bannalec and the men of Lorient fell upon them with pike and scythe and blunderbuss, and those who did not run away lie there below in the gravel pit now—thirty-eight of them."

"And the thirty-ninth skull?" I asked, finishing my cigarette.

The mayor had succeeded in filling his pipe, and now he began to put his tobacco pouch away.

"The thirty-ninth skull," he mumbled, holding the pipe stem between his defective teeth—"the thirty-ninth skull is no business of mine. I have told the Bannalec men to cease digging."

"But what is—whose is the missing skull?" I persisted curiously.

The mayor was busy trying to strike a spark to his tinder. Presently he set it aglow, applied it to his pipe, took the prescribed four puffs, knocked the ashes out of the bowl, and gravely replaced the pipe in his pocket.

"The missing skull?" he asked.

"Yes," said I, impatiently.

The mayor slowly unrolled the scroll and began to read, translating from the Breton into French. And this is what he read:

"On the Cliffs of St. Gildas,
April 13, 1760.

"On this day, by order of the Count of Soisic, general in chief of the Breton forces now lying in Kerselec Forest, the bodies of thirty-eight English soldiers of the 27th, 50th, and 72d regiments of Foot were buried in this spot, together with their arms and equipments."

The mayor paused and glanced at me reflectively.

"Go on, Le Bihan," I said.

"With them," continued the mayor, turning the scroll and reading on the other side, "was buried the body of that vile traitor who betrayed the fort to the English. The manner of his death was as follows: By order of the most noble Count of Soisic, the traitor was first branded upon the forehead with the brand of an arrowhead. The iron burned through the flesh and was pressed heavily so that the brand should even burn into the bone of the skull. The traitor was then led out and bidden to kneel. He admitted having guided the English from the island of Groix. Although a priest and a Frenchman, he had violated his priestly office to aid him in discovering the password to the fort. This password he extorted during confession from a young Breton girl who was in the habit of rowing across from the island of Groix to visit her husband in the fort. When the fort fell, this young girl, crazed by the death of her husband, sought the Count of Soisic and told how the priest had forced her to confess to him all she knew about the fort. The priest was arrested at St. Gildas as he was about to cross the river to Lorient. When arrested he cursed the girl, Marie Trevec—"

"What!" I exclaimed, "Marie Trevec!"

"Marie Trevec," repeated Le Bihan; "the priest cursed Marie Trevec, and all her family and descendants. He was shot as he knelt, having a mask of leather over his face, because the Bretons who composed the squad of execution refused to fire at a priest unless his face was concealed. The priest was l'Abbé Sorgue, commonly known as the Black Priest on account of his dark face and swarthy eyebrows. He was buried with a stake through his heart."

Le Bihan paused, hesitated, looked at me, and handed the manuscript back to Durand. The gendarme took it and slipped it into the brass cylinder.

"So," said I, "the thirty-ninth skull is the skull of the Black Priest."

"Yes," said Fortin. "I hope they won't find it."

"I have forbidden them to proceed," said the mayor querulously. "You heard me, Max Fortin."

I rose and picked up my gun. Môme came and pushed his head into my hand.

"That's a fine dog," observed Durand, also rising.

"Why don't you wish to find his skull?" I asked Le Bihan. "It would be curious to see whether the arrow brand really burned into the bone."

"There is something in that scroll that I didn't read to you," said the mayor grimly. "Do you wish to know what it is?"

"Of course," I replied in surprise.

"Give me the scroll again, Durand," he said; then he read from the bottom: "I, l'Abbé Sorgue, forced to write the above by my executioners, have written it in my own blood; and with it I leave my curse. My curse on St. Gildas, on Marie Trevec, and on her descendants. I will come back to St. Gildas when my remains are disturbed. Woe to that Englishman whom my branded skull shall touch!"

"What rot!" I said. "Do you believe it was really written in his own blood?"

"I am going to test it," said Fortin, "at the request of Monsieur le Maire. I am not anxious for the job, however."

"See," said Le Bihan, holding out the scroll to me, "it is signed, 'L'Abbé Sorgue.'"

I glanced curiously over the paper.

"It must be the Black Priest," I said. "He was the only man who wrote in the Breton language. This is a wonderfully interesting discovery, for now, at last, the mystery of the Black Priest's disappearance is cleared up. You will, of course, send this scroll to Paris, Le Bihan?"

"No," said the mayor obstinately, "it shall be buried in the pit below where the rest of the Black Priest lies."

I looked at him and recognized that argument would be useless. But still I said, "It will be a loss to history, Monsieur Le Bihan."

"All the worse for history, then," said the enlightened Mayor of St. Gildas.

We had sauntered back to the gravel pit while speaking. The men of Bannalec were carrying the bones of the English soldiers toward the St. Gildas cemetery, on the cliffs to the east, where already a knot of white-coiffed women stood in attitudes of prayer; and I saw the somber robe of a priest among the crosses of the little graveyard.

"They were thieves and assassins; they are dead now," muttered Max Fortin.

"Respect the dead," repeated the Mayor of St. Gildas, looking after the Bannalec men.

"It was written in that scroll that Marie Trevec, of Groix Island, was cursed by the priest—she and her descendants," I said, touching Le Bihan on the arm. "There was a Marie Trevec who married an Yves Trevec of St. Gildas—"

"It is the same," said Le Bihan, looking at me obliquely.

"Oh!" said I; "then they were ancestors of my wife."

"Do you fear the curse?" asked Le Bihan.

"What?" I laughed.

"There was the case of the Purple Emperor," said Max Fortin timidly.

Startled for a moment, I faced him, then shrugged my shoulders and kicked at a smooth bit of rock which lay near the edge of the pit, almost embedded in gravel.

"Do you suppose the Purple-Emperor drank himself crazy because he was descended from Marie Trevec?" I asked contemptuously.

"Of course not," said Max Fortin hastily.

"Of course not," piped the mayor. "I only—Hellow! what's that you're kicking?"

"What?" said I, glancing down, at the same time involuntarily giving another kick. The smooth bit of rock dislodged itself and rolled out of the loosened gravel at my feet.

"The thirty-ninth skull!" I exclaimed. "By jingo, it's the noddle of the Black Priest! See! there is the arrowhead branded on the front!"

The mayor stepped back. Max Fortin also retreated. There was a pause, during which I looked at them, and they looked anywhere but at me.

"I don't like it," said the mayor at last, in a husky, high voice. "I don't like it!

The scroll says he will come back to St. Gildas when his remains are disturbed. I—I don't like it, Monsieur Darrel—"

"Bosh!" said I; "the poor wicked devil is where he can't get out. For Heaven's sake, Le Bihan, what is this stuff you are talking in the year of grace 1896?"

The mayor gave me a look.

"And he says 'Englishman.' You are an Englishman, Monsieur Darrel," he announced.

"You know better. You know I'm an American."

"It's all the same," said the Mayor of St. Gildas, obstinately.

"No, it isn't!" I answered, much exasperated, and deliberately pushed the skull till it rolled into the bottom of the gravel pit below.

"Cover it up," said I; "bury the scroll with it too, if you insist, but I think you ought to send it to Paris. Don't look so gloomy, Fortin, unless you believe in werewolves and ghosts. Hey! what the—what the devil's the matter with you, anyway? What are you staring at, Le Bihan?"

"Come, come," muttered the mayor in a low, tremulous voice, "it's time we got out of this. Did you see? Did you see, Fortin?"

"I saw," whispered Max Fortin, pallid with fright.

The two men were almost running across the sunny pasture now, and I hastened after them, demanding to know what was the matter.

"Matter!" chattered the mayor, gasping with exasperation and terror. "The skull is rolling up hill again," and he burst into a terrified gallop, Max Fortin followed close behind.

I watched them stampeding across the pasture, then turned toward the gravel pit, mystified, incredulous. The skull was lying on the edge of the pit, exactly where it had been before I pushed it over the edge. For a second I stared at it; a singular chilly feeling crept up my spinal column, and I turned and walked away, sweat starting from the root of every hair on my head. Before I had gone twenty paces the absurdity of the whole thing struck me. I halted, hot with shame and annoyance, and retraced my steps.

There lay the skull.

"I rolled a stone down instead of the skull," I muttered to myself. Then with the butt of my gun I pushed the skull over the edge of the pit and watched it roll to the bottom; and as it struck the bottom of the pit, Môme, my dog, suddenly whipped his tail between his legs, whimpered, and made off across the moor.

"Môme!" I shouted, angry and astonished; but the dog only fled the faster, and I ceased calling from sheer surprise.

"What the mischief is the matter with that dog!" I thought. He had never before played me such a trick.

Mechanically I glanced into the pit, but I could not see the skull. I looked down. The skull lay at my feet again, touching them.

"Good heavens!" I stammered, and struck at it blindly with my gunstock. The ghastly thing flew into the air, whirling over and over, and rolled again down the sides of the pit to the bottom. Breathlessly I stared at it, then, confused and scarcely comprehending, I stepped back from the pit, still facing it, one, ten, twenty paces, my eyes almost starting from my head, as though I expected to see the thing roll up from the bottom of the pit under my very gaze. At last I turned my back to the pit and strode out across the gorse-covered moorland toward my home. As I reached the road that winds from St. Gildas to St. Julien I gave one hasty glance at the pit over my shoulder. The sun shone hot on the sod about the excavation. There was something white and bare and round on the turf at the edge of the pit. It might have been a stone; there were plenty of them lying about.

II

When I entered my garden I saw Môme sprawling on the stone doorstep. He eyed me sideways and flopped his tail.

"Are you not mortified, you idiot dog?" I said, looking about the upper windows for Lys.

Môme rolled over on his back and raised one deprecating forepaw, as though to ward off calamity.

"Don't act as though I was in the habit of beating you to death," I said, disgusted. I had never in my life raised whip to the brute. "But you are a fool dog," I continued. "No, you needn't come to be babied and wept over; Lys can do that, if she insists, but I am ashamed of you, and you can go to the devil."

Môme slunk off into the house, and I followed, mounting directly to my wife's boudoir. It was empty.

"Where has she gone?" I said, looking hard at Môme, who had followed me. "Oh! I see you don't know. Don't pretend you do. Come off that lounge! Do you think Lys wants tan-colored hairs all over her lounge?"

I rang the bell for Catherine and Fine, but they didn't know where "madame" had gone; so I went into my room, bathed, exchanged my somewhat grimy shooting clothes for a suit of warm, soft knickerbockers, and, after lingering some extra moments over my toilet—for I was particular, now that I had married Lys—I went down to the garden and took a chair out under the fig-trees.

"Where can she be?" I wondered, Môme came sneaking out to be comforted, and I forgave him for Lys's sake, whereupon he frisked.

"You bounding cur," said I, "now what on earth started you off across the moor? If you do it again I'll push you along with a charge of dust shot."

As yet I had scarcely dared think about the ghastly hallucination of which I had been a victim, but now I faced it squarely, flushing a little with mortification at the thought of my hasty retreat from the gravel pit.

"To think," I said aloud, "that those old woman's tales of Max Fortin and Le Bihan should have actually made me see what didn't exist at all! I lost my nerve like a schoolboy in a dark bedroom." For I knew now that I had mistaken a round stone for a skull each time, and had pushed a couple of big pebbles into the pit instead of the skull itself.

"By jingo!" said I, "I'm nervous; my liver must be in a devil of a condition if I see such things when I'm awake! Lys will know what to give me."

I felt mortified and irritated and sulky, and thought disgustedly of Le Bihan and Max Fortin.

But after a while I ceased speculating, dismissed the mayor, the chemist, and the skull from my mind, and smoked pensively, watching the sun low dipping in the western ocean. As the twilight fell for a moment over ocean and moorland, a wistful, restless happiness filled my heart, the happiness that all men know—all men who have loved.

Slowly the purple mist crept out over the sea; the cliffs darkened; the forest was shrouded.

Suddenly the sky above burned with the afterglow, and the world was alight again.

Cloud after cloud caught the rose dye; the cliffs were tinted with it; moor and pasture, heather and forest burned and pulsated with the gentle flush. I saw the gulls turning and tossing above the sand bar, their snowy wings tipped with pink; I saw the sea swallows sheering the surface of the still river, stained to its placid depths with warm reflections of the clouds. The twitter of drowsy hedge birds broke out in the stillness; a salmon rolled its shining side above tidewater.

The interminable monotone of the ocean intensified the silence. I sat motionless, holding my breath as one who listens to the first low rumor of an organ. All at once the pure whistle of a nightingale cut the silence, and the first moonbeam silvered the wastes of mist-hung waters.

I raised my head.

Lys stood before me in the garden.

When we had kissed each other, we linked arms and moved up and down the gravel walks, watching the moonbeams sparkle on the sand bar as the tide ebbed and ebbed. The broad beds of white pinks about us were atremble with hovering white moths; the October roses hung all abloom, perfuming the salt wind.

"Sweetheart," I said, "where is Yvonne? Has she promised to spend Christmas with us?"

"Yes, Dick; she drove me down from Plougat this afternoon. She sent her love to you. I am not jealous. What did you shoot?"

"A hare and four partridges. They are in the gun room. I told Catherine not to touch them until you had seen them."

Now I suppose I knew that Lys could not be particularly enthusiastic over game or guns; but she pretended she was, and always scornfully denied that it was for my sake and not for the pure love of sport. So she dragged me off to inspect the rather meager game bag, and she paid me pretty compliments, and gave a little cry of delight and pity as I lifted the enormous hare out of the sack by his ears.

"He'll eat no more of our lettuce," I said attempting to justify the assassination.

"Unhappy little bunny—and what a beauty! O Dick, you are a splendid shot, are you not?"

I evaded the question and hauled out a partridge.

"Poor little dead things'" said Lys in a whisper; "it seems a pity—doesn't it, Dick? But then you are so clever—"

"We'll have them broiled," I said guardedly, "tell Catherine."

Catherine came in to take away the game, and presently 'Fine Lelocard, Lys's maid, announced dinner, and Lys tripped away to her boudoir.

I stood an instant contemplating her blissfully, thinking, "My boy, you're the happiest fellow in the world—you're in love with your wife'"

I walked into the dining-room, beamed at the plates, walked out again; met Tregunc in the hallway, beamed on him; glanced into the kitchen, beamed at Catherine, and went up stairs, still beaming.

Before I could knock at Lys's door it opened, and Lys came hastily out. When she saw me she gave a little cry of relief, and nestled close to my breast.

"There is something peering in at my window," she said.

"What!" I cried angrily.

"A man, I think, disguised as a priest, and he has a mask on. He must have climbed up by the bay tree."

I was down the stairs and out of doors in no time. The moonlit garden was absolutely deserted. Tregunc came up, and together we searched the hedge and shrubbery around the house and out to the road.

"Jean Marie," said I at length, "loose my bulldog—he knows you—and take your supper on the porch where you can watch. My wife says the fellow is disguised as a priest, and wears a mask."

Tregunc showed his white teeth in a smile. "He will not care to venture in here again, I think, Monsieur Darrel."

I went back and found Lys seated quietly at the table.

"The soup is ready, dear," she said. "Don't worry; it was only some foolish lout from Bannalec. No one in St. Gildas or St. Julien would do such a thing."

I was too much exasperated to reply at first, but Lys treated it as a stupid joke, and after a while I began to look at it in that light.

Lys told me about Yvonne, and reminded me of my promise to have Herbert Stuart down to meet her.

"You wicked diplomat!" I protested. "Herbert is in Paris, and hard at work for the Salon."

"Don't you think he might spare a week to flirt with the prettiest girl in Finistere?" inquired Lys innocently.

"Prettiest girl! Not much!" I said.

"Who is, then?" urged Lys.

I laughed a trifle sheepishly.

"I suppose you mean me, Dick," said Lys, coloring up.

"Now I bore you, don't I?"

"Bore me? Ah, no, Dick."

After coffee and cigarettes were served I spoke about Tregunc, and Lys approved.

"Poor Jean! He will be glad, won't he? What a dear fellow you are!"

"Nonsense," said I; "we need a gardener; you said so yourself, Lys."

But Lys leaned over and kissed me, and then bent down and hugged Môme—who whistled through his nose in sentimental appreciation.

"I am a very happy woman," said Lys.

"Môme was a very bad dog to-day," I observed.

"Poor Môme!" said Lys, smiling.

When dinner was over and Môme lay snoring before the blaze—for the October nights are often chilly in Finistere—Lys curled up in the chimney corner with her embroidery, and gave me a swift glance from under her dropping lashes.

"You look like a schoolgirl, Lys," I said teasingly. "I don't believe you are sixteen yet."

She pushed back her heavy burnished hair thoughtfully. Her wrist was as white as surf foam.

"Have we been married four years? I don't believe it," I said.

She gave me another swift glance and touched the embroidery on her knee, smiling faintly.

"I see," said I, also smiling at the embroidered garment. "Do you think it will fit?"

"Fit?" repeated Lys. Then she laughed.

"And," I persisted, "are you perfectly sure that you—er—we shall need it?"

"Perfectly," said Lys. A delicate color touched her cheeks and neck. She held up the little garment, all fluffy with misty lace and wrought with quaint embroidery.

"It is very gorgeous," said I; "don't use your eyes too much, dearest. May I smoke a pipe?"

"Of course," she said selecting a skein of pale blue silk.

For a while I sat and smoked in silence, watching her slender fingers among the tinted silks and thread of gold.

Presently she spoke: "What did you say your crest is, Dick?"

"My crest? Oh, something or other rampant on a something or other—"

"Dick!"

"Dearest?"

"Don't be flippant."

"But I really forget. It's an ordinary crest; everybody in New York has them. No family should be without 'em."

"You are disagreeable, Dick. Send Josephine upstairs for my album."

"Are you going to put that crest on the—the—whatever it is?"

"I am; and my own crest, too."

I thought of the Purple Emperor and wondered a little.

"You didn't know I had one, did you?" she smiled.

"What is it?" I replied evasively.

"You shall see. Ring for Josephine."

I rang, and, when 'Fine appeared, Lys gave her some orders in a low voice, and Josephine trotted away, bobbing her white-coiffed head with a "Bien, Madame!"

After a few minutes she returned, bearing a tattered, musty volume, from which the gold and blue had mostly disappeared.

I took the book in my hands and examined the ancient emblazoned covers.

"Lilies!" I exclaimed.

"Fleur-de-lis," said my wife demurely.

"Oh!" said I, astonished, and opened the book.

"You have never before seen this book?" asked Lys, with a touch of malice in her eyes.

"You know I haven't. Hello! What's this? Oho! So there should be a de before Trevec? Lys de Trevec? Then why in the world did the Purple Emperor—"

"Dick!" cried Lys.

"All right," said I. "Shall I read about the Sieur de Trevec who rode to Saladin's tent alone to seek for medicine for St. Louise? Or shall I read about—what is it? Oh, here it is, all down in black and white—about the Marquis de Trevec who drowned himself before Alva's eyes rather than surrender the banner of the fleur-de-lis to Spain? It's all written here. But, dear, how about that soldier named Trevec who was killed in the old fort on the cliff yonder?"

"He dropped the de, and the Trevecs since then have been Republicans," said Lys—"all except me."

"That's quite right," said I; "it is time that we Republicans should agree upon some feudal system. My dear, I drink to the king!" and I raised my wine glass and looked at Lys.

"To the king," said Lys, flushing. She smoothed out the tiny garment on her knees; she touched the glass with her lips; her eyes were very sweet. I drained the glass to the king.

After a silence I said: "I will tell the king stories. His majesty shall be amused."

"His majesty," repeated Lys softly.

"Or hers," I laughed. "Who knows?"

"Who knows?" murmured Lys; with a gentle sigh.

"I know some stories about Jack the Giant-Killer," I announced. "Do you, Lys?"

"I? No, not about a giant-killer, but I know all about the werewolf, and Jeanne-la-Flamme, and the Man in Purple Tatters, and—O dear me, I know lots more."

"You are very wise," said I. "I shall teach his majesty, English."

"And I Breton," cried Lys jealously.

"I shall bring playthings to the king," said I—"big green lizards from the gorse, little gray mullets to swim in glass globes, baby rabbits from the forest of Kerselec —"

"And I," said Lys, "will bring the first primrose, the first branch of aubepine, the first jonquil, to the king—my king."

"Our king," said I; and there was peace in Finistere.

I lay back, idly turning the leaves of the curious old volume.

"I am looking," said I, "for the crest."

"The crest, dear? It is a priest's head with an arrow-shaped mark on the forehead, on a field—"

I sat up and stared at my wife.

"Dick, whatever is the matter?" she smiled. "The story is there in that book. Do you care to read it? No? Shall I tell it to you? Well, then: It happened in the third crusade. There was a monk whom men called the Black Priest. He turned apostate, and sold himself to the enemies of Christ. A Sieur de Trevec burst into the Saracen camp, at the head of only one hundred lances, and carried the Black Priest away out of the very midst of their army."

"So that is how you come by the crest," I said quietly; but I thought of the branded skull in the gravel pit, and wondered.

"Yes," said Lys. "The Sieur de Trevec cut the Black Priest's head off, but first he branded him with an arrow mark on the forehead. The book says it was a pious action, and the Sieur de Trevec got great merit by it. But I think it was cruel, the branding," she sighed.

"Did you ever hear of any other Black Priest?"

"Yes. There was one in the last century, here in St. Gildas. He cast a white shadow in the sun. He wrote in the Breton language. Chronicles, too, I believe. I never saw them. His name was the same as that of the old chronicler, and of the other priest, Jacques Sorgue. Some said he was a lineal descendant of the traitor. Of course the first Black Priest was bad enough for anything. But if he did have a child, it need not have been the ancestor of the last Jacques Sorgue. They say he was so good he was not allowed to die, but was caught up to heaven one day," added Lys, with believing eyes.

I smiled.

"But he disappeared," persisted Lys.

"I'm afraid his journey was in another direction," I said jestingly, and thoughtlessly told her the story of the morning. I had utterly forgotten the masked man at her window, but before I finished I remembered him fast enough, and realized what I had done as I saw her face whiten.

"Lys," I urged tenderly, "that was only some clumsy clown's trick. You said so yourself. You are not superstitious, my dear?"

Her eyes were on mine. She slowly drew the little gold cross from her bosom and kissed it. But her lips trembled as they pressed the symbol of faith.

III

About nine o'clock the next morning I walked into the Groix Inn and sat down at the long discolored oaken table, nodding good-day to Marianne Bruyere, who in turn bobbed her white coiffe at me.

"My clever Bannalec maid," said I, "what is good for a stirrup-cup at the Groix Inn?"

"Schist?" she inquired in Breton.

"With a dash of red wine, then," I replied.

She brought the delicious Quimperle cider, and I poured a little Bordeaux into it. Marianne watched me with laughing black eyes.

"What makes your cheeks so red, Marianne?" I asked. "Has Jean Marie been here?"

"We are to be married, Monsieur Darrel," she laughed.

"Ah! Since when has Jean Marie Tregunc lost his head?"

"His head? Oh, Monsieur Darrel—his heart, you mean!"

"So I do," said I. "Jean Marie is a practical fellow."

"It is all due to your kindness—" began the girl, but I raised my hand and held up the glass.

"It's due to himself. To your happiness, Marianne"; and I took a hearty draught of the schist. "Now," said I, "tell me where I can find Le Bihan and Max Fortin."

"Monsieur Le Bihan and Monsieur Fortin are above in the broad room. I believe they are examining the Red Admiral's effects."

"To send them to Paris? Oh, I know. May I go up, Marianne?"

"And God go with you," smiled the girl.

When I knocked at the door of the broad room above little Max Fortin opened it. Dust covered his spectacles and nose; his hat, with the tiny velvet ribbons fluttering, was all awry.

"Come in, Monsieur Darrel," he said; "the mayor and I are packing up the effects of the Purple Emperor and of the poor Red Admiral."

"The collections?" I asked, entering the room. "You must be very careful in packing those butterfly cases; the slightest jar might break wings and antennas, you know."

Le Bihan shook hands with me and pointed to the great pile of boxes.

"They're all cork lined," he said, "but Fortin and I are putting felt around each box. The Entomological Society of Paris pays the freight."

The combined collection of the Red Admiral and the Purple Emperor made a magnificent display.

I lifted and inspected case after case set with gorgeous butterflies and moths, each specimen carefully labelled with the name in Latin. There were cases filled with crimson tiger moths all aflame with color; cases devoted to the common yellow butterflies; symphonies in orange and pale yellow; cases of soft gray and dun-colored sphinx moths; and cases of grayish nettle-bed butterflies of the numerous family of Vanessa.

All alone in a great case by itself was pinned the purple emperor, the Apatura Iris, that fatal specimen that had given the Purple Emperor his name and quietus.

I remembered the butterfly, and stood looking at it with bent eyebrows.

Le Bihan glanced up from the floor where he was nailing down the lid of a box full of cases.

"It is settled, then," said he, "that madame, your wife, gives the Purple Emperor's entire Collection to the city of Paris?"

I nodded.

"Without accepting anything for it?"

"It is a gift," I said.

"Including the purple emperor there in the case? That butterfly is worth a great deal of money," persisted Le Bihan.

"You don't suppose that we would wish to sell that specimen, do you?" I answered a trifle sharply.

"If I were you I should destroy it," said the mayor in his high-pitched voice.

"That would be nonsense," said I, "like your burying the brass cylinder and scroll yesterday."

"It was not nonsense," said Le Bihan doggedly, "and I should prefer not to discuss the subject of the scroll."

I looked at Max Portin, who immediately avoided my eyes.

"You are a pair of superstitious old women," said I, digging my hands into my pockets; "you swallow every nursery tale that is invented."

"What of it?" said Le Bihan sulkily; "there's more truth than lies in most of 'em."

"Oh!" I sneered, "does the Mayor of St. Gildas and St. Julien believe in the loup-garou?"

"No, not in the loup-garou."

"In what, then—Jeanne-la-Flamme?"

"That," said Le Bihan with conviction, "is history."

"The devil it is!" said I; "and perhaps, Monsieur the mayor, your faith in giants is unimpaired?"

"There were giants—everybody knows it," growled Max Fortin.

"And you a chemist!" I observed scornfully.

"Listen, Monsieur Darrel," squeaked Le Bihan; "you know yourself that the Purple Emperor was a scientific man. Now suppose I should tell you that he always refused to include in his collection a Death's Messenger?"

"A what?" I exclaimed.

"You know what I mean—that moth that flies by night; some call it the Death's Head, but in St. Gildas we call it 'Death's Messenger.'"

"Oh!" said I, "you mean that big sphinx moth that is commonly known as the 'death's-head moth.' Why the mischief should the people here call it death's messenger?"

"For hundreds of years it has been known as death's messenger in St. Gildas," said Max Fortin. "Even Froissart speaks of it in his commentaries on Jacques Sorgue's *Chronicles*. The book is in your library."

"Sorgue? And who was Jacques Sorgue? I never read his book."

"Jacques Sorgue was the son of some unfrocked priest—I forget. It was during the crusades."

"Good Heavens!" I burst out, "I've been hearing of nothing but crusades and priests and death and sorcery ever since I kicked that skull into the gravel pit, and I am tired of it, I tell you frankly. One would think we lived in the dark ages. Do you know what year of our Lord it is, Le Bihan?"

"Eighteen hundred and ninety-six," replied the mayor.

"And yet you two hulking men are afraid of a death's-head moth."

"I don't care to have one fly into the window," said Max Fortin; "it means evil to the house and the people in it."

"God alone knows why he marked one of his creatures with a yellow death's head on the back," observed Le Bihan piously, "but I take it that he meant it as a warning; and I propose to profit by it," he added triumphantly.

"See here, Le Bihan," I said; "by a stretch of imagination one can make out a skull on the thorax of a certain big sphinx moth. What of it?"

"It is a bad thing to touch," said the mayor wagging his head.

"It squeaks when handled," added Max Fortin.

"Some creatures squeak all the time," I observed, looking hard at Le Bihan.

"Pigs," added the mayor.

"Yes, and asses," I replied. "Listen, Le Bihan: do you mean to tell me that you saw that skull roll uphill yesterday?"

The mayor shut his mouth tightly and picked up his hammer.

"Don't be obstinate," I said; "I asked you a question."

"And I refuse to answer," snapped Le Bihan. "Fortin saw what I saw; let him talk about it."

I looked searchingly at the little chemist.

"I don't say that I saw it actually roll up out of the pit, all by itself," said Fortin with a shiver, "but—but then, how did it come up out of the pit, if it didn't roll up all by itself?"

"It didn't come up at all; that was a yellow cobblestone that you mistook for the skull again," I replied. "You were nervous, Max."

"A—a very curious cobblestone, Monsieur Darrel," said Fortin.

"I also was a victim to the same hallucination," I continued, "and I regret to say that I took the trouble to roll two innocent cobblestones into the gravel pit, imagining each time that it was the skull I was rolling."

"It was," observed Le Bihan with a morose shrug.

"It just shows," said I, ignoring the mayor's remark, "how easy it is to fix up a train of coincidences so that the result seems to savor of the supernatural. Now, last night my wife imagined that she saw a priest in a mask peer in at her window—"

Fortin and Le Bihan scrambled hastily from their knees, dropping hammer and nails.

"W-h-a-t—what's that?" demanded the mayor.

I repeated what I had said. Max Fortin turned livid.

"My God!" muttered Le Bihan, "the Black Priest is in St. Gildas!"

"D-don't you—you know the old prophecy?" stammered Fortin; "Froissart quotes it from Jacques Sorgue:

> *"'When the Black Priest rises from the dead,*
> *St. Gildas folk shall shriek in bed;*
> *When the Black Priest rises from his grave,*
> *May the good God St. Gildas save!'"*

"Aristide Le Bihan," I said angrily, "and you, Max Fortin, I've got enough of this nonsense! Some foolish lout from Bannalec has been in St. Gildas playing tricks to frighten old fools like you. If you have nothing better to talk about than nursery legends I'll wait until you come to your senses. Good-morning." And I walked out, more disturbed than I cared to acknowledge to myself.

The day had become misty and overcast. Heavy, wet clouds hung in the east. I heard the surf thundering against the cliffs, and the gray gulls squealed as they tossed and turned high in the sky. The tide was creeping across the river sands, higher, higher, and I saw the seaweed floating on the beach, and the lancons springing from the foam, silvery threadlike flashes in the gloom. Curlew were flying up the river in twos and threes; the timid sea swallows skimmed across the moors toward some quiet, lonely pool, safe from the coming tempest. In every hedge field birds were gathering, huddling together, twittering restlessly.

When I reached the cliffs I sat down, resting my chin on my clenched hands. Already a vast curtain of rain, sweeping across the ocean miles away, hid the island of Groix. To the east, behind the white semaphore on the hills, black clouds crowded up over the horizon. After a little the thunder boomed, dull, distant, and slender skeins of lightning unraveled across the crest of the coming storm. Under the cliff at my feet the surf rushed foaming over the shore, and the lancons jumped and skipped and quivered until they seemed to be but the reflections of the meshed lightning.

I turned to the east. It was raining over Groix, it was raining at Sainte Barbe, it was raining now at the semaphore. High in the storm whirl a few gulls pitched; a nearer cloud trailed veils of rain in its wake; the sky was spattered with lightning; the thunder boomed.

As I rose to go, a cold raindrop fell upon the back of my hand, and another, and yet another on my face. I gave a last glance at the sea, where the waves were bursting into strange white shapes that seemed to fling out menacing arms toward me. Then something moved on the cliff, something black as the black rock it clutched—a filthy cormorant, craning its hideous head at the sky.

Slowly I plodded homeward across the somber moorland, where the gorse stems glimmered with a dull metallic green, and the heather, no longer violet and purple, hung drenched and dun-colored among the dreary rocks. The wet turf creaked under my heavy boots, the black-thorn scraped and grated against knee and elbow. Over all lay a strange light, pallid, ghastly, where the sea spray whirled across the landscape and drove into my face until it grew numb with the cold. In broad bands, rank after rank, billow on billow, the rain burst out across the endless moors, and yet there was no wind to drive it at such a pace.

Lys stood at the door as I turned into the garden, motioning me to hasten; and then for the first time I became conscious that I was soaked to the skin.

"However in the world did you come to stay out when such a storm threatened?" she said. "Oh, you are dripping! Go quickly and change; I have laid your warm underwear on the bed, Dick."

I kissed my wife, and went upstairs to change my dripping clothes for something more comfortable.

When I returned to the morning room there was a driftwood fire on the hearth, and Lys sat in the chimney corner embroidering.

"Catherine tells me that the fishing fleet from Lorient is out. Do you think they are in danger, dear?" asked Lys, raising her blue eyes to mine as I entered.

"There is no wind, and there will be no sea," said I, looking out of the window. Far across the moor I could see the black cliffs looming in the mist.

"How it rains!" murmured Lys; "come to the fire, Dick."

I threw myself on the fur rug, my hands in my pockets, my head on Lys's knees.

"Tell me a story," I said. "I feel like a boy of ten."

Lys raised a finger to her scarlet lips. I always waited for her to do that.

"Will you be very still, then?" she said.

"Still as death."

"Death," echoed a voice, very softly.

"Did you speak, Lys?" I asked, turning so that I could see her face.

"No; did you, Dick?"

"Who said 'death'?" I asked, startled.

"Death," echoed a voice, softly.

I sprang up and looked about. Lys rose too, her needles and embroidery falling to the floor. She seemed about to faint, leaning heavily on me, and I led her to the window and opened it a little way to give her air. As I did so the chain lightning split the zenith, the thunder crashed, and a sheet of rain swept into the room, driving with it something that fluttered—something that flapped, and squeaked, and beat upon the rug with soft, moist wings.

We bent over it together, Lys clinging to me, and we saw that it was a death's-head moth drenched with rain.

The dark day passed slowly as we sat beside the fire, hand in hand, her head against my breast, speaking of sorrow and mystery and death. For Lys believed that there were things on earth that none might understand, things that must be nameless forever and ever, until God rolls up the scroll of life and all is ended. We spoke of hope and fear and faith, and the mystery of the saints; we spoke of the beginning and the end, of the shadow of sin, of omens, and of love. The moth still lay on the floor quivering its somber wings in the warmth of the fire, the skull and ribs clearly etched upon its neck and body.

"If it is a messenger of death to this house," I said, "why should we fear, Lys?"

"Death should be welcome to those who love God," murmured Lys, and she drew the cross from her breast and kissed it.

"The moth might die if I threw it out into the storm," I said after a silence.

"Let it remain," sighed Lys.

Late that night my wife lay sleeping, and I sat beside her bed and read in the Chronicle of Jacques Sorgue. I shaded the candle, but Lys grew restless, and finally I took the book down into the morning room, where the ashes of the fire rustled and whitened on the hearth.

The death's-head moth lay on the rug before the fire where I had left it. At first I thought it was dead, but when I looked closer I saw a lambent fire in its amber eyes. The straight white shadow it cast across the floor wavered as the candle flickered.

The pages of the Chronicle of Jacques Sorgue were damp and sticky; the illuminated gold and blue initials left flakes of azure and gilt where my hand brushed them.

"It is not paper at all; it is thin parchment," I said to myself; and I held the discolored page close to the candle flame and read, translating laboriously:

"I, Jacques Sorgue, saw all these things. And I saw the Black Mass celebrated in the chapel of St. Gildas-on-the-Cliff. And it was said by the Abbé Sorgue, my kinsman: for which deadly sin the apostate priest was seized by the most noble Marquis of Plougastel and by him condemned to be burned with hot irons, until his seared soul quit its body and fly to its master the devil. But when the Black Priest lay in the crypt of Plougastel, his master Satan came at night and set him free, and carried him across land and sea to Mahmoud, which is Soldan or Saladin. And I, Jacques Sorgue, traveling afterward by sea, beheld with my own eyes my kinsman, the Black Priest of St. Gildas, borne along in the air upon a vast black wing, which was the wing of his master Satan. And this was seen also by two men of the crew."

I turned the page. The wings of the moth on the floor began to quiver. I read on and on, my eyes blurring under the shifting candle flame. I read of battles and of saints, and I learned how the Great Soldan made his pact with Satan, and then I came to the Sieur de Trevec, and read how he seized the Black Priest in the midst of Saladin's tents and carried him away and cut off his head first branding him on the forehead. "And before he suffered," said the Chronicle, "he cursed the Sieur de Trevec and his descendants, and he said he would surely return to St. Gildas. 'For the violence you do to me, I will do violence to you. For the evil I suffer at your hands, I will work evil on you and your descendants. Woe to your children, Sieur de Trevec!'" There was a whirr, a beating of strong wings, and my candle flashed up as in a sudden breeze. A humming filled the room; the great moth darted hither and thither, beating, buzzing, on ceiling and wall. I flung down my book and stepped forward. Now it lay fluttering upon the window sill, and for a moment I had it under my hand, but the thing squeaked and I shrank back. Then suddenly it darted across the candle flame; the light flared and went out, and at the same moment a shadow moved in the darkness outside. I raised my eyes to the window. A masked face was peering in at me.

Quick as thought I whipped out my revolver and fired every cartridge, but the face advanced beyond the window, the glass melting away before it like mist, and through the smoke of my revolver I saw something creep swiftly into the room. Then I tried to cry out, but the thing was at my throat, and I fell backward among the ashes of the hearth.

* * * *

When my eyes unclosed I was lying on the hearth, my head among the cold ashes. Slowly I got on my knees, rose painfully, and groped my way to a chair. On the floor lay my revolver, shining in the pale light of early morning. My mind clearing by degrees, I looked, shuddering, at the window. The glass was unbroken. I stooped stiffly, picked up my revolver and opened the cylinder. Every cartridge had been fired. Mechanically I closed the cylinder and placed the revolver in my pocket. The book, the Chronicles of Jacques Sorgue, lay on the table beside me, and as I started to close it I glanced at the page. It was all splashed with rain, and the lettering had run, so that the page was merely a confused blur of gold and red and black. As I stumbled toward the door I cast a fearful glance over my shoulder. The death's-head moth crawled shivering on the rug.

IV

The sun was about three hours high. I must have slept, for I was aroused by the sudden gallop of horses under our window. People were shouting and calling in the road. I sprang up and opened the sash. Le Bihan was there, an image of helplessness, and Max Fortin stood beside him polishing his glasses. Some gendarmes had just arrived from Quimperle, and I could hear them around the corner of the house, stamping, and rattling their sabres and carbines, as they led their horses into my stable.

Lys sat up, murmuring half-sleepy, half-anxious questions.

"I don't know," I answered. "I am going out to see what it means."

"It is like the day they came to arrest you," Lys said, giving me a troubled look. But I kissed her and laughed at her until she smiled too. Then I flung on coat and cap and hurried down the stairs.

The first person I saw standing in the road was the Brigadier Durand.

"Hello!" said I, "have you come to arrest me again? What the devil is all this fuss about, anyway?"

"We were telegraphed for an hour ago," said Durand briskly, "and for a sufficient reason, I think. Look there, Monsieur Darrel!"

He pointed to the ground almost under my feet.

"Good heavens!" I cried, "where did that puddle of blood come from?"

"That's what I want to know, Monsieur Darrel. Max Fortin found it at daybreak. See, it's splashed all over the grass, too. A trail of it leads into your garden, across the flower beds to your very window, the one that opens from the morning room. There is another trail leading from this spot across the road to the cliffs, then to the gravel pit, and thence across the moor to the forest of Kerselec. We are going to mount in a minute and search the bosquets. Will you join us? Bon Dieu! but the fellow bled like an ox. Max Fortin says it's human blood, or I should not have believed it."

The little chemist of Quimperle came up at that moment, rubbing his glasses with a colored handkerchief.

"Yes, it is human blood," he said, "but one thing puzzles me: the corpuscles are yellow. I never saw any human blood before with yellow corpuscles. But your English Doctor Thompson asserts that he has—"

"Well, it's human blood, anyway—isn't it?" insisted Durand, impatiently.

"Ye-es," admitted Max Fortin.

"Then it's my business to trail it," said the big gendarme, and he called his men and gave the order to mount.

"Did you hear anything last night?" asked Durand of me.

"I heard the rain. I wonder the rain did not wash away these traces."

"They must have come after the rain ceased. See this thick splash, how it lies over and weighs down the wet grass blades. Pah!"

It was a heavy, evil-looking clot, and I stepped back from it, my throat closing in disgust.

"My theory," said the brigadier, "is this: Some of those Biribi fishermen, probably the Icelanders, got an extra glass of cognac into their hides and quarreled on the road. Some of them were slashed, and staggered to your house. But there is only one trail, and yet—and yet, how could all that blood come from only one person? Well, the wounded man, let us say, staggered first to your house and then back here, and he wandered off, drunk and dying, God knows where. That's my theory."

"A very good one," said I calmly. "And you are going to trail him?"

"Yes."

"When?"

"At once. Will you come?"

"Not now. I'll gallop over by-and-bye. You are going to the edge of the Kerselec forest?"

"Yes; you will hear us calling. Are you coming, Max Fortin? And you, Le Bihan? Good; take the dog-cart."

The big gendarme tramped around the corner to the stable and presently returned mounted on a strong gray horse, his sabre shone on his saddle; his pale yellow and white facings were spotless. The little crowd of white-coiffed women with their children fell back as Durand touched spurs and clattered away followed by his two troopers. Soon after Le Bihan and Max Fortin also departed in the mayor's dingy dog-cart.

"Are you coming?" piped Le Bihan shrilly.

"In a quarter of an hour," I replied, and went back to the house.

When I opened the door of the morning room the death's-head moth was beating its strong wings against the window. For a second I hesitated, then walked over and opened the sash. The creature fluttered out, whirred over the flower beds a moment, then darted across the moorland toward the sea. I called the servants together and questioned them. Josephine, Catherine, Jean Marie Tregunc, not one of them had heard the slightest disturbance during the night. Then I told Jean Marie to saddle my horse, and while I was speaking Lys came down.

"Dearest," I began, going to her.

"You must tell me everything you know, Dick," she interrupted, looking me earnestly in the face.

"But there is nothing to tell—only a drunken brawl, and some one wounded."

"And you are going to ride—where, Dick?"

"Well, over to the edge of Kerselec forest. Durand and the mayor, and Max Fortin, have gone on, following a—a trail."

"What trail?"

"Some blood."

"Where did they find it?"

"Out in the road there." Lys crossed herself.

"Does it come near our house?"

"Yes."

"How near?"

"It comes up to the morning room window," said I, giving in.

Her hand on my arm grew heavy. "I dreamed last night—"

"So did I—" but I thought of the empty cartridges in my revolver, and stopped.

"I dreamed that you were in great danger, and I could not move hand or foot to save you; but you had your revolver, and I called out to you to fire—"

"I did fire!" I cried excitedly.

"You—you fired?"

I took her in my arms. "My darling," I said "something strange has happened—something that I cannot understand as yet. But, of course, there is an explanation. Last night I thought I fired at the Black Priest."

"Ah!" gasped Lys.

"Is that what you dreamed?"

"Yes, yes, that was it! I begged you to fire—"

"And I did."

Her heart was beating against my breast. I held her close in silence.

"Dick," she said at length, "perhaps you killed the—the thing."

"If it was human I did not miss," I answered grimly. "And it was human," I went on, pulling myself together, ashamed of having so nearly gone to pieces. "Of course it was human! The whole affair is plain enough. Not a drunken brawl, as Durand thinks; it was a drunken lout's practical joke, for which he has suffered. I suppose I must have filled him pretty full of bullets, and he has crawled away to die in Kerselec forest. It's a terrible affair; I'm sorry I fired so hastily; but that idiot Le Bihan and Max Fortin have been working on my nerves till I am as hysterical as a schoolgirl," I ended angrily.

"You fired—but the window glass was not shattered," said Lys in a low voice.

"Well, the window was open, then. And as for the—the rest—I've got nervous indigestion, and a doctor will settle the Black Priest for me, Lys."

I glanced out of the window at Tregunc waiting with my horse at the gate.

"Dearest, I think I had better go to join Durand and the others."

"I will go, too."

"Oh, no!"

"Yes, Dick."

"Don't, Lys."

"I shall suffer every moment you are away."

"The ride is too fatiguing, and we can't tell what unpleasant sight you may come upon. Lys, you don't really think there is anything supernatural in this affair?"

"Dick," she answered gently, "I am a Bretonne." With both arms around my neck, my wife said, "Death is the gift of God. I do not fear it when we are together. But alone—oh, my husband, I should fear a God who could take you away from me!"

We kissed each other soberly, simply, like two children. Then Lys hurried away to change her gown, and I paced up and down the garden waiting for her.

She came, drawing on her slender gauntlets. I swung her into the saddle, gave a hasty order to Jean Marie, and mounted.

Now, to quail under thoughts of terror on a morning like this, with Lys in the saddle beside me, no matter what had happened or might happen was impossible. Moreover, Môme came sneaking after us. I asked Tregunc to catch him, for I was afraid he might be brained by our horses' hoofs if he followed, but the wily puppy dodged and bolted after Lys, who was trotting along the highroad. "Never mind," I thought; "if he's hit he'll live, for he has no brains to lose."

Lys was waiting for me in the road beside the Shrine of Our Lady of St. Gildas when I joined her. She crossed herself, I doffed my cap, then we shook out our bridles and galloped toward the forest of Kerselec.

We said very little as we rode. I always loved to watch Lys in the saddle. Her exquisite figure and lovely face were the incarnation of youth and grace; her curling hair glistened like threaded gold.

Out of the corner of my eye I saw the spoiled puppy Môme come bounding cheerfully alongside, oblivious of our horses' heels. Our road swung close to the cliffs. A filthy cormorant rose from the black rocks and flapped heavily across our path. Lys's horse reared, but she pulled him down, and pointed at the bird with her riding crop.

"I see," said I; "it seems to be going our way. Curious to see a cormorant in a forest, isn't it?"

"It is a bad sign," said Lys. "You know the Morbihan proverb: 'When the cormorant turns from the sea, Death laughs in the forest, and wise woodsmen build boats.'"

"I wish," said I sincerely, "that there were fewer proverbs in Brittany."

We were in sight of the forest now; across the gorse I could see the sparkle of gendarmes' trappings, and the glitter of Le Bihan's silver-buttoned jacket. The hedge was low and we took it without difficulty, and trotted across the moor to where Le Bihan and Durand stood gesticulating.

They bowed ceremoniously to Lys as we rode up.

"The trail is horrible—it is a river," said the mayor in his squeaky voice. "Monsieur Darrel, I think perhaps madame would scarcely care to come any nearer."

Lys drew bridle and looked at me.

"It is horrible!" said Durand, walking up beside me; "it looks as though a bleeding regiment had passed this way. The trail winds and winds about here in the thickets; we lose it at times, but we always find it again. I can't understand how one man—no, nor twenty—could bleed like that!"

A halloo, answered by another, sounded from the depths of the forest.

"It's my men; they are following the trail," muttered the brigadier. "God alone knows what is at the end!"

"Shall we gallop back, Lys?" I asked.

"No; let us ride along the western edge of the woods and dismount. The sun is so hot now, and I should like to rest for a moment," she said.

"The western forest is clear of anything disagreeable," said Durand.

"Very well," I answered; "call me, Le Bihan, if you find anything."

Lys wheeled her mare, and I followed across the springy heather, Môme trotting cheerfully in the rear.

We entered the sunny woods about a quarter of a kilometer from where we left Durand. I took Lys from her horse, flung both bridles over a limb, and, giving my wife my arm, aided her to a flat mossy rock which overhung a shallow brook gurgling among the beech trees. Lys sat down and drew off her gauntlets. Môme pushed his head into her lap, received an undeserved caress, and came doubtfully toward me. I was weak enough to condone his offense, but I made him lie down at my feet, greatly to his disgust.

I rested my head on Lys's knees, looking up at the sky through the crossed branches of the trees.

"I suppose I have killed him," I said. "It shocks me terribly, Lys."

"You could not have known, dear. He may have been a robber, and—if—not—did—have you ever fired your revolver since that day four years ago when the Red Admiral's son tried to kill you? But I know you have not."

"No," said I, wondering. "It's a fact, I have not. Why?"

"And don't you remember that I asked you to let me load it for you the day when Yves went off, swearing to kill you and his father?"

"Yes, I do remember. Well?"

"Well, I—I took the cartridges first to St. Gildas chapel and dipped them in holy water. You must not laugh, Dick," said Lys gently, laying her cool hands on my lips.

"Laugh, my darling!"

Overhead the October sky was pale amethyst, and the sunlight burned like orange flame through the yellow leaves of beech and oak. Gnats and midges danced and wavered overhead; a spider dropped from a twig halfway to the ground and hung suspended on the end of his gossamer thread.

"Are you sleepy, dear?" asked Lys, bending over me.

"I am—a little; I scarcely slept two hours last night," I answered.

"You may sleep, if you wish," said Lys, and touched my eyes caressingly.

"Is my head heavy on your knees?"

"No, Dick."

I was already in a half doze; still I heard the brook babbling under the beeches and the humming of forest flies overhead. Presently even these were stilled.

The next thing I knew I was sitting bolt upright, my ears ringing with a scream, and I saw Lys cowering beside me, covering her white face with both hands.

As I sprang to my feet she cried again and clung to my knees. I saw my dog rush growling into a thicket, then I heard him whimper, and he came backing out, whining, ears flat, tail down. I stooped and disengaged Lys's hand.

"Don't go, Dick!" she cried. "O God, it's the Black Priest!"

In a moment I had leaped across the brook and pushed my way into the thicket. It was empty. I stared about me; I scanned every tree trunk, every bush. Suddenly I saw him. He was seated on a fallen log, his head resting in his hands, his rusty black robe gathered around him. For a moment my hair stirred under my cap; sweat started on forehead and cheek bone; then I recovered my reason, and understood that the man was human and was probably wounded to death. Ay, to death; for there at my feet, lay the wet trail of blood, over leaves and stones, down into the little hollow, across to the figure in black resting silently under the trees.

I saw that he could not escape even if he had the strength, for before him, almost at his very feet, lay a deep, shining swamp.

As I stepped forward my foot broke a twig. At the sound the figure started a little, then its head fell forward again. Its face was masked. Walking up to the man, I bade him tell where he was wounded. Durand and the others broke through the thicket at the same moment and hurried to my side.

"Who are you who hide a masked face in a priest's robe?" said the gendarme loudly.

There was no answer.

"See—see the stiff blood all over his robe," muttered Le Bihan to Fortin.

"He will not speak," said I.

"He may be too badly wounded," whispered Le Bihan.

"I saw him raise his head," I said, "my wife saw him creep up here."

Durand stepped forward and touched the figure.

"Speak!" he said.

"Speak!" quavered Fortin.

Durand waited a moment, then with a sudden upward movement he stripped off the mask and threw back the man's head. We were looking into the eye sockets of a skull. Durand stood rigid; the mayor shrieked. The skeleton burst out from its rot-ting robes and collapsed on the ground before us. From between the staring ribs and the grinning teeth spurted a torrent of black blood, showering the shrinking grasses; then the thing shuddered, and fell over into the black ooze of the bog. Little bubbles of iridescent air appeared from the mud; the bones were slowly engulfed, and, as the last fragments sank out of sight, up from the depths and along the bank crept a creature, shiny, shivering, quivering its wings.

It was a death's-head moth.

* * * *

I wish I had time to tell you how Lys outgrew superstitions—for she never knew the truth about the affair, and she never will know, since she has promised not to read this book. I wish I might tell you about the king and his coronation, and how the coronation robe fitted. I wish that I were able to write how Yvonne and Herbert Stuart rode to a boar hunt in Quimperle, and how the hounds raced the quarry right through the town, overturning three gendarmes, the notary, and an old woman. But I am becoming garrulous and Lys is calling me to come and hear the king say that he is sleepy. And his highness shall not be kept waiting.

THE KING'S CRADLE SONG

Seal with a seal of gold
The scroll of a life unrolled;
Swathe him deep in his purple stole;
Ashes of diamonds, crystalled coal,
Drops of gold in each scented fold.

Crimson wings of the Little Death,
Stir his hair with your silken breath;
Flaming wings of sins to be,
Splendid pinions of prophecy,
Smother his eyes with hues and dyes,
While the white moon spins and the winds arise,
And the stars drip through the skies.

Wave, O wings of the Little Death!
Seal his sight and stifle his breath,
Cover his breast with the gemmed shroud pressed;
From north to north, from west to west,
Wave, O wings of the Little Death!
Till the white moon reels in the cracking skies,
And the ghosts of God arise.

THE BEAST WITH FIVE FINGERS, by W. F. Harvey

When I was a little boy I once went with my father to call on Adrian Borlsover. I played on the floor with a black spaniel while my father appealed for a subscription. Just before we left my father said, "Mr. Borlsover, may my son here shake hands with you? It will be a thing to look back upon with pride when he grows to be a man."

I came up to the bed on which the old man was lying and put my hand in his, awed by the still beauty of his face. He spoke to me kindly, and hoped that I should always try to please my father. Then he placed his right hand on my head and asked for a blessing to rest upon me. "Amen!" said my father, and I followed him out of the room, feeling as if I wanted to cry. But my father was in excellent spirits.

"That old gentleman, Jim," said he, "is the most wonderful man in the whole town. For ten years he has been quite blind."

"But I saw his eyes," I said. "They were ever so black and shiny; they weren't shut up like Nora's puppies. Can't he see at all?"

And so I learnt for the first time that a man might have eyes that looked dark and beautiful and shining without being able to see.

"Just like Mrs. Tomlinson has big ears," I said, "and can't hear at all except when Mr. Tomlinson shouts."

"Jim," said my father, "it's not right to talk about a lady's ears. Remember what Mr. Borlsover said about pleasing me and being a good boy."

That was the only time I saw Adrian Borlsover. I soon forgot about him and the hand which he laid in blessing on my head. But for a week I prayed that those dark tender eyes might see.

"His spaniel may have puppies," I said in my prayers, "and he will never be able to know how funny they look with their eyes all closed up. Please let old Mr. Borlsover see."

* * * *

Adrian Borlsover, as my father had said, was a wonderful man. He came of an eccentric family. Borlsovers' sons, for some reason, always seemed to marry very ordinary women, which perhaps accounted for the fact that no Borlsover had been a genius, and only one Borlsover had been mad. But they were great champions of little causes, generous patrons of odd sciences, founders of querulous sects, trustworthy guides to the bypath meadows of erudition.

Adrian was an authority on the fertilization of orchids. He had held at one time the family living at Borlsover Conyers, until a congenital weakness of the lungs obliged him to seek a less rigorous climate in the sunny south coast watering-place where I had seen him. Occasionally he would relieve one or other of the local clergy. My father described him as a fine preacher, who gave long and inspiring sermons from what many men would have considered unprofitable texts. "An excellent proof," he would add, "of the truth of the doctrine of direct verbal inspiration."

Adrian Borlsover was exceedingly clever with his hands. His penmanship was exquisite. He illustrated all his scientific papers, made his own woodcuts, and carved the reredos that is at present the chief feature of interest in the church at Borlsover Conyers. He had an exceedingly clever knack in cutting silhouettes for young ladies and paper pigs and cows for little children, and made more than one complicated wind instrument of his own devising.

When he was fifty years old Adrian Borlsover lost his sight. In a wonderfully short time he had adapted himself to the new conditions of life. He quickly learned to read Braille. So marvelous indeed was his sense of touch that he was still able to maintain his interest in botany. The mere passing of his long supple fingers over a flower was sufficient means for its identification, though occasionally he would use his lips. I have found several letters of his among my father's correspondence. In no case was there anything to show that he was afflicted with blindness and this in spite of the fact that he exercised undue economy in the spacing of lines. Towards the close of his life the old man was credited with powers of touch that seemed almost uncanny: it has been said that he could tell at once the color of a ribbon placed between his fingers. My father would neither confirm nor deny the story.

I

Adrian Borlsover was a bachelor. His elder brother George had married late in life, leaving one son, Eustace, who lived in the gloomy Georgian mansion at Borlsover Conyers, where he could work undisturbed in collecting material for his great book on heredity.

Like his uncle, he was a remarkable man. The Borlsovers had always been born naturalists, but Eustace possessed in a special degree the power of systematizing his knowledge. He had received his university education in Germany, and then, after post-graduate work in Vienna and Naples, had traveled for four years in South America and the East, getting together a huge store of material for a new study into the processes of variation.

He lived alone at Borlsover Conyers with Saunders his secretary, a man who bore a somewhat dubious reputation in the district, but whose powers as a mathematician, combined with his business abilities, were invaluable to Eustace.

Uncle and nephew saw little of each other. The visits of Eustace were confined to a week in the summer or autumn: long weeks, that dragged almost as slowly as the bath-chair in which the old man was drawn along the sunny sea front. In their way the two men were fond of each other, though their intimacy would doubtless have been greater had they shared the same religious views. Adrian held to the old-fashioned evangelical dogmas of his early manhood; his nephew for many years had been thinking of embracing Buddhism. Both men possessed, too, the reticence the Borlsovers had always shown, and which their enemies sometimes called hypocrisy. With Adrian it was a reticence as to the things he had left undone; but with Eustace it seemed that the curtain which he was so careful to leave undrawn hid something more than a half-empty chamber.

* * * *

Two years before his death Adrian Borlsover developed, unknown to himself, the not uncommon power of automatic writing. Eustace made the discovery by accident. Adrian was sitting reading in bed, the forefinger of his left hand tracing the Braille characters, when his nephew noticed that a pencil the old man held in his right hand was moving slowly along the opposite page. He left his seat in the window and sat down beside the bed. The right hand continued to move, and now he could see plainly that they were letters and words which it was forming.

"Adrian Borlsover," wrote the hand, "Eustace Borlsover, George Borlsover, Francis Borlsover Sigismund Borlsover, Adrian Borlsover, Eustace Borlsover, Saville Borlsover. B, for Borlsover. Honesty is the Best Policy. Beautiful Belinda Borlsover."

"What curious nonsense!" said Eustace to himself.

"King George the Third ascended the throne in 1760," wrote the hand. "Crowd, a noun of multitude; a collection of individuals—Adrian Borlsover, Eustace Borlsover."

"It seems to me," said his uncle, closing the book, "that you had much better make the most of the afternoon sunshine and take your walk now."

"I think perhaps I will," Eustace answered as he picked up the volume. "I won't go far, and when I come back I can read to you those articles in *Nature* about which we were speaking."

He went along the promenade, but stopped at the first shelter, and seating himself in the corner best protected from the wind, he examined the book at leisure. Nearly every page was scored with a meaningless jungle of pencil marks: rows of capital letters, short words, long words, complete sentences, copy-book tags. The whole thing, in fact, had the appearance of a copy-book, and on a more careful scrutiny Eustace thought that there was ample evidence to show that the handwriting at the beginning of the book, good though it was was not nearly so good as the handwriting at the end.

He left his uncle at the end of October, with a promise to return early in December. It seemed to him quite clear that the old man's power of automatic writing was developing rapidly, and for the first time he looked forward to a visit that combined duty with interest.

But on his return he was at first disappointed. His uncle, he thought, looked older. He was listless too, preferring others to read to him and dictating nearly all his letters. Not until the day before he left had Eustace an opportunity of observing Adrian Borlsover's new-found faculty.

The old man, propped up in bed with pillows, had sunk into a light sleep. His two hands lay on the coverlet, his left hand tightly clasping his right. Eustace took an empty manuscript book and placed a pencil within reach of the fingers of the right hand. They snatched at it eagerly; then dropped the pencil to unloose the left hand from its restraining grasp.

"Perhaps to prevent interference I had better hold that hand," said Eustace to himself, as he watched the pencil. Almost immediately it began to write.

"Blundering Borlsovers, unnecessarily unnatural, extraordinarily eccentric, culpably curious."

"Who are you?" asked Eustace, in a low voice.

"Never you mind," wrote the hand of Adrian.

"Is it my uncle who is writing?"

"Oh, my prophetic soul, mine uncle."

"Is it anyone I know?"

"Silly Eustace, you'll see me very soon."

"When shall I see you?"

"When poor old Adrian's dead."

"Where shall I see you?"

"Where shall you not?"

Instead of speaking his next question, Borlsover wrote it. "What is the time?"

The fingers dropped the pencil and moved three or four times across the paper.

Then, picking up the pencil, they wrote:

"Ten minutes before four. Put your book away, Eustace. Adrian mustn't find us working at this sort of thing. He doesn't know what to make of it, and I won't have poor old Adrian disturbed. *Au revoir*."

Adrian Borlsover awoke with a start.

"I've been dreaming again," he said; "such queer dreams of leaguered cities and forgotten towns. You were mixed up in this one, Eustace, though I can't remember how. Eustace, I want to warn you. Don't walk in doubtful paths. Choose your friends well. Your poor grandfather—"

A fit of coughing put an end to what he was saying, but Eustace saw that the hand was still writing. He managed unnoticed to draw the book away. "I'll light the gas," he said, "and ring for tea." On the other side of the bed curtain he saw the last sentences that had been written.

"It's too late, Adrian," he read. "We're friends already; aren't we, Eustace Borlsover?"

On the following day Eustace Borlsover left. He thought his uncle looked ill when he said good-by, and the old man spoke despondently of the failure his life had been.

"Nonsense, uncle!" said his nephew. "You have got over your difficulties in a way not one in a hundred thousand would have done. Every one marvels at your splendid perseverance in teaching your hand to take the place of your lost sight. To me it's been a revelation of the possibilities of education."

"Education," said his uncle dreamily, as if the word had started a new train of thought, "education is good so long as you know to whom and for what purpose you give it. But with the lower orders of men, the base and more sordid spirits, I have grave doubts as to its results. Well, good-by, Eustace, I may not see you again. You are a true Borlsover, with all the Borlsover faults. Marry, Eustace. Marry some good, sensible girl. And if by any chance I don't see you again, my will is at my solicitor's. I've not left you any legacy, because I know you're well provided for, but I thought you might like to have my books. Oh, and there's just one other thing. You know, before the end people often lose control over themselves and make absurd requests. Don't pay any attention to them, Eustace. Good-by!" and he held out his hand. Eustace took it. It remained in his a fraction of a second longer than he had expected, and gripped him with a virility that was surprising. There was, too, in its touch a subtle sense of intimacy.

"Why, uncle!" he said, "I shall see you alive and well for many long years to come."

Two months later Adrian Borlsover died.

II

Eustace Borlsover was in Naples at the time. He read the obituary notice in the *Morning Post* on the day announced for the funeral.

"Poor old fellow!" he said. "I wonder where I shall find room for all his books."

The question occurred to him again with greater force when three days later he found himself standing in the library at Borlsover Conyers, a huge room built for use, and not for beauty, in the year of Waterloo by a Borlsover who was an ardent admirer of the great Napoleon. It was arranged on the plan of many college libraries, with tall, projecting bookcases forming deep recesses of dusty silence, fit graves for the old hates of forgotten controversy, the dead passions of forgotten lives. At the end of the room, behind the bust of some unknown eighteenth-century divine, an ugly iron corkscrew stair led to a shelf-lined gallery. Nearly every shelf was full.

"I must talk to Saunders about it," said Eustace. "I suppose that it will be necessary to have the billiard-room fitted up with book cases."

The two men met for the first time after many weeks in the dining-room that evening.

"Hullo!" said Eustace, standing before the fire with his hands in his pockets. "How goes the world, Saunders? Why these dress togs?" He himself was wearing an old shooting-jacket. He did not believe in mourning, as he had told his uncle on his last visit; and though he usually went in for quiet-colored ties, he wore this evening one of an ugly red, in order to shock Morton the butler, and to make them thrash out the whole question of mourning for themselves in the servants' hall. Eustace was a true Borlsover. "The world," said Saunders, "goes the same as usual, confoundedly slow. The dress togs are accounted for by an invitation from Captain Lockwood to bridge."

"How are you getting there?"

"I've told your coachman to drive me in your carriage. Any objection?"

"Oh, dear me, no! We've had all things in common for far too many years for me to raise objections at this hour of the day."

"You'll find your correspondence in the library," went on Saunders. "Most of it I've seen to. There are a few private letters I haven't opened. There's also a box with a rat, or something, inside it that came by the evening post. Very likely it's the six-toed albino. I didn't look, because I didn't want to mess up my things but I should gather from the way it's jumping about that it's pretty hungry."

"Oh, I'll see to it," said Eustace, "while you and the Captain earn an honest penny."

Dinner over and Saunders gone, Eustace went into the library. Though the fire had been lit the room was by no means cheerful.

"We'll have all the lights on at any rate," he said, as he turned the switches. "And, Morton," he added, when the butler brought the coffee, "get me a screw-driver or something to undo this box. Whatever the animal is, he's kicking up the deuce of a row. What is it? Why are you dawdling?"

"If you please, sir, when the postman brought it he told me that they'd bored the holes in the lid at the post-office. There were no breathin' holes in the lid, sir, and they didn't want the animal to die. That is all, sir."

"It's culpably careless of the man, whoever he was," said Eustace, as he removed the screws, "packing an animal like this in a wooden box with no means of getting air. Confound it all! I meant to ask Morton to bring me a cage to put it in. Now I suppose I shall have to get one myself."

He placed a heavy book on the lid from which the screws had been removed, and went into the billiard-room. As he came back into the library with an empty cage in his hand he heard the sound of something falling, and then of something scuttling along the floor.

"Bother it! The beast's got out. How in the world am I to find it again in this library!"

To search for it did indeed seem hopeless. He tried to follow the sound of the scuttling in one of the recesses where the animal seemed to be running behind the books in the shelves, but it was impossible to locate it. Eustace resolved to go on quietly reading. Very likely the animal might gain confidence and show itself. Saunders seemed to have dealt in his usual methodical manner with most of the correspondence. There were still the private letters.

What was that? Two sharp clicks and the lights in the hideous candelabra that hung from the ceiling suddenly went out.

"I wonder if something has gone wrong with the fuse," said Eustace, as he went to the switches by the door. Then he stopped. There was a noise at the other end of the room, as if something was crawling up the iron corkscrew stair. "If it's gone into the gallery," he said, "well and good." He hastily turned on the lights, crossed the room, and climbed up the stair. But he could see nothing. His grandfather had placed a little gate at the top of the stair, so that children could run and romp in the gallery without fear of accident. This Eustace closed, and having considerably narrowed the circle of his search, returned to his desk by the fire.

How gloomy the library was! There was no sense of intimacy about the room. The few busts that an eighteenth-century Borlsover had brought back from the grand tour, might have been in keeping in the old library. Here they seemed out of place. They made the room feel cold, in spite of the heavy red damask curtains and great gilt cornices.

With a crash two heavy books fell from the gallery to the floor; then, as Borlsover looked, another and yet another.

"Very well; you'll starve for this, my beauty!" he said. "We'll do some little experiments on the metabolism of rats deprived of water. Go on! Chuck them down! I think I've got the upper hand." He turned once again to his correspondence. The letter was from the family solicitor. It spoke of his uncle's death and of the valuable collection of books that had been left to him in the will.

"There was one request," he read, "which certainly came as a surprise to me. As you know, Mr. Adrian Borlsover had left instructions that his body was to be buried in as simple a manner as possible at Eastbourne. He expressed a desire that there should be neither wreaths nor flowers of any kind, and hoped that his friends and relatives would not consider it necessary to wear mourning. The day before his death we received a letter canceling these instructions. He wished his body to be embalmed (he gave us the address of the man we were to employ—Pennifer, Ludgate Hill), with orders that his right hand was to be sent to you, stating that it was at your special request. The other arrangements as to the funeral remained unaltered."

"Good Lord!" said Eustace; "what in the world was the old boy driving at? And what in the name of all that's holy is that?"

Someone was in the gallery. Someone had pulled the cord attached to one of the blinds, and it had rolled up with a snap. Someone must be in the gallery, for a second blind did the same. Someone must be walking round the gallery, for one after the other the blinds sprang up, letting in the moonlight.

"I haven't got to the bottom of this yet," said Eustace, "but I will do before the night is very much older," and he hurried up the corkscrew stair. He had just got to the top when the lights went out a second time, and he heard again the scuttling along the floor. Quickly he stole on tiptoe in the dim moonshine in the direction of the noise, feeling as he went for one of the switches. His fingers touched the metal knob at last. He turned on the electric light.

About ten yards in front of him, crawling along the floor, was a man's hand. Eustace stared at it in utter astonishment. It was moving quickly, in the manner of a geometer caterpillar, the fingers humped up one moment, flattened out the next; the thumb appeared to give a crab-like motion to the whole. While he was looking, too surprised to stir, the hand disappeared round the corner Eustace ran forward. He no longer saw it, but he could hear it as it squeezed its way behind the books on one of the shelves. A heavy volume had been displaced. There was a gap in the row of books where it had got in. In his fear lest it should escape him again, he seized the first book that came to his hand and plugged it into the hole. Then, emptying two shelves of their contents, he took the wooden boards and propped them up in front to make his barrier doubly sure.

"I wish Saunders was back," he said; "one can't tackle this sort of thing alone." It was after eleven, and there seemed little likelihood of Saunders returning before twelve. He did not dare to leave the shelf unwatched, even to run downstairs to ring the bell. Morton the butler often used to come round about eleven to see that the windows were fastened, but he might not come. Eustace was thoroughly unstrung. At last he heard steps down below.

"Morton!" he shouted; "Morton!"

"Sir?"

"Has Mr. Saunders got back yet?"

"Not yet, sir."

"Well, bring me some brandy, and hurry up about it. I'm up here in the gallery, you duffer."

"Thanks," said Eustace, as he emptied the glass. "Don't go to bed yet, Morton. There are a lot of books that have fallen down by accident; bring them up and put them back in their shelves."

Morton had never seen Borlsover in so talkative a mood as on that night. "Here," said Eustace, when the books had been put back and dusted, "you might hold up these boards for me, Morton. That beast in the box got out, and I've been chasing it all over the place."

"I think I can hear it chawing at the books, sir. They're not valuable, I hope? I think that's the carriage, sir; I'll go and call Mr. Saunders."

It seemed to Eustace that he was away for five minutes, but it could hardly have been more than one when he returned with Saunders. "All right, Morton, you can go now. I'm up here, Saunders."

"What's all the row?" asked Saunders, as he lounged forward with his hands in his pockets. The luck had been with him all the evening. He was completely satisfied, both with himself and with Captain Lockwood's taste in wines. "What's the matter? You look to me to be in an absolute blue funk."

"That old devil of an uncle of mine," began Eustace—"oh, I can't explain it all. It's his hand that's been playing old Harry all the evening. But I've got it cornered behind these books. You've got to help me catch it."

"What's up with you, Eustace? What's the game?"

"It's no game, you silly idiot! If you don't believe me take out one of those books and put your hand in and feel."

"All right," said Saunders; "but wait till I've rolled up my sleeve. The accumulated dust of centuries, eh?" He took off his coat, knelt down, and thrust his arm along the shelf.

"There's something there right enough," he said. "It's got a funny stumpy end to it, whatever it is, and nips like a crab. Ah, no, you don't!" He pulled his hand out in a flash. "Shove in a book quickly. Now it can't get out."

"What was it?" asked Eustace.

"It was something that wanted very much to get hold of me. I felt what seemed like a thumb and forefinger. Give me some brandy."

"How are we to get it out of there?"

"What about a landing net?"

"No good. It would be too smart for us. I tell you, Saunders, it can cover the ground far faster than I can walk. But I think I see how we can manage it. The two books at the end of the shelf are big ones that go right back against the wall. The others are very thin. I'll take out one at a time, and you slide the rest along until we have it squashed between the end two."

It certainly seemed to be the best plan. One by one, as they took out the books, the space behind grew smaller and smaller. There was something in it that was certainly very much alive. Once they caught sight of fingers pressing outward for a way of escape. At last they had it pressed between the two big books.

"There's muscle there, if there isn't flesh and blood," said Saunders, as he held them together. "It seems to be a hand right enough, too. I suppose this is a sort of infectious hallucination. I've read about such cases before."

"Infectious fiddlesticks!" said Eustace, his face white with anger; "bring the thing downstairs. We'll get it back into the box."

It was not altogether easy, but they were successful at last. "Drive in the screws," said Eustace, "we won't run any risks. Put the box in this old desk of mine. There's nothing in it that I want. Here's the key. Thank goodness, there's nothing wrong with the lock."

"Quite a lively evening," said Saunders. "Now let's hear more about your uncle."

They sat up together until early morning. Saunders had no desire for sleep. Eustace was trying to explain and to forget: to conceal from himself a fear that he had never felt before—the fear of walking alone down the long corridor to his bedroom.

III

"Whatever it was," said Eustace to Saunders on the following morning, "I propose that we drop the subject. There's nothing to keep us here for the next ten days. We'll motor up to the Lakes and get some climbing."

"And see nobody all day, and sit bored to death with each other every night. Not for me thanks. Why not run up to town? Run's the exact word in this case, isn't it? We're both in such a blessed funk. Pull yourself together Eustace, and let's have another look at the hand."

"As you like," said Eustace; "there's the key." They went into the library and opened the desk. The box was as they had left it on the previous night.

"What are you waiting for?" asked Eustace.

"I am waiting for you to volunteer to open the lid. However, since you seem to funk it, allow me. There doesn't seem to be the likelihood of any rumpus this morning, at all events." He opened the lid and picked out the hand.

"Cold?" asked Eustace.

"Tepid. A bit below blood-heat by the feel. Soft and supple too. If it's the embalming, it's a sort of embalming I've never seen before. Is it your uncle's hand?"

"Oh, yes, it's his all right," said Eustace. "I should know those long thin fingers anywhere. Put it back in the box, Saunders. Never mind about the screws. I'll lock the desk, so that there'll be no chance of its getting out. We'll compromise by motoring up to town for a week. If we get off soon after lunch we ought to be at Grantham or Stamford by night."

"Right," said Saunders; "and to-morrow—Oh, well, by to-morrow we shall have forgotten all about this beastly thing."

If when the morrow came they had not forgotten, it was certainly true that at the end of the week they were able to tell a very vivid ghost story at the little supper Eustace gave on Hallow E'en.

"You don't want us to believe that it's true, Mr. Borlsover? How perfectly awful!"

"I'll take my oath on it, and so would Saunders here; wouldn't you, old chap?"

"Any number of oaths," said Saunders. "It was a long thin hand, you know, and it gripped me just like that."

"Don't Mr. Saunders! Don't! How perfectly horrid! Now tell us another one, do. Only a really creepy one, please!"

* * * *

"Here's a pretty mess!" said Eustace on the following day as he threw a letter across the table to Saunders. "It's your affair, though. Mrs. Merrit, if I understand it, gives a month's notice."

"Oh, that's quite absurd on Mrs. Merrit's part," Saunders replied. "She doesn't know what she's talking about. Let's see what she says."

He read:

"Dear Sir,

"This is to let you know that I must give you a month's notice as from Tuesday the 13th. For a long time I've felt the place too big for me, but when Jane Parfit, and Emma Laidlaw go off with scarcely as much as an 'if you please,' after frightening the wits out of the other girls, so that they can't turn out a room by themselves or walk alone down the stairs for fear of treading on half-frozen toads or hearing it run along the passages at night, all I can say is that it's no place for me. So I must ask you, Mr. Borlsover, sir, to find a new housekeeper that has no objection to large and lonely houses, which some people do say, not that I believe them for a minute, my poor mother always having been a Wesleyan, are haunted.

"Yours faithfully, Elizabeth Merrit.

"P.S.—I should be obliged if you would give my respects to Mr. Saunders. I hope that he won't run no risks with his cold."

"Saunders," said Eustace, "you've always had a wonderful way with you in dealing with servants. You mustn't let poor old Merrit go."

"Of course she shan't go," said Saunders. "She's probably only angling for a rise in salary. I'll write to her this morning."

"No; there's nothing like a personal interview. We've had enough of town. We'll go back to-morrow, and you must work your cold for all it's worth. Don't forget that it's got on to the chest, and will require weeks of feeding up and nursing."

"All right. I think I can manage Mrs. Merrit."

But Mrs. Merrit was more obstinate than he had thought. She was very sorry to hear of Mr. Saunders's cold, and how he lay awake all night in London coughing; very sorry indeed. She'd change his room for him gladly, and get the south room aired. And wouldn't he have a basin of hot bread and milk last thing at night? But she was afraid that she would have to leave at the end of the month.

"Try her with an increase of salary," was the advice of Eustace.

It was no use. Mrs. Merrit was obdurate, though she knew of a Mrs. Handyside who had been housekeeper to Lord Gargrave, who might be glad to come at the salary mentioned.

"What's the matter with the servants, Morton?" asked Eustace that evening when he brought the coffee into the library. "What's all this about Mrs. Merrit wanting to leave?"

"If you please, sir, I was going to mention it myself. I have a confession to make, sir. When I found your note asking me to open that desk and take out the box with the rat, I broke the lock as you told me, and was glad to do it, because I could hear the animal in the box making a great noise, and I thought it wanted food. So I took out the box, sir, and got a cage, and was going to transfer it, when the animal got away."

"What in the world are you talking about? I never wrote any such note."

"Excuse me, sir, it was the note I picked up here on the floor on the day you and Mr. Saunders left. I have it in my pocket now."

It certainly seemed to be in Eustace's handwriting. It was written in pencil, and began somewhat abruptly.

"Get a hammer, Morton," he read, "or some other tool, and break open the lock in the old desk in the library. Take out the box that is inside. You need not do anything else. The lid is already open. Eustace Borlsover."

"And you opened the desk?"

"Yes, sir; and as I was getting the cage ready the animal hopped out."

"What animal?"

"The animal inside the box, sir."

"What did it look like?"

"Well, sir, I couldn't tell you," said Morton nervously; "my back was turned, and it was halfway down the room when I looked up."

"What was its color?" asked Saunders; "black?"

"Oh, no, sir, a grayish white. It crept along in a very funny way, sir. I don't think it had a tail."

"What did you do then?"

"I tried to catch it, but it was no use. So I set the rat-traps and kept the library shut. Then that girl Emma Laidlaw left the door open when she was cleaning, and I think it must have escaped."

"And you think it was the animal that's been frightening the maids?"

"Well, no, sir, not quite. They said it was—you'll excuse me, sir—a hand that they saw. Emma trod on it once at the bottom of the stairs. She thought then it was a half-frozen toad, only white. And then Parfit was washing up the dishes in the scullery. She wasn't thinking about anything in particular. It was close on dusk. She took her hands out of the water and was drying them absent-minded like on the roller towel, when she found that she was drying someone else's hand as well, only colder than hers."

"What nonsense!" exclaimed Saunders.

"Exactly, sir; that's what I told her; but we couldn't get her to stop."

"You don't believe all this?" said Eustace, turning suddenly towards the butler.

"Me, sir? Oh, no, sir! I've not seen anything."

"Nor heard anything?"

"Well, sir, if you must know, the bells do ring at odd times, and there's nobody there when we go; and when we go round to draw the blinds of a night, as often as not somebody's been there before us. But as I says to Mrs. Merrit, a young monkey might do wonderful things, and we all know that Mr. Borlsover has had some strange animals about the place."

"Very well, Morton, that will do."

"What do you make of it?" asked Saunders when they were alone. "I mean of the letter he said you wrote."

"Oh, that's simple enough," said Eustace. "See the paper it's written on? I stopped using that years ago, but there were a few odd sheets and envelopes left in the old desk. We never fastened up the lid of the box before locking it in. The hand got out, found a pencil, wrote this note, and shoved it through a crack on to the floor where Morton found it. That's plain as daylight."

"But the hand couldn't write?"

"Couldn't it? You've not seen it do the things I've seen," and he told Saunders more of what had happened at Eastbourne.

"Well," said Saunders, "in that case we have at least an explanation of the legacy. It was the hand which wrote unknown to your uncle that letter to your solicitor, bequeathing itself to you. Your uncle had no more to do with that request than I. In fact, it would seem that he had some idea of this automatic writing, and feared it."

"Then if it's not my uncle, what is it?"

"I suppose some people might say that a disembodied spirit had got your uncle to educate and prepare a little body for it. Now it's got into that little body and is off on its own."

"Well, what are we to do?"

"We'll keep our eyes open," said Saunders, "and try to catch it. If we can't do that, we shall have to wait till the bally clockwork runs down. After all, if it's flesh and blood, it can't live for ever."

For two days nothing happened. Then Saunders saw it sliding down the banister in the hall. He was taken unawares, and lost a full second before he started in pursuit, only to find that the thing had escaped him. Three days later, Eustace, writing alone in the library at night, saw it sitting on an open book at the other end of the room. The fingers crept over the page, feeling the print as if it were reading; but before he had time to get up from his seat, it had taken the alarm and was pulling itself up the curtains. Eustace watched it grimly as it hung on to the cornice with three fingers, flicking thumb and forefinger at him in an expression of scornful derision.

"I know what I'll do," he said. "If I only get it into the open I'll set the dogs on to it."

He spoke to Saunders of the suggestion.

"It's jolly good idea," he said; "only we won't wait till we find it out of doors. We'll get the dogs. There are the two terriers and the under-keeper's Irish mongrel that's on to rats like a flash. Your spaniel has not got spirit enough for this sort of game." They brought the dogs into the house, and the keeper's Irish mongrel chewed up the slippers, and the terriers tripped up Morton as he waited at table; but all three were welcome. Even false security is better than no security at all.

For a fortnight nothing happened. Then the hand was caught, not by the dogs, but by Mrs. Merrit's gray parrot. The bird was in the habit of periodically removing the pins that kept its seed and water tins in place, and of escaping through the holes in the side of the cage. When once at liberty Peter would show no inclination to return, and would often be about the house for days. Now, after six consecutive weeks of captivity, Peter had again discovered a new means of unloosing his bolts and was at large, exploring the tapestried forests of the curtains and singing songs in praise of liberty from cornice and picture rail.

"It's no use your trying to catch him," said Eustace to Mrs. Merrit, as she came into the study one afternoon towards dusk with a step-ladder. "You'd much better leave Peter alone. Starve him into surrender, Mrs. Merrit, and don't leave bananas and seed about for him to peck at when he fancies he's hungry. You're far too soft-hearted."

"Well, sir, I see he's right out of reach now on that picture rail, so if you wouldn't mind closing the door, sir, when you leave the room, I'll bring his cage in to-night and put some meat inside it. He's that fond of meat, though it does make him pull out his feathers to suck the quills. They *do* say that if you cook—"

"Never mind, Mrs. Merrit," said Eustace, who was busy writing. "That will do; I'll keep an eye on the bird."

There was silence in the room, unbroken but for the continuous whisper of his pen.

"Scratch poor Peter," said the bird. "Scratch poor old Peter!"

"Be quiet, you beastly bird!"

"Poor old Peter! Scratch poor Peter, do."

"I'm more likely to wring your neck if I get hold of you." He looked up at the picture rail, and there was the hand holding on to a hook with three fingers, and slowly scratching the head of the parrot with the fourth. Eustace ran to the bell and pressed it hard; then across to the window, which he closed with a bang. Frightened by the noise the parrot shook its wings preparatory to flight, and as it did so the fingers of the hand got hold of it by the throat. There was a shrill scream from Peter as he fluttered across the room, wheeling round in circles that ever descended, borne down under the weight that clung to him. The bird dropped at last quite suddenly, and Eustace saw fingers and feathers rolled into an inextricable mass on the floor. The struggle abruptly ceased as finger and thumb squeezed the neck; the bird's eyes rolled up to show the whites, and there was a faint, half-choked gurgle. But before the fingers had time to loose their hold, Eustace had them in his own.

"Send Mr. Saunders here at once," he said to the maid who came in answer to the bell. "Tell him I want him immediately."

Then he went with the hand to the fire. There was a ragged gash across the back where the bird's beak had torn it, but no blood oozed from the wound. He noticed with disgust that the nails had grown long and discolored.

"I'll burn the beastly thing," he said. But he could not burn it. He tried to throw it into the flames, but his own hands, as if restrained by some old primitive feeling, would not let him. And so Saunders found him pale and irresolute, with the hand still clasped tightly in his fingers.

"I've got it at last," he said in a tone of triumph.

"Good; let's have a look at it."

"Not when it's loose. Get me some nails and a hammer and a board of some sort."

"Can you hold it all right?"

"Yes, the thing's quite limp; tired out with throttling poor old Peter, I should say."

"And now," said Saunders when he returned with the things, "what are we going to do?"

"Drive a nail through it first, so that it can't get away; then we can take our time over examining it."

"Do it yourself," said Saunders. "I don't mind helping you with guinea-pigs occasionally when there's something to be learned; partly because I don't fear a guinea-pig's revenge. This thing's different."

"All right, you miserable skunk. I won't forget the way you've stood by me."

He took up a nail, and before Saunders had realised what he was doing had driven it through the hand, deep into the board.

"Oh, my aunt," he giggled hysterically, "look at it now," for the hand was writhing in agonized contortions, squirming and wriggling upon the nail like a worm upon the hook.

"Well," said Saunders, "you've done it now. I'll leave you to examine it."

"Don't go, in heaven's name. Cover it up, man, cover it up! Shove a cloth over it! Here!" and he pulled off the antimacassar from the back of a chair and wrapped the board in it. "Now get the keys from my pocket and open the safe. Chuck the other things out. Oh, Lord, it's getting itself into frightful knots! and open it quick!" He threw the thing in and banged the door.

"We'll keep it there till it dies," he said. "May I burn in hell if I ever open the door of that safe again."

* * * *

Mrs. Merrit departed at the end of the month. Her successor certainly was more successful in the management of the servants. Early in her rule she declared that she would stand no nonsense, and gossip soon withered and died. Eustace Borlsover went back to his old way of life. Old habits crept over and covered his new experience. He was, if anything, less morose, and showed a greater inclination to take his natural part in country society.

"I shouldn't be surprised if he marries one of these days," said Saunders. "Well, I'm in no hurry for such an event. I know Eustace far too well for the future Mrs. Borlsover to like me It will be the same old story again: a long friendship slowly made—marriage—and a long friendship quickly forgotten."

IV

But Eustace Borlsover did not follow the advice of his uncle and marry. He was too fond of old slippers and tobacco. The cooking, too, under Mrs. Handyside's management was excellent, and she seemed, too, to have a heaven-sent faculty in knowing when to stop dusting.

Little by little the old life resumed its old power. Then came the burglary. The men, it was said, broke into the house by way of the conservatory. It was really little more than an attempt, for they only succeeded in carrying away a few pieces of plate from the pantry. The safe in the study was certainly found open and empty, but, as Mr. Borlsover informed the police inspector, he had kept nothing of value in it during the last six months.

"Then you're lucky in getting off so easily, sir," the man replied. "By the way they have gone about their business, I should say they were experienced cracksmen. They must have caught the alarm when they were just beginning their evening's work."

"Yes," said Eustace, "I suppose I am lucky."

"I've no doubt," said the inspector, "that we shall be able to trace the men. I've said that they must have been old hands at the game. The way they got in and opened the safe shows that. But there's one little thing that puzzles me. One of them was careless enough not to wear gloves, and I'm bothered if I know what he was trying to do. I've traced his finger-marks on the new varnish on the window sashes in every one of the downstairs rooms. They are very distinct ones too."

"Right hand or left, or both?" asked Eustace.

"Oh, right every time. That's the funny thing. He must have been a foolhardy fellow, and I rather think it was him that wrote that." He took out a slip of paper from his pocket. "That's what he wrote, sir. 'I've got out, Eustace Borlsover, but I'll be back before long.' Some gaol bird just escaped, I suppose. It will make it all the easier for us to trace him. Do you know the writing, sir?"

"No," said Eustace; "it's not the writing of anyone I know."

"I'm not going to stay here any longer," said Eustace to Saunders at luncheon. "I've got on far better during the last six months than ever I expected, but I'm not going to run the risk of seeing that thing again. I shall go up to town this afternoon. Get Morton to put my things together, and join me with the car at Brighton on the day after to-morrow. And bring the proofs of those two papers with you. We'll run over them together."

"How long are you going to be away?"

"I can't say for certain, but be prepared to stay for some time. We've stuck to work pretty closely through the summer, and I for one need a holiday. I'll engage the rooms at Brighton. You'll find it best to break the journey at Hitchin. I'll wire to you there at the Crown to tell you the Brighton address."

The house he chose at Brighton was in a terrace. He had been there before. It was kept by his old college gyp, a man of discreet silence, who was admirably partnered by an excellent cook. The rooms were on the first floor. The two bedrooms were at the back, and opened out of each other. "Saunders can have the smaller one, though it is the only one with a fireplace," he said. "I'll stick to the larger of the two, since it's got a bathroom adjoining. I wonder what time he'll arrive with the car."

Saunders came about seven, cold and cross and dirty. "We'll light the fire in the dining-room," said Eustace, "and get Prince to unpack some of the things while we are at dinner. What were the roads like?"

"Rotten; swimming with mud, and a beastly cold wind against us all day. And this is July. Dear old England!"

"Yes," said Eustace, "I think we might do worse than leave dear old England for a few months."

They turned in soon after twelve.

"You oughtn't to feel cold, Saunders," said Eustace, "when you can afford to sport a great cat-skin lined coat like this. You do yourself very well, all things considered. Look at those gloves, for instance. Who could possibly feel cold when wearing them?"

"They are far too clumsy though for driving. Try them on and see," and he tossed them through the door on to Eustace's bed, and went on with his unpacking. A minute later he heard a shrill cry of terror. "Oh, Lord," he heard, "it's in the glove! Quick, Saunders, quick!" Then came a smacking thud. Eustace had thrown it from him. "I've chucked it into the bathroom," he gasped, "it's hit the wall and fallen into the bath. Come now if you want to help." Saunders, with a lighted candle in his hand, looked over the edge of the bath. There it was, old and maimed, dumb and blind, with a ragged hole in the middle, crawling, staggering, trying to creep up the slippery sides, only to fall back helpless.

"Stay there," said Saunders. "I'll empty a collar box or something, and we'll jam it in. It can't get out while I'm away."

"Yes, it can," shouted Eustace. "It's getting out now. It's climbing up the plug chain. No, you brute, you filthy brute, you don't! Come back, Saunders, it's getting away from me. I can't hold it; it's all slippery. Curse its claw! Shut the window, you idiot! The top too, as well as the bottom. You utter idiot! It's got out!" There was the sound of something dropping on to the hard flagstones below, and Eustace fell back fainting.

* * * *

For a fortnight he was ill.

"I don't know what to make of it," the doctor said to Saunders. "I can only suppose that Mr. Borlsover has suffered some great emotional shock. You had better let me send someone to help you nurse him. And by all means indulge that whim of his never to be left alone in the dark. I would keep a light burning all night if I were you. But he *must* have more fresh air. It's perfectly absurd this hatred of open windows."

Eustace, however, would have no one with him but Saunders. "I don't want the other men," he said. "They'd smuggle it in somehow. I know they would."

"Don't worry about it, old chap. This sort of thing can't go on indefinitely. You know I saw it this time as well as you. It wasn't half so active. It won't go on living much longer, especially after that fall. I heard it hit the flags myself. As soon as you're a bit stronger we'll leave this place; not bag and baggage, but with only the clothes on our backs, so that it won't be able to hide anywhere. We'll escape it that way. We won't give any address, and we won't have any parcels sent after us. Cheer up, Eustace! You'll be well enough to leave in a day or two. The doctor says I can take you out in a chair to-morrow."

"What have I done?" asked Eustace. "Why does it come after me? I'm no worse than other men. I'm no worse than you, Saunders; you know I'm not. It was you who were at the bottom of that dirty business in San Diego, and that was fifteen years ago."

"It's not that, of course," said Saunders. "We are in the twentieth century, and even the parsons have dropped the idea of your old sins finding you out. Before you caught the hand in the library it was filled with pure malevolence—to you and all mankind. After you spiked it through with that nail it naturally forgot about other people, and concentrated its attention on you. It was shut up in the safe, you know, for nearly six months. That gives plenty of time for thinking of revenge."

Eustace Borlsover would not leave his room, but he thought that there might be something in Saunders's suggestion to leave Brighton without notice. He began rapidly to regain his strength.

"We'll go on the first of September," he said.

* * * *

The evening of August 31st was oppressively warm. Though at midday the windows had been wide open, they had been shut an hour or so before dusk. Mrs. Prince had long since ceased to wonder at the strange habits of the gentlemen on the first floor. Soon after their arrival she had been told to take down the heavy window curtains in the two bedrooms, and day by day the rooms had seemed to grow more bare. Nothing was left lying about.

"Mr. Borlsover doesn't like to have any place where dirt can collect," Saunders had said as an excuse. "He likes to see into all the corners of the room."

"Couldn't I open the window just a little?" he said to Eustace that evening. "We're simply roasting in here, you know."

"No, leave well alone. We're not a couple of boarding-school misses fresh from a course of hygiene lectures. Get the chessboard out."

They sat down and played. At ten o'clock Mrs. Prince came to the door with a note. "I am sorry I didn't bring it before," she said, "but it was left in the letter-box."

"Open it, Saunders, and see if it wants answering."

It was very brief. There was neither address nor signature.

"Will eleven o'clock to-night be suitable for our last appointment?"

"Who is it from?" asked Borlsover.

"It was meant for me," said Saunders. "There's no answer, Mrs. Prince," and he put the paper into his pocket. "A dunning letter from a tailor; I suppose he must have got wind of our leaving."

It was a clever lie, and Eustace asked no more questions. They went on with their game.

On the landing outside Saunders could hear the grandfather's clock whispering the seconds, blurting out the quarter-hours.

"Check!" said Eustace. The clock struck eleven. At the same time there was a gentle knocking on the door; it seemed to come from the bottom panel.

"Who's there?" asked Eustace.

There was no answer.

"Mrs. Prince, is that you?"

"She is up above," said Saunders; "I can hear her walking about the room."

"Then lock the door; bolt it too. Your move, Saunders."

While Saunders sat with his eyes on the chessboard, Eustace walked over to the window and examined the fastenings. He did the same in Saunders's room and the bathroom. There were no doors between the three rooms, or he would have shut and locked them too.

"Now, Saunders," he said, "don't stay all night over your move. I've had time to smoke one cigarette already. It's bad to keep an invalid waiting. There's only one possible thing for you to do. What was that?"

"The ivy blowing against the window. There, it's your move now, Eustace."

"It wasn't the ivy, you idiot. It was someone tapping at the window," and he pulled up the blind. On the outer side of the window, clinging to the sash, was the hand.

"What is it that it's holding?"

"It's a pocket-knife. It's going to try to open the window by pushing back the fastener with the blade."

"Well, let it try," said Eustace. "Those fasteners screw down; they can't be opened that way. Anyhow, we'll close the shutters. It's your move, Saunders. I've played."

But Saunders found it impossible to fix his attention on the game. He could not understand Eustace, who seemed all at once to have lost his fear. "What do you say to some wine?" he asked. "You seem to be taking things coolly, but I don't mind confessing that I'm in a blessed funk."

"You've no need to be. There's nothing supernatural about that hand, Saunders. I mean it seems to be governed by the laws of time and space. It's not the sort of thing that vanishes into thin air or slides through oaken doors. And since that's so, I defy it to get in here. We'll leave the place in the morning. I for one have bottomed the depths of fear. Fill your glass, man! The windows are all shuttered, the door is locked and bolted. Pledge me my uncle Adrian! Drink, man! What are you waiting for?"

Saunders was standing with his glass half raised. "It can get in," he said hoarsely; "it can get in! We've forgotten. There's the fireplace in my bedroom. It will come down the chimney."

"Quick!" said Eustace, as he rushed into the other room; "we haven't a minute to lose. What can we do? Light the fire, Saunders. Give me a match, quick!"

"They must be all in the other room. I'll get them."

"Hurry, man, for goodness' sake! Look in the bookcase! Look in the bathroom! Here, come and stand here; I'll look."

"Be quick!" shouted Saunders. "I can hear something!"

"Then plug a sheet from your bed up the chimney. No, here's a match." He had found one at last that had slipped into a crack in the floor.

"Is the fire laid? Good, but it may not burn. I know—the oil from that old reading-lamp and this cotton-wool. Now the match, quick! Pull the sheet away, you fool! We don't want it now."

There was a great roar from the grate as the flames shot up. Saunders had been a fraction of a second too late with the sheet. The oil had fallen on to it. It, too, was burning.

"The whole place will be on fire!" cried Eustace, as he tried to beat out the flames with a blanket. "It's no good! I can't manage it. You must open the door, Saunders, and get help."

Saunders ran to the door and fumbled with the bolts. The key was stiff in the lock.

"Hurry!" shouted Eustace; "the whole place is ablaze!"

The key turned in the lock at last. For half a second Saunders stopped to look back. Afterwards he could never be quite sure as to what he had seen, but at the time he thought that something black and charred was creeping slowly, very slowly, from the mass of flames towards Eustace Borlsover. For a moment he thought of returning to his friend, but the noise and the smell of the burning sent him running down the passage crying, "Fire! Fire!" He rushed to the telephone to summon help, and then back to the bathroom—he should have thought of that before—for water. As he burst open the bedroom door there came a scream of terror which ended suddenly, and then the sound of a heavy fall.

WHAT WAS IT?,
by Fitz-James O'Brien

It is, I confess, with considerable diffidence, that I approach the strange narrative which I am about to relate. The events which I purpose detailing are of so extraordinary a character that I am quite prepared to meet with an unusual amount of incredulity and scorn. I accept all such beforehand. I have, I trust, the literary courage to face unbelief. I have, after mature consideration resolved to narrate, in as simple and straightforward a manner as I can compass, some facts that passed under my observation, in the month of July last, and which, in the annals of the mysteries of physical science, are wholly unparalleled.

I live at No. — Twenty-sixth Street, in New York. The house is in some respects a curious one. It has enjoyed for the last two years the reputation of being haunted. It is a large and stately residence, surrounded by what was once a garden, but which is now only a green enclosure used for bleaching clothes. The dry basin of what has been a fountain, and a few fruit trees ragged and unpruned, indicate that this spot in past days was a pleasant, shady retreat, filled with fruits and flowers and the sweet murmur of waters.

The house is very spacious. A hall of noble size leads to a large spiral staircase winding through its center, while the various apartments are of imposing dimensions. It was built some fifteen or twenty years since by Mr. A——, the well-known New York merchant, who five years ago threw the commercial world into convulsions by a stupendous bank fraud. Mr. A——, as everyone knows, escaped to Europe, and died not long after, of a broken heart. Almost immediately after the news of his decease reached this country and was verified, the report spread in Twenty-sixth Street that No. — was haunted. Legal measures had dispossessed the widow of its former owner, and it was inhabited merely by a caretaker and his wife, placed there by the house agent into whose hands it had passed for the purposes of renting or sale. These people declared that they were troubled with unnatural noises. Doors were opened without any visible agency. The remnants of furniture scattered through the various rooms were, during the night, piled one upon the other by unknown hands. Invisible feet passed up and down the stairs in broad daylight, accompanied by the rustle of unseen silk dresses, and the gliding of viewless hands along the massive balusters. The caretaker and his wife declared they would live there no longer. The house agent laughed, dismissed them, and put others in their place. The noises and supernatural manifestations continued. The neighborhood caught up the story, and the house remained untenanted for three years. Several persons negotiated for it; but, somehow, always before the bargain was closed they heard the unpleasant rumors and declined to treat any further.

It was in this state of things that my landlady, who at that time kept a boarding-house in Bleecker Street, and who wished to move further up town, conceived the bold idea of renting No. — Twenty-sixth Street. Happening to have in her house rather a plucky and philosophical set of boarders, she laid her scheme before us, stating candidly everything she had heard respecting the ghostly qualities of the establishment to which she wished to remove us. With the exception of two timid persons,—a sea-captain and a returned Californian, who immediately gave notice that they would leave,—all of Mrs. Moffat's guests declared that they would accompany her in her chivalric incursion into the abode of spirits.

Our removal was effected in the month of May, and we were charmed with our new residence. The portion of Twenty-sixth Street where our house is situated, between Seventh and Eighth Avenues, is one of the pleasantest localities in New York. The gardens back of the houses, running down nearly to the Hudson, form, in the summer time, a perfect avenue of verdure. The air is pure and invigorating, sweeping, as it does, straight across the river from the Weehawken heights, and even the ragged garden which surrounded the house, although displaying on washing days rather too much clothesline, still gave us a piece of greensward to look at, and a cool retreat in the summer evenings, where we smoked our cigars in the dusk, and watched the fireflies flashing their dark lanterns in the long grass.

Of course we had no sooner established ourselves at No. — than we began to expect ghosts. We absolutely awaited their advent with eagerness. Our dinner conversation was supernatural. One of the boarders, who had purchased Mrs. Crowe's *Night Side of Nature* for his own private delectation, was regarded as a public enemy by the entire household for not having bought twenty copies. The man led a life of supreme wretchedness while he was reading this volume. A system of espionage was established, of which he was the victim. If he incautiously laid the book down for an instant and left the room, it was immediately seized and read aloud in secret places to a select few. I found myself a person of immense importance, it having leaked out that I was tolerably well versed in the history of supernaturalism, and had once written a story the foundation of which was a ghost. If a table or a wainscot panel happened to warp when we were assembled in the large drawing-room, there was an instant silence, and everyone was prepared for an immediate clanking of chains and a spectral form.

After a month of psychological excitement, it was with the utmost dissatisfaction that we were forced to acknowledge that nothing in the remotest degree approaching the supernatural had manifested itself. Once the black butler asseverated that his candle had been blown out by some invisible agency while he was undressing himself for the night; but as I had more than once discovered this colored gentleman in a condition when one candle must have appeared to him like two, thought it possible that, by going a step further in his potations, he might have reversed this phenomenon, and seen no candle at all where he ought to have beheld one.

Things were in this state when an accident took place so awful and inexplicable in its character that my reason fairly reels at the bare memory of the occurrence. It was the tenth of July. After dinner was over I repaired, with my friend Dr. Hammond, to the garden to smoke my evening pipe. Independent of certain mental sympathies which existed between the Doctor and myself, we were linked together by a vice. We both smoked opium. We knew each other's secret, and respected it. We enjoyed together that wonderful expansion of thought, that marvelous intensifying of the perceptive faculties, that boundless feeling of existence when we seem to have points of contact with the whole universe,—in short, that unimaginable spiritual bliss, which I would not surrender for a throne, and which I hope you, reader, will never—never taste.

Those hours of opium happiness which the Doctor and I spent together in secret were regulated with a scientific accuracy. We did not blindly smoke the drug of paradise, and leave our dreams to chance. While smoking, we carefully steered our conversation through the brightest and calmest channels of thought. We talked of the East, and endeavored to recall the magical panorama of its glowing scenery. We criticized the most sensuous poets,—those who painted life ruddy with health, brimming with passion, happy in the possession of youth and strength and beauty. If we talked of Shakespeare's *Tempest*, we lingered over Ariel, and avoided Caliban. Like the Guebers, we turned our faces to the East, and saw only the sunny side of the world.

This skillful coloring of our train of thought produced in our subsequent visions a corresponding tone. The splendors of Arabian fairyland dyed our dreams. We paced the narrow strip of grass with the tread and port of kings. The song of the *rana arborea*, while he clung to the bark of the ragged plum-tree, sounded like the strains of divine musicians. Houses, walls, and streets melted like rain clouds, and vistas of unimaginable glory stretched away before us. It was a rapturous companionship. We enjoyed the vast delight more perfectly because, even in our most ecstatic moments, we were conscious of each other's presence. Our pleasures, while individual, were still twin, vibrating and moving in musical accord.

On the evening in question, the tenth of July, the Doctor and myself drifted into an unusually metaphysical mood. We lit our large meerschaums, filled with fine Turkish tobacco, in the core of which burned a little black nut of opium, that, like the nut in the fairy tale, held within its narrow limits wonders beyond the reach of kings; we paced to and fro, conversing. A strange perversity dominated the currents of our thought. They would *not* flow through the sun-lit channels into which we strove to divert them. For some unaccountable reason, they constantly diverged into dark and lonesome beds, where a continual gloom brooded. It was in vain that, after our old fashion, we flung ourselves on the shores of the East, and talked of its gay bazaars, of the splendors of the time of Haroun, of harems and golden palaces. Black afreets continually arose from the depths of our talk, and expanded, like the one the fisherman released from the copper vessel, until they blotted everything bright from our vision. Insensibly, we yielded to the occult force that swayed us, and indulged in gloomy speculation. We had talked some time upon the proneness of the human mind to mysticism, and the almost universal love of the terrible, when Hammond suddenly said to me. "What do you consider to be the greatest element of terror?"

The question puzzled me. That many things were terrible, I knew. Stumbling over a corpse in the dark; beholding, as I once did, a woman floating down a deep and rapid river, with wildly lifted arms, and awful, upturned face, uttering, as she drifted, shrieks that rent one's heart while we, spectators, stood frozen at a window which overhung the river at a height of sixty feet, unable to make the slightest effort to save her, but dumbly watching her last supreme agony and her disappearance. A shattered wreck, with no life visible, encountered floating listlessly on the ocean, is a terrible object, for it suggests a huge terror, the proportions of which are veiled. But it now struck me, for the first time, that there must be one great and ruling embodiment of fear,—a King of Terrors, to which all others must succumb. What might it be? To what train of circumstances would it owe its existence?

"I confess, Hammond," I replied to my friend, "I never considered the subject before. That there must be one Something more terrible than any other thing, I feel. I cannot attempt, however, even the most vague definition."

"I am somewhat like you, Harry," he answered. "I feel my capacity to experience a terror greater than anything yet conceived by the human mind;—something combining in fearful and unnatural amalgamation hitherto supposed incompatible elements. The calling of the voices in Brockden Brown's novel of *Wieland* is awful; so is the picture of the Dweller of the Threshold, in Bulwer's Zanoni; but," he added, shaking his head gloomily, "there is something more horrible still than those."

"Look here, Hammond," I rejoined, "let us drop this kind of talk, for Heaven's sake! We shall suffer for it, depend on it."

"I don't know what's the matter with me to-night," he replied, "but my brain is running upon all sorts of weird and awful thoughts. I feel as if I could write a story like Hoffman, to-night, if I were only master of a literary style."

"Well, if we are going to be Hoffmanesque in our talk, I'm off to bed. Opium and nightmares should never be brought together. How sultry it is! Good-night, Hammond."

"Good-night, Harry. Pleasant dreams to you."

"To you, gloomy wretch, afreets, ghouls, and enchanters."

We parted, and each sought his respective chamber. I undressed quickly and got into bed, taking with me, according to my usual custom, a book, over which I generally read myself to sleep. I opened the volume as soon as I had laid my head upon the pillow, and instantly flung it to the other side of the room. It was Goudon's *History of Monsters*,—a curious French work, which I had lately imported from Paris, but which, in the state of mind I had then reached, was anything but an agreeable companion. I resolved to go to sleep at once; so, turning down my gas until nothing but a little blue point of light glimmered on the top of the tube, I composed myself to rest.

The room was in total darkness. The atom of gas that still remained alight did not illuminate a distance of three inches round the burner. I desperately drew my arm across my eyes, as if to shut out even the darkness, and tried to think of nothing. It was in vain. The confounded themes touched on by Hammond in the garden kept obtruding themselves on my brain. I battled against them. I erected ramparts of would-be blackness of intellect to keep them out. They still crowded upon me. While I was lying still as a corpse, hoping that by a perfect physical inaction I should hasten mental repose, an awful incident occurred. A Something dropped, as it seemed, from the ceiling, plumb upon my chest, and the next instant I felt two bony hands encircling my throat, endeavoring to choke me.

I am no coward, and am possessed of considerable physical strength. The suddenness of the attack, instead of stunning me, strung every nerve to its highest tension. My body acted from instinct, before my brain had time to realize the terrors of my position. In an instant I wound two muscular arms around the creature, and squeezed it, with all the strength of despair, against my chest. In a few seconds the bony hands that had fastened on my throat loosened their hold, and I was free to breathe once more. Then commenced a struggle of awful intensity. Immersed in the most profound darkness, totally ignorant of the nature of the Thing by which I was so suddenly attacked, finding my grasp slipping every moment, by reason, it seemed to me, of the entire nakedness of my assailant, bitten with sharp teeth in the shoulder, neck, and chest, having every moment to protect my throat against a pair of sinewy, agile hands, which my utmost efforts could not confine,—these were a combination of circumstances to combat which required all the strength, skill, and courage that I possessed.

At last, after a silent, deadly, exhausting struggle, I got my assailant under by a series of incredible efforts of strength. Once pinned, with my knee on what I made out to be its chest, I knew that I was victor. I rested for a moment to breathe. I heard the creature beneath me panting in the darkness, and felt the violent throbbing of a heart. It was apparently as exhausted as I was; that was one comfort. At this moment I remembered that I usually placed under my pillow, before going to bed, a large yellow silk pocket handkerchief. I felt for it instantly; it was there. In a few seconds more I had, after a fashion, pinioned the creature's arms.

I now felt tolerably secure. There was nothing more to be done but to turn on the gas, and, having first seen what my midnight assailant was like, arouse the household. I will confess to being actuated by a certain pride in not giving the alarm before; I wished to make the capture alone and unaided.

Never losing my hold for an instant, I slipped from the bed to the floor, dragging my captive with me. I had but a few steps to make to reach the gas-burner; these I made with the greatest caution, holding the creature in a grip like a vice. At last I got within arm's length of the tiny speck of blue light which told me where the gas-burner lay. Quick as lightning I released my grasp with one hand and let on the full flood of light. Then I turned to look at my captive.

I cannot even attempt to give any definition of my sensations the instant after I turned on the gas. I suppose I must have shrieked with terror, for in less than a minute afterward my room was crowded with the inmates of the house. I shudder now as I think of that awful moment. *I saw nothing*! Yes; I had one arm firmly clasped round a breathing, panting, corporeal shape, my other hand gripped with all its strength a throat as warm, as apparently fleshy, as my own; and yet, with this living substance in my grasp, with its body pressed against my own, and all in the bright glare of a large jet of gas, I absolutely beheld nothing! Not even an outline, —a vapor!

I do not, even at this hour, realize the situation in which I found myself. I cannot recall the astounding incident thoroughly. Imagination in vain tries to compass the awful paradox.

It breathed. I felt its warm breath upon my cheek. It struggled fiercely. It had hands. They clutched me. Its skin was smooth, like my own. There it lay, pressed close up against me, solid as stone,—and yet utterly invisible!

I wonder that I did not faint or go mad on the instant. Some wonderful instinct must have sustained me; for, absolutely, in place of loosening my hold on the terrible Enigma, I seemed to gain an additional strength in my moment of horror, and tightened my grasp with such wonderful force that I felt the creature shivering with agony.

Just then Hammond entered my room at the head of the household. As soon as he beheld my face—which, I suppose, must have been an awful sight to look at—he hastened forward, crying, "Great heaven, Harry! what has happened?"

"Hammond! Hammond!" I cried, "come here. O, this is awful! I have been attacked in bed by something or other, which I have hold of; but I can't see it,—I can't see it!"

Hammond, doubtless struck by the unfeigned horror expressed in my countenance, made one or two steps forward with an anxious yet puzzled expression. A very audible titter burst from the remainder of my visitors. This suppressed laughter made me furious. To laugh at a human being in my position! It was the worst species of cruelty. *Now*, I can understand why the appearance of a man struggling violently, as it would seem, with an airy nothing, and calling for assistance against a vision, should have appeared ludicrous. *Then*, so great was my rage against the mocking crowd that had I the power I would have stricken them dead where they stood.

"Hammond! Hammond!" I cried again, despairingly, "for God's sake come to me. I can hold the—the thing but a short while longer. It is overpowering me. Help me! Help me!"

"Harry," whispered Hammond, approaching me, "you have been smoking too much opium."

"I swear to you, Hammond, that this is no vision," I answered, in the same low tone. "Don't you see how it shakes my whole frame with its struggles? If you don't believe me, convince yourself. Feel it,—touch it."

Hammond advanced and laid his hand in the spot I indicated. A wild cry of horror burst from him. He had felt it!

In a moment he had discovered somewhere in my room a long piece of cord, and was the next instant winding it and knotting it about the body of the unseen being that I clasped in my arms.

"Harry," he said, in a hoarse, agitated voice, for, though he preserved his presence of mind, he was deeply moved, "Harry, it's all safe now. You may let go, old fellow, if you're tired. The Thing can't move."

I was utterly exhausted, and I gladly loosed my hold.

Hammond stood holding the ends of the cord that bound the Invisible, twisted round his hand, while before him, self-supporting as it were, he beheld a rope laced and interlaced, and stretching tightly around a vacant space. I never saw a man look so thoroughly stricken with awe. Nevertheless his face expressed all the courage and determination which I knew him to possess. His lips, although white, were set firmly, and one could perceive at a glance that, although stricken with fear, he was not daunted.

The confusion that ensued among the guests of the house who were witnesses of this extraordinary scene between Hammond and myself,—who beheld the pantomime of binding this struggling Something,—who beheld me almost sinking from physical exhaustion when my task of jailer was over,—the confusion and terror that took possession of the bystanders, when they saw all this, was beyond description. The weaker ones fled from the apartment. The few who remained clustered near the door and could not be induced to approach Hammond and his Charge. Still incredulity broke out through their terror. They had not the courage to satisfy themselves, and yet they doubted. It was in vain that I begged of some of the men to come near and convince themselves by touch of the existence in that room of a living being which was invisible. They were incredulous, but did not dare to undeceive themselves. How could a solid, living, breathing body be invisible, they asked. My reply was this. I gave a sign to Hammond, and both of us—conquering our fearful repugnance to touch the invisible creature—lifted it from the ground, manacled as it was, and took it to my bed. Its weight was about that of a boy of fourteen.

"Now my friends," I said, as Hammond and myself held the creature suspended over the bed, "I can give you self-evident proof that here is a solid, ponderable body, which, nevertheless, you cannot see. Be good enough to watch the surface of the bed attentively."

I was astonished at my own courage in treating this strange event so calmly; but I had recovered from my first terror, and felt a sort of scientific pride in the affair, which dominated every other feeling.

The eyes of the bystanders were immediately fixed on my bed. At a given signal Hammond and I let the creature fall. There was a dull sound of a heavy body alighting on a soft mass. The timbers of the bed creaked. A deep impression marked itself distinctly on the pillow, and on the bed itself. The crowd who witnessed this gave a low cry, and rushed from the room. Hammond and I were left alone with our Mystery.

We remained silent for some time, listening to the low, irregular breathing of the creature on the bed, and watching the rustle of the bedclothes as it impotently struggled to free itself from confinement. Then Hammond spoke.

"Harry, this is awful."

"Ay, awful."

"But not unaccountable."

"Not unaccountable! What do you mean? Such a thing has never occurred since the birth of the world. I know not what to think, Hammond. God grant that I am not mad, and that this is not an insane fantasy!"

"Let us reason a little, Harry. Here is a solid body which we touch, but which we cannot see. The fact is so unusual that it strikes us with terror. Is there no parallel, though, for such a phenomenon? Take a piece of pure glass. It is tangible and transparent. A certain chemical coarseness is all that prevents its being so entirely transparent as to be totally invisible. It is not *theoretically impossible*, mind you, to make a glass which shall not reflect a single ray of light,—a glass so pure and homogeneous in its atoms that the rays from the sun will pass through it as they do through the air, refracted but not reflected. We do not see the air, and yet we feel it."

"That's all very well, Hammond, but these are inanimate substances. Glass does not breathe, air does not breathe. *This* thing has a heart that palpitates,—a will that moves it,—lungs that play, and inspire and respire."

"You forget the phenomena of which we have so often heard of late," answered the Doctor, gravely. "At the meetings called 'spirit circles,' invisible hands have been thrust into the hands of those persons round the table,—warm, fleshly hands that seemed to pulsate with mortal life."

"What? Do you think, then, that this thing is—"

"I don't know what it is," was the solemn reply; "but please the gods I will, with your assistance, thoroughly investigate it."

We watched together, smoking many pipes, all night long, by the bedside of the unearthly being that tossed and panted until it was apparently wearied out. Then we learned by the low, regular breathing that it slept.

The next morning the house was all astir. The boarders congregated on the landing outside my room, and Hammond and myself were lions. We had to answer a thousand questions as to the state of our extraordinary prisoner, for as yet not one person in the house except ourselves could be I induced to set foot in the apartment.

The creature was awake. This was evidenced by the convulsive manner in which the bedclothes were moved in its efforts to escape. There was something truly terrible in beholding, as it were, those second-hand indications of the terrible writhings and agonized struggles for liberty which themselves were invisible.

Hammond and myself had racked our brains during the long night to discover some means by which we might realize the shape and general appearance of the Enigma. As well as we could make out by passing our hands over the creature's form, its outlines and lineaments were human. There was a mouth; a round, smooth head without hair; a nose, which, however, was little elevated above the cheeks; and its hands and feet felt like those of a boy. At first we thought of placing the being on a smooth surface and tracing its outlines with chalk, as shoemakers trace the outline of the foot. This plan was given up as being of no value. Such an outline would give not the slightest idea of its conformation.

A happy thought struck me. We would take a cast of it in plaster of Paris. This would give us the solid figure, and satisfy all our wishes. But how to do it? The movements of the creature would disturb the setting of the plastic covering, and distort the mold. Another thought. Why not give it chloroform? It had respiratory organs,—that was evident by its breathing. Once reduced to a state of insensibility, we could do with it what we would. Doctor X—— was sent for; and after the worthy physician had recovered from the first shock of amazement, he proceeded to administer the chloroform. In three minutes afterward we were enabled to remove the fetters from the creature's body, and a modeler was busily engaged in covering the invisible form with the moist clay. In five minutes more we had a mold, and before evening a rough facsimile of the Mystery. It was shaped like a man—distorted, uncouth, and horrible, but still a man. It was small, not over four feet and some inches in height, and its limbs revealed a muscular development that was unparalleled. Its face surpassed in hideousness anything I had ever seen. Gustav Doré, or Callot, or Tony Johannot, never conceived anything so horrible. There is a face in one of the latter's illustrations to *Un Voyage où il vous plaira*, which somewhat approaches the countenance of this creature, but does not equal it. It was the physiognomy of what I should fancy a ghoul might be. It looked as if it was capable of feeding on human flesh.

Having satisfied our curiosity, and bound every one in the house to secrecy, it became a question what was to be done with our Enigma? It was impossible that we should keep such a horror in our house; it was equally impossible that such an awful being should be let loose upon the world. I confess that I would have gladly voted for the creature's destruction. But who would shoulder the responsibility? Who would undertake the execution of this horrible semblance of a human being? Day after day this question was deliberated gravely. The boarders all left the house. Mrs. Moffat was in despair, and threatened Hammond and myself with all sorts of legal penalties if we did not remove the Horror. Our answer was, "We will go if you like, but we decline taking this creature with us. Remove it yourself if you please. It appeared in your house. On you the responsibility rests." To this there was, of course, no answer. Mrs. Moffat could not obtain for love or money a person who would even approach the Mystery.

The most singular part of the affair was that we were entirely ignorant of what the creature habitually fed on. Everything in the way of nutriment that we could think of was placed before it, but was never touched. It was awful to stand by, day after day, and see the clothes toss, and hear the hard breathing, and know that it was starving.

Ten, twelve days, a fortnight passed, and it still lived. The pulsations of the heart, however, were daily growing fainter, and had now nearly ceased. It was evident that the creature was dying for want of sustenance. While this terrible life-struggle was going on, I felt miserable. I could not sleep. Horrible as the creature was, it was pitiful to think of the pangs it was suffering.

At last it died. Hammond and I found it cold and stiff one morning in the bed. The heart had ceased to beat, the lungs to inspire. We hastened to bury it in the garden. It was a strange funeral, the dropping of that viewless corpse into the damp hole. The cast of its form I gave to Doctor X——, who keeps it in his museum in Tenth Street.

As I am on the eve of a long journey from which I may not return, I have drawn up this narrative of an event the most singular that has ever come to my knowledge.

THE SHELL OF SENSE, by Olivia Howard Dunbar

It was intolerably unchanged, the dim, dark-toned room. In an agony of recognition my glance ran from one to another of the comfortable, familiar things that my earthly life had been passed among. Incredibly distant from it all as I essentially was. I noted sharply that the very gaps that I myself had left in my bookshelves still stood unfilled; that the delicate fingers of the ferns that I had tended were still stretched futilely toward the light; that the soft agreeable chuckle of my own little clock, like some elderly woman with whom conversation has become automatic, was undiminished.

Unchanged—or so it seemed at first. But there were certain trivial differences that shortly smote me. The windows were closed too tightly; for I had always kept the house very cool, although I had known that Theresa preferred warm rooms. And my work-basket was in disorder; it was preposterous that so small a thing should hurt me so. Then, for this was my first experience of the shadow-folded transition, the odd alteration of my emotions bewildered me. For at one moment the place seemed so humanly familiar, so distinctly my own proper envelope, that for love of it I could have laid my cheek against the wall; while in the next I was miserably conscious of strange new shrillnesses. How could they be endured—and had I ever endured them?—those harsh influences that I now perceived at the window; light and color so blinding that they obscured the form of the wind, tumult so discordant that one could scarcely hear the roses open in the garden below?

But Theresa did not seem to mind any of these things. Disorder, it is true, the dear child had never minded. She was sitting all this time at my desk—at *my* desk—occupied, I could only too easily surmise how. In the light of my own habits of precision it was plain that that sombre correspondence should have been attended to before; but I believe that I did not really reproach Theresa, for I knew that her notes, when she did write them, were perhaps less perfunctory than mine. She finished the last one as I watched her, and added it to the heap of black-bordered envelopes that lay on the desk. Poor girl! I saw now that they had cost her tears. Yet, living beside her day after day, year after year, I had never discovered what deep tenderness my sister possessed. Toward each other it had been our habit to display only a temperate affection, and I remember having always thought it distinctly fortunate for Theresa, since she was denied my happiness, that she could live so easily and pleasantly without emotions of the devastating sort.... And now, for the first time, I was really to behold her.... Could it be Theresa, after all, this tangle of subdued turbulences? Let no one suppose that it is an easy thing to bear, the relentlessly lucid understanding that I then first exercised; or that, in its first enfranchisement, the timid vision does not yearn for its old screens and mists.

Suddenly, as Theresa sat there, her head, filled with its tender thoughts of me, held in her gentle hands, I felt Allan's step on the carpeted stair outside. Theresa felt it, too,—but how? for it was not audible. She gave a start, swept the black envelopes out of sight, and pretended to be writing in a little book. Then I forgot to watch her any longer in my absorption in Allan's coming. It was he, of course, that

I was awaiting. It was for him that I had made this first lonely, frightened effort to return, to recover.... It was not that I had supposed he would allow himself to recognize my presence, for I had long been sufficiently familiar with his hard and fast denials of the invisible. He was so reasonable always, so sane—so blindfolded. But I had hoped that because of his very rejection of the ether that now contained me I could perhaps all the more safely, the more secretly, watch him, linger near him. He was near now, very near,—but why did Theresa, sitting there in the room that had never belonged to her, appropriate for herself his coming? It was so manifestly I who had drawn him, I whom he had come to seek.

The door was ajar. He knocked softly at it "Are you there, Theresa?" he called. He expected to find her, then, there in my room? I shrank back, fearing, almost, to stay.

"I shall have finished in a moment," Theresa told him, and he sat down to wait for her.

No spirit still unreleased can understand the pang that I felt with Allan sitting almost within my touch. Almost irresistibly the wish beset me to let him for an instant feel my nearness. Then I checked myself, remembering—oh, absurd, piteous human fears!—that my too unguarded closeness might alarm him. It was not so remote a time that I myself had known them, those blind, uncouth timidities. I came, therefore, somewhat nearer—but I did not touch him. I merely leaned toward him and with incredible softness whispered his name. That much I could not have forborne; the spell of life was still too strong in me.

But it gave him no comfort, no delight. "Theresa!" he called, in a voice dreadful with alarm—and in that instant the last veil fell, and desperately, scarce believingly, I beheld how it stood between them, those two.

She turned to him that gentle look of hers.

"Forgive me," came from him hoarsely. "But I had suddenly the most—unaccountable sensation. Can there be too many windows open? There is such a—chill—about."

"There are no windows open," Theresa assured him. "I took care to shut out the chill. You are not well, Allan!"

"Perhaps not." He embraced the suggestion. "And yet I feel no illness apart from this abominable sensation that persists—persists.... Theresa, you must tell me: do I fancy it, or do you, too, feel—something—strange here?"

"Oh, there is something very strange here," she half sobbed. "There always will be."

"Good heavens, child, I didn't mean that!" He rose and stood looking about him. "I know, of course, that you have your beliefs, and I respect them, but you know equally well that I have nothing of the sort! So—don't let us conjure up anything inexplicable."

I stayed impalpably, imponderably near him. Wretched and bereft though I was, I could not have left him while he stood denying me.

"What I mean," he went on, in his low, distinct voice, "is a special, an almost ominous sense of cold. Upon my soul, Theresa,"—he paused—"if I *were* superstitious, if I were a woman, I should probably imagine it to seem—a presence!"

He spoke the last word very faintly, but Theresa shrank from it nevertheless.

"*Don't* say that, Allan!" she cried out. "Don't think it, I beg of you! I've tried so hard myself not to think it—and you must help me. You know it is only perturbed, uneasy spirits that wander. With her it is quite different. She has always been so happy—she must still be."

I listened, stunned, to Theresa's sweet dogmatism. From what blind distances came her confident misapprehensions, how dense, both for her and for Allan, was the separating vapor!

Allan frowned. "Don't take me literally, Theresa," he explained; and I, who a moment before had almost touched him, now held myself aloof and heard him with a strange untried pity, new born in me. "I'm not speaking of what you call—spirits. It's something much more terrible." He allowed his head to sink heavily on his chest. "If I did not positively know that I had never done her any harm, I should suppose myself to be suffering from guilt, from remorse.... Theresa, you know better than I, perhaps. Was she content, always? Did she believe in me?"

"Believe in you?—when she knew you to be so good!—when you adored her!"

"She thought that? She said it? Then what in Heaven's name ails me?—unless it is all as you believe, Theresa, and she knows now what she didn't know then, poor dear, and minds—"

"Minds what? What do you mean, Allan?"

I, who with my perhaps illegitimate advantage saw so clear, knew that he had not meant to tell her: I did him that justice, even in my first jealousy. If I had not tortured him so by clinging near him, he would not have told her. But the moment came, and overflowed, and he did tell her—passionate, tumultuous story that it was. During all our life together, Allan's and mine, he had spared me, had kept me wrapped in the white cloak of an unblemished loyalty. But it would have been kinder, I now bitterly thought, if, like many husbands, he had years ago found for the story he now poured forth some clandestine listener; I should not have known. But he was faithful and good, and so he waited till I, mute and chained, was there to hear him. So well did I know him, as I thought, so thoroughly had he once been mine, that I saw it in his eyes, heard it in his voice, before the words came. And yet, when it came, it lashed me with the whips of an unbearable humiliation. For I, his wife, had not known how greatly he could love.

And that Theresa, soft little traitor, should, in her still way, have cared too! Where was the iron in her, I moaned within my stricken spirit, where the steadfastness? From the moment he bade her, she turned her soft little petals up to him—and my last delusion was spent. It was intolerable; and none the less so that in another moment she had, prompted by some belated thought of me, renounced him. Allan was hers, yet she put him from her; and it was my part to watch them both.

Then in the anguish of it all I remembered, awkward, untutored spirit that I was, that I now had the Great Recourse. Whatever human things were unbearable, I had no need to bear. I ceased, therefore, to make the effort that kept me with them. The pitiless poignancy was dulled, the sounds and the light ceased, the lovers faded from me, and again I was mercifully drawn into the dim, infinite spaces.

* * * *

There followed a period whose length I cannot measure and during which I was able to make no progress in the difficult, dizzying experience of release. "Earthbound" my jealousy relentlessly kept me. Though my two dear ones had forsworn each other, I could not trust them, for theirs seemed to me an affectation of a more than mortal magnanimity. Without a ghostly sentinel to prick them with sharp fears and recollections, who could believe that they would keep to it? Of the efficacy of my own vigilance, so long as I might choose to exercise it, I could have no doubt, for I had by this time come to have a dreadful exultation in the new power that lived in me. Repeated delicate experiment had taught me how a touch or a breath, a wish or a whisper, could control Allan's acts, could keep him from Theresa. I could manifest myself as palely, as transiently, as a thought. I could produce the merest necessary flicker, like the shadow of a just-opened leaf, on his trembling, tortured consciousness. And these unrealized perceptions of me he interpreted, as I had known that he would, as his soul's inevitable penance. He had come to believe that he had done evil in silently loving Theresa all these years, and it was my vengeance to allow him to believe this, to prod him ever to believe it afresh.

I am conscious that this frame of mind was not continuous in me. For I remember, too, that when Allan and Theresa were safely apart and sufficiently miserable I loved them as dearly as I ever had, more dearly perhaps. For it was impossible that I should not perceive, in my new emancipation, that they were, each of them, something more and greater than the two beings I had once ignorantly pictured them. For years they had practiced a selflessness of which I could once scarcely have conceived, and which even now I could only admire without entering into its mystery. While I had lived solely for myself, these two divine creatures had lived exquisitely for me. They had granted me everything, themselves nothing. For my undeserving sake their lives had been a constant torment of renunciation—a torment they had not sought to alleviate by the exchange of a single glance of understanding. There were even marvelous moments when, from the depths of my newly informed heart, I pitied them—poor creatures, who, withheld from the infinite solaces that I had come to know, were still utterly within that

Shell of sense
So frail, so piteously contrived for pain.

Within it, yes; yet exercising qualities that so sublimely transcended it. Yet the shy, hesitating compassion that thus had birth in me was far from being able to defeat the earlier, earthlier emotion. The two, I recognized, were in a sort of conflict; and I, regarding it, assumed that the conflict would never end; that for years, as Allan and Theresa reckoned time, I should be obliged to withhold myself from the great spaces and linger suffering, grudging, shamed, where they lingered.

* * * *

It can never have been explained, I suppose, what, to devitalized perception such as mine, the contact of mortal beings with each other appears to be. Once to have exercised this sense-freed perception is to realize that the gift of prophecy, although the subject of such frequent marvel, is no longer mysterious. The merest glance of our sensitive and uncloyed vision can detect the strength of the relation between two beings, and therefore instantly calculate its duration. If you see a heavy weight suspended from a slender string, you can know, without any wizardry, that in a few moments the string will snap; well, such, if you admit the analogy, is prophecy, is foreknowledge. And it was thus that I saw it with Theresa and Allan. For it was perfectly visible to me that they would very little longer have the strength to preserve, near each other, the denuded impersonal relation that they, and that I, behind them, insisted on; and that they would have to separate. It was my sister, perhaps the more sensitive, who first realized this. It had now become possible for me to observe them almost constantly, the effort necessary to visit them had so greatly diminished; so that I watched her, poor, anguished girl, prepare to leave him. I saw each reluctant movement that she made. I saw her eyes, worn from self-searching; I heard her step grown timid from inexplicable fears; I entered her very heart and heard its pitiful, wild beating. And still I did not interfere.

For at this time I had a wonderful, almost demoniacal sense of disposing of matters to suit my own selfish will. At any moment I could have checked their miseries, could have restored happiness and peace. Yet it gave me, and I could weep to admit it, a monstrous joy to know that Theresa thought she was leaving Allan of her own free intention, when it was I who was contriving, arranging, insisting.... And yet she wretchedly felt my presence near her; I am certain of that.

A few days before the time of her intended departure my sister told Allan that she must speak with him after dinner. Our beautiful old house branched out from a circular hall with great arched doors at either end; and it was through the rear doorway that always in summer, after dinner, we passed out into the garden adjoining. As usual, therefore, when the hour came, Theresa led the way. That dreadful daytime brilliance that in my present state I found so hard to endure was now becoming softer. A delicate, capricious twilight breeze danced inconsequently through languidly whispering leaves. Lovely pale flowers blossomed like little moons in the dusk, and over them the breath of mignonette hung heavily. It was a perfect place—and it had so long been ours, Allan's and mine. It made me restless and a little wicked that those two should be there together now.

For a little they walked about together, speaking of common, daily things. Then suddenly Theresa burst out:

"I am going away, Allan. I have stayed to do everything that needed to be done. Now your mother will be here to care for you, and it is time for me to go."

He stared at her and stood still. Theresa had been there so long, she so definitely, to his mind, belonged there. And she was, as I also had jealously known, so lovely there, the small, dark, dainty creature, in the old hall, on the wide staircases, in the garden.... Life there without Theresa, even the intentionally remote, the perpetually renounced Theresa—he had not dreamed of it, he could not, so suddenly, conceive of it.

"Sit here," he said, and drew her down beside him on a bench, "and tell me what it means, why you are going. Is it because of something that I have been—have done?"

She hesitated. I wondered if she would dare tell him. She looked out and away from him, and he waited long for her to speak.

The pale stars were sliding into their places. The whispering of the leaves was almost hushed. All about them it was still and shadowy and sweet. It was that wonderful moment when, for lack of a visible horizon, the not yet darkened world seems infinitely greater—a moment when anything can happen, anything be believed in. To me, watching, listening, hovering, there came a dreadful purpose and a dreadful courage. Suppose for one moment, Theresa should not only feel, but *see* me—would she dare to tell him then?

There came a brief space of terrible effort, all my fluttering, uncertain forces strained to the utmost. The instant of my struggle was endlessly long and the transition seemed to take place outside me—as one sitting in a train, motionless, sees the leagues of earth float by. And then, in a bright, terrible flash I knew I had achieved it—I had *attained visibility*. Shuddering, insubstantial, but luminously apparent, I stood there before them. And for the instant that I maintained the visible state I looked straight into Theresa's soul.

She gave a cry. And then, thing of silly, cruel impulses that I was, I saw what I had done. The very thing that I wished to avert I had precipitated. For Allan, in his sudden terror and pity, had bent and caught her in his arms. For the first time they were together; and it was I who had brought them.

Then, to his whispered urging to tell the reason of her cry, Theresa said:

"Frances was here. You did not see her, standing there, under the lilacs, with no smile on her face?"

"My dear, my dear!" was all that Allan said. I had so long now lived invisibly with them, he knew that she was right.

"I suppose you know what it means?" she asked him, calmly.

"Dear Theresa," Allan said, slowly, "if you and I should go away somewhere, could we not evade all this ghostliness? And will you come with me?"

"Distance would not banish her," my sister confidently asserted. And then she said, softly: "Have you thought what a lonely, awesome thing it must be to be so newly dead? Pity her, Allan. We who are warm and alive should pity her. She loves you still,—that is the meaning of it all, you know—and she wants us to understand that for that reason we must keep apart. Oh, it was so plain in her white face as she stood there. And you did not see her?"

"It was your face that I saw," Allan solemnly told her—oh, how different he had grown from the Allan that I had known!—"and yours is the only face that I shall ever see." And again he drew her to him.

She sprang from him. "You are defying her, Allan!" she cried. "And you must not. It is her right to keep us apart, if she wishes. It must be as she insists. I shall go, as I told you. And, Allan, I beg of you, leave me the courage to do as she demands!"

They stood facing each other in the deep dusk, and the wounds that I had dealt them gaped red and accusing. "We must pity her," Theresa had said. And as I remembered that extraordinary speech, and saw the agony in her face, and the greater agony in Allan's, there came the great irreparable cleavage between mortality and me. In a swift, merciful flame the last of my mortal emotions—gross and tenacious they must have been—was consumed. My cold grasp of Allan loosened and a new unearthly love of him bloomed in my heart.

I was now, however, in a difficulty with which my experience in the newer state was scarcely sufficient to deal. How could I make it plain to Allan and Theresa that I wished to bring them together, to heal the wounds that I had made?

Pityingly, remorsefully, I lingered near them all that night and the next day. And by that time had brought myself to the point of a great determination. In the little time that was left, before Theresa should be gone and Allan bereft and desolate, I saw the one way that lay open to me to convince them of my acquiescence in their destiny.

In the deepest darkness and silence of the next night I made a greater effort than it will ever be necessary for me to make again. When they think of me, Allan and Theresa, I pray now that they will recall what I did that night, and that my thousand frustrations and selfishnesses may shrivel and be blown from their indulgent memories.

Yet the following morning, as she had planned, Theresa appeared at breakfast dressed for her journey. Above in her room there were the sounds of departure. They spoke little during the brief meal, but when it was ended Allan said:

"Theresa, there is half an hour before you go. Will you come upstairs with me? I had a dream that I must tell you of."

"Allan!" She looked at him, frightened, but went with him. "It was of Frances you dreamed," she said, quietly, as they entered the library together.

"Did I say it was a dream? But I was awake—thoroughly awake. I had not been sleeping well, and I heard, twice, the striking of the clock. And as I lay there, looking out at the stars, and thinking—thinking of you, Theresa,—she came to me, stood there before me, in my room. It was no sheeted specter, you understand; it was Frances, literally she. In some inexplicable fashion I seemed to be aware that she wanted to make me know something, and I waited, watching her face. After a few moments it came. She did not speak, precisely. That is, I am sure I heard no sound. Yet the words that came from her were definite enough. She said: 'Don't let Theresa leave you. Take her and keep her.' Then she went away. Was that a dream?"

"I had not meant to tell you," Theresa eagerly answered, "but now I must. It is too wonderful. What time did your clock strike, Allan?"

"One, the last time."

"Yes; it was then that I awoke. And she had been with me. I had not seen her, but her arm had been about me and her kiss was on my cheek. Oh. I knew; it was unmistakable. And the sound of her voice was with me."

"Then she bade you, too—"

"Yes, to stay with you. I am glad we told each other." She smiled tearfully and began to fasten her wrap.

"But you are not going—*now*!" Allan cried. "You know that you cannot, now that she has asked you to stay."

"Then you believe, as I do, that it was she?" Theresa demanded.

"I can never understand, but I know," he answered her. "And now you will not go?"

* * * *

I am freed. There will be no further semblance of me in my old home, no sound of my voice, no dimmest echo of my earthly self. They have no further need of me, the two that I have brought together. Theirs is the fullest joy that the dwellers in the shell of sense can know. Mine is the transcendent joy of the unseen spaces.

THE WOMAN AT SEVEN BROTHERS, by Wilbur Daniel Steele

I tell you sir, I was innocent. I didn't know any more about the world at twenty-two than some do at twelve. My uncle and aunt in Duxbury brought me up strict; I studied hard in high school, I worked hard after hours, and I went to church twice on Sundays, and I can't see it's right to put me in a place like this, with crazy people. Oh yes, I know they're crazy—you can't tell *me*. As for what they said in court about finding her with her husband, that's the Inspector's lie, sir, because he's down on me, and wants to make it look like my fault.

No, sir, I can't say as I thought she was handsome—not at first. For one thing, her lips were too thin and white, and her color was bad. I'll tell you a fact, sir; that first day I came off to the Light I was sitting on my cot in the store-room (that's where the assistant keeper sleeps at the Seven Brothers), as lonesome as I could be, away from home for the first time, and the water all around me, and, even though it was a calm day, pounding enough on the ledge to send a kind of a *woom-woom-woom* whining up through all that solid rock of the tower. And when old Fedderson poked his head down from the living-room with the sunshine above making a kind of bright frame around his hair and whiskers, to give me a cheery, "Make yourself to home, son!" I remember I said to myself: "He's all right. I'll get along with him. But his wife's enough to sour milk." That was odd, because she was so much under him in age—'long about twenty-eight or so, and him nearer fifty. But that's what I said, sir.

Of course that feeling wore off, same as any feeling will wear off sooner or later in a place like the Seven Brothers. Cooped up in a place like that you come to know folks so well that you forget what they *do* look like. There was a long time I never noticed her, any more than you'd notice the cat. We used to sit of an evening around the table, as if you were Fedderson there, and me here, and her somewhere back there, in the rocker, knitting. Fedderson would be working on his Jacob's-ladder, and I'd be reading. He'd been working on that Jacob's-ladder a year, I guess, and every time the Inspector came off with the tender he was so astonished to see how good that ladder was that the old man would go to work and make it better. That's all he lived for.

If I was reading, as I say, I daren't take my eyes off the book, or Fedderson had me. And then he'd begin—what the Inspector said about him. How surprised the member of the board had been, that time, to see everything so clean about the light. What the Inspector had said about Fedderson's being stuck here in a second-class light—best keeper on the coast. And so on and so on, till either he or I had to go aloft and have a look at the wicks.

He'd been there twenty-three years, all told, and he'd got used to the feeling that he was kept down unfair—so used to it, I guess, that he fed on it, and told himself how folks ashore would talk when he was dead and gone—best keeper on the coast—kept down unfair. Not that he said that to me. No, he was far too loyal and humble and respectful, doing his duty without complaint, as anybody could see.

And all that time, night after night, hardly ever a word out of the woman. As I remember it, she seemed more like a piece of furniture than anything else—not even a very good cook, nor over and above tidy. One day, when he and I were trimming the lamp, he passed the remark that his *first* wife used to dust the lens and take a pride in it. Not that he said a word against Anna, though. He never said a word against any living mortal; he was too upright.

I don't know how it came about; or, rather, I *do* know, but it was so sudden, and so far away from my thoughts, that it shocked me, like the world turned over. It was at prayers. That night I remember Fedderson was uncommon long-winded. We'd had a batch of newspapers out by the tender, and at such times the old man always made a long watch of it, getting the world straightened out. For one thing, the United States minister to Turkey was dead. Well, from him and his soul, Fedderson got on to Turkey and the Presbyterian college there, and from that to heathen in general. He rambled on and on, like the surf on the ledge, woom-woom-woom, never coming to an end.

You know how you'll be at prayers sometimes. My mind strayed. I counted the canes in the chair-seat where I was kneeling; I plaited a corner of the table-cloth between my fingers for a spell, and by and by my eyes went wandering up the back of the chair.

The woman, sir, was looking at me. Her chair was back to mine, close, and both our heads were down in the shadow under the edge of the table, with Fedderson clear over on the other side by the stove. And there were her two eyes hunting mine between the spindles in the shadow. You won't believe me, sir, but I tell you I felt like jumping to my feet and running out of the room—it was so queer.

I don't know what her husband was praying about after that. His voice didn't mean anything, no more than the seas on the ledge away down there. I went to work to count the canes in the seat again, but all my eyes were in the top of my head. It got so I couldn't stand it. We were at the Lord's prayer, saying it singsong together, when I had to look up again. And there her two eyes were, between the spindles, hunting mine. Just then all of us were saying, "Forgive us our trespasses —" I thought of it afterward.

When we got up she was turned the other way, but I couldn't help seeing her cheeks were red. It was terrible. I wondered if Fedderson would notice, though I might have known he wouldn't—not him. He was in too much of a hurry to get at his Jacob's-ladder, and then he had to tell me for the tenth time what the Inspector'd said that day about getting him another light—Kingdom Come, maybe, he said.

I made some excuse or other and got away. Once in the store-room, I sat down on my cot and stayed there a long time, feeling queerer than anything. I read a chapter in the Bible, I don't know why. After I'd got my boots off I sat with them in my hands for as much as an hour, I guess, staring at the oil-tank and its lopsided shadow on the wall. I tell you, sir, I was shocked. I was only twenty-two remember, and I was shocked and horrified.

And when I did turn in, finally, I didn't sleep at all well. Two or three times I came to, sitting straight up in bed. Once I got up and opened the outer door to have a look. The water was like glass, dim, without a breath of wind, and the moon just going down. Over on the black shore I made out two lights in a village, like a pair of eyes watching. Lonely? My, yes! Lonely and nervous. I had a horror of her, sir. The dinghy-boat hung on its davits just there in front of the door, and for a minute I had an awful hankering to climb into it, lower away, and row off, no matter where. It sounds foolish.

Well, it seemed foolish next morning, with the sun shining and everything as usual—Fedderson sucking his pen and wagging his head over his eternal "log," and his wife down in the rocker with her head in the newspaper, and her breakfast work still waiting. I guess that jarred it out of me more than anything else—sight of her slouched down there, with her stringy, yellow hair and her dusty apron and the pale back of her neck, reading the Society Notes. *Society Notes*! Think of it! For the first time since I came to Seven Brothers I wanted to laugh.

I guess I did laugh when I went aloft to clean the lamp and found everything so free and breezy, gulls flying high and little whitecaps making under a westerly. It was like feeling a big load dropped off your shoulders. Fedderson came up with his dust-rag and cocked his head at me.

"What's the matter, Ray?" said he.

"Nothing," said I. And then I couldn't help it. "Seems kind of out of place for society notes," said I, "out here at Seven Brothers."

He was the other side of the lens, and when he looked at me he had a thousand eyes, all sober. For a minute I thought he was going on dusting, but then he came out and sat down on a sill.

"Sometimes," said he, "I get to thinking it may be a mite dull for her out here. She's pretty young, Ray. Not much more'n a girl, hardly."

"Not much more'n a *girl*!" It gave me a turn, sir, as though I'd seen my aunt in short dresses.

"It's a good home for her, though," he went on slow. "I've seen a lot worse ashore, Ray. Of course if I could get a shore light—"

"Kingdom Come's a shore light."

He looked at me out of his deep-set eyes, and then he turned them around the light-room, where he'd been so long.

"No," said he, wagging his head. "It ain't for such as me."

I never saw so humble a man.

"But look here," he went on, more cheerful. "As I was telling her just now, a month from yesterday's our fourth anniversary, and I'm going to take her ashore for the day and give her a holiday—new hat and everything. A girl wants a mite of excitement now and then, Ray."

There it was again, that "girl." It gave me the fidgets, sir. I had to do something about it. It's close quarters for last names in a light, and I'd taken to calling him Uncle Matt soon after I came. Now, when I was at table that noon I spoke over to where she was standing by the stove, getting him another help of chowder.

"I guess I'll have some, too, *Aunt* Anna," said I, matter of fact.

She never said a word nor gave a sign—just stood there kind of round-shouldered, dipping the chowder. And that night at prayers I hitched my chair around the table, with its back the other way.

You get awful lazy in a lighthouse, some ways. No matter how much tinkering you've got, there's still a lot of time and there's such a thing as too much reading. The changes in weather get monotonous, too, by and by; the light burns the same on a thick night as it does on a fair one. Of course there's the ships, north-bound, south-bound—wind-jammers, freighters, passenger-boats full of people. In the watches at night you can see their lights go by, and wonder what they are, how they're laden, where they'll fetch up, and all. I used to do that almost every evening when it was my first watch, sitting out on the walk-around up there with my legs hanging over the edge and my chin propped on the railing—lazy. The Boston boat was the prettiest to see, with her three tiers of port-holes lit, like a string of pearls wrapped round and round a woman's neck—well away, too, for the ledge must have made a couple of hundred fathoms off the Light, like a white dog-tooth of a breaker, even on the darkest night.

Well, I was lolling there one night, as I say, watching the Boston boat go by, not thinking of anything special, when I heard the door on the other side of the tower open and footsteps coming around to me.

By and by I nodded toward the boat and passed the remark that she was fetching in uncommon close to-night. No answer. I made nothing of that, for oftentimes Fedderson wouldn't answer, and after I'd watched the lights crawling on through the dark a spell, just to make conversation I said I guessed there'd be a bit of weather before long.

"I've noticed," said I, "when there's weather coming on, and the wind in the northeast, you can hear the orchestra playing aboard of her just over there. I make it out now. Do you?"

"Yes. Oh—yes—! *I hear it all right!*"

You can imagine I started. It wasn't him, but *her*. And there was something in the way she said that speech, sir—something—well—unnatural. Like a hungry animal snapping at a person's hand.

I turned and looked at her sidewise. She was standing by the railing, leaning a little outward, the top of her from the waist picked out bright by the lens behind her. I didn't know what in the world to say, and yet I had a feeling I ought not to sit there mum.

"I wonder," said I, "what that captain's thinking of, fetching in so handy to-night. It's no way. I tell you, if 'twasn't for this light, she'd go to work and pile up on the ledge some thick night—"

She turned at that and stared straight into the lens. I didn't like the look of her face. Somehow, with its edges cut hard all around and its two eyes closed down to slits, like a cat's, it made a kind of mask.

"And then," I went on, uneasy enough—"and then where'd all their music be of a sudden, and their goings-on and their singing—"

"And dancing!" She clipped me off so quick it took my breath.

"D-d-dancing?" said I.

"That's dance-music," said she. She was looking at the boat again.

"How do you know?" I felt I had to keep on talking.

Well, sir—she laughed. I looked at her. She had on a shawl of some stuff or other that shined in the light; she had it pulled tight around her with her two hands in front at her breast, and I saw her shoulders swaying in tune.

"How do I *know*?" she cried. Then she laughed again, the same kind of a laugh. It was queer, sir, to see her, and to hear her. She turned, as quick as that, and leaned toward me. "Don't you know how to dance, Ray?" said she.

"N-no," I managed, and I was going to say "*Aunt Anna*," but the thing choked in my throat.

I tell you she was looking square at me all the time with her two eyes and moving with the music as if she didn't know it. By heavens, sir, it came over me of a sudden that she wasn't so bad-looking, after all. I guess I must have sounded like a fool.

"You—you see," said I, "she's cleared the rip there now, and the music's gone. You—you hear?"

"Yes," said she, turning back slow. "That's where it stops every night—night after night—it stops just there—at the rip."

When she spoke again her voice was different. I never heard the like of it, thin and taut as a thread. It made me shiver, sir.

"I hate 'em!" That's what she said. "I hate 'em all. I'd like to see 'em dead. I'd love to see 'em torn apart on the rocks, night after night. I could bathe my hands in their blood, night after night."

And do you know, sir, I saw it with my own eyes, her hands moving in each other above the rail. But it was her voice, though. I didn't know what to do, or what to say, so I poked my head through the railing and looked down at the water. I don't think I'm a coward, sir, but it was like a cold—ice-cold—hand, taking hold of my beating heart.

When I looked up finally, she was gone. By and by I went in and had a look at the lamp, hardly knowing what I was about. Then, seeing by my watch it was time for the old man to come on duty, I started to go below. In the Seven Brothers, you understand, the stair goes down in a spiral through a well against the south wall and first there's the door to the keeper's room and then you come to another, and that's the living-room, and then down to the store-room. And at night, if you don't carry a lantern, it's as black as the pit.

Well, down I went, sliding my hand along the rail, and as usual I stopped to give a rap on the keeper's door, in case he was taking a nap after supper. Sometimes he did.

I stood there, blind as a bat, with my mind still up on the walk-around. There was no answer to my knock. I hadn't expected any. Just from habit, and with my right foot already hanging down for the next step, I reached out to give the door one more tap for luck.

Do you know, sir, my hand didn't fetch up on anything. The door had been there a second before, and now the door wasn't there. My hand just went on going through the dark, on and on, and I didn't seem to have sense or power enough to stop it. There didn't seem any air in the well to breathe, and my ears were drumming to the surf—that's how scared I was. And then my hand touched the flesh of a face, and something in the dark said, "Oh!" no louder than a sigh.

Next thing I knew, sir, I was down in the living-room, warm and yellow-lit, with Fedderson cocking his head at me across the table, where he was at that eternal Jacob's-ladder of his.

"What's the matter, Ray?" said he. "Lord's sake, Ray!"

"Nothing," said I. Then I think I told him I was sick. That night I wrote a letter to A.L. Peters, the grain-dealer in Duxbury, asking for a job—even though it wouldn't go ashore for a couple of weeks, just the writing of it made me feel better.

It's hard to tell you how those two weeks went by. I don't know why, but I felt like hiding in a corner all the time. I had to come to meals, but I didn't look at her, though, not once, unless it was by accident. Fedderson thought I was still ailing and nagged me to death with advice and so on. One thing I took care not to do, I can tell you, and that was to knock on his door till I'd made certain he wasn't below in the living-room—though I was tempted to.

Yes, sir; that's a queer thing, and I wouldn't tell you if I hadn't set out to give you the truth. Night after night, stopping there on the landing in that black pit, the air gone out of my lungs and the surf drumming in my ears and sweat standing cold on my neck—and one hand lifting up in the air—God forgive me, sir! Maybe I did wrong not to look at her more, drooping about her work in her gingham apron, with her hair stringing.

When the Inspector came off with the tender, that time, I told him I was through. That's when he took the dislike to me, I guess, for he looked at me kind of sneering and said, soft as I was, I'd have to put up with it till next relief. And then, said he, there'd be a whole house-cleaning at Seven Brothers, because he'd gotten Fedderson the berth at Kingdom Come. And with that he slapped the old man on the back.

I wish you could have seen Fedderson, sir. He sat down on my cot as if his knees had given 'way. Happy? You'd think he'd be happy, with all his dreams come true. Yes, he was happy, beaming all over—for a minute. Then, sir, he began to shrivel up. It was like seeing a man cut down in his prime before your eyes. He began to wag his head.

"No," said he. "No, no; it's not for such as me. I'm good enough for Seven Brothers, and that's all, Mr. Bayliss. That's all."

And for all the Inspector could say, that's what he stuck to. He'd figured himself a martyr so many years, nursed that injustice like a mother with her first-born, sir; and now in his old age, so to speak, they weren't to rob him of it. Fedderson was going to wear out his life in a second-class light, and folks would talk—that was his idea. I heard him hailing down as the tender was casting off:

"See you to-morrow, Mr. Bayliss. Yep. Coming ashore with the wife for a spree. Anniversary. Yep."

But he didn't sound much like a spree. They *had*, robbed him, partly, after all. I wondered what *she* thought about it. I didn't know till night. She didn't show up to supper, which Fedderson and I got ourselves—had a headache, be said. It was my early watch. I went and lit up and came back to read a spell. He was finishing off the Jacob's-ladder, and thoughtful, like a man that's lost a treasure. Once or twice I caught him looking about the room on the sly. It was pathetic, sir.

Going up the second time, I stepped out on the walk-around to have a look at things. She was there on the seaward side, wrapped in that silky thing. A fair sea was running across the ledge and it was coming on a little thick—not too thick. Off to the right the Boston boat was blowing, *whroom-whroom!* Creeping up on us, quarter-speed. There was another fellow behind her, and a fisherman's conch farther offshore.

I don't know why, but I stopped beside her and leaned on the rail. She didn't appear to notice me, one way or another. We stood and we stood, listening to the whistles, and the longer we stood the more it got on my nerves, her not noticing me. I suppose she'd been too much on my mind lately. I began to be put out. I scraped my feet. I coughed. By and by I said out loud:

"Look here, I guess I better get out the fog-horn and give those fellows a toot."

"Why?" said she, without moving her head—calm as that.

"*Why?*" It gave me a turn, sir. For a minute I stared at her. "Why? Because if she don't pick up this light before very many minutes she'll be too close in to wear—tide'll have her on the rocks—that's why!"

I couldn't see her face, but I could see one of her silk shoulders lift a little, like a shrug. And there I kept on staring at her, a dumb one, sure enough. I know what brought me to was hearing the Boston boat's three sharp toots as she picked up the light—mad as anything—and swung her helm a-port. I turned away from her, sweat stringing down my face, and walked around to the door. It was just as well, too, for the feed-pipe was plugged in the lamp and the wicks were popping. She'd have been out in another five minutes, sir.

When I'd finished, I saw that woman standing in the doorway. Her eyes were bright. I had a horror of her, sir, a living horror.

"If only the light had been out," said she, low and sweet.

"God forgive you," said I. "You don't know what you're saying."

She went down the stair into the well, winding out of sight, and as long as I could see her, her eyes were watching mine. When I went, myself, after a few minutes, she was waiting for me on that first landing, standing still in the dark. She took hold of my hand, though I tried to get it away.

"Good-by," said she in my ear.

"Good-by?" said I. I didn't understand.

"You heard what he said to-day—about Kingdom Come? Be it so—on his own head. I'll never come back here. Once I set foot ashore—I've got friends in Brightonboro, Ray."

I got away from her and started on down. But I stopped. "Brightonboro?" I whispered back. "Why do you tell *me*?" My throat was raw to the words, like a sore.

"So you'd know," said she.

Well, sir, I saw them off next morning, down that new Jacob's-ladder into the dinghy-boat, her in a dress of blue velvet and him in his best cutaway and derby—rowing away, smaller and smaller, the two of them. And then I went back and sat on my cot, leaving the door open and the ladder still hanging down the wall, along with the boat-falls.

I don't know whether it was relief, or what. I suppose I must have been worked up even more than I'd thought those past weeks, for now it was all over I was like a rag. I got down on my knees, sir, and prayed to God for the salvation of my soul, and when I got up and climbed to the living-room it was half past twelve by the clock. There was rain on the windows and the sea was running blue-black under the sun. I'd sat there all that time not knowing there was a squall.

It was funny; the glass stood high, but those black squalls kept coming and going all afternoon, while I was at work up in the light-room. And I worked hard, to keep myself busy. First thing I knew it was five, and no sign of the boat yet. It began to get dim and kind of purplish-gray over the land. The sun was down. I lit up, made everything snug, and got out the night-glasses to have another look for that boat. He'd said he intended to get back before five. No sign. And then, standing there, it came over me that of course he wouldn't be coming off—he'd be hunting *her*, poor old fool. It looked like I had to stand two men's watches that night.

Never mind. I felt like myself again, even if I hadn't had any dinner or supper. Pride came to me that night on the walk-around, watching the boats go by—little boats, big boats, the Boston boat with all her pearls and her dance-music. They couldn't see me; they didn't know who I was; but to the last of them, they depended on *me*. They say a man must be born again. Well, I was born again. I breathed deep in the wind.

Dawn broke hard and red as a dying coal. I put out the light and started to go below. Born again; yes, sir. I felt so good I whistled in the well, and when I came to the first door on the stair I reached out in the dark to give it a rap for luck. And then, sir, the hair prickled all over my scalp, when I found my hand just going on and on through the air, the same as it had gone once before, and all of a sudden I wanted to yell, because I thought I was going to touch flesh. It's funny what their just forgetting to close their door did to me, isn't it?

Well, I reached for the latch and pulled it to with a bang and ran down as if a ghost was after me. I got up some coffee and bread and bacon for breakfast. I drank the coffee. But somehow I couldn't eat, all along of that open door. The light in the room was blood. I got to thinking. I thought how she'd talked about those men, women, and children on the rocks, and how she'd made to bathe her hands over the rail. I almost jumped out of my chair then; it seemed for a wink she was there beside the stove watching me with that queer half-smile—really, I seemed to see her for a flash across the red table-cloth in the red light of dawn.

"Look here!" said I to myself, sharp enough; and then I gave myself a good laugh and went below. There I took a look out of the door, which was still open, with the ladder hanging down. I made sure to see the poor old fool come pulling around the point before very long now.

My boots were hurting a little, and, taking them off, I lay down on the cot to rest, and somehow I went to sleep. I had horrible dreams. I saw her again standing in that blood-red kitchen, and she seemed to be washing her hands, and the surf on the ledge was whining up the tower, louder and louder all the time, and what it whined was, "Night after night—night after night." What woke me was cold water in my face.

The store-room was in gloom. That scared me at first; I thought night had come, and remembered the light. But then I saw the gloom was of a storm. The floor was shining wet, and the water in my face was spray, flung up through the open door. When I ran to close it, it almost made me dizzy to see the gray-and-white breakers marching past. The land was gone; the sky shut down heavy overhead; there was a piece of wreckage on the back of a swell, and the Jacob's-ladder was carried clean away. How that sea had picked up so quick I can't think. I looked at my watch and it wasn't four in the afternoon yet.

When I closed the door, sir, it was almost dark in the store-room. I'd never been in the Light before in a gale of wind. I wondered why I was shivering so, till I found it was the floor below me shivering, and the walls and stair. Horrible crunchings and grindings ran away up the tower, and now and then there was a great thud somewhere, like a cannon-shot in a cave. I tell you, sir, I was alone, and I was in a mortal fright for a minute or so. And yet I had to get myself together. There was the light up there not tended to, and an early dark coming on and a heavy night and all, and I had to go. And I had to pass that door.

You'll say it's foolish, sir, and maybe it *was* foolish. Maybe it was because I hadn't eaten. But I began thinking of that door up there the minute I set foot on the stair, and all the way up through that howling dark well I dreaded to pass it. I told myself I wouldn't stop. I didn't stop. I felt the landing underfoot and I went on, four steps, five—and then I couldn't. I turned and went back. I put out my hand and it went on into nothing. That door, sir, was open again.

I left it be; I went on up to the light-room and set to work. It was Bedlam there, sir, screeching Bedlam, but I took no notice. I kept my eyes down. I trimmed those seven wicks, sir, as neat as ever they were trimmed; I polished the brass till it shone, and I dusted the lens. It wasn't till that was done that I let myself look back to see who it was standing there, half out of sight in the well. It was her, sir.

"Where'd you come from?" I asked. I remember my voice was sharp.

"Up Jacob's-ladder," said she, and hers was like the syrup of flowers.

I shook my head. I was savage, sir. "The ladder's carried away."

"I cast it off," said she, with a smile.

"Then," said I, "you must have come while I was asleep." Another thought came on me heavy as a ton of lead. "And where's *he*?" said I. "Where's the boat?"

"He's drowned," said she, as easy as that. "And I let the boat go adrift. You wouldn't hear me when I called."

"But look here," said I. "If you came through the store-room, why didn't you wake me up? Tell me that!" It sounds foolish enough, me standing like a lawyer in court, trying to prove she *couldn't* be there.

She didn't answer for a moment. I guess she sighed, though I couldn't hear for the gale, and her eyes grew soft, sir, so soft.

"I couldn't," said she. "You looked so peaceful—dear one."

My cheeks and neck went hot, sir, as if a warm iron was laid on them. I didn't know what to say. I began to stammer, "What do you mean—" but she was going back down the stair, out of sight. My God sir, and I used not to think she was good-looking!

I started to follow her. I wanted to know what she meant. Then I said to myself, "If I don't go—if I wait here—she'll come back." And I went to the weather side and stood looking out of the window. Not that there was much to see. It was growing dark, and the Seven Brothers looked like the mane of a running horse, a great, vast, white horse running into the wind. The air was a-welter with it. I caught one peep of a fisherman, lying down flat trying to weather the ledge, and I said, "God help them all to-night," and then I went hot at sound of that "God."

I was right about her, though. She was back again. I wanted her to speak first, before I turned, but she wouldn't. I didn't hear her go out; I didn't know what she was up to till I saw her coming outside on the walk-around, drenched wet already. I pounded on the glass for her to come in and not be a fool; if she heard she gave no sign of it.

There she stood, and there I stood watching her. Lord, sir—was it just that I'd never had eyes to see? Or are there women who bloom? Her clothes were shining on her, like a carving, and her hair was let down like a golden curtain tossing and streaming in the gale, and there she stood with her lips half open, drinking, and her eyes half closed, gazing straight away over the Seven Brothers, and her shoulders swaying, as if in tune with the wind and water and all the ruin. And when I looked at her hands over the rail, sir, they were moving in each other as if they bathed, and then I remembered, sir.

A cold horror took me. I knew now why she had come back again. She wasn't a woman—she was a devil. I turned my back on her. I said to myself: "It's time to light up. You've got to light up"—like that, over and over, out loud. My hand was shivering so I could hardly find a match; and when I scratched it, it only flared a second and then went out in the back draught from the open door. She was standing in the doorway, looking at me. It's queer, sir, but I felt like a child caught in mischief.

"I—I—was going to light up," I managed to say, finally.

"Why?" said she. No, I can't say it as she did.

"*Why?*" said I. "*My God!*"

She came nearer, laughing, as if with pity, low, you know. "Your God? And who is your God? What is God? What is anything on a night like this?"

I drew back from her. All I could say anything about was the light.

"Why not the dark?" said she. "Dark is softer than light—tenderer—dearer than light. From the dark up here, away up here in the wind and storm, we can watch the ships go by, you and I. And you love me so. You've loved me so long, Ray."

"I never have!" I struck out at her. "I don't! I don't!"

Her voice was lower than ever, but there was the same laughing pity in it. "Oh yes, you have." And she was near me again.

"I have?" I yelled. "I'll show you! I'll show you if I have!"

I got another match, sir, and scratched it on the brass. I gave it to the first wick, the little wick that's inside all the others. It bloomed like a yellow flower. "I *have*?" I yelled, and gave it to the next.

Then there was a shadow, and I saw she was leaning beside me, her two elbows on the brass, her two arms stretched out above the wicks, her bare forearms and wrists and hands. I gave a gasp:

"Take care! You'll burn them! For God's sake—"

She didn't move or speak. The match burned my fingers and went out, and all I could do was stare at those arms of hers, helpless. I'd never noticed her arms before. They were rounded and graceful and covered with a soft down, like a breath of gold. Then I heard her speaking close to my ear.

"Pretty arms," she said. "Pretty arms!"

I turned. Her eyes were fixed on mine. They seemed heavy, as if with sleep, and yet between their lids they were two wells, deep and deep, and as if they held all the things I'd ever thought or dreamed in them. I looked away from them, at her lips. Her lips were red as poppies, heavy with redness. They moved, and I heard them speaking:

"Poor boy, you love me so, and you want to kiss me—don't you?"

"No," said I. But I couldn't turn around. I looked at her hair. I'd always thought it was stringy hair. Some hair curls naturally with damp, they say, and perhaps that was it, for there were pearls of wet on it, and it was thick and shimmering around her face, making soft shadows by the temples. There was green in it, queer strands of green like braids.

"What is it?" said I.

"Nothing but weed," said she, with that slow, sleepy smile.

Somehow or other I felt calmer than I had any time. "Look here," said I. "I'm going to light this lamp." I took out a match, scratched it, and touched the third wick. The flame ran around, bigger than the other two together. But still her arms hung there. I bit my lip. "By God, I will!" said I to myself, and I lit the fourth.

It was fierce, sir, fierce! And yet those arms never trembled. I had to look around at her. Her eyes were still looking into mine, so deep and deep, and her red lips were still smiling with that queer, sleepy droop; the only thing was that tears were raining down her cheeks—big, glowing round, jewel tears. It wasn't human, sir. It was like a dream.

"Pretty arms," she sighed, and then, as if those words had broken something in her heart, there came a great sob bursting from her lips. To hear it drove me mad. I reached to drag her away, but she was too quick, sir; she cringed from me and slipped out from between my hands. It was like she faded away, sir, and went down in a bundle, nursing her poor arms and mourning over them with those terrible, broken sobs.

The sound of them took the manhood out of me—you'd have been the same, sir. I knelt down beside her on the floor and covered my face.

"Please!" I moaned. "Please! Please!" That's all I could say. I wanted her to forgive me. I reached out a hand, blind, for forgiveness, and I couldn't find her anywhere. I had hurt her so, and she was afraid of me, of *me*, sir, who loved her so deep it drove me crazy.

I could see her down the stair, though it was dim and my eyes were filled with tears. I stumbled after her, crying, "Please! Please!" The little wicks I'd lit were blowing in the wind from the door and smoking the glass beside them black. One went out. I pleaded with them, the same as I would plead with a human being. I said I'd be back in a second. I promised. And I went on down the stair, crying like a baby because I'd hurt her, and she was afraid of me—of *me*, sir.

She had gone into her room. The door was closed against me and I could hear her sobbing beyond it, broken-hearted. My heart was broken too. I beat on the door with my palms. I begged her to forgive me. I told her I loved her. And all the answer was that sobbing in the dark.

And then I lifted the latch and went in, groping, pleading. "Dearest—please! Because I love you!"

I heard her speak down near the floor. There wasn't any anger in her voice; nothing but sadness and despair.

"No," said she. "You don't love me, Ray. You never have."

"I do! I have!"

"No, no," said she, as if she was tired out.

"Where are you?" I was groping for her. I thought, and lit a match. She had got to the door and was standing there as if ready to fly. I went toward her, and she made me stop. She took my breath away. "I hurt your arms," said I, in a dream.

"No," said she, hardly moving her lips. She held them out to the match's light for me to look and there was never a scar on them—not even that soft, golden down was singed, sir. "You can't hurt my body," said she, sad as anything. "Only my heart, Ray; my poor heart."

I tell you again, she took my breath away. I lit another match. "How can you be so beautiful?" I wondered.

She answered in riddles—but oh, the sadness of her, sir.

"Because," said she, "I've always so wanted to be."

"How come your eyes so heavy?" said I.

"Because I've seen so many things I never dreamed of," said she.

"How come your hair so thick?"

"It's the seaweed makes it thick," said she smiling queer, queer.

"How come seaweed there?"

"Out of the bottom of the sea."

She talked in riddles, but it was like poetry to hear her, or a song.

"How come your lips so red?" said I.

"Because they've wanted so long to be kissed."

Fire was on me, sir. I reached out to catch her, but she was gone, out of the door and down the stair. I followed, stumbling. I must have tripped on the turn, for I remember going through the air and fetching up with a crash, and I didn't know anything for a spell—how long I can't say. When I came to, she was there, somewhere, bending over me, crooning, "My love—my love—" under her breath like, a song.

But then when I got up, she was not where my arms went; she was down the stair again, just ahead of me. I followed her. I was tottering and dizzy and full of pain. I tried to catch up with her in the dark of the store-room, but she was too quick for me, sir, always a little too quick for me. Oh, she was cruel to me, sir. I kept bumping against things, hurting myself still worse, and it was cold and wet and a horrible noise all the while, sir; and then, sir, I found the door was open, and a sea had parted the hinges.

I don't know how it all went, sir. I'd tell you if I could, but it's all so blurred—sometimes it seems more like a dream. I couldn't find her any more; I couldn't hear her; I went all over, everywhere. Once, I remember, I found myself hanging out of that door between the davits, looking down into those big black seas and crying like a baby. It's all riddles and blur. I can't seem to tell you much, sir. It was all—all—I don't know.

I was talking to somebody else—not her. It was the Inspector. I hardly knew it was the Inspector. His face was as gray as a blanket, and his eyes were bloodshot, and his lips were twisted. His left wrist hung down, awkward. It was broken coming aboard the Light in that sea. Yes, we were in the living-room. Yes, sir, it was daylight—gray daylight. I tell you, sir, the man looked crazy to me. He was waving his good arm toward the weather windows, and what he was saying, over and over, was this:

"*Look what you done, damn you! Look what you done*!"

And what I was saying was this:

"*I've lost her*!"

I didn't pay any attention to him, nor him to me. By and by he did, though. He stopped his talking all of a sudden, and his eyes looked like the devil's eyes. He put them up close to mine. He grabbed my arm with his good hand, and I cried, I was so weak.

"Johnson," said he, "is that it? By the living God—if you got a woman out here, Johnson!"

"No," said I. "I've lost her."

"What do you mean—lost her?"

"It was dark," said I—and it's funny how my head was clearing up—"and the door was open—the store-room door—and I was after her—and I guess she stumbled, maybe—and I lost her."

"Johnson," said he, "what do you mean? You sound crazy—downright crazy. Who?"

"Her," said I. "Fedderson's wife."

"*Who?*"

"Her," said I. And with that he gave my arm another jerk.

"Listen," said he, like a tiger. "Don't try that on me. It won't do any good—that kind of lies—not where *you're* going to. Fedderson and his wife, too—the both of 'em's drowned deader 'n a door-nail."

"I know," said I, nodding my head. I was so calm it made him wild.

"You're crazy! Crazy as a loon, Johnson!" And he was chewing his lip red. "I know, because it was me that found the old man laying on Back Water Flats yesterday morning—*me!* And she'd been with him in the boat, too, because he had a piece of her jacket tore off, tangled in his arm."

"I know," said I, nodding again, like that.

"You know *what*, you *crazy, murdering fool*?" Those were his words to me, sir.

"I know," said I, "what I know."

"And *I* know," said he, "what *I* know."

And there you are, sir. He's Inspector. I'm—nobody.

AT THE GATE,
by Myla Jo Closser

A shaggy Airedale scented his way along the highroad. He had not been there before, but he was guided by the trail of his brethren who had preceded him. He had gone unwillingly upon this journey, yet with the perfect training of dogs he had accepted it without complaint. The path had been lonely, and his heart would have failed him, traveling as he must without his people, had not these traces of countless dogs before him promised companionship of a sort at the end of the road.

The landscape had appeared arid at first, for the translation from recent agony into freedom from pain had been so numbing in its swiftness that it was some time before he could fully appreciate the pleasant dog-country through which he was passing. There were woods with leaves upon the ground through which to scurry, long grassy slopes for extended runs, and lakes into which he might plunge for sticks and bring them back to—But he did not complete his thought, for the boy was not with him. A little wave of homesickness possessed him.

It made his mind easier to see far ahead a great gate as high as the heavens, wide enough for all. He understood that only man built such barriers and by straining his eyes he fancied he could discern humans passing through to whatever lay beyond. He broke into a run that he might the more quickly gain this inclosure made beautiful by men and women; but his thoughts outran his pace, and he remembered that he had left the family behind, and again this lovely new compound became not perfect, since it would lack the family.

The scent of the dogs grew very strong now, and coming nearer, he discovered, to his astonishment that of the myriads of those who had arrived ahead of him thousands were still gathered on the outside of the portal. They sat in a wide circle spreading out on each side of the entrance, big, little, curly, handsome, mongrel, thoroughbred dogs of every age, complexion, and personality. All were apparently waiting for something, someone, and at the pad of the Airedale's feet on the hard road they arose and looked in his direction.

That the interest passed as soon as they discovered the new-comer to be a dog puzzled him. In his former dwelling-place a four-footed brother was greeted with enthusiasm when he was a friend, with suspicious diplomacy when a stranger, and with sharp reproof when an enemy; but never had he been utterly ignored.

He remembered something that he had read many times on great buildings with lofty entrances. "Dogs not admitted," the signs had said, and he feared this might be the reason for the waiting circle outside the gate. It might be that this noble portal stood as the dividing-line between mere dogs and humans. But he had been a member of the family, romping with them in the living-room, sitting at meals with them in the dining-room, going upstairs at night with them, and the thought that he was to be "kept out" would be unendurable.

He despised the passive dogs. They should be treating a barrier after the fashion of their old country, leaping against it, barking, and scratching the nicely painted door. He bounded up the last little hill to set them an example, for he was still full of the rebellion of the world; but he found no door to leap against. He could see beyond the entrance dear masses of people, yet no dog crossed the threshold. They continued in their patient ring, their gaze upon the winding road.

He now advanced cautiously to examine the gate. It occurred to him that it must be fly-time in this region, and he did not wish to make himself ridiculous before all these strangers by trying to bolt through an invisible mesh like the one that had baffled him when he was a little chap. Yet there were no screens, and despair entered his soul. What bitter punishment these poor beasts must have suffered before they learned to stay on this side the arch that led to human beings! What had they done on earth to merit this? Stolen bones troubled his conscience, runaway days, sleeping in the best chair until the key clicked in the lock. These were sins.

At that moment an English bull-terrier, white, with liver-colored spots and a jaunty manner, approached him, snuffling in a friendly way. No sooner had the bull-terrier smelt his collar than he fell to expressing his joy at meeting him. The Airedale's reserve was quite thawed by this welcome, though he did not know just what to make of it.

"I know you! I know you!" exclaimed the bull-terrier, adding inconsequently, "What's your name?"

"Tam o'Shanter. They call me Tammy," was the answer, with a pardonable break in the voice.

"I know them," said the bull-terrier. "Nice folks."

"Best ever," said the Airedale, trying to be nonchalant, and scratching a flea which was not there. "I don't remember you. When did you know them?"

"About fourteen tags ago, when they were first married. We keep track of time here by the license-tags. I had four."

"This is my first and only one. You were before my time, I guess." He felt young and shy.

"Come for a walk, and tell me all about them," was his new friend's invitation.

"Aren't we allowed in there?" asked Tam, looking toward the gate.

"Sure. You can go in whenever you want to. Some of us do at first, but we don't stay."

"Like it better outside?"

"No, no; it isn't that."

"Then why are all you fellows hanging around here? Any old dog can see it's better beyond the arch."

"You see, we're waiting for our folks to come."

The Airedale grasped it at once, and nodded understandingly.

"I felt that way when I came along the road. It wouldn't be what it's supposed to be without them. It wouldn't be the perfect place."

"Not to us," said the bull-terrier.

"Fine! I've stolen bones, but it must be that I have been forgiven, if I'm to see them here again. It's the great good place all right. But look here," he added as a new thought struck him, "do they wait for us?"

The older inhabitant coughed in slight embarrassment.

"The humans couldn't do that very well. It wouldn't be the thing to have them hang around outside for just a dog—not dignified."

"Quite right," agreed Tam. "I'm glad they go straight to their mansions. I'd—I'd hate to have them missing me as I am missing them." He sighed. "But, then, they wouldn't have to wait so long."

"Oh, well, they're getting on. Don't be discouraged," comforted the terrier. "And in the meantime it's like a big hotel in summer—watching the new arrivals. See, there is something doing now."

All the dogs were aroused to excitement by a little figure making its way uncertainly up the last slope. Half of them started to meet it, crowding about in a loving, eager pack.

"Look out; don't scare it," cautioned the older animals, while word was passed to those farthest from the gate: "Quick! Quick! A baby's come!"

Before they had entirely assembled, however, a gaunt yellow hound pushed through the crowd, gave one sniff at the small child, and with a yelp of joy crouched at its feet. The baby embraced the hound in recognition, and the two moved toward the gate. Just outside the hound stopped to speak to an aristocratic St. Bernard who had been friendly:

"Sorry to leave you, old fellow," he said, "but I'm going in to watch over the kid. You see, I'm all she has up here."

The bull-terrier looked at the Airedale for appreciation.

"That's the way we do it," he said proudly.

"Yes, but—" the Airedale put his head on one side in perplexity.

"Yes, but what?" asked the guide.

"The dogs that don't have any people—the nobodies' dogs?"

"That's the best of all. Oh, everything is thought out here. Crouch down,—you must be tired,—and watch," said the bull-terrier.

Soon they spied another small form making the turn in the road. He wore a Boy Scout's uniform, but he was a little fearful, for all that, so new was this adventure. The dogs rose again and snuffled, but the better groomed of the circle held back, and in their place a pack of odds and ends of the company ran down to meet him. The Boy Scout was reassured by their friendly attitude, and after petting them impartially, he chose an old-fashioned black and tan, and the two passed in.

Tam looked questioningly.

"They didn't know each other!" he exclaimed.

"But they've always wanted to. That's one of the boys who used to beg for a dog, but his father wouldn't let him have one. So all our strays wait for just such little fellows to come along. Every boy gets a dog, and every dog gets a master."

"I expect the boy's father would like to know that now," commented the Airedale. "No doubt he thinks quite often, 'I wish I'd let him have a dog.'"

The bull-terrier laughed.

"You're pretty near the earth yet, aren't you?"

Tam admitted it.

"I've a lot of sympathy with fathers and with boys, having them both in the family, and a mother as well."

The bull-terrier leaped up in astonishment.

"You don't mean to say they keep a boy?"

"Sure; greatest boy on earth. Ten this year."

"Well, well, this is news! I wish they'd kept a boy when I was there."

The Airedale looked at his new friend intently.

"See here, who are you?" he demanded.

But the other hurried on:

"I used to run away from them just to play with a boy. They'd punish me, and I always wanted to tell them it was their fault for not getting one."

"Who are you, anyway?" repeated Tam. "Talking all this interest in me, too. Whose dog *were* you?"

"You've already guessed. I see it in your quivering snout. I'm the old dog that had to leave them about ten years ago."

"Their old dog Bully?"

"Yes, I'm Bully." They nosed each other with deeper affection, then strolled about the glades shoulder to shoulder. Bully the more eagerly pressed for news. "Tell me, how are they getting along?"

"Very well indeed; they've paid for the house."

"I—I suppose you occupy the kennel?"

"No. They said they couldn't stand it to see another dog in your old place."

Bully stopped to howl gently.

"That touches me. It's generous in you to tell it. To think they missed me!"

For a little while they went on in silence, but as evening fell, and the light from the golden streets inside of the city gave the only glow to the scene, Bully grew nervous and suggested that they go back.

"We can't see so well at night, and I like to be pretty close to the path, especially toward morning."

Tam assented.

"And I will point them out. You might not know them just at first."

"Oh, we know them. Sometimes the babies have so grown up they're rather hazy in their recollection of how we look. They think we're bigger than we are; but you can't fool us dogs."

"It's understood," Tam cunningly arranged, "that when he or she arrives you'll sort of make them feel at home while I wait for the boy?"

"That's the best plan," assented Bully, kindly. "And if by any chance the little fellow should come first,—there's been a lot of them this summer—of course you'll introduce me?"

"I shall be proud to do it."

And so with muzzles sunk between their paws, and with their eyes straining down the pilgrims' road, they wait outside the gate.

LIGEIA,
by Edgar Allan Poe

And the will therein lieth, which dieth not. Who knoweth the mystery of the will, with its vigor? For God is but a great will pervading all things by nature of its intentness. Man doth not yield himself to the angels, nor unto death utterly, save only through the weakness of his feeble will.—Joseph Glanvill.

I cannot, for my soul, remember how, when, or even precisely where, I first became acquainted with the lady Ligeia. Long years have since elapsed, and my memory is feeble through much suffering. Or, perhaps, I cannot *now* bring these points to mind, because, in truth, the character of my beloved, her rare learning, her singular yet placid cast of beauty, and the thrilling and enthralling eloquence of her low musical language, made their way into my heart by paces so steadily and stealthily progressive, that they have been unnoticed and unknown. Yet I believe that I met her first and most frequently in some large, old, decaying city near the Rhine. Of her family—I have surely heard her speak. That it is of a remotely ancient date cannot be doubted. Ligeia! Ligeia! Buried in studies of a nature more than all else adapted to deaden impressions of the outward world, it is by that sweet word alone—by Ligeia—that I bring before mine eyes in fancy the image of her who is no more. And now, while I write, a recollection flashes upon me that I have never known the paternal name of her who was my friend and my bethrothed, and who became the partner of my studies, and finally the wife of my bosom. Was it a playful charge on the part of my Ligeia? or was it a test of my strength of affection, that I should institute no inquiries upon this point? or was it rather a caprice of my own—a wildly romantic offering on the shrine of the most passionate devotion? I but indistinctly recall the fact itself—what wonder that I have utterly forgotten the circumstances which originated or attended it? And, indeed, if ever that spirit which is entitled Romance—if ever she, the wan misty-winged Ashtophet of idolatrous Egypt, presided, as they tell, over marriages ill-omened, then most surely she presided over mine.

There is one dear topic, however, on which my memory fails me not. It is the *person* of Ligeia. In stature she was tall, somewhat slender, and, in her latter days, even emaciated. I would in vain attempt to portray the majesty, the quiet ease of her demeanor, or the incomprehensible lightness and elasticity of her footfall. She came and departed as a shadow. I was never made aware of her entrance into my closed study, save by the dear music of her low sweet voice, as she placed her marble hand upon my shoulder. In beauty of face no maiden ever equaled her. It was the radiance of an opium-dream—an airy and spirit-lifting vision more wildly divine than the phantasies which hovered about the slumbering souls of the daughters of Delos. Yet her features were not of that regular mold which we have been falsely taught to worship in the classical labors of the heathen. "There is no exquisite beauty," says Bacon, Lord Verulam, speaking truly of all the forms and genera of beauty, "without some strangeness in the proportion." Yet, although I saw that the features of Ligeia were not of a classic regularity—although I perceived that her loveliness was indeed "exquisite," and felt that there was much of "strangeness" pervading it, yet I have tried in vain to detect the irregularity and to trace home my own perception of "the strange." I examined the contour of the lofty and pale fore-head—it was faultless—how cold indeed that word when applied to a majesty so divine!—the skin rivaling the purest ivory, the commanding extent and repose, the gentle prominence of the regions above the temples; and then the raven-black, the glossy, the luxuriant, and naturally-curling tresses, setting forth the full force of the Homeric epithet, "hyacinthine!" I looked at the delicate outlines of the nose—and nowhere but in the graceful medallions of the Hebrews had I beheld a similar per-fection. There were the same luxurious smoothness of surface, the same scarcely perceptible tendency to the aquiline, the same harmoniously curved nostrils speak-ing the free spirit. I regarded the sweet mouth. Here was indeed the triumph of all things heavenly—the magnificent turn of the short upper lip—the soft, voluptuous slumber of the under—the dimples which sported, and the color which spoke—the teeth glancing back, with a brilliancy almost startling, every ray of the holy light which fell upon them in her serene and placid yet most exultingly radiant of all smiles. I scrutinized the formation of the chin—and, here, too, I found the gentle-ness of breadth, the softness and the majesty, the fullness and the spirituality, of the Greek—the contour which the god Apollo revealed but in a dream, to Cleomenes, the son of the Athenian. And then I peered into the large eyes of Ligeia.

For eyes we have no models in the remotely antique. It might have been, too, that in these eyes of my beloved lay the secret to which Lord Verulam alludes. They were, I must believe, far larger than the ordinary eyes of our own race. They were even fuller than the fullest of the gazelle eyes of the tribe of the valley of Nourjahad. Yet it was only at intervals—in moments of intense excitement—that this peculiarity became more than slightly noticeable in Ligeia. And at such mo-ments was her beauty—in my heated fancy thus it appeared perhaps—the beauty of beings either above or apart from the earth—the beauty of the fabulous Houri of the Turk. The hue of the orbs was the most brilliant of black, and, far over them, hung jetty lashes of great length. The brows, slightly irregular in outline, had the same tint. The "strangeness," however, which I found in the eyes was of a nature distinct from the formation, or the color, or the brilliancy of the features, and must, after all, be referred to the *expression*. Ah, word of no meaning! behind whose vast latitude of mere sound we intrench our ignorance of so much of the spiritual. The expres-sion of the eyes of Ligeia! How for long hours have I pondered upon it! How have I, through the whole of a midsummer night, struggled to fathom it! What was it—that something more profound than the well of Democritus—which lay far within the pupils of my beloved? What was it? I was possessed with a passion to discover. Those eyes! those large, those shining, those divine orbs! they became to me twin stars of Leda, and I to them devoutest of astrologers.

There is no point, among the many incomprehensible anomalies of the science of mind, more thrillingly exciting than the fact—never, I believe, noticed in the schools—than in our endeavors to recall to memory something long forgotten, we often find ourselves *upon the very verge* of remembrance, without being able, in the end, to remember. And thus how frequently, in my intense scrutiny of Ligeia's eyes, have I felt approaching the full knowledge of their expression—felt it ap-proaching—yet not quite be mine—and so at length entirely depart! And (strange, oh, strangest mystery of all!) I found, in the commonest objects of the universe, a circle of analogies to that expression. I mean to say that, subsequently to the period when Ligeia's beauty passed into my spirit, there dwelling as in a shrine, I derived, from many existences in the material world, a sentiment such as I felt always around, within me, by her large and luminous orbs. Yet not the more could I define that sentiment, or analyze, or even steadily view it. I recognized it, let me repeat, sometimes in the survey of a rapidly growing vine—in the contemplation of a moth, a butterfly, a chrysalis, a stream of running water. I have felt it in the ocean—in the falling of a meteor. I have felt it in the glances of unusually aged people. And there are one or two stars in heaven (one especially, a star of the sixth magnitude, double and changeable, to be found near the large star in Lyra) in a telescopic scrutiny of which I have been made aware of the feeling. I have been filled with it by certain sounds from stringed instruments, and not unfrequently by passages from books. Among innumerable other instances, I well remember something in a volume of Joseph Glanvill, which (perhaps merely from its quaintness—who shall say?) never failed to inspire me with the sentiment: "And the will therein lieth, which dieth not. Who knoweth the mysteries of the will, with its vigor? For God is but a great will pervading all things by nature of its intentness. Man doth not yield him to the angels, nor unto death utterly, save only through the weakness of his feeble will."

Length of years and subsequent reflection have enabled me to trace, indeed, some remote connection between this passage in the English moralist and a portion of the character of Ligeia. An *intensity* in thought, action, or speech was possibly, in her, a result, or at least an index, of that gigantic volition which, during our long intercourse, failed to give other and more immediate evidence of its existence. Of all the women whom I have ever known, she, the outwardly calm, the ever-placid Ligeia, was the most violently a prey to the tumultuous vultures of stern passion. And of such passion I could form no estimate, save by the miraculous expansion of those eyes which at once so delighted and appalled me,—by the almost magical melody, modulation, distinctness, and placidity of her very low voice,—and by the fierce energy (rendered doubly effective by contrast with her manner of utterance) of the wild words which she habitually uttered.

I have spoken of the learning of Ligeia: it was immense—such as I have never known in woman. In the classical tongues was she deeply proficient, and as far as my own acquaintance extended in regard to the modern dialects of Europe, I have never known her at fault. Indeed upon any theme of the most admired because simply the most abstruse of the boasted erudition of the Academy, have I *ever* found Ligeia at fault? How singularly—how thrillingly, this one point in the nature of my wife has forced itself, at this late period only, upon my attention! I said her knowledge was such as I have never known in woman—but where breathes the man who has traversed, and successfully, *all* the wide areas of moral, physical, and mathematical science? I saw not then what I now clearly perceive that the acquisitions of Ligeia were gigantic, were astounding; yet I was sufficiently aware of her infinite supremacy to resign myself, with a child-like confidence, to her guidance through the chaotic world of metaphysical investigation at which I was most busily occupied during the earlier years of our marriage. With how vast a triumph—with how vivid a delight—with how much of all that is ethereal in hope did I *feel*, as she bent over me in studies but little sought—but less known,—that delicious vista by slow degrees expanding before me, down whose long, gorgeous, and all untrodden path, I might at length pass onward to the goal of a wisdom too divinely precious not to be forbidden.

How poignant, then, must have been the grief with which, after some years, I beheld my well-grounded expectations take wings to themselves and fly away! Without Ligeia I was but as a child groping benighted. Her presence, her readings alone, rendered vividly luminous the many mysteries of the transcendentalism in which we were immersed. Wanting the radiant luster of her eyes, letters, lambent and golden, grew duller than Saturnian lead. And now those eyes shone less and less frequently upon the pages over which I pored. Ligeia grew ill. The wild eyes blazed with a too—too glorious effulgence; the pale fingers became of the transparent waxen hue of the grave; and the blue veins upon the lofty forehead swelled and sank impetuously with the tides of the most gentle emotion. I saw that she must die —and I struggled desperately in spirit with the grim Azrael. And the struggles of the passionate wife were, to my astonishment, even more energetic than my own. There had been much in her stern nature to impress me with the belief that, to her, death would have come without its terrors; but not so. Words are impotent to convey any just idea of the fierceness of resistance with which she wrestled with the Shadow. I groaned in anguish at the pitiable spectacle. I would have soothed—I would have reasoned; but in the intensity of her wild desire for life—for life—*but* for life—solace and reason were alike the uttermost of folly. Yet not until the last instance, amid the most convulsive writhings of her fierce spirit, was shaken the external placidity of her demeanor. Her voice grew more gentle—grew more low—yet I would not wish to dwell upon the wild meaning of the quietly uttered words. My brain reeled as I hearkened, entranced, to a melody more than mortal—to assumptions and aspirations which mortality had never before known.

That she loved me I should not have doubted; and I might have been easily aware that, in a bosom such as hers, love would have reigned no ordinary passion. But in death only was I fully impressed with the strength of her affection. For long hours, detaining my hand, would she pour out before me the overflowing of a heart whose more than passionate devotion amounted to idolatry. How had I deserved to be so blessed by such confessions?—how had I deserved to be so cursed with the removal of my beloved in the hour of my making them? But upon this subject I cannot bear to dilate. Let me say only, that in Ligeia's more than womanly abandonment to a love, alas! all unmerited, all unworthily bestowed, I at length, recognized the principle of her longing, with so wildly earnest a desire, for the life which was now fleeing so rapidly away. It is this wild longing—it is this eager vehemence of desire for life—*but* for life—that I have no power to portray—no utterance capable of expressing.

At high noon of the night in which she departed, beckoning me, peremptorily, to her side, she bade me repeat certain verses composed by herself not many days before. I obeyed her. They were these:—

Lo! 'tis a gala night
Within the lonesome latter years!
An angel throng, bewinged, bedight
In veils, and drowned in tears,
Sit in a theatre, to see
A play of hopes and fears,
While the orchestra breathes fitfully
The music of the spheres.
Mimes, in the form of God on high,
Mutter and mumble low,
And hither and thither fly;
Mere puppets they, who come and go
At bidding of vast formless things
That shift the scenery to and fro,
Flapping from out their condor wings
Invisible Wo!

That motley drama!—oh, be sure
It shall not be forgot!
With its Phantom chased for evermore
By a crowd that seize it not,
Through a circle that ever returneth in
To the self-same spot;
And much of Madness, and more of Sin
And Horror, the soul of the plot!
But see, amid the mimic rout,
A crawling shape intrude!
A blood-red thing that writhes from out
The scenic solitude!
It writhes!—it writhes!—with mortal pangs
The mimes become its food,
And the seraphs sob at vermin fangs
In human gore imbued.
Out—out are the lights—out all:
And over each quivering form,
The curtain, a funeral pall,
Comes down with the rush of a storm—
And the angels, all pallid and wan,
Uprising, unveiling, affirm
That the play is the tragedy, "Man,"
And its hero, the conqueror Worm.

"O God!" half shrieked Ligeia, leaping to her feet and extending her arms aloft with a spasmodic movement, as I made an end of these lines—"O God! O Divine Father!—shall these things be undeviatingly so?—shall this conqueror be not once conquered? Are we not part and parcel in Thee? Who—who knoweth the mysteries of the will with its vigor? Man doth not yield him to the angels, *nor unto death utterly*, save only through the weakness of his feeble will."

And now, as if exhausted with emotion, she suffered her white arms to fall, and returned solemnly to her bed of death. And as she breathed her last sighs, there came mingled with them a low murmur from her lips. I bent to them my ear, and distinguished, again, the concluding words of the passage in Glanvill: "*Man doth not yield him to the angels, nor unto death utterly, save only through the weakness of his feeble will.*"

She died: and I, crushed into the very dust with sorrow, could no longer endure the lonely desolation of my dwelling in the dim and decaying city by the Rhine. I had no lack of what the world calls wealth. Ligeia had brought me far more, very far more, than ordinarily falls to the lot of mortals. After a few months, therefore, of weary and aimless wandering, I purchased and put in some repair, an abbey, which I shall not name, in one of the wildest and least frequented portions of fair England. The gloomy and dreary grandeur of the building, the almost savage aspect of the domain, the many melancholy and time-honored memories connected with both, had much in unison with the feelings of utter abandonment which had driven me into that remote and unsocial region of the country. Yet although the external abbey, with its verdant decay hanging about it, suffered but little alteration, I gave way, with a child-like perversity, and perchance with a faint hope of alleviating my sorrows, to a display of more than regal magnificence within. For such follies, even in childhood, I had imbibed a taste, and now they came back to me as if in the dotage of grief. Alas, I feel how much even of incipient madness might have been discovered in the gorgeous and fantastic draperies, in the solemn carvings of Egypt, in the wild cornices and furniture, in the Bedlam patterns of the carpets of tufted gold! I had become a bounden slave in the trammels of opium, and my labors and my orders had taken a coloring from my dreams. But these absurdities I must not pause to detail. Let me speak only of that one chamber, ever accursed, whither, in a moment of mental alienation, I led from the altar as my bride—as the successor of the unforgotten Ligeia—the fair-haired and blue-eyed Lady Rowena Trevanion, of Tremaine.

There is no individual portion of the architecture and decoration of that bridal chamber which is not visibly before me. Where were the souls of the haughty family of the bride, when, through thirst of gold, they permitted to pass the threshold of an apartment *so* bedecked, a maiden and a daughter so beloved? I have said, that I minutely remember the details of the chamber—yet I am sadly forgetful on topics of deep moment; and here there was no system, no keeping, in the fantastic display to take hold upon the memory. The room lay in a high turret of the castellated abbey, was pentagonal in shape, and of capacious size. Occupying the whole southern face of the pentagonal was the sole window—an immense sheet of unbroken glass from Venice—a single pane, and tinted of a leaden hue, so that the rays of either the sun or moon passing through it, fell with a ghastly luster on the objects within. Over the upper portion of this huge window extended the trellis-work of an aged vine, which clambered up the massy walls of the turret. The ceiling, of gloomy-looking oak, was excessively lofty, vaulted, and elaborately fretted with the wildest and most grotesque specimens of a semi-Gothic, semi-Druidical device. From out the most central recess of this melancholy vaulting, depended, by a single chain of gold with long links, a huge censer of the same metal, Saracenic in pattern, and with many perforations so contrived that there writhed in and out of them, as if endued with a serpent vitality, a continual succession of parti-colored fires.

Some few ottomans and golden candelabra, of Eastern figure, were in various stations about; and there was the couch, too—the bridal couch—of an Indian model, and low, and sculptured of solid ebony, with a pall-like canopy above. In each of the angles of the chamber stood on end a gigantic sarcophagus of black granite, from the tombs of the kings over against Luxor, with their aged lids full of immemorial sculpture. But in the draping of the apartment lay, alas! the chief phantasy of all. The lofty walls, gigantic in height—even unproportionably so—were hung from summit to foot, in vast folds, with a heavy and massive-looking tapestry—tapestry of a material which was found alike as a carpet on the floor, as a covering for the ottomans and the ebony bed, as a canopy for the bed, and as the gorgeous volutes of the curtains which partially shaded the window. The material was the richest cloth of gold. It was spotted all over, at irregular intervals, with arabesque figures, about a foot in diameter, and wrought upon the cloth in patterns of the most jetty black. But these figures partook of the true character of the arabesque only when regarded from a single point of view. By a contrivance now common, and indeed traceable to a very remote period of antiquity, they were made changeable in aspect. To one entering the room, they bore the appearance of simple monstrosities; but upon a farther advance, this appearance gradually departed; and, step by step, as the visitor moved his station in the chamber, he saw himself surrounded by an endless succession of the ghastly forms which belong to the superstition of the Norman, or arise in the guilty slumbers of the monk. The phantasmagoric effect was vastly heightened by the artificial introduction of a strong continual current of wind behind the draperies—giving a hideous and uneasy animation to the whole.

In halls such as these—in a bridal chamber such as this—I passed, with the Lady of Tremaine, the unhallowed hours of the first month of our marriage—passed them with but little disquietude. That my wife dreaded the fierce moodiness of my temper—that she shunned me, and loved me but little—I could not help perceiving; but it gave me rather pleasure than otherwise. I loathed her with a hatred belonging more to demon than to man. My memory flew back (oh, with what intensity of regret!) to Ligeia, the beloved, the august, the beautiful, the entombed. I reveled in recollections of her purity, of her wisdom, of her lofty—her ethereal nature, of her passionate, her idolatrous love. Now, then, did my spirit fully and freely burn with more than all the fires of her own. In the excitement of my opium dreams (for I was habitually fettered in the shackles of the drug), I would call aloud upon her name, during the silence of the night, or among the sheltered recesses of the glens by day, as if, through the wild eagerness, the solemn passion, the consuming ardor of my longing for the departed, I could restore her to the pathways she had abandoned—ah, *could* it be forever?—upon the earth.

About the commencement of the second month of the marriage, the Lady Rowena was attacked with sudden illness, from which her recovery was slow. The fever which consumed her rendered her nights uneasy; and in her perturbed state of half-slumber, she spoke of sounds, and of motions, in and about the chamber of the turret, which I concluded had no origin save in the distemper of her fancy, or perhaps in the phantasmagoric influences of the chamber itself. She became at length convalescent—finally, well. Yet but a second more violent disorder again threw her upon a bed of suffering; and from this attack her frame, at all times feeble, never altogether recovered. Her illnesses were, after this epoch, of alarming character, and of more alarming recurrence, defying alike the knowledge and the great exertions of her physicians. With the increase of the chronic disease, which had thus, apparently, taken too sure hold upon her constitution to be eradicated by human means, I could not fail to observe a similar increase in the nervous irritation of her temperament, and in her excitability by trivial causes of fear. She spoke again, and now more frequently and pertinaciously, of the sounds—of the slight sounds—and of the unusual motions among the tapestries, to which she had formerly alluded.

One night, near the closing in of September, she pressed this distressing subject with more than usual emphasis upon my attention. She had just awakened from an unquiet slumber, and I had been watching, with feelings half of anxiety, half of vague terror, the workings of her emaciated countenance. I sat by the side of her ebony bed, upon one of the ottomans of India. She partly arose, and spoke, in an earnest low whisper, of sounds which she *then* heard, but which I could not hear—of motions which she then saw, but which I could not perceive. The wind was rushing hurriedly behind the tapestries, and I wished to show her (what, let me confess it, I could not all believe) that those almost inarticulate breathings, and those very gentle variations of the figures upon the wall, were but the natural effects of that customary rushing of the wind. But a deadly pallor, overspreading her face, had proved to me that my exertions to reassure her would be fruitless. She appeared to be fainting, and no attendants were within call. I remembered where was deposited a decanter of light wine which had been ordered by her physicians, and hastened across the chamber to procure it. But, as I stepped beneath the light of the censer, two circumstances of a startling nature attracted my attention. I had felt that some palpable although invisible object had passed lightly by my person; and I saw that there lay upon the golden carpet, in the very middle of the rich luster thrown from the censer, a shadow—a faint, indefinite shadow of angelic aspect—such as might be fancied for the shadow of a shade. But I was wild with the excitement of an immoderate dose of opium, and heeded these things but little, nor spoke of them to Rowena. Having found the wine, I recrossed the chamber, and poured out a gobletful, which I held to the lips of the fainting lady. She had now partially recovered, however, and took the vessel herself, while I sank upon an ottoman near me, with my eyes fastened upon her person. It was then that I became distinctly aware of a gentle footfall upon the carpet, and near the couch; and in a second thereafter, as Rowena was in the act of raising the wine to her lips, I saw, or may have dreamed that I saw, fall within the goblet, as if from some invisible spring in the atmosphere of the room, three or four large drops of a brilliant and ruby colored fluid. If this I saw—not so Rowena. She swallowed the wine unhesitatingly, and I forebore to speak to her of a circumstance which must, after all, I considered, have been but the suggestion of a vivid imagination, rendered morbidly active by the terror of the lady, by the opium, and by the hour.

Yet I cannot conceal it from my own perception that, immediately subsequent to the fall of the ruby drops, a rapid change for the worse took place in the disorder of my wife; so that, on the third subsequent night, the hands of her menials prepared her for the tomb, and on the fourth, I sat alone, with her shrouded body, in that fantastic chamber which had received her as my bride. Wild visions, opium-engendered, flitted, shadow-like, before me. I gazed with unquiet eye upon the sarcophagi in the angles of the room, upon the varying figures of the drapery, and upon the writhing of the parti-colored fires in the censer overhead. My eyes then fell, as I called to mind the circumstances of a former night, to the spot beneath the glare of the censer where I had seen the faint traces of the shadow. It was there, however, no longer; and breathing with greater freedom, I turned my glances to the pallid and rigid figure upon the bed. Then rushed upon me a thousand memories of Ligeia—and then came back upon my heart, with the turbulent violence of a flood, the whole of that unutterable woe with which I had regarded *her* thus enshrouded. The night waned; and still, with a bosom full of bitter thoughts of the one only and supremely beloved, I remained gazing upon the body of Rowena.

It might have been midnight, or perhaps earlier, or later, for I had taken no note of time, when a sob, low, gentle, but very distinct, startled me from my revery. I *felt* that it came from the bed of ebony—the bed of death. I listened in an agony of superstitious terror—but there was no repetition of the sound. I strained my vision to detect any motion in the corpse—but there was not the slightest perceptible. Yet I could not have been deceived. I *had* heard the noise, however faint, and my soul was awakened within me. I resolutely and perseveringly kept my attention riveted upon the body. Many minutes elapsed before any circumstance occurred tending to throw light upon the mystery. At length it became evident that a slight, a very feeble, and barely noticeable tinge of color had flushed up within the cheeks, and along the sunken small veins of the eyelids. Through a species of unutterable horror and awe, for which the language of mortality has no sufficiently energetic expression, I felt my heart cease to beat, my limbs grow rigid where I sat. Yet a sense of duty finally operated to restore my self-possession. I could no longer doubt that we had been precipitate in our preparations—that Rowena still lived. It was necessary that some immediate exertion be made; yet the turret was altogether apart from the portion of the abbey tenanted by the servants—there were none within call—I had no means of summoning them to my aid without leaving the room for many minutes—and this I could not venture to do. I therefore struggled alone in my endeavors to call back the spirit still hovering. In a short period it was certain, however, that a relapse had taken place; the color disappeared from both eyelid and cheek, leaving a wanness even more than that of marble; the lips became doubly shriveled and pinched up in the ghastly expression of death; a repulsive clamminess and coldness overspread rapidly the surface of the body; and all the usual rigorous stiffness immediately supervened. I fell back with a shudder upon the couch from which I had been so startlingly aroused, and again gave myself up to passionate waking visions of Ligeia.

An hour thus elapsed, when (could it be possible?) I was a second time aware of some vague sound issuing from the region of the bed. I listened—in extremity of horror. The sound came again—it was a sigh. Rushing to the corpse, I saw—distinctly saw—a tremor upon the lips. In a minute afterward they relaxed, disclosing a bright line of the pearly teeth. Amazement now struggled in my bosom with the profound awe which had hitherto reigned there alone. I felt that my vision grew dim, that my reason wandered; and it was only by a violent effort that I at length succeeded in nerving myself to the task which duty thus once more had pointed out. There was now a partial glow upon the forehead and upon the cheek and throat; a perceptible warmth pervaded the whole frame; there was even a slight pulsation at the heart. The lady *lived*; and with redoubled ardor I betook myself to the task of restoration. I chafed and bathed the temples and the hands and used every exertion which experience, and no little medical reading, could suggest. But in vain. Suddenly, the color fled, the pulsation ceased, the lips resumed the expression of the dead, and, in an instant afterward, the whole body took upon itself the icy chilliness, the livid hue, the intense rigidity, the sunken outline, and all the loathsome peculiarities of that which has been, for many days, a tenant of the tomb.

And again I sunk into visions of Ligeia—and again (what marvel that I shudder while I write?), *again* there reached my ears a low sob from the region of the ebony bed. But why shall I minutely detail the unspeakable horrors of that night? Why shall I pause to relate how, time after time, until near the period of the gray dawn, this hideous drama of revivification was repeated; how each terrific relapse was only into a sterner and apparently more irredeemable death; how each agony wore the aspect of a struggle with some invisible foe; and how each struggle was succeeded by I know not what of wild change in the personal appearance of the corpse? Let me hurry to a conclusion.

The greater part of the fearful night had worn away, and she who had been dead once again stirred—and now more vigorously than hitherto, although arousing from a dissolution more appalling in its utter hopelessness than any. I had long ceased to struggle or to move, and remained sitting rigidly upon the ottoman, a helpless prey to a whirl of violent emotions, of which extreme awe was perhaps the least terrible, the least consuming. The corpse, I repeat, stirred, and now more vigorously than before. The hues of life flushed up with unwonted energy into the countenance—the limbs relaxed—and, save that the eyelids were yet pressed heavily together, and that the bandages and draperies of the grave still imparted their charnel character to the figure, I might have dreamed that Rowena had indeed shaken off, utterly, the fetters of Death. But if this idea was not, even then, altogether adopted, I could at least doubt no longer, when, arising from the bed, tottering, with feeble steps, with closed eyes, and with the manner of one bewildered in a dream, the thing that was enshrouded advanced boldly and palpably into the middle of the apartment.

I trembled not—I stirred not—for a crowd of unutterable fancies connected with the air, the stature, the demeanor, of the figure, rushing hurriedly through my brain, had paralyzed—had chilled me into stone. I stirred not—but gazed upon the apparition. There was a mad disorder in my thoughts—a tumult unappeasable. Could it, indeed, be the *living* Rowena who confronted me? Could it, indeed, be Rowena *at all*—the fair-haired, the blue-eyed Lady Rowena Trevanion of Tremaine? Why,

why should I doubt it? The bandage lay heavily about the mouth—but then might it not be the mouth of the breathing Lady of Tremaine? And the cheeks—there were the roses as in her noon of life—yes, these might indeed be the fair cheeks of the living Lady of Tremaine. And the chin, with its dimples, as in health, might it not be hers?—but *had she then grown taller since her malady?* What inexpressible madness seized me with that thought? One bound, and I had reached her feet! Shrinking from my touch, she let fall from her head, unloosened, the ghastly cerements which had confined it, and there streamed forth into the rushing atmosphere of the chamber huge masses of long and disheveled hair; *it was blacker than the raven wings of midnight.* And now slowly opened *the eyes* of the figure which stood before me. "Here then, at least," I shrieked aloud, "can I never—can I never be mistaken—these are the full, and the black, and the wild eyes—of my lost love —of the Lady—of the LADY LIGEIA."

THE HAUNTED ORCHARD, by Richard Le Gallienne

Spring was once more in the world. As she sang to herself in the faraway woodlands her voice reached even the ears of the city, weary with the long winter. Daffodils flowered at the entrances to the Subway, furniture removing vans blocked the side streets, children clustered like blossoms on the doorsteps, the open cars were running, and the cry of the "cash clo'" man was once more heard in the land.

Yes, it was the spring, and the city dreamed wistfully of lilacs and the dewy piping of birds in gnarled old apple-trees, of dogwood lighting up with sudden silver the thickening woods, of water-plants unfolding their glossy scrolls in pools of morning freshness.

On Sunday mornings, the outbound trains were thronged with eager pilgrims, hastening out of the city, to behold once more the ancient marvel of the spring; and, on Sunday evenings, the railway termini were aflower with banners of blossom from rifled woodland and orchard carried in the hands of the returning pilgrims, whose eyes still shone with the spring magic, in whose ears still sang the fairy music.

And as I beheld these signs of the vernal equinox I knew that I, too, must follow the music, forsake awhile the beautiful siren we call the city, and in the green silences meet once more my sweetheart Solitude.

As the train drew out of the Grand Central, I hummed to myself,

"I've a neater, sweeter maiden, in a greener, cleaner land"

and so I said good-by to the city, and went forth with beating heart to meet the spring.

I had been told of an almost forgotten corner on the south coast of Connecticut, where the spring and I could live in an inviolate loneliness—a place uninhabited save by birds and blossoms, woods and thick grass, and an occasional silent farmer, and pervaded by the breath and shimmer of the Sound.

Nor had rumor lied, for when the train set me down at my destination I stepped out into the most wonderful green hush, a leafy Sabbath silence through which the very train, as it went farther on its way, seemed to steal as noiselessly as possible for fear of breaking the spell.

After a winter in the town, to be dropped thus suddenly into the intense quiet of the country-side makes an almost ghostly impression upon one, as of an enchanted silence, a silence that listens and watches but never speaks, finger on lip. There is a spectral quality about everything upon which the eye falls: the woods, like great green clouds, the wayside flowers, the still farm-houses half lost in orchard bloom—all seem to exist in a dream. Everything is so still, everything so supernaturally green. Nothing moves or talks, except the gentle susurrus of the spring wind swaying the young buds high up in the quiet sky, or a bird now and again, or a little brook singing softly to itself among the crowding rushes.

Though, from the houses one notes here and there, there are evidently human inhabitants of this green silence, none are to be seen. I have often wondered where the countryfolk hide themselves, as I have walked hour after hour, past farm and croft and lonely door-yards, and never caught sight of a human face. If you should want to ask the way, a farmer is as shy as a squirrel, and if you knock at a farm-house door, all is as silent as a rabbit-warren.

As I walked along in the enchanted stillness, I came at length to a quaint old farm-house—"old Colonial" in its architecture—embowered in white lilacs, and surrounded by an orchard of ancient apple-trees which cast a rich shade on the deep spring grass. The orchard had the impressiveness of those old religious groves, dedicated to the strange worship of sylvan gods, gods to be found now only in Horace or Catullus, and in the hearts of young poets to whom the beautiful antique Latin is still dear.

The old house seemed already the abode of Solitude. As I lifted the latch of the white gate and walked across the forgotten grass, and up on to the veranda already festooned with wistaria, and looked into the window, I saw Solitude sitting by an old piano, on which no composer later than Bach had ever been played.

In other words, the house was empty; and going round to the back, where old barns and stables leaned together as if falling asleep, I found a broken pane, and so climbed in and walked through the echoing rooms. The house was very lonely. Evidently no one had lived in it for a long time. Yet it was all ready for some occupant, for whom it seemed to be waiting. Quaint old four-poster bedsteads stood in three rooms—dimity curtains and spotless linen—old oak chests and mahogany presses; and, opening drawers in Chippendale sideboards, I came upon beautiful frail old silver and exquisite china that set me thinking of a beautiful grandmother of mine, made out of old lace and laughing wrinkles and mischievous old blue eyes.

There was one little room that particularly interested me, a tiny bedroom all white, and at the window the red roses were already in bud. But what caught my eye with peculiar sympathy was a small bookcase, in which were some twenty or thirty volumes, wearing the same forgotten expression—forgotten and yet cared for—which lay like a kind of memorial charm upon everything in the old house. Yes, everything seemed forgotten and yet everything, curiously—even religiously—remembered. I took out book after book from the shelves, once or twice flowers fell out from the pages—and I caught sight of a delicate handwriting here and there and frail markings. It was evidently the little intimate library of a young girl. What surprised me most was to find that quite half the books were in French—French poets and French romancers: a charming, very rare edition of Ronsard, a beautifully printed edition of Alfred de Musset, and a copy of Théophile Gautier's *Mademoiselle de Maupin*. How did these exotic books come to be there alone in a deserted New England farm-house?

This question was to be answered later in a strange way. Meanwhile I had fallen in love with the sad, old, silent place, and as I closed the white gate and was once more on the road, I looked about for someone who could tell me whether or not this house of ghosts might be rented for the summer by a comparatively living man.

I was referred to a fine old New England farm-house shining white through the trees a quarter of a mile away. There I met an ancient couple, a typical New England farmer and his wife; the old man, lean, chin-bearded, with keen gray eyes flickering occasionally with a shrewd humor, the old lady with a kindly old face of the withered-apple type and ruddy. They were evidently prosperous people, but their minds—for some reason I could not at the moment divine—seemed to be divided between their New England desire to drive a hard bargain and their disinclination to let the house at all.

Over and over again they spoke of the loneliness of the place. They feared I would find it very lonely. No one had lived in it for a long time, and so on. It seemed to me that afterwards I understood their curious hesitation, but at the moment only regarded it as a part of the circuitous New England method of bargaining. At all events, the rent I offered finally overcame their disinclination, whatever its cause, and so I came into possession—for four months—of that silent old house, with the white lilacs, and the drowsy barns, and the old piano, and the strange orchard; and, as the summer came on, and the year changed its name from May to June, I used to lie under the apple-trees in the afternoons, dreamily reading some old book, and through half-sleepy eyelids watching the silken shimmer of the Sound.

I had lived in the old house for about a month, when one afternoon a strange thing happened to me. I remember the date well. It was the afternoon of Tuesday, June 13th. I was reading, or rather dipping here and there, in Burton's *Anatomy of Melancholy*. As I read, I remember that a little unripe apple, with a petal or two of blossom still clinging to it, fell upon the old yellow page. Then I suppose I must have fallen into a dream, though it seemed to me that both my eyes and my ears were wide open, for I suddenly became aware of a beautiful young voice singing very softly somewhere among the leaves. The singing was very frail, almost imperceptible, as though it came out of the air. It came and went fitfully, like the elusive fragrance of sweetbrier—as though a girl was walking to and fro, dreamily humming to herself in the still afternoon. Yet there was no one to be seen. The orchard had never seemed more lonely. And another fact that struck me as strange was that the words that floated to me out of the aerial music were French, half sad, half gay snatches of some long-dead singer of old France, I looked about for the origin of the sweet sounds, but in vain. Could it be the birds that were singing in French in this strange orchard? Presently the voice seemed to come quite close to me, so near that it might have been the voice of a dryad singing to me out of the tree against which I was leaning. And this time I distinctly caught the words of the sad little song:

"Chante, rossignol, chante,
Toi qui as le cœur gai;
Tu as le cœur à rire,
Moi, je l'ai-t-à pleurer."

But, though the voice was at my shoulder, I could see no one, and then the singing stopped with what sounded like a sob; and a moment or two later I seemed to hear a sound of sobbing far down the orchard. Then there followed silence, and I was left to ponder on the strange occurrence. Naturally, I decided that it was just a day-dream between sleeping and waking over the pages of an old book; yet when next day and the day after the invisible singer was in the orchard again, I could not be satisfied with such mere matter-of-fact explanation.

"A la claire fontaine,"

went the voice to and fro through the thick orchard boughs,

"M'en allant promener,
J'ai trouvé l'eau si belle
Que je m'y suis baigné,
Lui y a longtemps que je t'aime,
Jamais je ne t'oubliai."

It was certainly uncanny to hear that voice going to and fro the orchard, there somewhere amid the bright sun-dazzled boughs—yet not a human creature to be seen—not another house even within half a mile. The most materialistic mind could hardly but conclude that here was something "not dreamed of in our philosophy." It seemed to me that the only reasonable explanation was the entirely irrational one—that my orchard was haunted: haunted by some beautiful young spirit, with some sorrow of lost joy that would not let her sleep quietly in her grave.

And next day I had a curious confirmation of my theory. Once more I was lying under my favorite apple-tree, half reading and half watching the Sound, lulled into a dream by the whir of insects and the spices called up from the earth by the hot sun. As I bent over the page, I suddenly had the startling impression that someone was leaning over my shoulder and reading with me, and that a girl's long hair was falling over me down on to the page. The book was the Ronsard I had found in the little bedroom. I turned, but again there was nothing there. Yet this time I knew that I had not been dreaming, and I cried out:

"Poor child! tell me of your grief—that I may help your sorrowing heart to rest."

But, of course, there was no answer; yet that night I dreamed a strange dream. I thought I was in the orchard again in the afternoon and once again heard the strange singing—but this time, as I looked up, the singer was no longer invisible. Coming toward me was a young girl with wonderful blue eyes filled with tears and gold hair that fell to her waist. She wore a straight, white robe that might have been a shroud or a bridal dress. She appeared not to see me, though she came directly to the tree where I was sitting. And there she knelt and buried her face in the grass and sobbed as if her heart would break. Her long hair fell over her like a mantle, and in my dream I stroked it pityingly and murmured words of comfort for a sorrow I did not understand.... Then I woke suddenly as one does from dreams. The moon was shining brightly into the room. Rising from my bed, I looked out into the orchard. It was almost as bright as day. I could plainly see the tree of which I had been dreaming, and then a fantastic notion possessed me. Slipping on my clothes, I went out into one of the old barns and found a spade. Then I went to the tree where I had seen the girl weeping in my dream and dug down at its foot.

I had dug little more than a foot when my spade struck upon some hard substance, and in a few more moments I had uncovered and exhumed a small box, which, on examination, proved to be one of those pretty old-fashioned Chippendale work-boxes used by our grandmothers to keep their thimbles and needles in, their reels of cotton and skeins of silk. After smoothing down the little grave in which I had found it, I carried the box into the house, and under the lamplight examined its contents.

Then at once I understood why that sad young spirit went to and fro the orchard singing those little French songs—for the treasure-trove I had found under the apple-tree, the buried treasure of an unquiet, suffering soul, proved to be a number of love-letters written mostly in French in a very picturesque hand—letters, too, written but some five or six years before. Perhaps I should not have read them—yet I read them with such reverence for the beautiful, impassioned love that animated them, and literally made them "smell sweet and blossom in the dust," that I felt I had the sanction of the dead to make myself the confidant of their story. Among the letters were little songs, two of which I had heard the strange young voice singing in the orchard, and, of course, there were many withered flowers and such like remembrances of bygone rapture.

Not that night could I make out all the story, though it was not difficult to define its essential tragedy, and later on a gossip in the neighborhood and a headstone in the churchyard told me the rest. The unquiet young soul that had sung so wistfully to and fro the orchard was my landlord's daughter. She was the only child of her parents, a beautiful, willful girl, exotically unlike those from whom she was sprung and among whom she lived with a disdainful air of exile. She was, as a child, a little creature of fairy fancies, and as she grew up it was plain to her father and mother that she had come from another world than theirs. To them she seemed like a child in an old fairy-tale strangely found on his hearth by some shepherd as he returns from the fields at evening—a little fairy girl swaddled in fine linen, and dowered with a mysterious bag of gold.

Soon she developed delicate spiritual needs to which her simple parents were strangers. From long truancies in the woods she would come home laden with mysterious flowers, and soon she came to ask for books and pictures and music, of which the poor souls that had given her birth had never heard. Finally she had her way, and went to study at a certain fashionable college; and there the brief romance of her life began. There she met a romantic young Frenchman who had read Ronsard to her and written her those picturesque letters I had found in the old mahogany work-box. And after a while the young Frenchman had gone back to France, and the letters had ceased. Month by month went by, and at length one day, as she sat wistful at the window, looking out at the foolish sunlit road, a message came. He was dead. That headstone in the village churchyard tells the rest. She was very young to die—scarcely nineteen years; and the dead who have died young, with all their hopes and dreams still like unfolded buds within their hearts, do not rest so quietly in the grave as those who have gone through the long day from morning until evening and are only too glad to sleep.

* * * *

Next day I took the little box to a quiet corner of the orchard, and made a little pyre of fragrant boughs—for so I interpreted the wish of that young, unquiet spirit—and the beautiful words are now safe, taken up again into the aerial spaces from which they came.

But since then the birds sing no more little French songs in my old orchard.

KERFOL, by Edith Wharton

I

"You ought to buy it," said my host; "it's just the place for a solitary-minded devil like you. And it would be rather worth while to own the most romantic house in Brittany. The present people are dead broke, and it's going for a song—you ought to buy it."

It was not with the least idea of living up to the character my friend Lanrivain ascribed to me (as a matter of fact, under my unsociable exterior I have always had secret yearnings for domesticity) that I took his hint one autumn afternoon and went to Kerfol. My friend was motoring over to Quimper on business: he dropped me on the way, at a cross-road on a heath, and said: "First turn to the right and second to the left. Then straight ahead till you see an avenue. If you meet any peasants, don't ask your way. They don't understand French, and they would pretend they did and mix you up. I'll be back for you here by sunset—and don't forget the tombs in the chapel."

I followed Lanrivain's directions with the hesitation occasioned by the usual difficulty of remembering whether he had said the first turn to the right and second to the left, or the contrary. If I had met a peasant I should certainly have asked, and probably been sent astray; but I had the desert landscape to myself, and so stumbled on the right turn and walked across the heath till I came to an avenue. It was so unlike any other avenue I have ever seen that I instantly knew it must be *the* avenue. The grey-trunked trees sprang up straight to a great height and then interwove their pale-grey branches in a long tunnel through which the autumn light fell faintly. I know most trees by name, but I haven't to this day been able to decide what those trees were. They had the tall curve of elms, the tenuity of poplars, the ashen colour of olives under a rainy sky; and they stretched ahead of me for half a mile or more without a break in their arch. If ever I saw an avenue that unmistakably led to something, it was the avenue at Kerfol. My heart beat a little as I began to walk down it.

Presently the trees ended and I came to a fortified gate in a long wall. Between me and the wall was an open space of grass, with other grey avenues radiating from it. Behind the wall were tall slate roofs mossed with silver, a chapel belfry, the top of a keep. A moat filled with wild shrubs and brambles surrounded the place; the drawbridge had been replaced by a stone arch, and the portcullis by an iron gate. I stood for a long time on the hither side of the moat, gazing about me, and letting the influence of the place sink in. I said to myself: "If I wait long enough, the guardian will turn up and show me the tombs—" and I rather hoped he wouldn't turn up too soon.

I sat down on a stone and lit a cigarette. As soon as I had done it, it struck me as a puerile and portentous thing to do, with that great blind house looking down at me, and all the empty avenues converging on me. It may have been the depth of the silence that made me so conscious of my gesture. The squeak of my match sounded as loud as the scraping of a brake, and I almost fancied I heard it fall when I tossed it onto the grass. But there was more than that: a sense of irrelevance, of littleness, of futile bravado, in sitting there puffing my cigarette-smoke into the face of such a past.

I knew nothing of the history of Kerfol—I was new to Brittany, and Lanrivain had never mentioned the name to me till the day before—but one couldn't as much as glance at that pile without feeling in it a long accumulation of history. What kind of history I was not prepared to guess: perhaps only that sheer weight of many associated lives and deaths which gives a majesty to all old houses. But the aspect of Kerfol suggested something more—a perspective of stern and cruel memories stretching away, like its own grey avenues, into a blur of darkness.

Certainly no house had ever more completely and finally broken with the present. As it stood there, lifting its proud roofs and gables to the sky, it might have been its own funeral monument. "Tombs in the chapel? The whole place is a tomb!" I reflected. I hoped more and more that the guardian would not come. The details of the place, however striking, would seem trivial compared with its collective impressiveness; and I wanted only to sit there and be penetrated by the weight of its silence.

"It's the very place for you!" Lanrivain had said; and I was overcome by the almost blasphemous frivolity of suggesting to any living being that Kerfol was the place for him. "Is it possible that any one could *not* see—?" I wondered. I did not finish the thought: what I meant was undefinable. I stood up and wandered toward the gate. I was beginning to want to know more; not to *see* more—I was by now so sure it was not a question of seeing—but to feel more: feel all the place had to communicate. "But to get in one will have to rout out the keeper," I thought reluctantly, and hesitated. Finally I crossed the bridge and tried the iron gate. It yielded, and I walked through the tunnel formed by the thickness of the *chemin de ronde*. At the farther end, a wooden barricade had been laid across the entrance, and beyond it was a court enclosed in noble architecture. The main building faced me; and I now saw that one half was a mere ruined front, with gaping windows through which the wild growths of the moat and the trees of the park were visible. The rest of the house was still in its robust beauty. One end abutted on the round tower, the other on the small traceried chapel, and in an angle of the building stood a graceful well-head crowned with mossy urns. A few roses grew against the walls, and on an upper window-sill I remember noticing a pot of fuchsias.

My sense of the pressure of the invisible began to yield to my architectural interest. The building was so fine that I felt a desire to explore it for its own sake. I looked about the court, wondering in which corner the guardian lodged. Then I pushed open the barrier and went in. As I did so, a dog barred my way. He was such a remarkably beautiful little dog that for a moment he made me forget the splendid place he was defending. I was not sure of his breed at the time, but have since learned that it was Chinese, and that he was of a rare variety called the "Sleeve-dog." He was very small and golden brown, with large brown eyes and a ruffled throat: he looked like a large tawny chrysanthemum. I said to myself: "These little beasts always snap and scream, and somebody will be out in a minute."

The little animal stood before me, forbidding, almost menacing: there was anger in his large brown eyes. But he made no sound, he came no nearer. Instead, as I advanced, he gradually fell back, and I noticed that another dog, a vague rough brindled thing, had limped up. "There'll be a hubbub now," I thought; for at the same moment a third dog, a long-haired white mongrel, slipped out of a doorway and joined the others. All three stood looking at me with grave eyes; but not a sound came from them. As I advanced they continued to fall back on muffled paws, still watching me. "At a given point, they'll all charge at my ankles: it's one of the jokes that dogs who live together put up on one," I thought. I was not alarmed, for they were neither large nor formidable. But they let me wander about the court as I pleased, following me at a little distance—always the same distance—and always keeping their eyes on me. Presently I looked across at the ruined facade, and saw that in one of its empty window-frames another dog stood: a white pointer with one brown ear. He was an old grave dog, much more experienced than the others; and he seemed to be observing me with a deeper intentness. "I'll hear from *him*," I said to myself; but he stood in the window-frame, against the trees of the park, and continued to watch me without moving. I stared back at him for a time, to see if the sense that he was being watched would not rouse him. Half the width of the court lay between us, and we gazed at each other silently across it. But he did not stir, and at last I turned away. Behind me I found the rest of the pack, with a newcomer added: a small black greyhound with pale agate-coloured eyes. He was shivering a little, and his expression was more timid than that of the others. I noticed that he kept a little behind them. And still there was not a sound.

I stood there for fully five minutes, the circle about me—waiting, as they seemed to be waiting. At last I went up to the little golden-brown dog and stooped to pat him. As I did so, I heard myself give a nervous laugh. The little dog did not start, or growl, or take his eyes from me—he simply slipped back about a yard, and then paused and continued to look at me. "Oh, hang it!" I exclaimed, and walked across the court toward the well.

As I advanced, the dogs separated and slid away into different corners of the court. I examined the urns on the well, tried a locked door or two, and looked up and down the dumb façade; then I faced about toward the chapel. When I turned I perceived that all the dogs had disappeared except the old pointer, who still watched me from the window. It was rather a relief to be rid of that cloud of witnesses; and I began to look about me for a way to the back of the house. "Perhaps there'll be somebody in the garden," I thought. I found a way across the moat, scrambled over a wall smothered in brambles, and got into the garden. A few lean hydrangeas and geraniums pined in the flower-beds, and the ancient house looked down on them indifferently. Its garden side was plainer and severer than the other: the long granite front, with its few windows and steep roof, looked like a fortress-prison. I walked around the farther wing, went up some disjointed steps, and entered the deep twilight of a narrow and incredibly old box-walk. The walk was just wide enough for one person to slip through, and its branches met overhead. It was like the ghost of a box-walk, its lustrous green all turning to the shadowy greyness of the avenues. I walked on and on, the branches hitting me in the face and springing back with a dry rattle; and at length I came out on the grassy top of the *chemin de ronde*. I walked along it to the gate-tower, looking down into the court, which was just below me. Not a human being was in sight; and neither were the dogs. I found a flight of steps in the thickness of the wall and went down them; and when I emerged again into the court, there stood the circle of dogs, the golden-brown one a little ahead of the others, the black greyhound shivering in the rear.

"Oh, hang it—you uncomfortable beasts, you!" I exclaimed, my voice startling me with a sudden echo. The dogs stood motionless, watching me. I knew by this time that they would not try to prevent my approaching the house, and the knowledge left me free to examine them. I had a feeling that they must be horribly cowed to be so silent and inert. Yet they did not look hungry or ill-treated. Their coats were smooth and they were not thin, except the shivering greyhound. It was more as if they had lived a long time with people who never spoke to them or looked at them: as though the silence of the place had gradually benumbed their busy inquisitive natures. And this strange passivity, this almost human lassitude, seemed to me sadder than the misery of starved and beaten animals. I should have liked to rouse them for a minute, to coax them into a game or a scamper; but the longer I looked into their fixed and weary eyes the more preposterous the idea became. With the windows of that house looking down on us, how could I have imagined such a thing? The dogs knew better: *they* knew what the house would tolerate and what it would not. I even fancied that they knew what was passing through my mind, and pitied me for my frivolity. But even that feeling probably reached them through a thick fog of listlessness. I had an idea that their distance from me was as nothing to my remoteness from them. The impression they produced was that of having in common one memory so deep and dark that nothing that had happened since was worth either a growl or a wag.

"I say," I broke out abruptly, addressing myself to the dumb circle, "do you know what you look like, the whole lot of you? You look as if you'd seen a ghost—that's how you look! I wonder if there *is* a ghost here, and nobody but you left for it to appear to?" The dogs continued to gaze at me without moving....

* * * *

It was dark when I saw Lanrivain's motor lamps at the cross-roads—and I wasn't exactly sorry to see them. I had the sense of having escaped from the loneliest place in the whole world, and of not liking loneliness—to that degree—as much as I had imagined I should. My friend had brought his solicitor back from Quimper for the night, and seated beside a fat and affable stranger I felt no inclination to talk of Kerfol....

But that evening, when Lanrivain and the solicitor were closeted in the study, Madame de Lanrivain began to question me in the drawing-room.

"Well—are you going to buy Kerfol?" she asked, tilting up her gay chin from her embroidery.

"I haven't decided yet. The fact is, I couldn't get into the house," I said, as if I had simply postponed my decision, and meant to go back for another look.

"You couldn't get in? Why, what happened? The family are mad to sell the place, and the old guardian has orders—"

"Very likely. But the old guardian wasn't there."

"What a pity! He must have gone to market. But his daughter—?"

"There was nobody about. At least I saw no one."

"How extraordinary! Literally nobody?"

"Nobody but a lot of dogs—a whole pack of them—who seemed to have the place to themselves."

Madame de Lanrivain let the embroidery slip to her knee and folded her hands on it. For several minutes she looked at me thoughtfully.

"A pack of dogs—you *saw* them?"

"Saw them? I saw nothing else!"

"How many?" She dropped her voice a little. "I've always wondered—"

I looked at her with surprise: I had supposed the place to be familiar to her. "Have you never been to Kerfol?" I asked.

"Oh, yes: often. But never on that day."

"What day?"

"I'd quite forgotten—and so had Hervé, I'm sure. If we'd remembered, we never should have sent you to-day—but then, after all, one doesn't half believe that sort of thing, does one?"

"What sort of thing?" I asked, involuntarily sinking my voice to the level of hers. Inwardly I was thinking: "I *knew* there was something...."

Madame de Lanrivain cleared her throat and produced a reassuring smile. "Didn't Hervé tell you the story of Kerfol? An ancestor of his was mixed up in it. You know every Breton house has its ghost-story; and some of them are rather unpleasant."

"Yes—but those dogs?"

"Well, those dogs are the ghosts of Kerfol. At least, the peasants say there's one day in the year when a lot of dogs appear there; and that day the keeper and his daughter go off to Morlaix and get drunk. The women in Brittany drink dreadfully." She stooped to match a silk; then she lifted her charming inquisitive Parisian face. "Did you *really* see a lot of dogs? There isn't one at Kerfol," she said.

II

Lanrivain, the next day, hunted out a shabby calf volume from the back of an upper shelf of his library.

"Yes—here it is. What does it call itself? *A History of the Assizes of the Duchy of Brittany. Quimper, 1702.* The book was written about a hundred years later than the Kerfol affair; but I believe the account is transcribed pretty literally from the judicial records. Anyhow, it's queer reading. And there's a Hervé de Lanrivain mixed up in it—not exactly *my* style, as you'll see. But then he's only a collateral. Here, take the book up to bed with you. I don't exactly remember the details; but after you've read it I'll bet anything you'll leave your light burning all night!"

I left my light burning all night, as he had predicted; but it was chiefly because, till near dawn, I was absorbed in my reading. The account of the trial of Anne de Cornault, wife of the lord of Kerfol, was long and closely printed. It was, as my friend had said, probably an almost literal transcription of what took place in the court-room; and the trial lasted nearly a month. Besides, the type of the book was detestable.

At first I thought of translating the old record. But it is full of wearisome repetitions, and the main lines of the story are forever straying off into side issues. So I have tried to disentangle it, and give it here in a simpler form. At times, however, I have reverted to the text because no other words could have conveyed so exactly the sense of what I felt at Kerfol; and nowhere have I added anything of my own.

III

It was in the year 16— that Yves de Cornault, lord of the domain of Kerfol, went to the *pardon* of Locronan to perform his religious duties. He was a rich and powerful noble, then in his sixty-second year, but hale and sturdy, a great horseman and hunter and a pious man. So all his neighbours attested. In appearance he was short and broad, with a swarthy face, legs slightly bowed from the saddle, a hanging nose and broad hands with black hairs on them. He had married young and lost his wife and son soon after, and since then had lived alone at Kerfol. Twice a year he went to Morlaix, where he had a handsome house by the river, and spent a week or ten days there; and occasionally he rode to Rennes on business. Witnesses were found to declare that during these absences he led a life different from the one he was known to lead at Kerfol, where he busied himself with his estate, attended mass daily, and found his only amusement in hunting the wild boar and water-fowl. But these rumours are not particularly relevant, and it is certain that among people of his own class in the neighbourhood he passed for a stern and even austere man, observant of his religious obligations, and keeping strictly to himself. There was no talk of any familiarity with the women on his estate, though at that time the nobility were very free with their peasants. Some people said he had never looked at a woman since his wife's death; but such things are hard to prove, and the evidence on this point was not worth much.

Well, in his sixty-second year, Yves de Cornault went to the *pardon* at Locronan, and saw there a young lady of Douarnenez, who had ridden over pillion behind her father to do her duty to the saint. Her name was Anne de Barrigan, and she came of good old Breton stock, but much less great and powerful than that of Yves de Cornault; and her father had squandered his fortune at cards, and lived almost like a peasant in his little granite manor on the moors.... I have said I would add nothing of my own to this bald statement of a strange case; but I must interrupt myself here to describe the young lady who rode up to the lych-gate of Locronan at the very moment when the Baron de Cornault was also dismounting there. I take my description from a faded drawing in red crayon, sober and truthful enough to be by a late pupil of the Clouets, which hangs in Lanrivain's study, and is said to be a portrait of Anne de Barrigan. It is unsigned and has no mark of identity but the initials A. B., and the date 16—, the year after her marriage. It represents a young woman with a small oval face, almost pointed, yet wide enough for a full mouth with a tender depression at the corners. The nose is small, and the eyebrows are set rather high, far apart, and as lightly pencilled as the eyebrows in a Chinese painting. The forehead is high and serious, and the hair, which one feels to be fine and thick and fair, is drawn off it and lies close like a cap. The eyes are neither large nor small, hazel probably, with a look at once shy and steady. A pair of beautiful long hands are crossed below the lady's breast....

The chaplain of Kerfol, and other witnesses, averred that when the Baron came back from Locronan he jumped from his horse, ordered another to be instantly saddled, called to a young page to come with him, and rode away that same evening to the south. His steward followed the next morning with coffers laden on a pair of pack mules. The following week Yves de Cornault rode back to Kerfol, sent for his vassals and tenants, and told them he was to be married at All Saints to Anne de Barrigan of Douarnenez. And on All Saints' Day the marriage took place.

As to the next few years, the evidence on both sides seems to show that they passed happily for the couple. No one was found to say that Yves de Cornault had been unkind to his wife, and it was plain to all that he was content with his bargain. Indeed, it was admitted by the chaplain and other witnesses for the prosecution that the young lady had a softening influence on her husband, and that he became less exacting with his tenants, less harsh to peasants and dependents, and less subject to the fits of gloomy silence which had darkened his widowhood. As to his wife, the only grievance her champions could call up in her behalf was that Kerfol was a lonely place, and that when her husband was away on business at Rennes or Morlaix—whither she was never taken—she was not allowed so much as to walk in the park unaccompanied. But no one asserted that she was unhappy, though one servant-woman said she had surprised her crying, and had heard her say that she was a woman accursed to have no child, and nothing in life to call her own. But that was a natural enough feeling in a wife attached to her husband; and certainly it must have been a great grief to Yves de Cornault that she bore no son. Yet he never made her feel her childlessness as a reproach—she admits this in her evidence—but seemed to try to make her forget it by showering gifts and favours on her. Rich though he was, he had never been openhanded; but nothing was too fine for his wife, in the way of silks or gems or linen, or whatever else she fancied. Every wandering merchant was welcome at Kerfol, and when the master was called away he never came back without bringing his wife a handsome present—something curious and particular—from Morlaix or Rennes or Quimper. One of the waiting-women gave, in cross-examination, an interesting list of one year's gifts, which I copy. From Morlaix, a carved ivory junk, with Chinamen at the oars, that a strange sailor had brought back as a votive offering for Notre Dame de la Clarté, above Ploumanac'h; from Quimper, an embroidered gown, worked by the nuns of the Assumption; from Rennes, a silver rose that opened and showed an amber Virgin with a crown of garnets; from Morlaix, again, a length of Damascus velvet shot with gold, bought of a Jew from Syria; and for Michaelmas that same year, from Rennes, a necklet or bracelet of round stones—emeralds and pearls and rubies—strung like beads on a fine gold chain. This was the present that pleased the lady best, the woman said. Later on, as it happened, it was produced at the trial, and appears to have struck the Judges and the public as a curious and valuable jewel.

The very same winter, the Baron absented himself again, this time as far as Bordeaux, and on his return he brought his wife something even odder and prettier than the bracelet. It was a winter evening when he rode up to Kerfol and, walking into the hall, found her sitting by the hearth, her chin on her hand, looking into the fire. He carried a velvet box in his hand and, setting it down, lifted the lid and let out a little golden-brown dog.

Anne de Cornault exclaimed with pleasure as the little creature bounded toward her. "Oh, it looks like a bird or a butterfly!" she cried as she picked it up; and the dog put its paws on her shoulders and looked at her with eyes "like a Christian's." After that she would never have it out of her sight, and petted and talked to it as if it had been a child—as indeed it was the nearest thing to a child she was to know. Yves de Cornault was much pleased with his purchase. The dog had been brought to him by a sailor from an East India merchantman, and the sailor had bought it of a pilgrim in a bazaar at Jaffa, who had stolen it from a nobleman's wife in China: a perfectly permissible thing to do, since the pilgrim was a Christian and the nobleman a heathen doomed to hell-fire.

Yves de Cornault had paid a long price for the dog, for they were beginning to be in demand at the French court, and the sailor knew he had got hold of a good thing; but Anne's pleasure was so great that, to see her laugh and play with the little animal, her husband would doubtless have given twice the sum.

* * * *

So far, all the evidence is at one, and the narrative plain sailing; but now the steering becomes difficult. I will try to keep as nearly as possible to Anne's own statements; though toward the end, poor thing....

Well, to go back. The very year after the little brown dog was brought to Kerfol, Yves de Cornault, one winter night, was found dead at the head of a narrow flight of stairs leading down from his wife's rooms to a door opening on the court. It was his wife who found him and gave the alarm, so distracted, poor wretch, with fear and horror—for his blood was all over her—that at first the roused household could not make out what she was saying, and thought she had suddenly gone mad. But there, sure enough, at the top of the stairs lay her husband, stone dead, and head foremost, the blood from his wounds dripping down to the steps below him. He had been dreadfully scratched and gashed about the face and throat, as if with curious pointed weapons; and one of his legs had a deep tear in it which had cut an artery, and probably caused his death. But how did he come there, and who had murdered him?

His wife declared that she had been asleep in her bed, and hearing his cry had rushed out to find him lying on the stairs; but this was immediately questioned. In the first place, it was proved that from her room she could not have heard the struggle on the stairs, owing to the thickness of the walls and the length of the intervening passage; then it was evident that she had not been in bed and asleep, since she was dressed when she roused the house, and her bed had not been slept in. Moreover, the door at the bottom of the stairs was ajar, and it was noticed by the chaplain (an observant man) that the dress she wore was stained with blood about the knees, and that there were traces of small blood-stained hands low down on the staircase walls, so that it was conjectured that she had really been at the postern-door when her husband fell and, feeling her way up to him in the darkness on her hands and knees, had been stained by his blood dripping down on her. Of course it was argued on the other side that the blood-marks on her dress might have been caused by her kneeling down by her husband when she rushed out of her room; but there was the open door below, and the fact that the finger-marks in the staircase all pointed upward.

The accused held to her statement for the first two days, in spite of its improbability; but on the third day word was brought to her that Hervé de Lanrivain, a young nobleman of the neighbourhood, had been arrested for complicity in the crime. Two or three witnesses thereupon came forward to say that it was known throughout the country that Lanrivain had formerly been on good terms with the lady of Cornault; but that he had been absent from Brittany for over a year, and people had ceased to associate their names. The witnesses who made this statement were not of a very reputable sort. One was an old herb-gatherer suspected of witchcraft, another a drunken clerk from a neighbouring parish, the third a half-witted shepherd who could be made to say anything; and it was clear that the prosecution was not satisfied with its case, and would have liked to find more definite proof of Lanrivain's complicity than the statement of the herb-gatherer, who swore to having seen him climbing the wall of the park on the night of the murder. One way of patching out incomplete proofs in those days was to put some sort of pressure, moral or physical, on the accused person. It is not clear what pressure was put on Anne de Cornault; but on the third day, when she was brought into court, she "appeared weak and wandering," and after being encouraged to collect herself and speak the truth, on her honour and the wounds of her Blessed Redeemer, she confessed that she had in fact gone down the stairs to speak with Hervé de Lanrivain (who denied everything), and had been surprised there by the sound of her husband's fall. That was better; and the prosecution rubbed its hands with satisfaction. The satisfaction increased when various dependents living at Kerfol were induced to say—with apparent sincerity—that during the year or two preceding his death their master had once more grown uncertain and irascible, and subject to the fits of brooding silence which his household had learned to dread before his second marriage. This seemed to show that things had not been going well at Kerfol; though no one could be found to say that there had been any signs of open disagreement between husband and wife.

Anne de Cornault, when questioned as to her reason for going down at night to open the door to Hervé de Lanrivain, made an answer which must have sent a smile around the court. She said it was because she was lonely and wanted to talk with the young man. Was this the only reason? she was asked; and replied: "Yes, by the Cross over your Lordships' heads."

"But why at midnight?" the court asked.

"Because I could see him in no other way."

I can see the exchange of glances across the ermine collars under the Crucifix.

Anne de Cornault, further questioned, said that her married life had been extremely lonely: "desolate" was the word she used. It was true that her husband seldom spoke harshly to her; but there were days when he did not speak at all. It was true that he had never struck or threatened her; but he kept her like a prisoner at Kerfol, and when he rode away to Morlaix or Quimper or Rennes he set so close a watch on her that she could not pick a flower in the garden without having a waiting-woman at her heels. "I am no Queen, to need such honours," she once said to him; and he had answered that a man who has a treasure does not leave the key in the lock when he goes out. "Then take me with you," she urged; but to this he said that towns were pernicious places, and young wives better off at their own firesides.

"But what did you want to say to Hervé de Lanrivain?" the court asked; and she answered: "To ask him to take me away."

"Ah—you confess that you went down to him with adulterous thoughts?"

"Then why did you want him to take you away?"

"Because I was afraid for my life."

"Of whom were you afraid?"

"Of my husband."

"Why were you afraid of your husband?"

"Because he had strangled my little dog."

Another smile must have passed around the courtroom: in days when any nobleman had a right to hang his peasants—and most of them exercised it—pinching a pet animal's wind-pipe was nothing to make a fuss about.

At this point one of the Judges, who appears to have had a certain sympathy for the accused, suggested that she should be allowed to explain herself in her own way; and she thereupon made the following statement.

The first years of her marriage had been lonely; but her husband had not been unkind to her. If she had had a child she would not have been unhappy; but the days were long, and it rained too much.

It was true that her husband, whenever he went away and left her, brought her a handsome present on his return; but this did not make up for the loneliness. At least nothing had, till he brought her the little brown dog from the East: after that she was much less unhappy. Her husband seemed pleased that she was so fond of the dog; he gave her leave to put her jewelled bracelet around its neck, and to keep it always with her.

One day she had fallen asleep in her room, with the dog at her feet, as his habit was. Her feet were bare and resting on his back. Suddenly she was waked by her husband: he stood beside her, smiling not unkindly.

"You look like my great-grandmother, Juliane de Cornault, lying in the chapel with her feet on a little dog," he said.

The analogy sent a chill through her, but she laughed and answered: "Well, when I am dead you must put me beside her, carved in marble, with my dog at my feet."

"Oho—we'll wait and see," he said, laughing also, but with his black brows close together. "The dog is the emblem of fidelity."

"And do you doubt my right to lie with mine at my feet?"

"When I'm in doubt I find out," he answered. "I am an old man," he added, "and people say I make you lead a lonely life. But I swear you shall have your monument if you earn it."

"And I swear to be faithful," she returned, "if only for the sake of having my little dog at my feet."

Not long afterward he went on business to the Quimper Assizes; and while he was away his aunt, the widow of a great nobleman of the duchy, came to spend a night at Kerfol on her way to the *pardon* of Ste. Barbe. She was a woman of piety and consequence, and much respected by Yves de Cornault, and when she proposed to Anne to go with her to Ste. Barbe no one could object, and even the chaplain declared himself in favour of the pilgrimage. So Anne set out for Ste. Barbe, and there for the first time she talked with Hervé de Lanrivain. He had come once or twice to Kerfol with his father, but she had never before exchanged a dozen words with him. They did not talk for more than five minutes now: it was under the chestnuts, as the procession was coming out of the chapel. He said: "I pity you," and she was surprised, for she had not supposed that any one thought her an object of pity. He added: "Call for me when you need me," and she smiled a little, but was glad afterward, and thought often of the meeting.

She confessed to having seen him three times afterward: not more. How or where she would not say—one had the impression that she feared to implicate some one. Their meetings had been rare and brief; and at the last he had told her that he was starting the next day for a foreign country, on a mission which was not without peril and might keep him for many months absent. He asked her for a remembrance, and she had none to give him but the collar about the little dog's neck. She was sorry afterward that she had given it, but he was so unhappy at going that she had not had the courage to refuse.

Her husband was away at the time. When he returned a few days later he picked up the little dog to pet it, and noticed that its collar was missing. His wife told him that the dog had lost it in the undergrowth of the park, and that she and her maids had hunted a whole day for it. It was true, she explained to the court, that she had made the maids search for the necklet—they all believed the dog had lost it in the park....

Her husband made no comment, and that evening at supper he was in his usual mood, between good and bad: you could never tell which. He talked a good deal, describing what he had seen and done at Rennes; but now and then he stopped and looked hard at her, and when she went to bed she found her little dog strangled on her pillow. The little thing was dead, but still warm; she stooped to lift it, and her distress turned to horror when she discovered that it had been strangled by twisting twice round its throat the necklet she had given to Lanrivain.

The next morning at dawn she buried the dog in the garden, and hid the necklet in her breast. She said nothing to her husband, then or later, and he said nothing to her; but that day he had a peasant hanged for stealing a faggot in the park, and the next day he nearly beat to death a young horse he was breaking.

Winter set in, and the short days passed, and the long nights, one by one; and she heard nothing of Hervé de Lanrivain. It might be that her husband had killed him; or merely that he had been robbed of the necklet. Day after day by the hearth among the spinning maids, night after night alone on her bed, she wondered and trembled. Sometimes at table her husband looked across at her and smiled; and then she felt sure that Lanrivain was dead. She dared not try to get news of him, for she was sure her husband would find out if she did: she had an idea that he could find out anything. Even when a witchwoman who was a noted seer, and could show you the whole world in her crystal, came to the castle for a night's shelter, and the maids flocked to her, Anne held back.

The winter was long and black and rainy. One day, in Yves de Cornault's absence, some gypsies came to Kerfol with a troop of performing dogs. Anne bought the smallest and cleverest, a white dog with a feathery coat and one blue and one brown eye. It seemed to have been ill-treated by the gypsies, and clung to her plaintively when she took it from them. That evening her husband came back, and when she went to bed she found the dog strangled on her pillow.

After that she said to herself that she would never have another dog; but one bitter cold evening a poor lean greyhound was found whining at the castle-gate, and she took him in and forbade the maids to speak of him to her husband. She hid him in a room that no one went to, smuggled food to him from her own plate, made him a warm bed to lie on and petted him like a child.

Yves de Cornault came home, and the next day she found the greyhound strangled on her pillow. She wept in secret, but said nothing, and resolved that even if she met a dog dying of hunger she would never bring him into the castle; but one day she found a young sheepdog, a brindled puppy with good blue eyes, lying with a broken leg in the snow of the park. Yves de Cornault was at Rennes, and she brought the dog in, warmed and fed it, tied up its leg and hid it in the castle till her husband's return. The day before, she gave it to a peasant woman who lived a long way off, and paid her handsomely to care for it and say nothing; but that night she heard a whining and scratching at her door, and when she opened it the lame puppy, drenched and shivering, jumped up on her with little sobbing barks. She hid him in her bed, and the next morning was about to have him taken back to the peasant woman when she heard her husband ride into the court. She shut the dog in a chest, and went down to receive him. An hour or two later, when she returned to her room, the puppy lay strangled on her pillow....

After that she dared not make a pet of any other dog; and her loneliness became almost unendurable. Sometimes, when she crossed the court of the castle, and thought no one was looking, she stopped to pat the old pointer at the gate. But one day as she was caressing him her husband came out of the chapel; and the next day the old dog was gone....

This curious narrative was not told in one sitting of the court, or received without impatience and incredulous comment. It was plain that the Judges were surprised by its puerility, and that it did not help the accused in the eyes of the public. It was an odd tale, certainly; but what did it prove? That Yves de Cornault disliked dogs, and that his wife, to gratify her own fancy, persistently ignored this dislike. As for pleading this trivial disagreement as an excuse for her relations—whatever their nature—with her supposed accomplice, the argument was so absurd that her own lawyer manifestly regretted having let her make use of it, and tried several times to cut short her story. But she went on to the end, with a kind of hypnotized insistence, as though the scenes she evoked were so real to her that she had forgotten where she was and imagined herself to be re-living them.

At length the Judge who had previously shown a certain kindness to her said (leaning forward a little, one may suppose, from his row of dozing colleagues): "Then you would have us believe that you murdered your husband because he would not let you keep a pet dog?"

"I did not murder my husband."

"Who did, then? Hervé de Lanrivain?"

"No."

"Who then? Can you tell us?"

"Yes, I can tell you. The dogs—" At that point she was carried out of the court in a swoon.

* * * *

It was evident that her lawyer tried to get her to abandon this line of defense. Possibly her explanation, whatever it was, had seemed convincing when she poured it out to him in the heat of their first private colloquy; but now that it was exposed to the cold daylight of judicial scrutiny, and the banter of the town, he was thoroughly ashamed of it, and would have sacrificed her without a scruple to save his professional reputation. But the obstinate Judge—who perhaps, after all, was more inquisitive than kindly—evidently wanted to hear the story out, and she was ordered, the next day, to continue her deposition.

She said that after the disappearance of the old watchdog nothing particular happened for a month or two. Her husband was much as usual: she did not remember any special incident. But one evening a pedlar woman came to the castle and was selling trinkets to the maids. She had no heart for trinkets, but she stood looking on while the women made their choice. And then, she did not know how, but the pedlar coaxed her into buying for herself a pear-shaped pomander with a strong scent in it—she had once seen something of the kind on a gypsy woman. She had no desire for the pomander, and did not know why she had bought it. The pedlar said that whoever wore it had the power to read the future; but she did not really believe that, or care much either. However, she bought the thing and took it up to her room, where she sat turning it about in her hand. Then the strange scent attracted her and she began to wonder what kind of spice was in the box. She opened it and found a grey bean rolled in a strip of paper; and on the paper she saw a sign she knew, and a message from Hervé de Lanrivain, saying that he was at home again and would be at the door in the court that night after the moon had set....

She burned the paper and sat down to think. It was nightfall, and her husband was at home.... She had no way of warning Lanrivain, and there was nothing to do but to wait....

At this point I fancy the drowsy court-room beginning to wake up. Even to the oldest hand on the bench there must have been a certain relish in picturing the feelings of a woman on receiving such a message at nightfall from a man living twenty miles away, to whom she had no means of sending a warning....

She was not a clever woman, I imagine; and as the first result of her cogitation she appears to have made the mistake of being, that evening, too kind to her husband. She could not ply him with wine, according to the traditional expedient, for though he drank heavily at times he had a strong head; and when he drank beyond its strength it was because he chose to, and not because a woman coaxed him. Not his wife, at any rate—she was an old story by now. As I read the case, I fancy there was no feeling for her left in him but the hatred occasioned by his supposed dishonour.

At any rate, she tried to call up her old graces; but early in the evening he complained of pains and fever, and left the hall to go up to the room where he sometimes slept. His servant carried him a cup of hot wine, and brought back word that he was sleeping and not to be disturbed; and an hour later, when Anne lifted the tapestry and listened at his door, she heard his loud regular breathing. She thought it might be a feint, and stayed a long time barefooted in the passage, her ear to the crack; but the breathing went on too steadily and naturally to be other than that of a man in a sound sleep. She crept back to her room reassured, and stood in the window watching the moon set through the trees of the park. The sky was misty and starless, and after the moon went down the night was black as pitch. She knew the time had come, and stole along the passage, past her husband's door—where she stopped again to listen to his breathing—to the top of the stairs. There she paused a moment, and assured herself that no one was following her; then she began to go down the stairs in the darkness. They were so steep and winding that she had to go very slowly, for fear of stumbling. Her one thought was to get the door unbolted, tell Lanrivain to make his escape, and hasten back to her room. She had tried the bolt earlier in the evening, and managed to put a little grease on it; but nevertheless, when she drew it, it gave a squeak…not loud, but it made her heart stop; and the next minute, overhead, she heard a noise.…

"What noise?" the prosecution interposed.

"My husband's voice calling out my name and cursing me."

"What did you hear after that?"

"A terrible scream and a fall."

"Where was Hervé de Lanrivain at this time?"

"He was standing outside in the court. I just made him out in the darkness. I told him for God's sake to go, and then I pushed the door shut."

"What did you do next?"

"I stood at the foot of the stairs and listened."

"What did you hear?"

"I heard dogs snarling and panting." (Visible discouragement of the bench, boredom of the public, and exasperation of the lawyer for the defense. Dogs again—! But the inquisitive Judge insisted.)

"What dogs?"

She bent her head and spoke so low that she had to be told to repeat her answer: "I don't know."

"How do you mean—you don't know?"

"I don't know what dogs.…"

The Judge again intervened: "Try to tell us exactly what happened. How long did you remain at the foot of the stairs?"

"Only a few minutes."

"And what was going on meanwhile overhead?"

"The dogs kept on snarling and panting. Once or twice he cried out. I think he moaned once. Then he was quiet."

"Then what happened?"

"Then I heard a sound like the noise of a pack when the wolf is thrown to them —gulping and lapping."

(There was a groan of disgust and repulsion through the court, and another attempted intervention by the distracted lawyer. But the inquisitive Judge was still inquisitive.)

"And all the while you did not go up?"

"Yes—I went up then—to drive them off."

"The dogs?"

"Yes."

"Well—?"

"When I got there it was quite dark. I found my husband's flint and steel and struck a spark. I saw him lying there. He was dead."

"And the dogs?"

"The dogs were gone."

"Gone—whereto?"

"I don't know. There was no way out—and there were no dogs at Kerfol."

She straightened herself to her full height, threw her arms above her head, and fell down on the stone floor with a long scream. There was a moment of confusion in the court-room. Some one on the bench was heard to say: "This is clearly a case for the ecclesiastical authorities"—and the prisoner's lawyer doubtless jumped at the suggestion.

After this, the trial loses itself in a maze of cross-questioning and squabbling. Every witness who was called corroborated Anne de Cornault's statement that there were no dogs at Kerfol: had been none for several months. The master of the house had taken a dislike to dogs, there was no denying it But, on the other hand, at the inquest, there had been long and bitter discussions as to the nature of the dead man's wounds. One of the surgeons called in had spoken of marks that looked like bites. The suggestion of witchcraft was revived, and the opposing lawyers hurled tomes of necromancy at each other.

At last Anne de Cornault was brought back into court—at the instance of the same Judge—and asked if she knew where the dogs she spoke of could have come from. On the body of her Redeemer she swore that she did not. Then the Judge put his final question: "If the dogs you think you heard had been known to you, do you think you would have recognized them by their barking?"

"Yes."

"Did you recognize them?"

"Yes."

"What dogs do you take them to have been?"

"My dead dogs," she said in a whisper.... She was taken out of court, not to reappear there again. There was some kind of ecclesiastical investigation, and the end of the business was that the Judges disagreed with each other, and with the ecclesiastical committee, and that Anne de Cornault was finally handed over to the keeping of her husband's family, who shut her up in the keep of Kerfol, where she is said to have died many years later, a harmless mad-woman.

So ends her story. As for that of Hervé de Lanrivain, I had only to apply to his collateral descendant for its subsequent details. The evidence against the young man being insufficient, and his family influence in the duchy considerable, he was set free, and left soon afterward for Paris. He was probably in no mood for a worldly life, and he appears to have come almost immediately under the influence of the famous M. Arnauld d'Andilly and the gentlemen of Port Royal. A year or two later he was received into their Order, and without achieving any particular distinction he followed its good and evil fortunes till his death some twenty years later. Lanrivain showed me a portrait of him by a pupil of Philippe de Champaigne: sad eyes, an impulsive mouth and a narrow brow. Poor Hervé de Lanrivain: it was a grey ending. Yet as I looked at his stiff and sallow effigy, in the dark dress of the Jansénistes, I almost found myself envying his fate. After all, in the course of his life two great things had happened to him: he had loved romantically, and he must have talked with Pascal....

THE WIND IN THE ROSE-BUSH, by Mary E. Wilkins Freeman

Ford village has no railroad station, being on the other side of the river from Porter's Falls, and accessible only by the ford which gives it its name, and a ferry line.

The ferry-boat was waiting when Rebecca Flint got off the train with her bag and lunch basket. When she and her small trunk were safely embarked she sat stiff and straight and calm in the ferry-boat as it shot swiftly and smoothly across stream. There was a horse attached to a light country wagon on board, and he pawed the deck uneasily. His owner stood near, with a wary eye upon him, although he was chewing, with as dully reflective an expression as a cow. Beside Rebecca sat a woman of about her own age, who kept looking at her with furtive curiosity; her husband, short and stout and saturnine, stood near her. Rebecca paid no attention to either of them. She was tall and spare and pale, the type of a spinster, yet with rudimentary lines and expressions of matronhood. She all unconsciously held her shawl, rolled up in a canvas bag, on her left hip, as if it had been a child. She wore a settled frown of dissent at life, but it was the frown of a mother who regarded life as a froward child, rather than as an overwhelming fate.

The other woman continued staring at her; she was mildly stupid, except for an overdeveloped curiosity which made her at times sharp beyond belief. Her eyes glittered, red spots came on her flaccid cheeks; she kept opening her mouth to speak, making little abortive motions. Finally she could endure it no longer; she nudged Rebecca boldly.

"A pleasant day," said she.

Rebecca looked at her and nodded coldly.

"Yes, very," she assented.

"Have you come far?"

"I have come from Michigan."

"Oh!" said the woman, with awe. "It's a long way," she remarked, presently.

"Yes, it is," replied Rebecca, conclusively.

Still the other woman was not daunted; there was something which she determined to know, possibly roused thereto by a vague sense of incongruity in the other's appearance. "It's a long ways to come and leave a family," she remarked with painful slyness.

"I ain't got any family to leave," returned Rebecca, shortly.

"Then you ain't—"

"No, I ain't."

"Oh!" said the woman.

Rebecca looked straight ahead at the race of the river.

It was a long ferry. Finally Rebecca herself waxed unexpectedly loquacious. She turned to the older woman and inquired if she knew Jolin Dent's widow who lived in Ford Village. "Her husband died about three years ago," said she, by way of detail.

The woman started violently. She turned pale, then she flushed; she cast a strange glance at her husband, who was regarding both women with a sort of stolid keenness.

"Yes, I guess I do," faltered the woman, finally.

"Well, his first wife was my sister," said Rebecca with the air of one imparting important intelligence.

"Was she?" responded the other woman, feebly. She glanced at her husband with an expression of doubt and terror, and he shook his head forbiddingly.

"I'm going to see her and take my niece Agnes home with me," said Rebecca.

Then the woman gave such a violent start that she noticed it.

"What is the matter?" she asked.

"Nothin', I guess," replied the woman, with eyes on her husband, who was slowly shaking his head, like a Chinese toy.

"Is my niece sick?" asked Rebecca with quick suspicion.

"No, she ain't sick," replied the woman with alacrity, then she caught her breath with a gasp.

"When did you see her?"

"Let me see; I ain't seen her for some little time," replied the woman. Then she caught her breath again.

"She ought to have grown up real pretty, if she takes after my sister. She was a real pretty woman," Rebecca said, wistfully.

"Yes, I guess she did grow up pretty," replied the woman in a trembling voice.

"What kind of a woman is the second wife?"

The woman glanced at her husband's warning face. She continued to gaze at him while she replied in a choking voice to Rebecca:

"I—guess she's a nice woman," she replied. "I—don't know, I guess so. I—don't see much of her."

"I felt kind of hurt that John married again so quick," said Rebecca; "but I suppose he wanted his house kept, and Agnes wanted care. I wasn't so situated that I could take her when her mother died. I had my own mother to care for, and I was school-teaching. Now mother has gone, and my uncle died six months ago and left me quite a little property, and I've given up my school and I've come for Agnes. I guess she'll be glad to go with me, though I suppose her stepmother is a good woman and has always done for her."

The man's warning shake at his wife was fairly portentous.

"I guess so," said she.

"John always wrote that she was a beautiful woman," said Rebecca.

Then the ferry-boat grated on the shore.

John Dent's widow had sent a horse and wagon to meet her sister-in-law. When the woman and her husband went down the road, on which Rebecca in the wagon with her trunk soon passed them, she said, reproachfully:

"Seems as if I'd ought to have told her, Thomas."

"Let her find it out herself," replied the man. "Don't you go to burnin' your fingers in other folks' puddin', Maria."

"Do you s'pose she'll see anything?" asked the woman with a spasmodic shudder and a terrified roll of her eyes.

"See!" returned her husband with stolid scorn. "Better be sure there's anything to see."

"Oh, Thomas, they say—"

"Lord, ain't you found out that what they say is mostly lies?"

"But if it should be true, and she's a nervous woman, she might be scared enough to lose her wits," said his wife, staring uneasily after Rebecca's erect figure in the wagon disappearing over the crest of the hilly road.

"Wits that's so easy upset ain't worth much," declared the man. "You keep out of it, Maria."

Rebecca in the meantime rode on in the wagon, beside a flaxen-headed boy, who looked, to her understanding, not very bright. She asked him a question, and he paid no attention. She repeated it, and he responded with a bewildered and incoherent grunt. Then she let him alone, after making sure that he knew how to drive straight.

They had traveled about half a mile, passed the village square, and gone a short distance beyond, when the boy drew up with a sudden Whoa! before a very prosperous-looking house. It had been one of the aboriginal cottages of the vicinity, small and white, with a roof extending on one side over a piazza, and a tiny "L" jutting out in the rear, on the right hand. Now the cottage was transformed by dormer windows, a bay window on the piazzaless side, a carved railing down the front steps, and a modern hardwood door.

"Is this John Dent's house?" asked Rebecca.

The boy was as sparing of speech as a philosopher. His only response was in flinging the reins over the horse's back, stretching out one foot to the shaft, and leaping out of the wagon, then going around to the rear for the trunk. Rebecca got out and went toward the house. Its white paint had a new gloss; its blinds were an immaculate apple green; the lawn was trimmed as smooth as velvet, and it was dotted with scrupulous groups of hydrangeas and cannas.

"I always understood that John Dent was well-to-do," Rebecca reflected, comfortably. "I guess Agnes will have considerable. I've got enough, but it will come in handy for her schooling. She can have advantages."

The boy dragged the trunk up the fine gravel walk, but before he reached the steps leading up to the piazza, for the house stood on a terrace, the front door opened and a fair, frizzled head of a very large and handsome woman appeared. She held up her black silk skirt, disclosing voluminous ruffles of starched embroidery, and waited for Rebecca. She smiled placidly, her pink, double-chinned face widened and dimpled, but her blue eyes were wary and calculating. She extended her hand as Rebecca climbed the steps.

"This is Miss Flint, I suppose," said she.

"Yes, ma'am," replied Rebecca, noticing with bewilderment a curious expression compounded of fear and defiance on the other's face.

"Your letter only arrived this morning," said Mrs. Dent, in a steady voice. Her great face was a uniform pink, and her china-blue eyes were at once aggressive and veiled with secrecy.

"Yes, I hardly thought you'd get my letter," replied Rebecca. "I felt as if I could not wait to hear from you before I came. I supposed you would be so situated that you could have me a little while without putting you out too much, from what John used to write me about his circumstances, and when I had that money so unexpected I felt as if I must come for Agnes. I suppose you will be willing to give her up. You know she's my own blood, and of course she's no relation to you, though you must have got attached to her. I know from her picture what a sweet girl she must be, and John always said she looked like her own mother, and Grace was a beautiful woman, if she was my sister."

Rebecca stopped and stared at the other woman in amazement and alarm. The great handsome blonde creature stood speechless, livid, gasping, with her hand to her heart, her lips parted in a horrible caricature of a smile.

"Are you sick!" cried Rebecca, drawing near. "Don't you want me to get you some water!"

Then Mrs. Dent recovered herself with a great effort. "It is nothing," she said. "I am subject to—spells. I am over it now. Won't you come in, Miss Flint?"

As she spoke, the beautiful deep-rose color suffused her face, her blue eyes met her visitor's with the opaqueness of turquoise—with a revelation of blue, but a concealment of all behind.

Rebecca followed her hostess in, and the boy, who had waited quiescently, climbed the steps with the trunk. But before they entered the door a strange thing happened. On the upper terrace, close to the piazza post, grew a great rose-bush, and on it, late in the season though it was, one small red, perfect rose.

Rebecca looked at it, and the other woman extended her hand with a quick gesture. "Don't you pick that rose!" she brusquely cried.

Rebecca drew herself up with stiff dignity.

"I ain't in the habit of picking other folks' roses without leave," said she.

As Rebecca spoke she started violently and lost sight of her resentment, for something singular happened. Suddenly the rosebush was agitated violently as if by a gust of wind, yet it was a remarkably still day. Not a leaf of the hydrangea standing on the terrace close to the rose trembled.

"What on earth—" began Rebecca; then she stopped with a gasp at the sight of the other woman's face. Although a face, it gave somehow the impression of a desperately clutched hand of secrecy.

"Come in!" said she in a harsh voice, which seemed to come forth from her chest with no intervention of the organs of speech. "Come into the house. I'm getting cold out here."

"What makes that rose-bush blow so when there isn't any wind?" asked Rebecca, trembling with vague horror, yet resolute.

"I don't see as it is blowing," returned the woman, calmly. And as she spoke, indeed, the bush was quiet.

"It was blowing," declared Rebecca.

"It isn't now," said Mrs. Dent. "I can't try to account for everything that blows out-of-doors. I have too much to do."

She spoke scornfully and confidently, with defiant, unflinching eyes, first on the bush, then on Rebecca, and led the way into the house.

"It looked queer," persisted Rebecca, but she followed, and also the boy with the trunk.

Rebecca entered an interior, prosperous, even elegant, according to her simple ideas. There were Brussels carpets, lace curtains, and plenty of brilliant upholstery and polished wood.

"You're real nicely situated," remarked Rebecca after she had become a little accustomed to her new surroundings and the two women were seated at the tea-table.

Mrs. Dent stared with a hard complacency from behind her silver-plated service. "Yes, I be," said she.

"You got all the things new?" said Rebecca, hesitatingly, with a jealous memory of her dead sister's bridal furnishings.

"Yes," said Mrs. Dent. "I was never one to want dead folks' things, and I had money enough of my own, so I wasn't beholden to John. I had the old duds put up at auction. They didn't bring much."

"I suppose you saved some for Agnes. She'll want some of her poor mother's things when she is grown up," said Rebecca with some indignation.

The defiant stare of Mrs. Dent's blue eyes waxed more intense. "There's a few things up garret," said she.

"She'll be likely to value them," remarked Rebecca. As she spoke she glanced at the window. "Isn't it 'most time for her to be coming home?" she asked.

"'Most time," answered Mrs. Dent, carelessly; "but when she gets over to Addie Slocum's she never knows when to come home."

"Is Addie Slocum her intimate friend?"

"Intimate as any."

"Maybe we can have her come out to see Agnes when she's living with me," said Rebecca, wistfully. "I suppose she'll be likely to be homesick at first."

"Most likely," answered Mrs. Dent.

"Does she call you mother?" Rebecca asked.

"No, she calls me Aunt Emeline," replied the other woman, shortly. "When did you say you were going home?"

"In about a week, I thought, if she can be ready to go so soon," answered Rebecca with a surprised look.

She reflected that she would not remain a day longer than she could help after such an inhospitable look and question.

"Oh, as far as that goes," said Mrs. Dent, "it wouldn't make any difference about her being ready. You could go home whenever you felt that you must, and she could come afterward."

"Alone?"

"Why not? She's a big girl now, and you don't have to change cars."

"My niece will go home when I do, and not travel alone; and if I can't wait here for her, in the house that used to be her mother's and my sister's home, I'll go and board somewhere," returned Rebecca with warmth.

"Oh, you can stay here as long as you want to. You're welcome," said Mrs. Dent.

Then Rebecca started. "There she is!" she declared in a trembling, exultant voice. Nobody knew how she longed to see the girl.

"She isn't as late as I thought she'd be," said Mrs. Dent, and again that curious, subtle change passed over her face, and again it settled into that stony impassiveness.

Rebecca stared at the door, waiting for it to open. "Where is she?" she asked, presently.

"I guess she's stopped to take off her hat in the entry," suggested Mrs. Dent.

Rebecca waited. "Why don't she come? It can't take her all this time to take off her hat."

For answer Mrs. Dent rose with a stiff jerk and threw open the door.

"Agnes!" she called. "Agnes!" Then she turned and eyed Rebecca. "She ain't there."

"I saw her pass the window," said Rebecca in bewilderment.

"You must have been mistaken."

"I know I did," persisted Rebecca.

"You couldn't have."

"I did. I saw first a shadow go over the ceiling, then I saw her in the glass there"—she pointed to a mirror over the sideboard opposite—"and then the shadow passed the window."

"How did she look in the glass?"

"Little and light-haired, with the light hair kind of tossing over her forehead."

"You couldn't have seen her."

"Was that like Agnes?"

"Like enough; but of course you didn't see her. You've been thinking so much about her that you thought you did."

"You thought *you* did."

"I thought I saw a shadow pass the window, but I must have been mistaken. She didn't come in, or we would have seen her before now. I knew it was too early for her to get home from Addie Slocum's, anyhow."

When Rebecca went to bed Agnes had not returned. Rebecca had resolved that she would not retire until the girl came, but she was very tired, and she reasoned with herself that she was foolish. Besides, Mrs. Dent suggested that Agnes might go to the church social with Addie Slocum. When Rebecca suggested that she be sent for and told that her aunt had come, Mrs. Dent laughed meaningly.

"I guess you'll find out that a young girl ain't so ready to leave a sociable, where there's boys, to see her aunt," said she.

"She's too young," said Rebecca, incredulously and indignantly.

"She's sixteen," replied Mrs. Dent; "and she's always been great for the boys."

"She's going to school four years after I get her before she thinks of boys," declared Rebecca.

"We'll see," laughed the other woman.

After Rebecca went to bed, she lay awake a long time listening for the sound of girlish laughter and a boy's voice under her window; then she fell asleep.

The next morning she was down early. Mrs. Dent, who kept no servants, was busily preparing breakfast.

"Don't Agnes help you about breakfast?" asked Rebecca. "No, I let her lay," replied Mrs. Dent, shortly.

"What time did she get home last night?"

"She didn't get home."

"What?"

"She didn't get home. She stayed with Addie. She often does."

"Without sending you word?"

"Oh, she knew I wouldn't worry."

"When will she be home?"

"Oh, I guess she'll be along pretty soon."

Rebecca was uneasy, but she tried to conceal it, for she knew of no good reason for uneasiness. What was there to occasion alarm in the fact of one young girl staying overnight with another? She could not eat much breakfast. Afterward she went out on the little piazza, although her hostess strove furtively to stop her.

"Why don't you go out back of the house? It's real pretty—a view over the river," she said.

"I guess I'll go out here," replied Rebecca. She had a purpose—to watch for the absent girl.

Presently Rebecca came hustling into the house through the sitting room, into the kitchen where Mrs. Dent was cooking.

"That rose-bush!" she gasped.

Mrs. Dent turned and faced her.

"What of it?"

"It's a-blowing."

"What of it?"

"There isn't a mite of wind this morning."

Mrs. Dent turned with an inimitable toss of her fair head. "If you think I can spend my time puzzling over such nonsense as—" she began, but Rebecca interrupted her with a cry and a rush to the door.

"There she is now!" she cried.

She flung the door wide open, and curiously enough a breeze came in and her own gray hair tossed, and a paper blew off the table to the floor with a loud rustle, but there was nobody in sight.

"There's nobody here," Rebecca said.

She looked blankly at the other woman, who brought her rolling-pin down on a slab of pie crust with a thud.

"I didn't hear anybody," she said, calmly.

"*I saw somebody pass that window!*"

"You were mistaken again."

"I *know* I saw somebody."

"You couldn't have. Please shut that door."

Rebecca shut the door. She sat down beside the window and looked out on the autumnal yard, with its little curve of footpath to the kitchen door.

"What smells so strong of roses in this room?" she said, presently. She sniffed hard.

"I don't smell anything but these nutmegs."

"It is not nutmeg."

"I don't smell anything else."

"Where do you suppose Agnes is?"

"Oh, perhaps she has gone over the ferry to Porter's Falls with Addie. She often does. Addie's got an aunt over there, and Addie's got a cousin, a real pretty boy."

"You suppose she's gone over there?"

"Mebbe. I shouldn't wonder."

"When should she be home?"

"Oh, not before afternoon."

Rebecca waited with all the patience she could muster. She kept reassuring herself, telling herself that it was all natural, that the other woman could not help it, but she made up her mind that if Agnes did not return that afternoon she should be sent for.

When it was four o'clock she started up with resolution. She had been furtively watching the onyx clock on the sitting-room mantel; she had timed herself. She had said that if Agnes was not home by that time she should demand that she be sent for. She rose and stood before Mrs. Dent, who looked up coolly from her embroidery.

"I've waited just as long as I'm going to," she said. "I've come 'way from Michigan to see my own sister's daughter and take her home with me. I've been here ever since yesterday—twenty-four hours—and I haven't seen her. Now I'm going to. I want her sent for."

Mrs. Dent folded her embroidery and rose.

"Well, I don't blame you," she said. "It is high time she came home. I'll go right over and get her myself."

Rebecca heaved a sigh of relief. She hardly knew what she had suspected or feared, but she knew that her position had been one of antagonism if not accusation, and she was sensible of relief.

"I wish you would," she said, gratefully, and went back to her chair, while Mrs. Dent got her shawl and her little white head-tie. "I wouldn't trouble you, but I do feel as if I couldn't wait any longer to see her," she remarked, apologetically.

"Oh, it ain't any trouble at all," said Mrs. Dent as she went out. "I don't blame you; you have waited long enough."

Rebecca sat at the window watching breathlessly until Mrs. Dent came stepping through the yard alone. She ran to the door and saw, hardly noticing it this time, that the rose-bush was again violently agitated, yet with no wind evident elsewhere.

"Where is she?" she cried.

Mrs. Dent laughed with stiff lips as she came up the steps over the terrace. "Girls will be girls," said she. "She's gone with Addie to Lincoln. Addie's got an uncle who's conductor on the train, and lives there, and he got 'em passes, and they're goin' to stay to Addie's Aunt Margaret's a few days Mrs. Slocum said Agnes didn't have time to come over and ask me before the train went, but she took it on herself to say it would be all right, and—"

"Why hadn't she been over to tell you?" Rebecca was angry, though not suspicious. She even saw no reason for her anger.

"Oh, she was putting up grapes. She was coming over just as soon as she got the black off her hands. She heard I had company, and her hands were a sight. She was holding them over sulphur matches."

"You say she's going to stay a few days?" repeated Rebecca, dazedly.

"Yes; till Thursday, Mrs. Slocum said."

"How far is Lincoln from here?"

"About fifty miles. It'll be a real treat to her. Mrs. Slocum's sister is a real nice woman."

"It is goin' to make it pretty late about my goin' home."

"If you don't feel as if you could wait, I'll get her ready and send her on just as soon as I can," Mrs. Dent said, sweetly.

"I'm going to wait," said Rebecca, grimly.

The two women sat down again, and Mrs. Dent took up her embroidery.

"Is there any sewing I can do for her?" Rebecca asked, finally, in a desperate way. "If I can get her sewing along some—"

Mrs. Dent arose with alacrity and fetched a mass of white from the closet. "Here," she said, "if you want to sew the lace on this nightgown. I was going to put her to it, but she'll be glad enough to get rid of it. She ought to have this and one more before she goes. I don't like to send her away without some good underclothing."

Rebecca snatched at the little white garment and sewed feverishly.

That night she wakened from a deep sleep a little after midnight and lay a minute trying to collect her faculties and explain to herself what she was listening to. At last she discovered that it was the then popular strains of "The Maiden's Prayer" floating up through the floor from the piano in the sitting room below. She jumped up, threw a shawl over her nightgown, and hurried downstairs trembling. There was nobody in the sitting room: the piano was silent. She ran to Mrs. Dent's bedroom and called hysterically:

"Emeline! Emeline!"

"What is it?" asked Mrs. Dent's voice from the bed. The voice was stern, but had a note of consciousness in it.

"Who—who was that playing 'The Maiden's Prayer' in the sitting room, on the piano?"

"I didn't hear anybody."

"There was some one."

"I didn't hear anything."

"I tell you there was some one. But—*there ain't anybody there.*"

"I didn't hear anything."

"I did—somebody playing 'The Maiden's Prayer' on the piano. Has Agnes got home? I *want to know.*"

"Of course Agnes hasn't got home," answered Mrs. Dent with rising inflection.

"Be you gone crazy over that girl? The last boat from Porter's Falls was in before we went to bed. Of course she ain't come."

"I heard—"

"You were dreaming."

"I wasn't; I was broad awake."

Rebecca went back to her chamber and kept her lamp burning all night.

The next morning her eyes upon Mrs. Dent were wary and blazing with suppressed excitement. She kept opening her mouth as if to speak, then frowning, and setting her lips hard. After breakfast she went upstairs, and came down presently with her coat and bonnet.

"Now, Emeline," she said, "I want to know where the Slocums live."

Mrs. Dent gave a strange, long, half-lidded glance at her. She was finishing her coffee.

"Why?" she asked.

"I'm going over there and find out if they have heard anything from her daughter and Agnes since they went away. I don't like what I heard last night."

"You must have been dreaming."

"It don't make any odds whether I was or not. Does she play 'The Maiden's Prayer' on the piano? I want to know."

"What if she does? She plays it a little, I believe. I don't know. She don't half play it, anyhow; she ain't got an ear."

"That wasn't half played last night. I don't like such things happening. I ain't superstitious, but I don't like it. I'm going. Where do the Slocums live?"

"You go down the road over the bridge past the old grist mill, then you turn to the left; it's the only house for half a mile. You can't miss it. It has a barn with a ship in full sail on the cupola."

"Well, I'm going. I don't feel easy."

About two hours later Rebecca returned. There were red spots on her cheeks. She looked wild. "I've been there," she said, "and there isn't a soul at home. Something *has* happened."

"What has happened?"

"I don't know. Something. I had a warning last night. There wasn't a soul there. They've been sent for to Lincoln."

"Did you see anybody to ask?" asked Mrs. Dent with thinly concealed anxiety.

"I asked the woman that lives on the turn of the road. She's stone deaf. I suppose you know. She listened while I screamed at her to know where the Slocums were, and then she said, 'Mrs. Smith don't live here.' I didn't see anybody on the road, and that's the only house. What do you suppose it means?"

"I don't suppose it means much of anything," replied Mrs. Dent, coolly. "Mr. Slocum is conductor on the railroad, and he'd be away, anyway, and Mrs. Slocum often goes early when he does, to spend the day with her sister in Porter's Falls. She'd be more likely to go away than Addie."

"And you don't think anything has happened?" Rebecca asked with diminishing distrust before the reasonableness of it.

"Land, no!"

Rebecca went upstairs to lay aside her coat and bonnet. But she came hurrying back with them still on.

"Who's been in my room?" she gasped. Her face was pale as ashes.

Mrs. Dent also paled as she regarded her.

"What do you mean?" she asked, slowly.

"I found when I went upstairs that—little nightgown of—Agnes's on—the bed, laid out. It was—*laid out.* The sleeves were folded across the bosom, and there was that little red rose between them. Emeline, what is it? Emeline, what's the matter? Oh!"

Mrs. Dent was struggling for breath in great, choking gasps. She clung to the back of a chair. Rebecca, trembling herself so she could scarcely keep on her feet, got her some water.

As soon as she recovered herself Mrs. Dent regarded her with eyes full of the strangest mixture of fear and horror and hostility. "What do you mean talking so?" she said in a hard voice.

"It is there."

"Nonsense. You threw it down and it fell that way."

"It was folded in my bureau drawer."

"It couldn't have been."

"Who picked that red rose?"

"Look on the bush," Mrs. Dent replied shortly.

Rebecca looked at her; her mouth gaped. She hurried out of the room. When she came back her eyes seemed to protrude. (She had in the meantime hastened upstairs, and come down with tottering steps, clinging to the banister.)

"Now I want to know what all this means?" she demanded.

"What what means?"

"The rose is on the bush, and it's gone from the bed in my room! Is this house haunted, or what?"

"I don't know anything about a house being haunted. I don't believe in such things. Be you crazy?" Mrs. Dent spoke with gathering force. The color flashed back to her cheeks.

"No," said Rebecca, shortly, "I ain't crazy yet, but I shall be if this keeps on much longer. I'm going to find out where that girl is before night."

Mrs. Dent eyed her. "What be you going to do?"

"I'm going to Lincoln."

A faint triumphant smile overspread Mrs. Dent's large face.

"You can't," said she; "there ain't any train."

"No train?"

"No; there ain't any afternoon train from the Falls to Lincoln."

"Then I'm going over to the Slocums' again to-night."

However, Rebecca did not go; such a rain came up as deterred even her resolution, and she had only her best dresses with her. Then in the evening came the letter from the Michigan village which she had left nearly a week ago. It was from her cousin, a single woman, who had come to keep her house while she was away. It was a pleasant unexciting letter enough, all the first of it, and related mostly how she missed Rebecca; how she hoped she was having pleasant weather and kept her health; and how her friend, Mrs. Greenaway, had come to stay with her since she had felt lonesome the first night in the house; how she hoped Rebecca would have no objections to this, although nothing had been said about it, since she had not realized that she might be nervous alone. The cousin was painfully conscientious, hence the letter. Rebecca smiled in spite of her disturbed mind as she read it; then her eye caught the postscript. That was in a different hand, purporting to be written by the friend, Mrs. Hannah Greenaway, informing her that the cousin had fallen down the cellar stairs and broken her hip, and was in a dangerous condition, and begging Rebecca to return at once, as she herself was rheumatic and unable to nurse her properly, and no one else could be obtained.

Rebecca looked at Mrs. Dent, who had come to her room with the letter quite late; it was half-past nine, and she had gone upstairs for the night.

"Where did this come from?" she asked.

"Mr. Amblecrom brought it," she replied.

"Who's he?"

"The postmaster. He often brings the letters that come on the late mail. He knows I ain't anybody to send. He brought yours about your coming. He said he and his wife came over on the ferry-boat with you."

"I remember him," Rebecca replied, shortly. "There's bad news in this letter."

Mrs. Dent's face took on an expression of serious inquiry.

"Yes, my Cousin Harriet has fallen down the cellar stairs—they were always dangerous—and she's broken her hip, and I've got to take the first train home to-morrow."

"You don't say so. I'm dreadfully sorry."

"No, you ain't sorry!" said Rebecca with a look as if she leaped. "You're glad. I don't know why, but you're glad. You've wanted to get rid of me for some reason ever since I came. I don't know why. You're a strange woman. Now you've got your way, and I hope you're satisfied."

"How you talk."

Mrs. Dent spoke in a faintly injured voice, but there was a light in her eyes.

"I talk the way it is. Well, I'm going to-morrow morning, and I want you, just as soon as Agnes Dent comes home, to send her out to me. Don't you wait for anything. You pack what clothes she's got, and don't wait even to mend them, and you buy her ticket. I'll leave the money, and you send her along. She don't have to change cars. You start her off, when she gets home, on the next train!"

"Very well," replied the other woman. She had an expression of covert amusement.

"Mind you do it."

"Very well, Rebecca."

* * * *

Rebecca started on her journey the next morning. When she arrived, two days later, she found her cousin in perfect health. She found, moreover, that the friend had not written the postscript in the cousin's letter. Rebecca would have returned to Ford Village the next morning, but the fatigue and nervous strain had been too much for her. She was not able to move from her bed. She had a species of low fever induced by anxiety and fatigue. But she could write, and she did, to the Slocums, and she received no answer. She also wrote to Mrs. Dent; she even sent numerous telegrams, with no response. Finally she wrote to the postmaster, and an answer arrived by the first possible mail. The letter was short, curt, and to the purpose. Mr. Amblecrom, the post-master, was a man of few words, and especially wary as to his expressions in a letter.

"Dear madam," he wrote, "your favour rec'ed. No Slocums in Ford's Village. All dead. Addie ten years ago, her mother two years later, her father five. House vacant. Mrs. John Dent said to have neglected stepdaughter. Girl was sick. Medicine not given. Talk of taking action. Not enough evidence. House said to be haunted. Strange sights and sounds. Your niece, Agnes Dent, died a year ago, about this time.

"Yours truly,

"THOMAS AMBLECROM."

THE STORY OF MING-Y, by Lafcadio Hearn

The ancient Words of Kouei—Master of Musicians in the Courts of the Emperor Yao:—

When ye make to resound the stone melodious, the Ming-Khieou,—
When ye touch the lyre that is called Kin, or the guitar that is called Ssé,—
Accompanying their sound with song,—
Then do the grandfather and the father return;
Then do the ghosts of the ancestors come to hear.

THE STORY OF MING-Y

Sang the Poet Tching-Kou: "Surely the Peach-Flowers blossom over the tomb of Siĕ-Thao."

Do you ask me who she was,—the beautiful Siĕ-Thao? For a thousand years and more the trees have been whispering above her bed of stone. And the syllables of her name come to the listener with the lisping of the leaves; with the quivering of many-fingered boughs; with the fluttering of lights and shadows; with the breath, sweet as a woman's presence, of numberless savage flowers,—*Siĕ-Thao*. But, saving the whispering of her name, what the trees say cannot be understood; and they alone remember the years of Siĕ-Thao. Something about her you might, nevertheless, learn from any of those *Kiang-kou-jin*,—those famous Chinese story-tellers, who nightly narrate to listening crowds, in consideration of a few *tsien*, the legends of the past. Something concerning her you may also find in the book entitled "Kin-Kou-Ki-Koan," which signifies in our tongue: "The Marvellous Happenings of Ancient and of Recent Times." And perhaps of all things therein written, the most marvellous is this memory of Siĕ-Thao:—

Five hundred years ago, in the reign of the Emperor Houng-Wou, whose dynasty was *Ming*, there lived in the City of Genii, the city of Kwang-tchau-fu, a man celebrated for his learning and for his piety, named Tien-Pelou. This Tien-Pelou had one son, a beautiful boy, who for scholarship and for bodily grace and for polite accomplishments had no superior among the youths of his age. And his name was Ming-Y.

Now when the lad was in his eighteenth summer, it came to pass that Pelou, his father, was appointed Inspector of Public Instruction at the city of Tching-tou; and Ming-Y accompanied his parents thither. Near the city of Tching-tou lived a rich man of rank, a high commissioner of the government, whose name was Tchang, and who wanted to find a worthy teacher for his children. On hearing of the arrival of the new Inspector of Public Instruction, the noble Tchang visited him to obtain advice in this matter; and happening to meet and converse with Pelou's accomplished son, immediately engaged Ming-Y as a private tutor for his family.

Now as the house of this Lord Tchang was situated several miles from town, it was deemed best that Ming-Y should abide in the house of his employer. Accordingly the youth made ready all things necessary for his new sojourn; and his parents, bidding him farewell, counselled him wisely, and cited to him the words of Lao-tseu and of the ancient sages:

> "By a beautiful face the world is filled with love; but Heaven may never be deceived thereby. Shouldst thou behold a woman coming from the East, look thou to the West; shouldst thou perceive a maiden approaching from the West, turn thine eyes to the East."

If Ming-Y did not heed this counsel in after days, it was only because of his youth and the thoughtlessness of a naturally joyous heart.

And he departed to abide in the house of Lord Tchang, while the autumn passed, and the winter also.

* * * *

When the time of the second moon of spring was drawing near, and that happy day which the Chinese call *Hoa-tchao*, or, "The Birthday of a Hundred Flowers," a longing came upon Ming-Y to see his parents; and he opened his heart to the good Tchang, who not only gave him the permission he desired, but also pressed into his hand a silver gift of two ounces, thinking that the lad might wish to bring some little memento to his father and mother. For it is the Chinese custom, on the feast of Hoa-tchao, to make presents to friends and relations.

That day all the air was drowsy with blossom perfume, and vibrant with the droning of bees. It seemed to Ming-Y that the path he followed had not been trodden by any other for many long years; the grass was tall upon it; vast trees on either side interlocked their mighty and moss-grown arms above him, beshadowing the way; but the leafy obscurities quivered with bird-song, and the deep vistas of the wood were glorified by vapors of gold, and odorous with flower-breathings as a temple with incense. The dreamy joy of the day entered into the heart of Ming-Y; and he sat him down among the young blossoms, under the branches swaying against the violet sky, to drink in the perfume and the light, and to enjoy the great sweet silence. Even while thus reposing, a sound caused him to turn his eyes toward a shady place where wild peach-trees were in bloom; and he beheld a young woman, beautiful as the pinkening blossoms themselves, trying to hide among them. Though he looked for a moment only, Ming-Y could not avoid discerning the loveliness of her face, the golden purity of her complexion, and the brightness of her long eyes, that sparkled under a pair of brows as daintily curved as the wings of the silkworm butterfly outspread. Ming-Y at once turned his gaze away, and, rising quickly, proceeded on his journey. But so much embarrassed did he feel at the idea of those charming eyes peeping at him through the leaves, that he suffered the money he had been carrying in his sleeve to fall, without being aware of it. A few moments later he heard the patter of light feet running behind him, and a woman's voice calling him by name. Turning his face in great surprise, he saw a comely servant-maid, who said to him, "Sir, my mistress bade me pick up and return you this silver which you dropped upon the road." Ming-Y thanked the girl gracefully, and requested her to convey his compliments to her mistress. Then he proceeded on his way through the perfumed silence, athwart the shadows that dreamed along the forgotten path, dreaming himself also, and feeling his heart beating with strange quickness at the thought of the beautiful being that he had seen.

It was just such another day when Ming-Y, returning by the same path, paused once more at the spot where the gracious figure had momentarily appeared before him. But this time he was surprised to perceive, through a long vista of immense trees, a dwelling that had previously escaped his notice,—a country residence, not large, yet elegant to an unusual degree. The bright blue tiles of its curved and serrated double roof, rising above the foliage, seemed to blend their color with the luminous azure of the day; the green-and-gold designs of its carven porticos were exquisite artistic mockeries of leaves and flowers bathed in sunshine. And at the summit of terrace-steps before it, guarded by greatporcelain tortoises, Ming-Y saw standing the mistress of the mansion,—the idol of his passionate fancy,—accompanied by the same waiting-maid who had borne to her his message of gratitude. While Ming-Y looked, he perceived that their eyes were upon him; they smiled and conversed together as if speaking about him; and, shy though he was, the youth found courage to salute the fair one from a distance. To his astonishment, the young servant beckoned him to approach; and opening a rustic gate half veiled by trailing plants bearing crimson flowers, Ming-Y advanced along the verdant alley leading to the terrace, with mingled feelings of surprise and timid joy. As he drew near, the beautiful lady withdrew from sight; but the maid waited at the broad steps to receive him, and said as he ascended:

"Sir, my mistress understands you wish to thank her for the trifling service she recently bade me do you, and requests that you will enter the house, as she knows you already by repute, and desires to have the pleasure of bidding you good-day."

Ming-Y entered bashfully, his feet making no sound upon a matting elastically soft as forest moss, and found himself in a reception-chamber vast, cool, and fragrant with scent of blossoms freshly gathered. A delicious quiet pervaded the mansion; shadows of flying birds passed over the bands of light that fell through the half-blinds of bamboo; great butterflies, with pinions of fiery color, found their way in, to hover a moment about the painted vases, and pass out again into the mysterious woods. And noiselessly as they, the young mistress of the mansion entered by another door, and kindly greeted the boy, who lifted his hands to his breast and bowed low in salutation. She was taller than he had deemed her, and supplely-slender as a beauteous lily; her black hair was interwoven with the creamy blossoms of the *chu-sha-kih*; her robes of pale silk took shifting tints when she moved, as vapors change hue with the changing of the light.

"If I be not mistaken," she said, when both had seated themselves after having exchanged the customary formalities of politeness, "my honored visitor is none other than Tien-chou, surnamed Ming-Y, educator of the children of my respected relative, the High Commissioner Tchang. As the family of Lord Tchang is my family also, I cannot but consider the teacher of his children as one of my own kin."

"Lady," replied Ming-Y, not a little astonished, "may I dare to inquire the name of your honored family, and to ask the relation which you hold to my noble patron?"

"The name of my poor family," responded the comely lady, "is *Ping*,—an ancient family of the city of Tching-tou. I am the daughter of a certain Sië of Moun-hao; Sië is my name, likewise; and I was married to a young man of the Ping family, whose name was Khang. By this marriage I became related to your excellent patron; but my husband died soon after our wedding, and I have chosen this solitary place to reside in during the period of my widowhood."

There was a drowsy music in her voice, as of the melody of brooks, the murmurings of spring; and such a strange grace in the manner of her speech as Ming-Y had never heard before. Yet, on learning that she was a widow, the youth would not have presumed to remain long in her presence without a formal invitation; and after having sipped the cup of rich tea presented to him, he arose to depart. Sië would not suffer him to go so quickly.

"Nay, friend," she said; "stay yet a little while in my house, I pray you; for, should your honored patron ever learn that you had been here, and that I had not treated you as a respected guest, and regaled you even as I would him, I know that he would be greatly angered. Remain at least to supper."

So Ming-Y remained, rejoicing secretly in his heart, for Siĕ seemed to him the fairest and sweetest being he had ever known, and he felt that he loved her even more than his father and his mother. And while they talked the long shadows of the evening slowly blended into one violet darkness; the great citron-light of the sunset faded out; and those starry beings that are called the Three Councillors, who preside over life and death and the destinies of men, opened their cold bright eyes in the northern sky. Within the mansion of Siĕ the painted lanterns were lighted; the table was laid for the evening repast; and Ming-Y took his place at it, feeling little inclination to eat, and thinking only of the charming face before him. Observing that he scarcely tasted the dainties laid upon his plate, Siĕ pressed her young guest to partake of wine; and they drank several cups together. It was a purple wine, so cool that the cup into which it was poured became covered with vapory dew; yet it seemed to warm the veins with strange fire. To Ming-Y, as he drank, all things became more luminous as by enchantment; the walls of the chamber appeared to recede, and the roof to heighten; the lamps glowed like stars in their chains, and the voice of Siĕ floated to the boy's ears like some far melody heard through the spaces of a drowsy night. His heart swelled; his tongue loosened; and words flitted from his lips that he had fancied he could never dare to utter. Yet Siĕ sought not to restrain him; her lips gave no smile; but her long bright eyes seemed to laugh with pleasure at his words of praise, and to return his gaze of passionate admiration with affectionate interest.

"I have heard," she said, "of your rare talent, and of your many elegant accomplishments. I know how to sing a little, although I cannot claim to possess any musical learning; and now that I have the honor of finding myself in the society of a musical professor, I will venture to lay modesty aside, and beg you to sing a few songs with me. I should deem it no small gratification if you would condescend to examine my musical compositions."

"The honor and the gratification, dear lady," replied Ming-Y, "will be mine; and I feel helpless to express the gratitude which the offer of so rare a favor deserves."

The serving-maid, obedient to the summons of a little silver gong, brought in the music and retired. Ming-Y took the manuscripts, and began to examine them with eager delight. The paper upon which they were written had a pale yellow tint, and was light as a fabric of gossamer; but the characters were antiquely beautiful, as though they had been traced by the brush of Heï-song Ché-Tchoo himself,—that divine Genius of Ink, who is no bigger than a fly; and the signatures attached to the compositions were the signatures of Youen-tchin, Kao-pien, and Thou-mou,—mighty poets and musicians of the dynasty of Thang! Ming-Y could not repress a scream of delight at the sight of treasures so inestimable and so unique; scarcely could he summon resolution enough to permit them to leave his hands even for a moment. "O Lady!" he cried, "these are veritably priceless things, surpassing in worth the treasures of all kings. This indeed is the handwriting of those great masters who sang five hundred years before our birth. How marvellously it has been preserved! Is not this the wondrous ink of which it was written: *Po-nien-jou-chi, i-tien-jou-ki,*—'After centuries I remain firm as stone, and the letters that I make like lacquer'? And how divine the charm of this composition!—the song of Kao-pien, prince of poets, and Governor of Sze-tchouen five hundred years ago!"

"Kao-pien! darling Kao-pien!" murmured Siĕ, with a singular light in her eyes. "Kao-pien is also my favorite. Dear Ming-Y, let us chant his verses together, to the melody of old,—the music of those grand years when men were nobler and wiser than to-day."

* * * *

And their voices rose through the perfumed night like the voices of the wonder-birds,—of the Fung-hoang,—blending together in liquid sweetness. Yet a moment, and Ming-Y, overcome by the witchery of his companion's voice, could only listen in speechless ecstasy, while the lights of the chamber swam dim before his sight, and tears of pleasure trickled down his cheeks.

So the ninth hour passed; and they continued to converse, and to drink the cool purple wine, and to sing the songs of the years of Thang, until far into the night. More than once Ming-Y thought of departing; but each time Sië would begin, in that silver-sweet voice of hers, so wondrous a story of the great poets of the past, and of the women whom they loved, that he became as one entranced; or she would sing for him a song so strange that all his senses seemed to die except that of hearing. And at last, as she paused to pledge him in a cup of wine, Ming-Y could not restrain himself from putting his arm about her round neck and drawing her dainty head closer to him, and kissing the lips that were so much ruddier and sweeter than the wine. Then their lips separated no more;—the night grew old, and they knew it not.

* * * *

The birds awakened, the flowers opened their eyes to the rising sun, and Ming-Y found himself at last compelled to bid his lovely enchantress farewell. Sië, accompanying him to the terrace, kissed him fondly and said, "Dear boy, come hither as often as you are able,—as often as your heart whispers you to come. I know that you are not of those without faith and truth, who betray secrets; yet, being so young, you might also be sometimes thoughtless; and I pray you never to forget that only the stars have been the witnesses of our love. Speak of it to no living person, dearest; and take with you this little souvenir of our happy night."

And she presented him with an exquisite and curious little thing,—apaper-weight in likeness of a couchant lion, wrought from a jade-stone yellow as that created by a rainbow in honor of Kong-fu-tze. Tenderly the boy kissed the gift and the beautiful hand that gave it. "May the Spirits punish me," he vowed, "if ever I knowingly give you cause to reproach me, sweetheart!" And they separated with mutual vows.

That morning, on returning to the house of Lord Tchang, Ming-Y told the first falsehood which had ever passed his lips. He averred that his mother had requested him thenceforward to pass his nights at home, now that the weather had become so pleasant; for, though the way was somewhat long, he was strong and active, and needed both air and healthy exercise. Tchang believed all Ming-Y said, and offered no objection. Accordingly the lad found himself enabled to pass all his evenings at the house of the beautiful Sië. Each night they devoted to the same pleasures which had made their first acquaintance so charming: they sang and conversed by turns; they played at chess,—the learned game invented by Wu-Wang, which is an imitation of war; they composed pieces of eighty rhymes upon the flowers, the trees, the clouds, the streams, the birds, the bees. But in all accomplishments Sië far excelled her young sweetheart. Whenever they played at chess, it was always Ming-Y's general, Ming-Y's *tsiang*, who was surrounded and vanquished; when they composed verses, Sië's poems were ever superior to his in harmony of word-coloring, in elegance of form, in classic loftiness of thought. And the themes they selected were always the most difficult,—those of the poets of the Thang dynasty; the songs they sang were also the songs of five hundred years before,—the songs of Youen-tchin, of Thou-mou, of Kao-pien above all, high poet and ruler of the province of Sze-tchouen.

So the summer waxed and waned upon their love, and the luminous autumn came, with its vapors of phantom gold, its shadows of magical purple.

* * * *

Then it unexpectedly happened that the father of Ming-Y, meeting his son's employer at Tching-tou, was asked by him: "Why must your boy continue to travel every evening to the city, now that the winter is approaching? The way is long, and when he returns in the morning he looks fordone with weariness. Why not permit him to slumber in my house during the season of snow?" And the father of Ming-Y, greatly astonished, responded: "Sir, my son has not visited the city, nor has he been to our house all this summer. I fear that he must have acquired wicked habits, and that he passes his nights in evil company,—perhaps in gaming, or in drinking with the women of the flower-boats." But the High Commissioner returned: "Nay! that is not to be thought of. I have never found any evil in the boy, and there are no taverns nor flower-boats nor any places of dissipation in our neighborhood. No doubt Ming-Y has found some amiable youth of his own age with whom to spend his evenings, and only told me an untruth for fear that I would not otherwise permit him to leave my residence. I beg that you will say nothing to him until I shall have sought to discover this mystery; and this very evening I shall send my servant to follow after him, and to watch whither he goes."

Pelou readily assented to this proposal, and promising to visit Tchang the following morning, returned to his home. In the evening, when Ming-Y left the house of Tchang, a servant followed him unobserved at a distance. But on reaching the most obscure portion of the road, the boy disappeared from sight as suddenly as though the earth had swallowed him. After having long sought after him in vain, the domestic returned in great bewilderment to the house, and related what had taken place. Tchang immediately sent a messenger to Pelou.

In the mean time Ming-Y, entering the chamber of his beloved, was surprised and deeply pained to find her in tears. "Sweetheart," she sobbed, wreathing her arms around his neck, "we are about to be separated forever, because of reasons which I cannot tell you. From the very first I knew this must come to pass; and nevertheless it seemed to me for the moment so cruelly sudden a loss, so unexpected a misfortune, that I could not prevent myself from weeping! After this night we shall never see each other again, beloved, and I know that you will not be able to forget me while you live; but I know also that you will become a great scholar, and that honors and riches will be showered upon you, and that some beautiful and loving woman will console you for my loss. And now let us speak no more of grief; but let us pass this last evening joyously, so that your recollection of me may not be a painful one, and that you may remember my laughter rather than my tears."

She brushed the bright drops away, and brought wine and music and the melodious *kin* of seven silken strings, and would not suffer Ming-Y to speak for one moment of the coming separation. And she sang him an ancient song about the calmness of summer lakes reflecting the blue of heaven only, and the calmness of the heart also, before the clouds of care and of grief and of weariness darken its little world. Soon they forgot their sorrow in the joy of song and wine; and those last hours seemed to Ming-Y more celestial than even the hours of their first bliss.

But when the yellow beauty of morning came their sadness returned, and they wept. Once more Sië accompanied her lover to the terrace-steps; and as she kissed him farewell, she pressed into his hand a parting gift,—a little brush-case of agate, wonderfully chiselled, and worthy the table of a great poet. And they separated forever, shedding many tears.

* * * *

Still Ming-Y could not believe it was an eternal parting. "No!" he thought, "I shall visit her tomorrow; for I cannot now live without her, and I feel assured that she cannot refuse to receive me." Such were the thoughts that filled his mind as he reached the house of Tchang, to find his father and his patron standing on the porch awaiting him. Ere he could speak a word, Pelou demanded: "Son, in what place have you been passing your nights?"

Seeing that his falsehood had been discovered, Ming-Y dared not make any reply, and remained abashed and silent, with bowed head, in the presence of his father. Then Pelou, striking the boy violently with his staff, commanded him to divulge the secret; and at last, partly through fear of his parent, and partly through fear of the law which ordains that "*the son refusing to obey his father shall be punished with one hundred blows of the bamboo,*" Ming-Y faltered out the history of his love.

Tchang changed color at the boy's tale. "Child," exclaimed the High Commissioner, "I have no relative of the name of Ping; I have never heard of the woman you describe; I have never heard even of the house which you speak of. But I know also that you cannot dare to lie to Pelou, your honored father; there is some strange delusion in all this affair."

Then Ming-Y produced the gifts that Sië had given him,—the lion of yellow jade, the brush-case of carven agate, also some original compositions made by the beautiful lady herself. The astonishment of Tchang was now shared by Pelou. Both observed that the brush-case of agate and the lion of jade bore the appearance of objects that had lain buried in the earth for centuries, and were of a workmanship beyond the power of living man to imitate; while the compositions proved to be veritable master-pieces of poetry, written in the style of the poets of the dynasty of Thang.

"Friend Pelou," cried the High Commissioner, "let us immediately accompany the boy to the place where he obtained these miraculous things, and apply the testimony of our senses to this mystery. The boy is no doubt telling the truth; yet his story passes my understanding." And all three proceeded toward the place of the habitation of Sië.

* * * *

But when they had arrived at the shadiest part of the road, where the perfumes were most sweet and the mosses were greenest, and the fruits of the wild peach flushed most pinkly, Ming-Y, gazing through the groves, uttered a cry of dismay. Where the azure-tiled roof had risen against the sky, there was now only the blue emptiness of air; where the green-and-gold facade had been, there was visible only the flickering of leaves under the aureate autumn light; and where the broad terrace had extended, could be discerned only a ruin,—a tomb so ancient, so deeply gnawed by moss, that the name graven upon it was no longer decipherable. The home of Sië had disappeared!

All suddenly the High Commissioner smote his forehead with his hand, and turning to Pelou, recited the well-known verse of the ancient poet Tching-Kou:—

> *"Surely the peach-flowers blossom over*
> *the tomb of SIË-THAO."*

"Friend Pelou," continued Tchang, "the beauty who bewitched your son was no other than she whose tomb stands there in ruin before us! Did she not say she was wedded to Ping-Khang? There is no family of that name, but Ping-Khang is indeed the name of a broad alley in the city near. There was a dark riddle in all that she said. She called herself Sië of Moun-Hiao: there is no person of that name; there is no street of that name; but the Chinese characters *Moun* and *hiao*, placed together, form the character 'Kiao.' Listen! The alley Ping-Khang, situated in the street Kiao, was the place where dwelt the great courtesans of the dynasty of Thang! Did she not sing the songs of Kao-pien? And upon the brush-case and the paper-weight she gave your son, are there not characters which read, '*Pure object of art belonging to Kao, of the city of Pho-hai*'? That city no longer exists; but the memory of Kao-pien remains, for he was governor of the province of Sze-tchouen, and a mighty poet. And when he dwelt in the land of Chou, was not his favorite the beautiful wanton Sië,—Sië-Thao, unmatched for grace among all the women of her day? It was he who made her a gift of those manuscripts of song; it was he who gave her those objects of rare art. Sië-Thao died not as other women die. Her limbs may have crumbled to dust; yet something of her still lives in this deep wood,—her Shadow still haunts this shadowy place."

Tchang ceased to speak. A vague fear fell upon the three. The thin mists of the morning made dim the distances of green, and deepened the ghostly beauty of the woods. A faint breeze passed by, leaving a trail of blossom-scent,—a last odor of dying flowers,—thin as that which clings to the silk of a forgotten robe; and, as it passed, the trees seemed to whisper across the silence, "*Sië-Thao.*"

* * * *

Fearing greatly for his son, Pelou sent the lad away at once to the city of Kwang-tchau-fu. And there, in after years, Ming-Y obtained high dignities and honors by reason of his talents and his learning; and he married the daughter of an illustrious house, by whom he became the father of sons and daughters famous for their virtues and their accomplishments. Never could he forget Sië-Thao; and yet it is said that he never spoke of her,—not even when his children begged him to tell them the story of two beautiful objects that always lay upon his writing-table: a lion of yellow jade, and a brush-case of carven agate.

www.ingramcontent.com/pod-product-compliance
Lightning Source LLC
Chambersburg PA
CBHW020613260626
47157CB00003B/993
* 9 7 8 1 4 7 9 4 5 0 2 6 8 *